THE REBELLION

Deidrea DeWitt

THE REBELLION

BY

DEIDREA DEWITT

"Victorious warriors win first and then go to war, while defeated warriors go to war first and then seek to win."

— Sun Tzu, The Art of War

*To all the first loves we've never forgotten,
and to the new loves who shape us into
what we truly are.*

CHAPTER 1

PAST ESCAPES

"You can't take him!" I screamed.

The guards grabbed me before I reached the door, pulling me back into the living room. I was strong, but not strong enough to twist from their hold. My younger brother looked at me over his shoulder as the emperor's guards dragged him outside into the darkness. They forced him to his knees, pointing a sword at his throat.

A man in heavy boots stepped between us, his broad shoulders bringing back memories I had thrown away long ago. He had once been a shadow of my past, but now, he was a shadow that divided me from my brother.

"It's too late, Jaehwa," the shadow replied, not turning to face me.

I narrowed my eyes, the guards' hands gripping hard into my arms as I struggled to step forward.

"You expect me to back down?" I asked. "He's all I have left, Saejun! You know that!"

The shadow turned and stepped back into the house, his dark eyes showing no regrets nor sympathy as the living room candles lit his face. The crimson robes of the emperor clung to his skin like blood, a testament to his position of power. He stood tall and arrogant, as if he had never been the poor farmer's son he once was.

"He's a murderer," Saejun said. "He brought this upon himself."

"You're wrong!" I tried to twist out of the guards' hold, but they held fast. "Kiwan would never commit treason against the emperor! You know that. How can you take him away to be executed?"

I tried to catch my breath, my eyes beginning to burn. Saejun stepped in closer, but I only stared at his expensive boots, refusing to let him intimidate me. His fingers curled under my chin, lifting my head up to look at him. His features were just as I remembered - his sharp eyes and strong jaw - but there was a new darkness in him that wasn't caused by the late hour.

"Stop fighting against me," he replied. "You won't win. You know *that*."

I jerked my face from his hand. "Get out of my house."

"I hate to say this," he said, his hand dropping to his side, "but this house is no longer yours."

I looked up at him. "What do you mean?"

His jaw clenched before he opened his mouth again. "This house was in your brother's name. Now that he's been arrested, it has defaulted to the emperor."

"Saejun —"

"You can live here for the time being," he continued, "but you can be thrown out at any time. These are the orders of the emperor."

I twisted hard, breaking free from the guards, but only for a moment. They pulled me back again, bringing me down to my knees.

"Who the hell do you think you are?" I spat at Saejun.

"Enough," he warned.

"You disappear for five years, become captain of the guards, and then show up at my door to take my brother and my home away from me?" The guards twisted my arms in an attempt to silence me, but I continued. "Who the hell do you think you are? What right do you have to come back here?"

"Put her under house arrest," he told the guards, not even blinking. "Secure the first floor."

He turned his back on me. It was something he was good at.

"Saejun!" I called.

He stopped. With two heavy footsteps, he turned back.

"That…" he said, "will be the last time I allow you to say my name and live."

Before I could say anything else, he stepped out and slammed the door behind him. A new guard blocked the door, his face as hard as the walls that were now closing me in.

"Unhand me!" I yelled, throwing the guards off. They stepped back, not attempting to handle me again. Instead, they went to block the entryways.

"You are under strict house arrest by decree of the emperor," one of the guards said. "Should you oppose this, we will have to take physical measures to subdue you."

"Of course I oppose this, you wolves!"

I spun towards the doorway to escape, but pain exploded in my side before I could take a step forward. I crumbled to the floor in pain. The guard towered above me, holding his spear.

"Be grateful I didn't use the sharp end," he muttered.

Pain echoing in my side, I came to my feet.

"You can move about the house as you like," he continued, "but you can't leave."

I took a deep breath to ease the pain. "And how long will that be?"

"Until Captain Kim has signaled for your release."

Captain Kim. I wanted to vomit at the title.

Saejun. His name is Saejun.

At least... it used to be.

"Do you understand the rules as I've stated to you?" the guard asked.

I nodded, not looking at him.

"Good. You can move freely now. Take care not to ruin that freedom."

He narrowed his eyes. I returned the favor.

I tried not to show how much my side throbbed as I sat in the chair next to the window. There was nothing outside but darkness, not even a trace of my brother being arrested and dragged off in chains. My baby brother was gone.

And Saejun was gone. Again. He returned as easily as he had left... only to leave again.

"I hope you're living the life you always wanted," I whispered bitterly.

"What are you muttering to yourself?" the guard next to the door asked. His head cocked to the side as his eyes raked over me.

"Nothing," I replied. "I simply said that I was hungry."

I stood and started for the kitchen, but the guard's fingers snaked across my arm before clasping onto it.

"You're not allowed to do whatever you want, you know," he said, eyebrow raised.

"The rules were that I'm allowed to move about my home freely. Were you not here for that exchange?"

His jaw ticked, but he smoothed it out into a smile. "In that case, I'll take whatever you're having."

"Get your own food. I'm not your servant."

The guard gripped onto me harder. "But you're a servant of the emperor, aren't you?" He pulled me in closer, his rancid breath curling my toes. "Let me explain it this way. Captain Kim obeys the emperor. We obey Captain Kim. You obey us." He smiled, his lips pulling back to show the yellow of his teeth. "I suggest you listen if you know what's good for you."

"Kyungsuk," another guard said. "Back off the girl. Captain Kim doesn't allow us to touch women."

The guard didn't take his eyes off me as he spoke. "Yes… Captain Kim doesn't let us do a lot of things."

He released his grip and shoved me forward, biting his lip at me as I went to the kitchen. Disgusting. The thought of him and others like him watching me as I slept made me want to slit my own throat before they had the chance.

Dinner was the usual: a quarter bowl of rice and a handful of half-rotten vegetables. Crops were low this harvest, and everyone was struggling on the same diet. Not that the emperor gave a damn. The more people that died the better, as far as he was concerned. Less people to feed. Less people to plot against him.

Boots echoed behind me as I ate. "Smells good."

It was the guard who had been staring at me earlier, no doubt wanting to harass me any chance he got. What was his name? Kyungsuk?

"If you're hungry, I suggest you call your superiors," I replied. "It's not my job to feed you."

I stood to leave. The guard jumped forward and slammed his hand against the wall to intimidate me. How childish.

"Are you saying you wouldn't offer the emperor a single grain of rice?"

I looked him dead in the eyes. "Since when did you become the emperor? You're just a subordinate. All you can do is submit."

He grabbed me by the waist. "I'll show you submission."

I elbowed him hard in the stomach. He doubled over, and I struck my elbow against his forehead. With a grunt, he landed face down on the floor. I ran out of the room, only to be faced with two more guards who were drawing their swords.

To hell with them.

I bolted for the door. One of them stepped in to grab me, but I jumped back, sending a low kick to his gut. As the other lunged forward, I grabbed him and kneed him in the chest. I turned and ran back up the stairs. There were muffled yells and angry words below, but it didn't matter. I had to escape.

I ran past my room and into my brother's, a small ache wishing I had enough time to take something of his with me.

Instead, I kicked open the window.

A spear hit the wall next to me. I turned back to the guard standing in the doorway.

"You're sentencing yourself to death," he said.

I looked at his spear deep in the wall.

"Then consider this my seal," I said.

I jumped out the window.

CHAPTER 2

HOT MEETINGS

I fell from the second story onto the haystacks below with a thunk.

"Find her!" a voice rang out. "Drag her back here!"

I jumped off the haystack and away from the voices, the air in my lungs burning.

If they catch me, I'm dead. And so is Kiwan.

Without even a last glance at my childhood home, I threw myself into the dirty streets of the city.

Hold on, Kiwan. I'm coming.

There had to be a way to find him. Saejun hadn't left long ago. I could gain on them and free my brother —

I stopped. Two men blocked the road, crossing their swords in front of me, blocking the path.

"Wrong choice," one of the men said.

They raised their swords, readying themselves to strike me.

I pulled my foot back, ready to return the favor.

"Come with us," one of the men commanded, "and we won't harm you."

"The hell you won't," I spat back. "But come at me, and I promise you'll feel it tomorrow."

The man in front of me curled his lip as he raised his sword.

"You had your chance."

He charged. I ran towards him with the same speed. When he swung his sword, I dove under it, sliding past him. Coming back to my feet, I kicked him hard in the side, sending him into his friend.

I ran farther down the road, my lungs burning like fire. My feet were weak, but they were quick, and I was able to run much farther than the men weighed down by armor and weapons. My greatest weapon was my speed. I was grateful for that.

The city was not far on foot, and I flew towards it, sure I would be able to find a hiding spot within the safety of the town square. Though it was far past sunset, there was plenty of nightlife to hide away in, the drunkards and their female hostesses now coming out of the walls like swarms of spiders.

Despite the burning in my throat, I had no time for water. Saejun's guards would be behind me soon. I had to hide.

At the sound of drunken laughter and loud singing, I threw myself into the first door I found. It was a tavern. I was instantly overwhelmed by the amount of bodies in a single room, all singing off-pitch, their alcohol splattered on the floor. I edged myself along the wall, trying not to bring any attention to myself. It proved useless, however. I ran into one of the tables, knocking drinks from it. A handful of people turned their heads to glare at me.

I bolted out of the room and ran further down the hall, entering an empty dining room and shutting the door behind me. I tried to calm my heart and my breath. After a few deep breaths, I slid onto one of the cushions next to the table, leaning back against the wall.

Kiwan... how do I get to you?

I couldn't go directly to the prison. Everyone knew that the emperor's prison was crawling with guards, each trained daily by Saejun. There were at least thirty. I had confidence in my abilities, but I was no fool. Thirty against one was a suicide odd.

But how to get into the prison? Wear a disguise? Women could not be guards, and Saejun would know it was me right away. Sneaking in wasn't an option.

I could bring down the guards if I had someone to help me. But who would hate the emperor enough to go up against him?

"Did you find her?" a voice outside the window asked.

The hair on my neck stood on end.

"We'll find her soon enough," another voice said.

I looked around the room, trying to find anything I could use to defend myself. My eyes settled on a long wooden staff in the corner, possibly forgotten by a customer in his drunken stupor. I was glad for the owner's foolishness. I picked it up, its weight easy for me to handle. The voices on the other side of the window got louder, and I held the staff firm, ready to attack.

The door flew open behind me. With a quick turn, I jabbed the staff forward, right at a man who was standing in the entrance. He stepped to the side, grabbing the tip of the staff and shoving it away from his torso before it struck him. He looked at me, raising an eyebrow.

"That's the third attempt on my life today," he said with an accomplished smile. "A new record."

In a breath, I saw that he was not dressed as one of the emperor's guards. His robes were a rich blue and black, showing a man of great wealth. His wide and bright eyes had a dark mischief in them, but an undeniable power. He yanked the staff from my hold, proving that he not only had power of wealth, but power of strength.

He gave a crooked smile with full lips as he set the staff upright and leaned against it.

"Have we met?" he asked, his tone soft and friendly.

I glared at him.

"The silent type, huh?" he asked with a smile. "Or are you an assassin sent to kill me? I'm sorry if I've interrupted your assignment. Perhaps if you had used a sharper object, you would have completed your objective."

"If you were my objective," I countered. "I wouldn't need any weapon at all."

He gave a genuine laugh. "I like your confidence, sweetheart, but you have no idea what you're up against."

There was a scream outside. The man narrowed his eyes, looking past me as though he could see through the wall. He snapped back into a soft smile again, dropping the staff.

"That's my cue," he said. "You may want to leave out that window behind you. The front door is about to become unavailable."

He pointed at the window. I looked over my shoulder quickly, turning back to him as he winked.

"Until next time, sweetheart," he said.

With that, he disappeared.

There was another scream.

"Get out!" someone yelled from the main room. "Fire!"

I stepped out to see the main room in flames, fire rolling through it and filling the hallway. With no other option, I jumped back into the dining room and jumped out the window.

That was two windows in one day. There had to be more creative escape routes.

Panic reigned the town square. Multiple buildings were up in flames, people pouring out of them with chaotic screams. The emperor's guards were now distracted in putting out the flames, giving me the chance to slip away.

I snuck around the bar and found a drop leading to the river. It would be easy to hide myself and make my way towards the prison from there. Throwing myself into the drop, I hit the ground and rolled, the mud of the riverbank slopping beneath me and splattering my clothes. I looked over my shoulder at the flames.

Why were there so many fires suddenly…?

There was the pounding of horse hooves. I ducked behind some shrubs as a string of the emperor's horses made their way down the trail on the opposite side of the river. There were two horses in front, two in back. A whip cracked, followed by a small, high-pitched wail.

A child.

Between the horses was a trail of children, hands chained to each other in a line. One of them fell, and the whip sounded again, followed by another cry.

My stomach turned to ice.

"Get up!" one of the men atop his horse yelled. "Keep moving!"

Another crack of the whip.

"Please stop!" one of the girls cried, standing in front of the other. "She's sick!"

"Then we leave her to die and you can take her lashes!"

The whip sounded again, and it raised me to my feet. But before I could cross the river to reach the path, the man on the horse fell with a gurgled gasp, an arrow in his throat.

"The Rebellion!"

A group of men burst from the trees - maybe half a dozen - their faces covered in scarves. But their faces were not as important as the swords in their hands. They cut down the horses and their riders in a matter of moments, silently, swiftly like the wind. The girls in chains wailed in terror, dropping to the ground.

"Killing the horses was a bit dramatic," a voice said over the cries. "We could have used those."

One of the men turned and bowed. "Forgive us, Master."

The first speaker stayed hidden among the trees, not coming out to reveal his face. But he didn't need to. I could see his blue and black robes from where I stood.

"Release them and get them to the safehouse," he said cooly.

"Yes, Master," the men said in unison.

The group of men cut the chains of the girls and lifted them into their arms, disappearing into the trees as easily as they had came. The so-called *master* disappeared just as quickly, his robe slipping between the trees. I dug my feet into the earth.

The Rebellion.

A group known for their defiance against the emperor. They were his largest enemy in our country, and the most feared.

And possibly... the answer to my prayers.

CHAPTER 3

PROPERTY

I climbed the cliff, pressing myself against the small
ridge. Heights didn't bother me. To stand above the
world and look out on it gave me a sense of peace. In
these moments, it felt like I owned the world and not
the other way around.

In the darkness, there was nothing to see but
shadows… but that was all I needed.

Everyone knew that the Rebellion lived beyond the
forest outside of the city, but no one in their right minds
dared to look for them. Men and women alike were cut
down if they trespassed too deep into the forest. The Rebellion had no mercy on their enemies, and sometimes,
no mercy on their own allies.

In the city, there were stories on top of stories about
the Rebellion: slaughtered guards, poisoned food, destroyed buildings, and burned carriages. They were the
barbarians of the country, but the only ones to survive in
their mission.

Many opposed the emperor. The Rebellion was the only group to go up against him and live. Which meant that they had the strength I needed to get my brother back.

I hid on the cliffside and waited. The moonlight gave enough glow to show who was passing through.

Sooner or later, they would come.

***

After half a night of waiting, six shadows rode across the hills. I could barely make out the sound of the hooves, as if the horses knew they needed to be silent.

I watched as they disappeared into the forest; until there was neither a sound nor a rustle carrying on the wind. There was no way to tell where they had gone, but their tracks were still fresh and I could trace them.

It was a quick drop down the cliffside and a steady run across the lavender fields into the forests. The cicadas were loud as always, but better a summer cicada to block the sound of my steps than the autumn leaves that would give me away.

I tracked them through the forest, going deeper and deeper into the trees until everything around me was nearly covered in darkness. The tree silhouettes stood strong in the moonlight, but the tracks faded the further I walked.

The townsfolk always said that the Rebellion was cloaked in the devil's darkness. Maybe they were right.

Suddenly, my feet were knocked out under me. The world turned upside down and I was looking up at the stars.

And also to a man with a sword at my throat.

His eyes were as dark as the sky behind him, his black and blue robes swirling around his feet. He smirked.

"This is a very dangerous place for you, sweetheart," his gravelly voice hummed, dark as the shadows around his face. "Haven't you heard the rumors? I went through an awful lot of trouble to spread them."

I looked at the sword pointed at my throat, then back up at my attacker. It was the man I had struck with the staff - the same man the Rebellion had called *Master*.

"Are you part of the Rebellion?" I asked.

A single dimple showed in the pale light as he brightly smiled. "What makes you ask that? Shouldn't you be asking me to spare your life instead?"

"If you're the Rebellion, I have something for you. If you're not, then you should plead for your life instead."

He cocked his head to the side. "Bold words. But even in the darkness, I can see your fingers tremble."

I gripped hard into the ground.

"Why would you risk getting slaughtered for an audience with the Rebellion?" he asked.

"If you're not the Rebellion, I have no reason to tell you."

He chuckled, not removing his sword from my throat. "Then I have no reason to tell you whether or not I'm part of the Rebellion."

He was enjoying this conversation circle, and I refused to be part of his game.

"If that's that case," I said, "I suppose I'll have to go find someone else."

"Who said I'd let you live?"

I blinked and smiled. "Who said I was asking for your permission?"

I hooked one foot behind his ankle and kicked his hip with the other. He fell to the ground, just long enough for me to spring to my feet and dash through the trees.

His footsteps rustled behind me. Then they were to the side. Then the front. He stood before me, his sword sheathed and his arms wide in a taunt.

"Don't start a fight you can't finish, sweetheart."

He scratched the faint stubble on his chin with a confident smirk. It made me want to beat his lips off his face.

I brought my hands up to my face in fists. "Same to you."

His eyebrow twitched as he smiled wider. He leapt for me, but I dodged the attack. I scraped the tree beside me, however, and couldn't hold back a hiss as the bark tore my skin open. He advanced again, throwing a kick towards my face. I blocked, then hooked my arm under, pushing him back. I intended for him to fall, but he maneuvered out of the technique effortlessly.

"You know a few takedowns," he acknowledged, "but that won't help you against me."

He threw a double kick this time, landing the second kick in my shoulder. I yelped, but jumped in with a counter palm strike to the chest. He absorbed it, barely wincing, then locked my arm behind my back. He spun me so that my back faced him, his breath against my ear.

"Good try," he whispered, "but you should surrender. I'm the best there is."

I elbowed him to the gut, then spun around and grabbed him by the neck. Bending him over, I kneed him in the stomach and ran. I heard him grunt, then laugh, his footsteps following.

The world turned upside down again.

He straddled me, peering down at me with pride as he climbed on top of me and pinned my arms to the sides. I tried to buck him off, but he stayed on top of me, his knees firm in the earth on both sides of my hips.

"You fight well," he said. "Not as good as me, but well enough. Where did you learn?"

His eyes were playful and keen, like a cat playing with its supper. I glared at him, not answering his question. Instead I only watched him, waiting for his next move so that I could counter it.

He raised an eyebrow, then laughed again. "Alright. You've convinced me."

"Convinced you of what?" I replied.

He rolled off of me and pulled me up by my wrist. "Come with me."

Forcing my hands behind my back, he led me through the forest to a large, dark horse.

"Goyanggi will be happy to escort you to your prison," the man said in my ear. "It's either prison or death, and I'm feeling gracious today."

I squirmed. "There's no chance in hell I'm going anywhere with you."

"You wanted to be taken to the Rebellion, yes?" he asked. "Don't tell me you've changed your mind."

I turned my head, only to see his eyes glitter. There was something playful and seductive about them. Something daring me to follow him.

And he was part of the Rebellion. I knew he was.

It was the only chance to rescue my brother.

Clenching my teeth, I got on the horse. The man jumped up, nestling himself right behind me. The fabric of his robes brushed against my arms, his chest pressing up against my back. I shifted forward, but his hand snaked around my waist, pulling me back into him.

"Don't try escaping from me now, sweetheart," he whispered in my ear. "I guarantee it won't go well for you."

"My name is Jaehwa," I replied. "Not sweetheart."

"Your name doesn't make any difference to me." He grinned right before pulling a scarf from his belt and tying it around my eyes. "You're the property of Sok Haneul now."

CHAPTER 4

LEADER

"Why do you have a surname?"

The blindfolded ride on horseback was excruciatingly dull. Haneul refused to answer my questions despite his insistence that I come with him.

"You know," he said, "you're making me wish that I had a second scarf for your mouth."

"Only the upper class and royalty have a surname. How did you get the name Sok if you're part of the Rebellion?"

"*Am* I part of the Rebellion?" he teased. "I don't remember saying that."

I elbowed him. "Enough of your stupid games! Why won't you answer my questions?"

His hand came to my mouth, forcing my head back against his chest as his breath came to my ear.

"I can't guarantee your safety," he growled, "if you don't stop barking."

His fingers were rough against my lips - a sign of a man who had fought in battles for some time. Saejun had similar calluses on his hands when we were younger, but

I could tell that Haneul's calluses were those of someone with far more fighting experience even though I was sure him and Saejun were the same age.

I had asked Haneul what his age was, but he only replied that he outranked me. Even if he was younger, he said, I would still have to speak formally to him.

Like hell I would.

"We're here," he sang in my ear. "Try to make a good impression, sweetheart. I taught my men to kill strangers."

He pulled the blindfold from my eyes as he slid off the horse. When my eyes adjusted to the darkness, I could make out the silhouettes of small, thatched houses scattered around an empty clearing.

Haneul held a hand out and flicked his fingers to command me to get off the horse. I complied. As soon as I dropped next to him, however, he wrapped the scarf around my mouth.

"What do you think you're doing?" I protested, my words half-covered with the scarf.

"Much better," he replied. "That tongue is going to get both of us into trouble."

His arm wrapped around my waist, pulling me close to him. I pushed back against his chest, protesting through the scarf around my mouth.

"You know," he said, "this is a camp full of men that don't get to leave base often. I can only imagine what they'd do with a cute little thing such as yourself."

I let the words process while looking around the base. Shadows walked from one hut to the next, the moonlight hitting the whites of their eyes as they turned to look at us. I curled my fingers against Haneul's robes, wondering if I was seeing ghosts instead of human beings.

He only chuckled.

"Stick with me," he said. "You won't get out of this alive otherwise."

Putting my hands against my back, he pushed me deeper into camp. I could have easily thrown him off, but his grip was possessive; and by the looks in the eyes of the men we passed, it was safer to be possessed. Their eyes made it clear that they had no reservations to kill. I assumed they already had.

There must have been at least two dozen small houses in the clearing, with recently used fire pits between them. I could smell the charred meat, making my stomach turn in jealousy. I couldn't remember the last time my brother and I had eaten meat, if I was honest.

Haneul turned me to face him, knocking me out of my thoughts.

"Once we enter," he said, "don't speak unless you're spoken to. This will either go well or tragically for you."

"And why should I listen to you?" I asked through a mouthful of scarf.

He smiled again, his teeth showing. It made my stomach shudder.

"Because," he said, "whether you like it or not, sweetheart, I'm your only hope."

"Haneul!" a smoky voice called from inside the hut. "Why do I hear your babbling at the devil's hour?"

"Are you decent?" Haneul yelled back.

"Why should I be?" the voice returned. "God knows you never are."

"Put on a robe. I have something to show you."

There was muttering as someone lit a candle on the other side of the house. A man's silhouette appeared in the doorway.

"What the devil -"

The man threw open the door, meeting my eyes immediately. His voice had been so deep and blunt that I thought he would be an older man with a graying beard, but in reality, he looked no more than twenty-five; his dark, unbraided hair hanging past his collarbone. His eyes were small, but they were strong and sharp. They practically absorbed the shadows.

No... they looked like they could *control* the shadows.

"What stupid thing have you done now?" the man growled as he stared at me.

"Let's talk," Haneul replied.

The man stared at me for a long moment, then without a word, he turned back into the house and shut the door. Haneul pointed his chin at the entrance, then brought me inside. The belongings inside were simple: a bed mat, a water pitcher, and some robes hanging next to the wall. There were knives next to the clothes, and a long sword in the corner.

"Why did you bring a woman here?" the man asked.

"I wanted to show off my new present to myself," Haneul said, raising my arm. I jerked it away.

The man raised a thin eyebrow. "Don't you have enough women?"

"Not that kind of present," Haneul returned. "A recruit."

The man stopped and turned, his sharp eyes cutting into me. He frowned.

"No women on base. You know the rules."

"Come on, Kangdae," Haneul teased. "It's been years since that rule. I think it's time we took on a new pet."

"Pet?" I objected through my gag.

The man stepped forward, looking down into my eyes. His eyes would have been beautiful if they weren't so intimidating. He yanked the scarf from my mouth, glancing at my lips for a moment as if he was trying to decide whether or not to cut them off of my face.

"What's the real reason?" the man asked me. "Why did you come here?"

I stood as tall as I could. "The emperor's guards have taken my brother into custody for murder. He's innocent."

"How is that my problem?"

"I want your help."

He smirked. "Why would I help you? You're nothing to me."

"Yes, but I have something you want: information on Saejun, head of the emperor's guards."

I looked at both Haneul and Kangdae. Haneul raised an eyebrow. Kangdae did nothing at all.

"You expect me to risk my men's lives because you have some information?" Kangdae rolled his eyes. "Rich. For all I know, it's false information and you're here to lead me into a trap."

"I knew him before he became captain," I explained. "Whatever information you need, I can give you. Whatever information I don't have, I can get."

Kangdae stepped closer, leaning to my ear. "I have men that can do the same just as easily. Do you expect me to believe you're better than my own men?"

The scent of his breath was sweet despite his bitter words. He pulled back, sighing as he looked at Haneul.

"On the other hand," he continued. "Haneul was stupid enough to bring you here and give away our coordinates."

Haneul gave a half-shrug, grinning. "Oops."

"I won't kill you," Kangdae continued, "but I can't let you leave either."

His eyes drifted up and down my body. He curled his lip like he was looking at broken furniture.

"You can do whatever you want with her, Haneul," he said. "But keep her away from the men and the frontlines."

Haneul clapped his hands and rubbed them together, smiling. "I was hoping you'd say that, Boss."

"Wait!" I objected. "I need to save my brother."

"Then you shouldn't have come here," the man said. "That was your mistake."

"He'll be executed."

"You're lucky I won't execute you." He leaned back on his heels, a scarred collarbone peeking out of his robe. "If you want my help that badly, you need to give me something in return. Something I can't get anywhere else. I'll be waiting here when you figure out what that is. Now, get out. I need to sleep."

He nodded to Haneul. Haneul bowed and grabbed my arm, pulling me out of the hut.

"Wait!" I said, "I'm not finished -"

"You are for now," Haneul replied. "Kangdae is finished with you. We can try again when he's in a better mood, which is as rare as the full moon."

"You expect me to sit around and wait then? I have things to do."

Haneul's head cocked to the side in amusement. "How do you know Captain Kim?"

I swallowed. "We grew up together."

"And you would betray him so easily?"

"He took my brother. My brother is all I have left. I have no other family."

Haneul put his arm around me. "You have me now."

I shoved my hand in his face and threw him off. "I don't want you."

He chuckled, stumbling in front of me. "You don't really have a choice in this, sweetheart. I already told you. You're property of Sok Haneul now."

"Stop saying your own name. It's weird."

He winked and put his tongue between his teeth. "I can make you say it instead."

"Drop dead."

I was about to shove him away again, but he grabbed my wrist and pulled me with him.

"Come on," he said. "I want to show you a special room of mine."

I wasn't surprised that Haneul had a special room. I was, however, surprised about what was in it.

It was a large training center, with high walls and a display of weapons and gear. There were wooden columns to match the floors, swords and knives on the walls, as well as scrolls of ancient creeds.

"What is this place?" I asked.

"This is my domain," he replied. "I don't believe I've formally introduced myself yet."

"Sok Haneul. Yes, I've heard it a few times now."

"Ah, but you don't know my actual job title, sweet-heart." He grabbed a knife from the wall, spinning it between his fingers. "So let me introduce myself one last time to you. My name is Sok Haneul… the combat master of the Rebellion. And you… you're my new project."

CHAPTER 5

TRADE

I slept with Haneul.

Only in the literal sense.

"I can leave you with the wolves," he had said after we left the training center. "But you're better off with me."

I curled my lip at him. "So my choice is between the pack of wolves or their leader?"

"If you're going to be amongst the wolves, sweetheart, you might as well be on the leader's side."

I couldn't argue with him. And although the look in his eyes was dangerous, it wasn't murderous, so I took my chances.

His home was large but empty. A single mat was on the floor, a collection of swords and staves in the corner. His laundry was scattered in the corners of the room, crumpled pieces of paper decorating the floor along with his dirty clothing.

"Welcome home," he said.

I wrapped my arms around myself from the sudden thought of my family home occupied by the emperor's guards.

Saejun's guards.

How could you take everything, Saejun? When did you start to hate me that much…?

"What's with the look?" Haneul asked. "My place doesn't smell that bad."

I shook my head at him, shoving down any emotion he might see as weakness.

"Master?" a voice asked outside the hut.

Haneul opened the door, and a man holding a bed mat walked in. His copper skin and black hair were so pure that they glowed in the darkness. He looked to be the same age as Kiwan - around twenty, perhaps - but he showed no fragility in his physique despite his youth.

His eyes met mine. His jaw tightened as his eyes narrowed, the look in his eyes anything but welcoming.

"Enough staring, Intak," Haneul said, taking the bed mat from him. "She's not that easily intimidated."

Haneul smirked as he rolled the bed out on the ground.

"At least, she pretends not to be," he muttered in my direction.

"Does the boss know?" Intak asked, still staring at me.

Haneul hummed.

"And he's okay with it?"

"That's between me and him," Haneul replied. "You've done your job. Get out of my house."

The man looked me over one last time, then swung the door open and left us both behind without another word. The air chilled.

"Don't worry about him," Haneul said. "He's edgy, but harmless. The opposite of you."

"What?" I asked.

"Sleep," he commanded, pointing to the new mat on the ground. He wrapped a blanket around me, turning my shoulders to face him. "You'll need all the rest you can get for tomorrow. I can promise you that."

He fell asleep in an instant, but I didn't have the same luck. All I could do was imagine Kiwan alone, tortured by the guards and other prisoners in Saejun's hands.

The emperor didn't execute right away. There was three months between an arrest and an execution. He took his time, slowly making murderers suffer until they were begging for death on the day of their execution.

Someday… I would return the favor.

***

"We need to put you to work," Haneul said the next morning as he tied his sword onto his hip.

"Why are you helping me?" I asked, raising an eyebrow at him. It was something I had been wondering since he agreed to bring me to the Rebellion.

He grinned as he cinched his belt around his waist. "Because I plan on you helping me, sweetheart."

Haneul led us towards the middle of the camp, meeting with a man wearing a white robe covered in blood.

"Morning, Dolshik," Haneul said. "I came to introduce you to my new pet, Jaehwa."

The man's eyes narrowed. "You're pushing your luck these days, Han."

"I have plenty to spare," Haneul replied, shrugging.

The man pulled a long knife from his robe. I stepped back. His eyes widened, then he burst into happy laughter.

"Paranoid?" the man asked.

"Quick," Haneul corrected.

"I see." The man with the knife looked me over. "If she stays, she'll want to eat. If she wants to eat, she needs to work."

Haneul grabbed my hands, pulling me forward and fanning my hands out flat.

"Farmer's hands," Haneul said. "Put her in the gardens. You're short-handed, right?"

Dolshik cocked his head to the side. "You'll have to share your portion with her today. We're still waiting for the other half of the hunters to come back."

Haneul nodded. "Fair enough."

I looked over my shoulder as three men came towards me, carrying a large, dead buck. Dolshik waved them over to another large house, walking inside with his knife in hand.

Haneul led me further into the camp, towards a long, wooden building. It didn't have walls, but it had a roof that stretched out above several long tables. Haneul motioned for me to sit at one of the tables, then sat next to me.

Everyone's heads turned.

Haneul smiled. "As you were, soldiers."

They turned their heads back down. No one breathed a word.

I smelled breakfast before I saw it. Each man got a bowl of soup, not large, but still bigger than anything I had seen in awhile. A single bowl was placed between Haneul and me, with cabbage, rice, and chunks of meat floating in the broth.

How did they eat so well?

Haneul took a spoon and handed it to me. "Why are your eyes so wide? The emperor eats far more than this."

I looked away. It was more than I could ever feed Kiwan and myself.

He forced the spoon into my hand. I rubbed it between my fingers, afraid to dip it in. Haneul nudged me. I finally took a spoonful, sucking it down and letting the broth settle on my tongue. I could make broth, but it didn't have this much flavor. It was usually bean sprout broth, with random vegetables our garden spat out on occasion. This was an actual bone broth, heavy and dense with flavor.

I gripped the spoon.

Haneul's chewing slowed. He swallowed his mouthful and wrinkled his nose. "Dolshik used cabbage again. It ruins the whole thing, if you ask me. You okay with cabbage?"

I nodded. He slid the bowl over.

"Eat up." His eyebrows bounced. "You'll need the strength if you're going to survive what I have prepared for you."

***

After breakfast, Haneul led me to the gardens. There was a clearing in the forest, twice the size of my family's fields. Plenty of different crops were growing, healthy and wild. I wished I could say the same about my own family's crops.

"If you can keep these alive, I'll keep you alive," Haneul said. "You'll come here in the mornings, and come back to me in the afternoons. I have other uses for you besides talking to plants all day."

"And what uses are those?"

"Something I think you're going to like."

He wiggled his eyebrows.

"I'll kill you if you try anything on me," I replied.

"I have no doubts you'd try," he said, "but you wouldn't succeed."

Haneul showed me around the gardens, explaining each crop and the target production for the crew. By the numbers, there were maybe a hundred men, but not more.

As he showed me how to work the fields, a shadow crossed our path. I looked up, recognizing the cut of the man's jaw even though I had only seen it once in the dark. I stood, rushing to block his path.

Kangdae stopped, raising an eyebrow. "Why are you in front of me?"

I gripped my hands into fists. "I won't leave until you help me."

"You're not in a place to negotiate," he said. "You're on my property and you have no value to me. You're already overstepping your bounds."

He sidestepped, but I blocked his path again.

"Let me prove myself," I said.

He scoffed. "Haneul."

Haneul stepped in next to Kangdae. "Yes, Boss?"

Kangdae's eyes went straight through me as he spoke.

"If you insist on keeping this woman in camp," he said, "make sure to handle her properly. She should know her place."

He glanced down at my soiled hands, then side-stepped again, passing me. I clenched my fists tight, the knuckles completely white.

"I think he likes you," Haneul said as he watched Kangdae walk off.

I growled. "What makes you say that?"

"He didn't try to break my arm when you spoke out of turn. That's a good sign."

He walked forward, past the gardens and towards the other side of the forest.

"Enough talking, and enough gardening," he said. "It's time to start the fun stuff."

"As in…?"

He turned towards me, dimples accompanying his smile. "All pets need training, sweetheart."

CHAPTER 6

MISSING

"*The soil is bad.*"

"*What do you mean? Soil is soil.*"

"*No, Jaehwa, look. The soil here is damaged and can't produce anything. It needs to rest. It needs to heal.*"

"*We don't have that option. If we don't try and plant now, there will be nothing for the harvest, and our family will starve this winter.*"

"*I wouldn't let you starve. You know that.*"

"*And what if your farms can't produce enough, Sae-jun? What if there's only enough for your family?*"

"*Idiot. I just said I wouldn't let you starve. When I make you a promise, you need to believe it.*"

I dug the soil out of my nails.

I had been working in the gardens for two days now. I hadn't seen Kangdae in that time, but I saw far too much of Haneul. He was never too busy to annoy me with his twisted sense of humor, it seemed.

Since I had experience in working our family fields, Dolshik didn't spend much time teaching me about the gardens. I was usually left to myself in the mornings while Dolshik prepared the afternoon meals and Haneul trained the Rebellion.

I wished I could train with them. I needed something to take my mind off the memories.

The soil in these gardens was rich and dark, unlike our farmland. Maybe if our soil had been like this, Mother would still be alive.

I missed her. I missed her so much that it hurt. Even though as a child I rarely saw her during the day, it felt so warm when she came home at night. I remembered her dirtied hands from the fields, her soiled clothes, and her bright smile. Even after Father left, she still smiled like our dry, empty fields grew gold.

And worse… I missed *him*. Not that arrogant, vile captain of the guards, but Saejun, the righteous farmer's son long before he was given the name Captain Kim. After seeing him again, dozens of memories I had shoved down to my gut were now bubbling up, no matter how hard I tried to stop them.

I couldn't forget those days in the farmlands, back when I trusted him. Back when he made all those stupid promises to protect me.

No, the promises weren't stupid. I was.

"What are you thinking about?" Haneul asked, interrupting my thoughts.

I frowned as I turned my head up towards him at him, coming to my feet and dusting the dirt from my knees.

"I'm thinking about how much I don't trust you," I replied.

He pursed his lips and bounced his eyebrow. "So you were thinking about me?"

"Why are you here so early?" I asked, ignoring his terrible flirting.

"I've come to take you someplace beautiful," he replied. He wiggled his fingers to command me to follow. "And for the record, sweetheart, I don't trust you, either."

The forest opened up to a wide field, the scent of lavender and grass hitting my nose. My heart sank at the smell. It brought up even more memories I was tired of. But the sun glistening on the lake in front of us was enough to distract me from the annoyance; the gentle ripples from the water bugs on the water's surface calming my spirit.

"What is this place?" I asked.

Haneul rested his hands behind his back as he looked out on the water. "I knew you'd like it. It's a special place of mine."

"You have a lot of special places."

He lifted an eyebrow and smiled suggestively. I frowned back at him.

"Can you swim?" he asked as we walked along the edge of a lake.

"Of course," I replied. "I was raised around the —"

He shoved me in the lake. The cold water struck me in the face, and I spit out water as I came back to the surface. My hair and clothes were completely drenched.

"What the hell!" I yelled.

"Just checking," Haneul replied, shrugging. "Come on out."

I pulled myself out, the weight of my clothes pulling down against me. The summer breeze suddenly felt colder than it had moments ago.

"I don't have any spare clothes, you know," I growled, wringing the water out of my robes.

"You can strip if you want."

"Drop dead."

He chuckled. "You're ready for your resistance training now. Come with me."

He took me past the lake to a cleared area, surrounded by trees.

"You ready?" he asked.

"For what?"

"Private training. You should feel honored that I'm not charging you for it."

"It only means that you'll ask for a trade later."

He put his finger against his nose and winked. Licking his bottom lip he turned to face me, his irises shifting from playful to predatory as his right heel shifted back. I tensed.

"What is it you want from me?" I asked.

"I want you to fight me."

"What?"

He swung. I dodged his arm before the punch landed. He jumped towards me and swung again, and this time I brought my hand up to block right before returning a punch towards his face myself. He dipped his head sideways, anticipating the move and avoiding it gracefully. I stepped back again, waiting for him.

His eyes narrowed for a moment before he sprung at me again. This time, he tried to kick to my shoulder, but I turned, blocking it with both my forearms. He clicked his tongue, then kicked again. I did the same block, the pain vibrating through my arms.

"No good," he said.

His leg swept under me, sending me on my back. As he charged, I kicked into his gut, jumping back up to my feet. I raised my hands ready to fight again, now aware of the fact that his core was rock solid. His neck muscles seized right before he lunged for me again, and I spun to kick him. Before I could land the kick, however, he intercepted the spin and pressed my back against his front, his hand around my neck.

"This is how you get your throat slit, sweetheart," he said in my ear. "Don't ever give your back to your opponent."

His arms tightened around me as I struggled.

I grunted. "I could do it properly if you hadn't shoved me in the lake and ruined my clo— are you smelling my hair?"

"…no."

I elbowed him and spun out of his grip. I raised my hands, waiting for him to attack again.

"Wet clothes are the least of your problems," Haneul said. "Your moves are too rigid. They're easy to predict. That may work if you have a weapon to back you up or if you're fighting someone with the same style, but it won't work in the streets. You fight like fire. I need you to fight like water."

I scrunched my nose. "What does that even mean?"

He smiled. "You'll see."

Time passed painfully. Haneul directed intervals of sparring, running, and balancing. He gave me two breaks, allowing only enough time for water. By the time we finished, my wet clothes had dried and drenched again from sweat.

"Let's go back," he said finally as the sun fell a couple of hours past noon. "Mid-afternoon training starts at camp soon."

"What?" I asked, panting. "There's more?"

"You didn't think I was finished with you, did you? I have plans for you, my pet. We're just beginning."

***

It was like that every day for two weeks. I worked the gardens in the mornings, trained privately with Haneul afterwards, and then trained with his men in the late afternoon. None of them questioned his decision, but they also treated me as if I was completely invisible.

Except for Intak. He stood at the highest rank among the soldiers, wasting no opportunity to glare at me from across the room. The coldness in his eyes was borderline murderous, and I had no doubts that if Haneul paired us as sparring partners that Intak would do his best to end me.

Why, I didn't know.

Breakfast was the heartiest meal of the day, usually a soup of some sort with meat and vegetables. Lunch was only bean sprout broth, while dinner was usually rice and vegetable side dishes.

Kangdae ate with everyone for dinner, but I never saw him at any other meal. He also never acknowledged me inside or outside the dining hall. Sometimes I stared at him for the entire meal, but he never glanced back. Not once.

I was completely invisible to him.

"Are you doing alright, miss?"

Two bright, sparkly eyes looked back at me, accompanied by a child-like smile. It was Dolshik's assistant, Geonho. I had seen his face in passing, but this was the first time he had ever ventured to speak with me. He was certainly the youngest one at camp, perhaps not even breaking nineteen.

He set down my and Haneul's broth on the table, then plopped down on the other side, grabbing his knees as he crossed his legs.

"It's been awhile since I've seen a woman stay so long," he said with a cheerful round face. "A pretty one, too. Are we keeping her, Haneul?"

"Of course," Haneul replied, slurping from his bowl. "She's my pet."

I frowned at him.

"It'll be nice to have a woman around again," the happy kid continued, rocking back and forth. "As much as I love my brothers here, it's nice to have a little variety to mix things up —"

"Mix things up and eat more of my food," Dolshik said, coming up behind the happy little kid and making him cower. "There's enough going on here. We don't need variety."

The happy kid looked up at Dolshik. "Even you said yesterday that it was good to see —"

Dolshik kicked him before he could finish. The kid stood up, rubbing his backside.

"Get back to work, Geonho," Dolshik said. "Your job is to serve the food. Not make small talk."

Still rubbing his back, the kid bowed, flashing a smile before wandering back to the kitchen. Dolshik's eyes fell back between Haneul and me, his eyebrow raised.

"How long should I expect this to continue?" Dolshik asked. "If I have to keep feeding this girl —"

"This girl is under my command until I decide otherwise," Haneul replied. He stuffed part of his vegetable pancake in his cheek. "Your job is to feed whoever sits at these tables."

Dolshik turned his head back towards Kangdae. Kangdae looked at him, then in my direction. It was the first time he had looked at me in the last two weeks. I straightened. His jaw ticked, but he made no other attempts at acknowledging me before averting his eyes back down to his food.

"The Boss hasn't said anything?" Dolshik asked.

Haneul shrugged. "Only that she's mine."

"And why do you need a woman in the Rebellion?" a new voice cut in. "What use do you have for her, despite the obvious?"

Dolshik stepped back as Intak came forward, his fists clenched at his sides.

"Intak…" Haneul warned.

"You have dozens of women outside of the camp," Intak continued. "Why the hell do you need one inside?"

Haneul chuckled. "Dozens is a bit of an exaggeration. Twenty or so, maybe…"

"And why are you training her every day? Privately."

The other men looked at us, their chopsticks still. Kangdae included.

Haneul's eyelashes fluttered before he put down his chopsticks and leaned back. "Is that what you're worried about? That I'm replacing you?"

Intak's fists unclenched and clenched again. Haneul stood from the table, facing him.

"Are you training your whore to be your replacement?" Intak asked, voice low.

This time I stood from the table. "I'm not his whore."

"I can't think of any other reason he would keep you around," Intak spat back. "And I can't think of any reason he would train you to fight at all. You're a poor excuse for a fighter."

"Make your move and see if you say the same thing after I slice you to pieces."

Intak stepped forward, but Haneul put a hand out, stopping him.

"She's not my whore," Haneul said, sounding bored. "And she's not my replacement. She's my pet. And a project you don't need to worry about right now."

"Why would you keep this from me?" Intak asked.

Haneul reached out and ripped Intak's robe open. There was a deep cut from Intak's collarbone to his ribs; red, barely scabbing over.

"Why did you keep *this* from me?" Haneul returned.

Intak's eyes widened. He lowered his head.

"I shouldn't even let you do afternoon training in this condition," Haneul continued, "but I was waiting for you to be honest with me. Tell me, has it been healing the way it's supposed to?"

Intak bit his lip.

"I didn't think so." Haneul sighed. "For now, she's taking your time slot. When you've fully healed, I'll continue to train you as my successor. But remember: your future position can be taken from you. Don't get so attached to it that you forget who *I* am."

Intak bowed. "Yes, Master. Forgive me."

"And you," Haneul said, turning back towards me. "You're not strong enough to fight my men. So don't provoke them."

I scoffed. "What do you mean I'm not strong enough? I train every day with you —"

"— Because you're not anywhere close to where you need to be. I train you eight hours a day because you're weak. Only I get to decide when you're strong enough to fight."

I looked at Kangdae. He brought his tea up to his lips, keeping eye contact with me as he sipped. He lowered his cup back to the table, leaning back against the pillar behind him and shutting his eyes.

With one last look at Haneul and Intak, I turned on my heel and left. As hungry as I was, the humiliation was too much to bear.

Weak. He called me weak. In front of Kangdae, nonetheless.

If he had known the things I'd been through, he wouldn't have thrown that word around so easily. The arrogant, stupid bastard.

I walked away from the dining hall, towards the edge of the camp. I couldn't leave - I wasn't sure how to find my way out, and I didn't have a plan even if I did. How could I save Kiwan if I didn't have the Rebellion's help? And where would I live? I was homeless and - worse - helpless.

How could I get the Rebellion to help me?

***

The moon rose high, but shed no light on my unanswered questions. I held tight to my frustrations: Saejun, Haneul, Intak, Dolshik, Kangdae… a list of people with no other objective but to hold me back. Shutting my eyes, I imagined each one of their faces.

I could use my anger. My anger could fuel me to beat them.

To hell with all of them. If they thought I was weak, all I needed to do was prove them wrong.

"There you are," a low voice said in my ear, right before an arm snaked around my shoulders.

"I'm not in the mood for your games, Han—"

I stopped as I turned around. It wasn't Haneul.

The heartless leader of the Rebellion was standing behind me, his eyes soft in the moonlight.

"I was looking all over for you," Kangdae said, his hand reaching up for my face. His fingertips were cold, but his touch was warm; uncharacteristically delicate and smooth.

He stepped in closer. My heart raced as his natural airy scent invaded my space, and I could only freeze as he held my gaze.

He chuckled softly as he touched my cheek. "I've missed you… Yeojin."

CHAPTER 7

TRUST

"Yeojin?" I asked. "Who is —"

His arms wrapped tight around me, his face burying into my shoulder. I swallowed. Was he drunk? He didn't smell drunk. He would have to be completely intoxicated to even speak to me, let alone touch me.

Or hold me… like this…

His warm arms blocked the cool summer wind from my skin. It even blocked the humiliation of dinner that was still prickling against my chest. He held me tight; tighter than anyone had held me in years.

But something was wrong.

"Kangdae?" I asked, bringing my hands up to pull away.

Suddenly his full weight fell against me, knocking me off balance. I grabbed him to keep both of us from falling over.

"Kangdae, what's wrong? Answer me."

He curled up and pulled back, standing straight again. His eyes were warm, but glossed over. He smiled once more before turning around and walking back towards camp. I followed, staying a few feet behind and keeping silent. He wasn't stumbling around like a drunkard or someone high on opium. An allergic reaction? A poison?

He returned to his hut and stepped inside. Before I could follow him further, a hand reached out and pulled me back.

Dolshik's assistant, Geonho, had a rare frown as he shook his head at me.

"What's going on?" I asked Geonho.

He pulled on my arm, leading us away from the hut. "You shouldn't be seen here. Come with me."

His hand was gentle and his face was matted in a thousand concerned little lines, so I complied. He led us back towards Haneul's hut, but stopped out of earshot.

"What did I just witness?" I asked. "What's wrong with Kangdae?"

Geonho fanned the air, motioning me to keep my voice quiet. "Nothing's wrong with him."

"He *hugged* me. Of course something is wrong with him. Is he drunk? Taking opium?"

Geonho scrunched his nose and laughed. "He doesn't drink or do opium. That would compromise his focus."

"Then what's wrong?"

Geonho sighed, shoulders dropping. He looked back to Kangdae's hut.

"Ghosts," he said.

I raised an eyebrow. "Say again?"

"Ghosts. Of the past. Ones that haunt him every night."

I cocked my head to the side, looking back at Kangdae's hut. "Are you saying spirits torment him?"

"I'm saying his spirit is tormented." His eyes fell, and he folded his arms. "You can't be the leader of the Rebellion and not suffer in some way. And our leader suffers in many."

I looked back at Kangdae's hut. What would torment the heartless leader of the Rebellion?

"Please, miss," Geonho said, grabbing my hand. "Don't tell anyone what you've seen or heard tonight. It will put you in a very bad position."

My thoughts returned to dinner. It seemed I was already in a terrible position as it was. I didn't need to agitate it further. Not if I wanted Kiwan back.

I nodded in agreement, fully intending to break my promise later.

Yeojin. If that was a name that Kangdae said in the middle of the night incoherently, then it had to be important. Whoever Yeojin was, she might be a key to getting the upper hand on Kangdae. At the same time, I had to be cautious.

Geonho puffed out some air, dropping his head. "Thank you, miss. I know our group hasn't been the most welcoming."

"They hate me."

Geonho weakly smiled and shook his head. "That's not it. To them, mixing you in with us is like sentencing an innocent woman to her death."

I scoffed and rolled my eyes. "So Intak's death stare is out of compassionate concern?"

"Oh, no. Intak probably hates you."

He laughed with such innocence that I couldn't help but smile in return. He gave a small bow, patting me on the shoulder.

"Get some rest," Geonho encouraged. "It's past curfew and I don't want you in any more trouble."

With a childish wave he trotted back to his hut. I wasn't ready to face Haneul, but maybe at this late hour he had given up on me and fallen asleep.

He was sure to put me through worse training tomorrow for my attitude at dinner. Fine. He could go ahead and make me stronger.

He was laying in bed when I opened the hut, his eyes shut.

"You're late," he muttered, keeping his eyes closed.

I didn't reply as I crawled into my bed. I curled up, back towards him.

"I can't guarantee your protection if you wander off," he said.

"I don't want your protection."

"Want and need are two different things. I never said anything about you *wanting* my protection."

"You never said anything about me needing it, either."

He huffed through his nose. I heard his blankets shift before his arm landed in front of my face. He hovered above me, eyes burning deep into mine.

"I'm the only reason you're here," he whispered, "and I'm the only way you're going to survive. If your brother means anything to you, you need to learn to keep your mouth shut."

I glared. "Because I'm an outsider? Or because I'm a woman?"

"Because I'm your master." He grabbed my chin and forced me to look at him. "A pet always obeys her master. Because if she doesn't, she ends up wandering off alone… eventually crossing paths with someone who slits her throat for barking too much."

He let go of my face. I turned away from him.

"You and Intak both need to learn silence," he continued. "You ruin your advantages. Which, in turn, ruins my advantages. You both belong to me, so you will both learn it. Understand?"

I didn't answer.

"I asked you a question."

"Yes."

"Yes, what?"

"Yes, I understand."

He pulled my face back towards his. "Yes, *Master.*"

I sneered at him. He smiled.

"You'll say it one day," he said, rolling off me. "I'll make you say it sooner than you think."

He returned to his own bed. I covered myself, wrapping my arms tight around my shoulders.

Despite Haneul's scolding, I could only think about Kangdae. The man who never looked in my direction had me tight in his arms only moments ago. His hold was so warm and desperate, the opposite of his day-to-day demeanor.

Who was Yeojin?

But more importantly… who was Kangdae?

***

It was too quiet.

I didn't dare move from my position. I crouched, hoping to get a more advantageous angle in the darkness. It didn't work. I couldn't see anything through the forest trees, no sounds to give away any positions.

Snap.

I looked down at the twig under my foot that had just betrayed me.

Damn. He had heard that.

I jumped up and grabbed a low hanging branch, pulling myself up. Even at the top, it was useless to try and see through the thick sea of trees. I couldn't go anywhere, and even if I could, Haneul would find me. He always found me. Yet, I could never find him.

Where was he now?

A knife whirled past my ear and slammed into the tree trunk next to my shoulder. The branch bent as I jumped back, sending me back to the ground with a thud. I groaned, pain echoing through my hip and shoulder.

"No good," Haneul's voice said among the trees. "Get my knife and start again."

I picked myself up off the ground, climbed up for his knife, and pulled it out of the trunk.

"Where are you?" I asked.

"Come find me."

I dropped back to the ground - softly, this time - and looked around. There wasn't a shadow out of place, but it was so dark that I could have been wrong. The moon was hiding tonight along with Haneul.

"If you want your brother back, you'll need to be stealthy and resourceful," he said. "At this rate, you're not ready."

"You want me to wait for your approval? He'll be dead before then."

"Traitors are tortured for three months. It's been three weeks. You have time."

Anger burned in my throat and eyes. "And why should I let my brother endure torture for so long?"

An arm struck my neck as it wrapped around it, another hand breaking the knife out of my grip. Haneul's heavy, earthy musk flooded me from behind as he cut off my air supply.

"Because if you don't listen to me," he growled in my ear, "you're both dead."

He released me, casually picking up his knife as I coughed. I rubbed my neck as it throbbed from the bone of his arm striking it.

"You let your emotions control you," he said. "Fail. Again."

That was the sixth time he had failed me in the past two days. Stealth was not something I was trained in, and it wasn't something picked up easily. I couldn't even tell if I had improved. The frustration was suffocating.

"I think we need to raise the stakes," he continued. "You trust me too much."

"Trust you?" I asked with a laugh. "Whatever gave you that idea?"

He raised the knife, pressing it against my cheek. I didn't blink. Locking eyes with him, he dragged the knife from my cheek to my throat.

"I could end you with a flick of my wrist," he whispered, "but you're not even flinching. You trust me, Jaehwa. You're foolish enough to trust me with your life."

I clenched my teeth. "I don't trust you with anything."

His eyes drifted down my arms to my hands. He cocked his head to the side, pressing his lips together and meeting my eyes once more. There was something enchanting about his eyes, even with a knife in his hand. Confident and playful, like he knew he could hold my attention.

He wet his lips with his tongue and smiled.

"Your body tells me otherwise," he said.

"My body isn't yours to talk to."

"Your nerves speak louder than your mouth. They betray you every time you speak." He leaned in close to my ear. "And trust me, sweetheart, if I wanted your body for myself… you wouldn't stand a chance against me."

He stepped back, holding his knife out to his side.

"Intak," he commanded.

Intak's footsteps were completely silent as he stepped out from the trees. He walked towards us like a ghost; as if his feet never touched the ground. He took the knife from Haneul's hand, twirling it in his fingers as he glared.

"Yes, Master?" Intak replied.

Haneul took a few more steps back. "Hide and seek."

Intak nodded, his lips pulling smugly to the side. "Yes, Master."

"What are you doing?" I asked.

"You have until the count of twenty to hide, sweetheart," Haneul said, his teeth shining in the darkness. "And if Intak finds you, he has my permission to mark you… in any way he wants."

CHAPTER 8

SEEK

"One…" Haneul counted, flashing his teeth.

Intak flipped the knife in his fingers, staring deep into me.

What the…?

"Two," Haneul continued. "Losing time, sweetheart. Three…"

Intak gripped the knife handle.

I ran.

Fatigue consumed me as much as adrenaline. Hours of training with Haneul had drained me and now I had to fight for my life.

I knew Intak could hear my heavy footsteps. I didn't have any stealth before training, and now drained of all energy and patience, I had even less.

There has to be another way. Not hiding. Not being sneaky. Maybe… maybe the opposite is the answer.

The trees got thicker, their roots tripping me and their bark scraping my arms as I squeezed through. I didn't know if I was getting deeper into the forest or coming out of it, but I knew one thing…

It had been twenty counts.

I ran down the path, then took off my shoes, tucking them into my robe. I backtracked down the path I came, trying only to leave faint steps in the ground. The leaves and branches nipped at my feet. I winced but made no sound. Finding a large trunk with a low branch, I began to climb, cursing internally at the rustling leaves.

I sank low in one of the branches, flattening myself against it.

Intak came not long after. His skin and knife glistened in what little light there was, sending my heart back in my throat. He looked around, then crouched low.

He followed my path, his moves light and effortless. There wasn't a single sound in nature as he walked, as if he had the earth at his command.

He reached the end of the path and stopped. I inched up to a sitting position. Finding a gap in the roof of leaves above me, I tossed one of my shoes far above the trees and over Intak's head. There was a *swish* as it hit the trees in the distance.

Intak paused, then moved towards the sound. Even with sudden sounds, he made no quick movements. In all my training, I had never seen such control.

He disappeared into the forest, and I sighed with relief.

Safe.

But wait…

Haneul never said how to finish the game.

I held to the tree a bit longer. Every muscle ached as I waited, and I couldn't tell if laying in the tree was solving the problem or adding to it. The bark cut into my stomach like hunger pains, making me think of dinner that was hours ago, long forgotten by my body since I burned it all off in my training.

Haneul had been feeding me extra this week. I acted like I hadn't noticed that his portions were smaller than mine at every meal. I had to loosen the ties on my robe yesterday - a first in almost five years. When I looked down at my bare body after bathing, I actually saw some fat hugging my hips and ribs.

For the last three years I had been too scared to eat, giving my portions to Kiwan out of fear that I would watch him starve to death, just like Mother. I was always afraid I would be the next one to die of starvation.

If the king hadn't increased taxes on the farmers... and if Saejun hadn't left...

The anger from my memories brought strength back to my bones, and the ache in my muscles numbed.

And more than that, my curiosity drove me.

Haneul was feeding me, training me, and pushing me to my limits. But why? It had to be more than just charity. Haneul was anything but generous.

I dropped down from the tree, starting back the way I came. But before I could take more than three steps, a ghost sprung from the trees.

"Amateur," Intak said, clutching his knife. "You think I can't tell a difference between a noise coming from the sky or from the earth?"

I bent my knees, ready for his attack. "I wasn't sure you could hear anything over your ego."

"You should talk. You act like everyone here owes you something because your precious little brother is in prison. Guess what, princess, we don't work for you.

We're not obligated to help you. You don't seem to be understanding that."

"You hate the king and his guards. We have the same objective."

He hissed through his teeth. "Our objective is to work as a force to resist oppression on behalf of all citizens. Your objective is to protect your own personal treasures. What are you going to do? Snatch your criminal brother out of prison so you can die of treason or starvation?"

"He's not a criminal."

"Not my point."

He twirled the knife between his fingers, not taking his eyes off me.

"Master Sok always says that pain is a good teacher," he said. "But it seems he's not willing to teach you what you need to know."

I dug my back heel into the dirt. "And what do I need to be taught?"

His fingers gripped around the handle once more, his arm dropping down to his side. "That failure to submit results in death."

He lunged.

I jumped to the side, twigs digging into my bare feet. I round-housed him in the chest, sending him back for a moment. He grunted as he stepped forward again, raising the knife to strike. I dodged to the side, but not fast enough. It grazed the skin on my shoulder, tearing my robe. I kicked out his knee. As he stumbled to the side, I sprinted into the forest.

The trees showed no mercy. The roots grabbed at my toes as I rushed past. I could feel the blood starting to drip from my shoulder, reminding me that I could lose a lot more if I stopped.

Intak followed close behind, his quick and quiet footsteps threatening to take me over at any moment. I turned hard, scraping against the trees in the process. I could hear him breathing. Panting. Ready for the kill.

I turned hard once again, only to face a pathway blocked by a mountain of rocks. I leaped for it, sticking my bare toes in the crevices. I scrambled up the rocks, reaching a third of the way up before finding a suitable position to look back. Intak was still on my tail, cautiously climbing up the rocks after me.

He looked up at me, his eyes threatening me from the darkness below.

I jammed my foot into the rock under me, leaping for the next one before it crumbled beneath me. I ripped more rocks out of their positions as I climbed. The hollow clang of them hitting each other on the way down was the only sound in the forest besides my heavy breathing.

Until Intak screamed.

I jerked my head back to look down the mountain of rocks, only to see Intak sprawled out against the ground. He curled up in a ball, hissing and grunting. He crawled to the nearest tree, propping himself up against it. Even this far away in the darkness, I could see the drastic way his chest was rising and falling, and I could hear his ragged breath from where I stood.

Did I kill the bastard?

I called out for Intak, but he didn't answer. I then called out for Haneul, immediately shaking my head at my foolishness. He wouldn't rescue us. He'd want to see what I did next.

I scrambled back down the mountain of rocks, calling for Intak again as I climbed down. When he didn't answer again, I dropped to the ground completely, approaching him with caution.

His eyes were open, but barely. The top of his robe was pulled apart, showing his shallow and quick breaths.

And blood…. blood gushing from his chest.

His hand pressed against his old wound, which was now ripped open and spurting fresh blood. He glared at me as I stepped forward.

"Stay where you are," he commanded.

"You're going to bleed to death," I returned.

"Isn't that what you want?"

"Yes. But Haneul seems rather fond of you for some ridiculous reason."

"Funny. I say the same about you."

I stepped forward. "Let's both go back to him, then."

Intak eyed me for a moment. I held out my hand.

"Can you stand?" I asked.

He looked down at my hand, inches from his face. Reaching up, he wrapped a weak hand around my wrist, then pulled out his knife and cut me deep across the arm. I snarled, stumbling backwards.

"Don't play with the snakes, princess," he growled. "You're not experienced enough to know which ones are harmless and which ones have venom."

The blood trickled down my arm, making everything in my sight turn red. I jumped back and bared my teeth.

"Die then," I barked.

I ran back down the path we came, trying to recall the way. The sights and sounds were the same - complete nothingness.

Suddenly, there was nothing below my feet.

I tumbled down a large hill, the ground cutting up my feet and face even more. Hitting the bottom, pain ripped through my body and burst from my bloodied arm and shoulder. Cursing, I curled up in a ball, shuddering against the twigs pressing against my face and shoulder.

Everything ached. Fatigue took me over in a moment. And worse, complete hopelessness dominated my thoughts.

I'd die here as a murderer or Haneul would kill me. My brother would die an innocent child. I had no strength to fight anymore. I had nothing left.

"So…" a cool voice said behind me. "It looks like you've run out of options."

CHAPTER 9

MEDIC

I turned over on my side to find the two cool eyes that matched the voice.

Kangdae.

"Why are you here?" he asked.

I stared at him. His tone was smooth and soft. Was this the Leader of the Rebellion Kangdae? Or was it the Haunted Kangdae who was kind to me in his sleep?

He stepped forward and nudged me in the back with his foot. "Answer me, woman."

Leader of the Rebellion Kangdae. Definitely.

My stomach sank in disappointment. This was a moment I wished someone would hold me and tell me everything would sort itself out. Leader Kangdae wasn't the one to do it.

Only Saejun had ever done that for me.

I tried to sit up, breath shallow. My body felt like lead, my arms sinking back down towards the ground.

He sighed. "This is exactly why I didn't want women here."

I narrowed my eyes at him. "If you're saying I'm wea—"

He swept me off the ground into his arms before I could finish the sentence. My arms automatically wrapped around his neck from surprise, all words draining from my throat as the shadows in his eyes consumed me.

"Stop talking," he whispered. "Or I'll leave you here to bleed."

The words made me think of Intak, whom I had left to do just that. The thought of his pale body on the forest ground made my stomach coil. I hated him... but I couldn't leave a man to die. I didn't have that in me.

"Intak is badly bleeding," I said. "He's in the forest."

"Was this training Haneul's idea?"

I nodded.

"Then he's already taken care of it." He started to walk us both out of the forest.

"Are you sure —"

Kangdae shook me. "I told you to stop talking."

I grit my teeth as my body ached. It was bad enough that Kangdae had to carry me through the forest. He already thought I was weak. I couldn't give him any indication that it was true.

I stayed silent as he commanded, trying not to think about the way the skin of his neck felt against my hands, or the light scent of his breath that beat against me as he carried me. Even though his arms weren't large, they were strong underneath me, and he didn't seem to have trouble carrying me for such a long distance. He wasn't even bothered by the blood dripping down my arms and onto his clothes.

I thought about the night he hugged me, his warm embrace surrounding me. The way he held me now wasn't affectionate, but it still had warmth to it, and I decided to let my guard down again - just one more time - in case I never felt it again.

Who was Yeojin? And why did she bring out such an affectionate side of him?

I was too lost in my thoughts to notice the time it took to get back to camp, but it seemed short. The men that were still awake stared at Kangdae as he carried me across the camp. I ducked my head.

Just what I needed... more people thinking I was weak.

I expected Kangdae to drop me in Haneul's hut or training area, but he didn't stop. He didn't even stop at the medic hut.

"Where are you —"

"I said don't talk."

He carried me to his own house, kicking open the door with his foot. He set me down on the floor next to his blankets, then went to his shelves in the corner. He took a flask of water and poured water in his mouth without touching the rim to his lips, then handed it to me.

"All of it," he commanded.

I finished it, not realizing how thirsty I was. He crouched in front of me with a wooden box the size of my head. He opened it, taking out strange bottles and strips of cloth.

"This is going to hurt," he said. "A lot."

I stilled as he doused a cloth in some liquid and pulled down the shoulder of my robe. I barely had time to think about my bare shoulder being exposed to him before the wet cloth hit my skin, intense pain following straight after.

I grit my teeth trying not to scream. It got worse and worse the longer it sat on my shoulder, like fire peeling off my skin.

"Are you going to pretend you're not in pain?" Kangdae asked.

I clenched my teeth hard, holding back tears.

I can't cry in front of him. Anything but cry.

"Stop pretending," he said. "It annoys me."

I held for a few seconds longer, before huffing out air in a struggled half-sob. Kangdae took the cloth off then doused it again. I shook my head at him in protest, but he didn't bother looking up. He slapped it against the deep cut in my other arm, and this time I couldn't hold back a scream.

He smirked. "That's better."

Tears of defeat and anger rolled down my face. "What the hell is that?"

"A medicine for deep wounds. Made it myself."

I tried to keep my trembling hands still as the pain burned through my muscles. My head throbbed. Not only from the pain, but from the list of questions I now had.

"Why are you helping me?" I asked.

Kangdae paused. "Because you're important to Haneul."

"Why am I important to Haneul?"

"I don't know," he said, shrugging with one shoulder.

"Then… what do you think of me?"

He threw the cloth on top of the box and looked up into my eyes. His gaze was strong, reminding me again that he had commanded me to silence. But this was the only chance I had to ask him any questions, and I couldn't hold back.

"I don't," he said. "You're nothing to me. You're not allowed to mean anything to me."

I opened my mouth, but someone else spoke before I did.

"Boss."

I swallowed.

Haneul.

Kangdae told him to enter, and Haneul's eyes drifted to me as he came in, raising an eyebrow.

"This is a surprise," he said.

"Where's Intak?" Kangdae returned.

"On his way to the medic now. A few of the others are carrying him in." He looked between the two of us. "What happened here?"

Kangdae closed the box of medicine and put it away, not saying anything. I wasn't certain what to say. Haneul stared at me for a long moment, and I realized my shoulder was still exposed. I quickly adjusted my robe. Haneul stooped down and looked me over, stopping at the cut in my arm.

"You've been marked," he said. "Disappointing."

"You'll get her killed," Kangdae said.

"Maybe. But she's useful to me."

"Do I want to know why?"

"Maybe, but it's not useful to you." He looked over my cut. "You treated her?"

Kangdae nodded. "I don't want to do it again."

"I'm surprised you did it at all."

Kangdae stopped, looking at his fingertips. Haneul took in a breath, his eyes going wild for a moment.

"I just meant that it's been awhile since you treated someone," Haneul corrected. "That's all."

"Have her drink this," Kangdae said, handing Haneul a flask. "Then she can bathe and rest. Keep track of your pets from now on."

Haneul nodded. He jerked his chin at me to get up. I obeyed, getting to my feet as best as possible. Kangdae didn't look at me as I left, lost in his own world as he started to strip for bed. Haneul pulled me out of the hut.

"Are you alright?" he asked, his voice lined with concern.

I nodded.

"Good. Because you failed. Again. Rest until tomorrow afternoon, then we try this again."

He started to walk away. I followed him.

"Wait! Why do you keep failing me? I escaped Intak—"

Haneul turned around. "No, you offered to help Intak, then left him. You simultaneously turned to help your enemy out of pity and left your superior to die. Fail."

"And how exactly was I supposed to pass? What are your requirements for success?"

"Anything I don't consider a failure."

He stepped forward, invading my space. Even with how tired I was, there was a powerful charge when he stood this close to me, as if my life depended on my senses.

"You're really not understanding who we are, sweetheart," he said. "And you definitely don't understand what we do. You're wanting to be part of us and you haven't earned it."

"You brought me here."

"Which is why you belong to me. You're not under-standing that your life is solely in my hands. I need you to get that. Because if you don't, my men are at risk. Do you think I'll put you above my own men?"

I didn't answer.

His hands came around my neck, his thumbs press-ing up under my chin to tilt my head towards him.

"My men trust me, and they submit to my command because otherwise they die," he said. "That's why they call me *master*, sweetheart. Now it's your turn. Say it."

I clenched my teeth, my emotions churning in my stomach. He stared and waited, but I didn't say it. I wouldn't.

He dropped his hands.

"I won't help you until you say it," he said. "I can't risk putting my men in danger because of you. So if you want to save your brother, you better say it within the next week."

"And if I don't?"

He pulled back his lips to show his teeth. "If you don't, you'll regret it. I have something fun planned. I think you'll want to come."

Curiosity got the best of me. "What is it?"

He pulled his shoulders back and licked his lips. "We're going to spy… on Kim Saejun."

CHAPTER 10

BET

"*M*other says Father will come back. I think she's lying. He would have come back by now."

"*He would have if he was able to. You know what they do to people at the border, Jaehwa. If he tried to escape…*"

"*Maybe he just gave up. Maybe he didn't want to come back.*"

"*Of course he wanted to come back. He loved you.*"

"*He never would have left if he did.*"

"*Should he have stayed then? Should he have stayed only to watch your mom, you, and Kiwan starve to death? If I was him, I would do the same thing.*"

"*Then will you leave too, Saejun…?*"

"*If it meant keeping you alive? I'd go to the edge of the world.*"

Training intensified.

Haneul was relentless from sunrise to midnight, drilling us with combatives and endurance exercises. We trained with swords and knives, with no armor to protect us during the training. I was not as skilled as the others and it showed. The cuts in my arms ached as my skin stretched during training, but it was nothing compared to the heavy weight of my muscles. I collapsed at least once a day, sometimes twice.

Today was no exception.

"Jump!" Haneul commanded. "Fall! Prepare!"

I followed orders, jumping in the air, falling to the ground with my hands and feet sprawled like a stretching tiger, then jumping back into a fighting stance. We had done at least thirty, and my stomach was twisting horribly from the exercise.

I couldn't be weak. It was not an option. I couldn't be less than the others.

My body, however, did not have the same ambition.

As I fell for our next drill, my muscles gave way, and I collapsed completely. I tried to jump back to my feet, but my knees refused to hold my weight. I fell to the ground, limbs shaking.

Haneul was on me in a moment, his shoes stepping in front of my sight. I made the mistake of looking into his eyes.

"Get up," Haneul said, staring down at me. "There is no time for weakness."

The others waited.

I pressed my hands to the ground, trying to come up to my feet. As I attempted to stand straight, my knees gave out again. I fell forward. Haneul caught me in his arms, sighing through his nose. The men around us snickered.

Haneul's hands came to my waist. He pulled me in, pressing my body against his. I stiffened.

"What are you doing?" you asked.

He didn't answer. He only pressed in closer, crowding my space. His hands came to my neck, lifting my chin to look him straight in his dark eyes. A smile danced across his lips as his breath fanned my cheek, sending fire down my spine. With a satisfied chuckle, he then stepped back, leaving me to stand on my own. The adrenaline from his body against mine kept me on my feet.

The twitch of his mouth indicated that he knew it.

"There's something I want you all to remember," Haneul said, stepping away and addressing the other men in training. "If one of you fails, you all fail. If one of you succeeds, you all succeed. There are no individuals here. Do you understand?"

"Yes, Master," the men said in unison.

"As long as you keep my commands, you will continue to succeed. As a group. I don't acknowledge proud recruits."

"Yes, Master," the men said again.

I didn't speak. My eyes were stinging.

Haneul turned back to face me, a flicker of pity tracing the creases around his eyes. I hated that pity more than I hated his commands.

"I want you to go to the medic," Haneul said.

I gritted my teeth and shook my head.

"It's a command, Jaehwa."

"I can still train."

"I decide whether you train or not."

He tapped the back of my knee with his foot. Too weak to withhold even a gentle tap, I fell to the ground again, coughing as I sucked dirt down my throat.

"Your muscles haven't rested," Haneul said. "You've been training outside of my instructions and now your muscles are weak. They need to rest to get stronger. You know that."

I gripped chunks of dirt on the ground. He was right about the training. I should have known he would figure it out. Every night, after I was sure he was fast asleep, I got up and trained by myself. I couldn't sleep at the thought of seeing Saejun again... repressed memories bubbling up in my brain ever since Haneul had mentioned his name five days ago.

"Take her to the medic," Haneul said to the men next to him. "Make sure she stays."

"Yes, Master," two voices said in unison.

Two pairs of arms lifted me up to my feet and escorted me to the medic hut. I didn't bother to look at their faces, or the faces around me as I was carried off. All I could do was chant the same thing over and over inside my head.

I won't be weak. I won't be weak. I won't...

They escorted me into the hut and laid me on one of the floor pads.

"Miss?" a sweet voice asked.

I looked up to a pair of puppy eyes. Geonho smiled sympathetically, crouching down next to me.

"Don't take this the wrong way," he said, "but you look awful."

I snickered, too tired to smile.

"I've brought some broth for everyone here," he said. "There's a bit more. I'll get it for you."

He bounced away from my side, retrieving the broth. As my eyes wandered after him, they connected with another person in the corner. A person I was not in the mood to see.

"So the mighty have fallen," Intak muttered, smirking.

I puffed out some air. "Sorry I'm late. You must have been bored here by yourself."

His eye twitched. Geonho brought over the broth, as one of the medics brought over some herbal tea to drink. The broth was bitter and the tea was too strong, both as completely unsatisfying as my current situation.

"It looks like you won't be joining Haneul's mission," Intak continued.

"Says who?" I replied.

Geonho's eyes widened. "You can't help Haneul like this, Miss. You'll get yourself killed."

"Or someone else killed," Intak replied. "A weak link affects the whole chain."

I grunted. "Who are you to call me weak?"

"Someone who's been stuck in this damn hut, mostly because of you. This will be the first mission I've missed in two years. I've been commanded to stay back for the safety of the group. You will be too. You should obey the command."

"I need to get my brother," I said, trying to sit up.

Geonho stopped me and eased me back down on the mat. He shook his head. "Not now, Miss. Both you and your brother would die."

"They're going to find Saejun," I continued. "He took my brother. I need to —"

"You need to get your head on straight," Intak interrupted. "You can't run up to the leader of the emperor's guards and demand your brother back. He'll slit your throat. Then he'll slit your brother's throat. Your entire family will be lost. Just stay here. You can fight the guards later when you're not risking everyone's lives."

"I have two days. I can heal in one."

Geonho's eyes scrunched together as he gave me more broth. "Two days? I thought Haneul said that he was leaving tomorrow?"

Intak cleared his throat. Geonho suddenly went pink, covering his mouth with his hand.

"Tomorrow?" I asked. "What do you mean, tomorrow?"

"Nothing, Miss. You're right, it's two days from now. I got confused."

He gave a sweet smile, but it was hollow. I sank back into the bed, looking at the roof of the hut.

Haneul couldn't leave without me. I had to see Saejun.

***

"Will you be a farmer, like your father?"

"Being a farmer is good, I guess. But I'd rather be something exciting. Like a warrior. Or an undercover spy."

"You? A spy? Saejun, you can't even sneak out of the house properly."

"Shut up. What about you? Do you want to be a farmer like your parents?"

"I don't know. I think I'd like to try to make bottled perfumes like those ladies in the market. They're expensive to make, but those ladies have a lot of nice clothes, so they must make good money."

"Yeah? If you were going to make a perfume after me, what would it be made out of?"

"Hmm... I think... sweat and lavender. I'd call it Sticky Jun."

"Tsk. You're an idiot, Jaehwa."

"You're a bigger idiot for spending time with me, Saejun."

Even in the medic hut, I couldn't sleep. Maybe it was because Intak was ten feet from me. His breathing was harsh compared to Haneul's, and had a completely different rhythm. Or maybe it was the continuous thoughts of Saejun clouding my head. Maybe it was the pulsating ache in my bones. Whatever it was, it kept me up all night.

Light had barely dusted the camp when I heard footsteps. It wasn't just one pair, but a dozen. I crawled to the hut entrance, pulling the door back to see what was causing the noise.

Haneul was walking towards the front of camp, a crew behind him. They had packs on their backs, their faces solemn and focused.

So it was true. They were leaving.

I stumbled out the hut and followed after them, my knees still wobbling from yesterday's training. Adrenaline kicked in, giving me enough strength to reach them before they could make it out of the camp.

"Master," one of them said when I approached.

Haneul turned around. He scoffed and shook his head. "I should have known."

I gripped my hands into fists. "You said two days."

"I changed my mind," he said. "Even if I kept my plan, you're still not ready. You need to go back and rest."

"I'm well enough."

"This isn't up for discussion. My command is final."

"Then fight me," I said. "If I win the match, I go. If you win the match, I stay."

Pity creased his eyes again. "Jaehwa…"

"It's a simple solution, isn't it? If you think I'm as weak as you say, I'll lose and you can go without me. If you refuse my challenge, then I'll be forced to follow you."

He cussed, dropping his head back to look at the sky. He then rolled his neck around as if it were stiff, and nodded.

"I could tie you to the hut, but I have no doubt you'd torture every living soul at camp after I left." He sighed. "So be it. If that's what it takes."

He motioned me to follow him, and motioned for the others to stay put. He led us away from the group, towards the training center. He threw open the door and motioned me to enter. He followed me in, his tongue grazing his lip.

"Three point rule," Haneul said. "Whoever hits their opponent's head, chest, and gut first, wins."

I nodded. Haneul waited.

Normally, Haneul was the one to start the fight. This time, he was waiting for me. He was taunting me. He was calling me weak by holding back.

I jumped forward, my right knee going weak as I took my stance. He kicked it out, sending me to the floor. His fist tapped my temple.

"Head," he said, stepping back.

I came to my feet again, starting with a front punch. He stepped out of the way, allowing me to rush past. When I turned, he slammed his palm into my ribs, knocking me back.

"Chest," he said.

I grit my teeth, eyes stinging. I wouldn't lose. I didn't have the luxury.

I rushed forward again and went for a high kick, realizing too late that I was slow and easy to read. Haneul caught it in his arm and shoved my leg above my head, knocking me completely to the ground. He put his foot on my stomach.

"Gut," he said. "You lost in a matter of seconds, sweetheart. A deal is a deal. You're too weak to follow my men."

He lifted his leg off me. Blood rushing into my ears, I lifted my hips and horse-kicked him in the stomach, sending him back into the wall. He grunted as his full body slammed against it, shaking the weapons that hung there. Haneul grabbed the back of his neck as he dropped down to the floor, and it took me a moment to realize there was a spear on the wall directly behind him.

He hissed, right before three other spears dropped from the wall on top of him… and he screamed as one of them went straight through his leg.

CHAPTER 11

MASTER

"You wait outside."

It was a command, not a suggestion. The two men carrying Haneul to the medic hut glared at me as they went inside.

After a few moments, one of them came back out, standing next to the door as if to block me from going in. As much as I wanted to defy him, I couldn't. I didn't have the strength.

Lowering myself to the ground, I tried to catch my breath as the familiar ache of self-pity and defeat rushed over me.

Haneul was right. I pushed myself too hard. I didn't obey orders. I didn't listen to him.

And now he was in the medic hut, bleeding to death because of me. All because of me.

Haneul was the only damn person in five years who had...

I shuttered, grabbing my elbows to keep my hands from shaking. I wanted to vomit. I bit my lip, as if somehow it would help the ache in my gut. Every muscle throbbed, taunting my weakness and my shame until I wanted to rip off my own skin.

Footsteps shuffled behind me, and a shadow spread across the dirt.

Kangdae always looked cold, but now he looked heartless.

He glanced at me for a moment, then looked to the men in front of the medic hut. "What happened here?"

I opened my mouth to speak, but remembered Haneul's words:

He didn't try to break my arm when you spoke out of turn.

I bit down hard on my tongue, deciding not to speak.

"The woman stabbed him," one of the men said. "He's bleeding from the neck and leg."

Kangdae raised an eyebrow. "Was it an ambush?"

When a heartbeat passed and no one spoke, I answered, "No, sir. I challenged him to fight and he accepted."

"*Sir*?" Kangdae echoed ironically. His eyebrows crashed together. "Did you say that you challenged him? Is this true?"

The other men confirmed.

Kangdae hissed as he laughed. "How in the hell did you pull that off?"

I trembled, bowing my forehead completely to the ground until the gravel bit into my skin. "Please forgive me. I didn't mean to hurt him."

"You challenged him to fight, but didn't mean to hurt him? That's the opposite of a challenge." He huffed. "Stay here, woman. Your forgiveness will be based on the damage you've dealt."

When I dared to lift my head, Kangdae was gone.

"Miss?" a new voice called out. "What are you doing on the ground? Why aren't you in your bed?"

A pair of soft hands came to my arms, Geonho's light voice encouraging me to get up. I shook my head at him, staying low to the ground.

"My place is here," I said.

Geonho looked up to the others, asking what happened. One of the men quickly reiterated the events. Geonho sighed, rubbing the back of his head.

"It's all my fault," he said. "I mentioned the mission day. If it wasn't for me…"

"It wasn't you, Geonho," I said. "This was my doing. I had the choice to obey orders."

Silence passed as I tried to steady my trembling lips. Geonho crouched down next to me, his hand on my back in quiet reassurance. All I could do was stare at the ground in front of me, thinking of the ways Haneul had watched over me.

"My brother is all I have left. I have no other family."
"You have me."
"I don't want you."

Suddenly, I'd do anything to take back those words.

After some time, the hut door swung open and Kangdae walked out. His gaze met mine and he rolled his eyes.

"Good God, woman," he said. "All you did was stab him in the leg. Why are you so noisy?"

He walked away before I could even put an answer together.

The other men walked inside, leaving me with Geonho. He didn't say anything, only continuing to pat the top of my back reassuringly.

After a bit of time, the men came out again, glaring at me. One of them jerked his head, signaling for me to go inside. Geonho helped me to my feet and walked me in.

Haneul had a wrap around his neck and one around his leg. He was fiddling with the leg bandage as I walked in. His color had mostly returned; his smirk fully resurrected.

"I appreciate you getting the last word," he said as we approached his bed, "but you still lost the challenge."

I collapsed next to him, my hands shaking as they reached out for his wraps. I stopped myself, putting my hands in my lap and trying to hold them still.

"*Heol…* What is this reaction?" he asked. "I thought you'd be gloating."

I dropped my head. His breathing softened.

"You're not supposed to fall in love with me, sweetheart."

I raised my head and frowned at him. He laughed.

"There's the scowl I've become so fond of," he said. He sighed and looked around. "Would someone get me off this damn mat? Leave this bed for someone who's really injured."

He started to stand, but I raised my hands to stop him. "You're injured. Stay."

"I'm fine. I've been stabbed far worse than this."

Geonho helped Haneul to his feet and helped him limp towards the entrance. I jumped up after them, putting Haneul's other arm over my shoulder. I barely had enough strength to stand on my own, but this was the least I could do.

Haneul smiled, his hand wrapping around to pinch my cheek.

"You're cute when you're concerned," he said.

"Don't make me regret it," I returned, shrugging off his fingers.

His lips pressed together, a smile curling at the ends.

"I think that'll be a problem," he said. "Because your regret is what fascinates me the most."

***

Haneul slept most of the afternoon, and I stayed with him, only dozing from time to time. Night fell hard, the evening chill taking over the hut. Watching Haneul in his restful state - his eyes closed, his entire body vulnerable to threat - my heart tightened in my ribs.

He protected me. He fed me. He trained me. He did more for me in the last month than anyone had in five years. Watching him sleep, thinking of these things, made my entire body ache.

I threw my blanket on him, taking care not to hurt any of his wounds as I tucked in the sides of it.

"If you pack me in this blanket any tighter," Haneul said, eyes still shut, "I'm going to turn into a butterfly in three days."

He opened one eye, then the other. A smile flashed across his face before he sat up and removed the blanket. He threw it over my head.

"Rest, Jaehwa," he said. "You're not in any better shape than I am."

I lowered my head under the blanket. "Forgive me."

"What did you say?"

"Forgive me."

He chuckled. "Forgive you for what?"

"For disobeying you."

"And why should I forgive that?"

I didn't answer. He ripped the blanket off my head, and all I saw was his playful grin.

"You know," he said, "you're starting to become the most complicated burden I've ever given myself,"

Burden.

That's what I was, wasn't I? A burden to my family. A burden to my brother. A burden to myself. To everyone.

Weak and helpless. Nothing else.

Sobs struck my chest and fell from my lips mercilessly. Haneul grabbed my arms and pulled me against his chest, his hands stroking my back and hair as I sobbed.

"It's alright," he whispered into my hair. "It's alright."

"You're hurt because of me."

"I made my own decisions."

"If I had only followed your orders, then…"

I sat up, sniffling. He brushed the hair from my face.

"Are you ready to follow my orders, then?" he asked. "If you want to be equal to my men, then you have to sacrifice the same things they have. You have to give up complete control to me. Are you willing to do that?"

I traced my fingers over the wrap on his neck, careful not to apply any pressure and hurt him further.

"You're the only one in the last five years who's helped me," I said. "I had to fight alone to keep Kiwan and me alive. There was no one else. I had to be the strongest. If I submitted, then we were dead. But even with all my fighting, my family is now…"

I couldn't finish, sobs threatening to take over again. Haneul's eyes never left mine as he took my hand from his wound and held it. His fingers traced mine, the touch making me feel both comforted and weak.

"I wasn't strong enough," I whispered through my tears. "He's going to die because of me."

"If he dies, it won't be because of you."

"It's all my fault. I could have stopped it."

"How, sweetheart?" he asked, the nickname lacking its usual condescending edge. "There's nothing you could have done. This guilt will drain your life faster than a cut from any sword."

He grabbed my face between his hands and forced me to look at him.

"*If he dies,*" he said, "*it's not my fault.* I want you to say that. I want you to say it every time you inhale until you believe it."

My jaw trembled between his hands as I continued to keep sniffling. I forced the sobs back, but my gut felt like it would rip apart if I kept them down any longer.

"Say it," he commanded.

I tried to steady my breath.

"It's not… if he dies…"

I couldn't get through the sentence. Haneul brought me back to his chest, the fabric of his robe brushing against my tears. He stroked my back, holding my hand in his.

"He's all I have left," I whispered.

"You have me now. I wouldn't leave a stray out in the cold to wander. What kind of master would I be?"

His cheek grazed against mine as he leaned into my ear.

"Let me be your master, Jaehwa," he whispered, "You trust me more than you want to admit. Submit to my command. I'll keep you safe."

Safe.

I couldn't remember the last time I felt that emotion.

I didn't answer. I could only grip his robe as I leaned against his chest. He chuckled softly into my ear.

"Alright then, my pet," he said. "I think it's time for you to take your place in the pack."

CHAPTER 12

THE REASON

A nd because both the cow herder and the weaver neglected their responsibilities, the Sky King separated them for all eternity."

"That's awful. Why would the king be so cruel to two people in love?"

"The town suffered because of them. Should being in love mean letting the people around you suffer?"

"I suppose not. That would be selfish."

"Love can take two paths... it can be a beautiful self-lessness that builds a kingdom or an evil selfishness that destroys one."

"Have you ever been in love, Saejun? ...Saejun?"

"If I was in love, I wouldn't allow it to become a selfish one that leads to destruction. If I did - if I allowed everything around me to fall into ruin - then it would hurt the one I love most."

Three days passed. Haneul ordered me to rest, and I obeyed regardless of the painful memories that kept me awake at night. It would have been better to train. It would have given me something to focus on. But all I could focus on now was the night sky and the memories that came along with it.

Haneul healed easily. He didn't even limp after three days. It didn't make his mood any better, however. He had sent a dozen men to scout Saejun to gain information on what he was doing, where he was going, and anything else that might be useful. But Haneul wasn't happy about leaving his men without himself or Intak to lead. The mission was too important for that.

What was his plan for scouting Saejun, anyways?

"They should have been back by now," Haneul muttered, looking up at the moon. "I gave them explicit instructions."

Intak adjusted his robe, wincing in pain as he shifted in front of the fire. "They'll return."

Haneul clicked his tongue. "Something's off."

"Do you think Gaemin was ready to lead such a mission?"

"He's completed his training. He's one of the best in stealth and strategy. But…" Haneul kept his eyes on the sky. "…being the best doesn't mean being above mistakes."

I added another log to the fire, hoping it would warm up my thoughts. I felt an eerie chill, same as Haneul, but I tried to convince myself that it was nothing. But Saejun was smart. He knew strategy and the psychology of battle better than anyone. It wouldn't have been hard for him to figure out that he was being spied on. And with the men alone out there - without Haneul or Intak as their leader - who knew what trouble they could have been in?

I hated to admit it, but Intak was a better leader than I had given him credit for. His demeanor was harsher than Haneul's and he was unbearable as a person, but he cared about the men as much as Haneul did.

Regardless, I still didn't like him.

I felt him eyeing me. I raised my head to face him and lifted both my eyebrows, waiting for him to tell me why he was staring.

"You're too quiet," Intak said, nodding at me. "I don't like it."

"I'm not interested in what you don't like," I replied. "I'm only here to bring firewood."

"That's probably the most useful thing you've done here." He turned to Haneul. "I still don't understand her purpose here, Master."

Haneul brought his finger to his lips, eyes still on the sky. Intak and I both went silent, looking up with him. His eyes widened, and he pointed.

"There!" he said, jumping up.

I tried to follow his sight, but there was only darkness. A small dot flickered across the stars, then dropped out of the sky. There was a shrill cry, and Haneul ran to the middle of the campsite to greet the creature who had called.

There was a flap of wings against a wooden cage. Haneul ran over to it and reached inside, pulling out a small messenger pigeon. He took the scroll from its foot and checked the paper.

"What is it?" you asked.

"A messenger pigeon," Intak said. "It's to bring us messages without leading enemies to our location."

"I knew that," I snapped back. "I meant, what's written on the scroll?"

Haneul clicked his tongue again, sighing. He handed the paper over to Intak, who grunted in response.

"Captured," Intak said. "All of them, you think?"

"More than half," Haneul replied. "If they're sending a message it means there aren't enough men to return safely. Captain Kim probably has most of them in prison, if not all of them."

Captain Kim.

Saejun.

Haneul stepped away and walked towards the cluster of huts in the middle of the campsite. Intak followed, and not knowing what else to do, I did as well.

When we reached the destination, I wished I hadn't.

Haneul approached Kangdae, who took the scroll in his hand and read it over carefully. His jaw tightened as he handed it back, his eyes narrowing as Haneul began to speak. Their voices were too low for me to clearly hear their words, but with the vein jutting out of Kangdae's neck, I didn't need much of a commentary.

"Intak," Haneul commanded. "Get the Higher Five. We'll meet in the training hut."

Intak bowed and ran off. I stepped forward, expecting directions as well.

Kangdae's lip curled. "I blame you for this, woman."

"Me?" I asked, not meaning to react out loud.

"Yes, you. If you hadn't put a piercing through Haneul's leg, he would have led the mission. There are men in prison because of your poorly controlled emotions."

I grit my teeth, but hung my head. I couldn't argue with the consequences of my actions.

"Some good came of it," Haneul said with a slight glimmer in his eye.

I tried not to blush at the thought of the night I cried in his arms. It was humiliating. The way he held me as if I were some sort of child instead of one of his soldiers... I hated that he had to care for me more than the others.

And yet, on the other hand, I felt myself seeking his attention even when I hated it most.

"I think she's ready for her first mission," Haneul continued.

Kangdae looked confused. I was too.

"Mission?" Kangdae echoed. "We have a quarter of our men under Kim's thumb. I'm not going to put the rest of them in danger because of this... this... whatever she is."

"She's my weapon," Haneul returned. "And the best one I've had so far."

Kangdae laughed. "This one? Care to explain?"

Haneul's eyes darted around the campsite.

"This woman put a hole in your leg, and you claim she's useful?" Kangdae continued, looking at me.

I gripped my hands into fists.

Haneul raised his hand to signal me to back down. "She has a purpose. I need you to trust me on this."

"You never should have brought another woman in this place," Kangdae said to Haneul. "You knew the rule."

"I'm the reason for the rule, aren't I?" Haneul returned.

Kangdae didn't answer.

"Old rules won't work for new times," Haneul continued. "If we want to win the next round, we need to take control of the game."

"Not like this. Not with a woman. I won't allow her to go on missions. I won't allow the dangers."

"You think I would allow her to be in danger, then? After everything?"

Kangdae looked at Haneul, then at me. He stepped forward, his eyes looking down on me as they always did. I could see him evaluate my worth as I stared back at him.

"I have an important use for her," Haneul replied to a question that hadn't been asked.

Kangdae's eyebrow bounced as he continued to stare at me. "Do you pay her for it?"

I snarled. "You bastard—"

I raised my hand to slap him across the face, but he grabbed it. He didn't even blink, his dark eyes locked on mine.

"I'm training her for the Underground," Haneul announced.

Kangdae's eyes shot between him and me.

"Are you insane?" he asked.

Haneul chuckled darkly. "Have I ever claimed to be otherwise?"

"That's a death trap."

"Life is a death trap. The Underground is just collecting intelligence."

"Unless you're caught."

"She won't get caught. She'll be with me."

I pulled out of Kangdae's hold, grunting at all the information I didn't understand. "What are you two talking about?"

"She fights like him," Haneul said, ignoring me.

They stared at each other for a long moment, Kangdae's fingers twitching. Haneul didn't have an expression at all.

"That's why, then?" Kangdae asked.

Haneul dropped his head in a single nod. The silence between them was unbearable and didn't answer any of the questions hanging in the air.

Kangdae finally huffed, shaking his head. "Her blood is on your hands. Remember that."

"I know," Haneul replied. "I don't plan for any blood to be wasted this time."

Haneul took my arm and pulled me away from Kangdae. An aura of frustration was pouring off of him, his grip on my arm tighter than usual. This wasn't the combat master of the Rebellion. This was Haneul. A tense, serious Haneul.

We reached halfway to the training hut before I pulled out of his grip. He looked back at me, unamused.

"What was all that back there?" I asked. "What is the Underground?"

He stared for a long moment, then reached up to graze his own lip with his thumb. "Where did you learn to fight, sweetheart?"

I stayed silent, not answering.

Haneul stepped closer. He leaned down over me like he was about to swallow me whole, his lips stretching until his teeth appeared.

"You learned from him, didn't you?" he whispered. "He fights like you, doesn't he?"

I swallowed.

"You didn't realize you were giving me information all this time, did you?" His fingers came up and traced around my cheek. "Your weaknesses show me his. Your strengths show me his. Your techniques show me everything I need to know about him."

I stepped back, shaking off his fingers. "Stop babbling. What are you even talking about?"

His grin widened. "You weren't lying when you said you knew Kim Saejun. You knew him well. He was your teacher."

CHAPTER 13

PURPOSE

"Pick up your heel," Saejun commanded. "You keep dropping it."

"I have a cramp in my foot."

"Your enemy won't care. He wants you dead, Jaehwa. Pick it up."

I picked up my heel, the pain surging through my calf.

Saejun trained me daily, when Mother and Kiwan went to the fields and I was left to watch over the house. Saejun's family owned farmland next to mine, and he took it on himself to train me out in the lavender fields that connected our fields together. He always said that there might be a day he wouldn't be there to protect me.

Maybe he had always planned to leave.

"Bring your hands up more," he said, slapping my low hands. "Don't ever drop them below your jaw."

We sparred every afternoon, summer or winter. I liked the training, though. I liked fighting against the elements, feeling myself get stronger.

Most of all, I liked seeing him.

Sweat poured down his face, his strong arms throwing punch after punch against me. He tried to sweep me, but I could always dodge his sweeps. I spun and kicked his chest, earning a grunt and a smile from him.

"More power next time," he said. "Don't hold back."

He made me stronger. Physically, emotionally. He made sure I never allowed myself to back down from any challenge that would come up against me.

He then locked me in a chokehold, my guard going down for a moment as my skin pressed against his. I shook myself to my senses, breaking the hold to face him. He kicked my feet out. I grabbed the collar of his robe, taking him down to the ground with me.

He fell on top of me and his face hovered over mine, his eyes shimmering in the sunlight despite their darkness. I could feel his fingers on the edges of my hair, curling.

He was close. Closer than he should have been.

"Jaehwa…" he whispered. "Will… your mother be home tonight?"

I swallowed. "No, why?"

He chewed his lip then shook his head and looked away. "Nothing. I wanted… I wanted to ask her something."

He leaned back and I sat up.

"What would you possibly want to ask my mother?" I joked.

He rubbed the back of his neck as if it were aching, but I didn't remember hitting him there. "It's nothing."

He stood up, his clothes clasping to the muscles of his back and chest. I bit my lip, hoping he wouldn't turn around to see me stare. He put on his outer robe, indicating he was done training for the day.

"Kiwan will be home tonight," I offered.

He nodded. "I know."

"Will you come over then? Or do you need my mother to make an appearance?"

"I'll come over." He stole a glance back at me, lips pulling to the side. "But who said either one of them was the reason?"

A horse neighed in the distance. Saejun's face hardened.

Three men on horseback approached us, their steeds carrying the blood-red flag of the emperor. My heart seized as I came to my knees. Would they demand more food from the farmers again? Taxes? Something else? The emperor's wishes changed more frequently than the weather, and it was always the lower class that paid for it most.

Saejun held out his hand to signal me to be still. His steel nerves took the tension out of my body. Whatever the possibilities, he wouldn't let any harm come to me. I believed that with every fiber of my being.

The horses approached us. One of the guards spoke.

"We're looking for Saejun, son of Hangbak. Do you know him?"

"I'm him," Saejun replied without hesitation.

"These fields are your family's, correct?"

He nodded.

"Your family has served the Emperor well with your provisions."

Saejun sealed his lips and nodded again. I knew what he was really thinking:

Yes, we serve the Emperor well… and he lets us starve to death.

What the guards didn't know was that Saejun and his family hid away a small percentage of crops to feed starving people in the village. His family had saved ours more times than I ever wanted to admit. He would never let us starve. I never doubted that.

"The Emperor has received your request for admission into the guards."

I started to my feet. "Saejun, you —"

"Quiet," he commanded, his eyes shooting me a warning glance.

He had never reprimanded me like that before. I sank back on my ankles.

"I'm honored that the emperor would seek me out personally," Saejun replied to the guards, bowing.

"We would like to discuss your admittance," the guard said. "Would you be able to attend city hall this evening?"

"Yes, of course."

The guards nodded. "Then we look forward to your attendance."

They arranged the time and location, while I sat there, dazed.

Saejun? Part of the Emperor's guards? Why? Those men were crooked and evil. They preyed upon the weak and tortured the strong. Why the hell would Saejun apply for such a position?

The guards left the field, and Saejun let out a long breath.

"I'm so sorry, Jaehwa," he said. "Are you okay?"

I jumped to my feet. "Am I okay? Are you insane? You applied to become one of the emperor's guards, but never breathed a word about it? Why would you do such a thing?"

His head dropped as he shifted his weight. "I knew you wouldn't approve."

"Who the hell would?"

"It's not working anymore," he said. "Our family crops aren't producing like they used to. We're going dry. We can't help everyone anymore. The emperor is becoming harsher with food rations and we can't pacify him."

It's not like I could disagree. Mother had to work from sunrise to sunset to make enough for the small bags of rice and wilted vegetables that got me and Kiwan through the week.

"I can't do any more from the outside," he continued. "I have to get inside."

"You moron," I whispered back, my insides trembling. "They'll kill you."

He shook his head. "Not if I'm careful."

He stepped in close, the scent of mixed lavender from the fields and his sweat mixing in the air. They were two smells I still remembered vividly.

"I can't watch our families and the townspeople die off so easily. At least one person I know dies every week from starvation or flogging. I can't take it anymore."

His chest heaved as he dropped his head again.

"So you'll join them?" I asked. "You'll become one of them?"

"I'll change things," he replied. "I promise you."

"You're largely outnumbered. In the end, you'll be the one that changes."

I tried not to cry. Imagining Saejun in the midst of the guards demanding taxes and crops from the farmers and arresting innocent citizens was more than I could bear.

And worse, he would be leaving us. Just like Father did.

Suddenly, my hand was warm. His fingers had wrapped around mine, and he brought our intertwined hands up to his chest.

"Let me speak with them tonight," he said. "It's a long shot, but we're running out of options."

I turned my head away from him, not knowing what to say. Silence passed between us as the wind grazed over our hands.

"No matter what happens, Jaehwa, I'll come back to you," he said. "Please believe me."

He lifted my hand higher, staring into my eyes. He brought my knuckle to his lips and pecked it softly, then let my hand fall back to my side.

I believed him.

But he never returned.

Not until the night he arrested Kiwan for murder and put me under house arrest.

My fingers grazed the knuckle Saejun had kissed five years ago. I wished I could wash away the memory. Every memory.

Maybe I couldn't rinse my brain of him, but I could at least wash away today's training.

Haneul had forbidden me from training after sundown, but he said nothing about bathing. I had been going to the lake past the gardens at midnight when I wasn't able to sleep. I knew the men wouldn't go past the gardens after certain times, and since the training ground was off-limits after hours, they were sure not to come by. It was the perfect place to clear my head and bathe away from the men.

None of them had made an inappropriate advance on me, and I was grateful… but part of me wondered if that was because they thought I was Haneul's woman. Haneul had never claimed me as his, but he certainly didn't let anyone else near me.

And as time went on, I didn't reject his ownership.

Upon reaching the lake, I disrobed and slid into the water, letting the cool water lap at my collarbone. I dipped under a couple of times, trying to get the stench of the day's training out of my hair and skin.

My first mission. Haneul was letting me go on my first mission.

He still hadn't explained the Underground. Not really.

"Our goal is to take down the emperor," Haneul had explained. "My goal is to weaken him until he can't stand on his own two feet. You'll be helping us in that. That piques your interest, doesn't it?"

He was right. The emperor had taken everything from me - Father, Mother, my brother, my home… and even Saejun. He took all of it. It would be my greatest pleasure to make sure he ended up with nothing in return.

But what about Kiwan? How would I save my brother? Haneul had never fully agreed to help me save him, and as time went on, I was beginning to believe Haneul had no intentions to rescue him. If I was honest,

I had no idea what Haneul's intentions truly were... and that made me nervous.

I looked to the stars for answers, but they didn't offer any. They only burned above, silent and steady.

My eyes drifted back down to land. A shadow hung next to one of the trees near the lake. I blinked, hoping it was a trick of the eyes.

It wasn't. There was a man watching me.

"Show yourself!" I yelled, trying not to let my heartbeat strangle my vocal cords.

There was a small chuckle. "Do you really want me to?"

The shadow stepped into the moonlight more, resting himself against another tree.

...Kangdae?

"How long have you been there?" I demanded.

He stared, not answering.

"Are you some sort of pervert?" I asked.

"Everyone's some sort of pervert, woman."

He walked towards the edge of the lake, hands on the belt of his robes. I dipped down lower in the water. I was sure he couldn't see anything, but just in case, I covered myself.

"Do you often sneak past the camp to come here?" he asked.

"If I did, I wouldn't tell you."

"I own you. You need to tell me everything."

I rolled my eyes. "Property of Kangdae? Isn't that Haneul's line?"

"I own Haneul. He can't own you without my permission."

"Didn't you give him permission to do whatever he wanted with me?"

He nodded. "Within reason. But I still own you both."

He crouched next to the lake, still staring. Was he trying to see me naked? This bastard —

"What do you want?" I asked, unable to understand his deep stare.

He looked down at his fingertips as if there was something stuck to them. His eyes drifted to the side and back down to his fingers.

"I want you to come to me," he said.

I froze in the water, stomach sinking. "What?"

"I want you to work for me instead of Haneul."

I narrowed my eyes. What was he talking about?

"It shouldn't be hard for you," Kangdae continued. "You don't like following orders anyways."

"What do you mean, work for you? I thought you gave me to Haneul?"

"That was until he decided to train you for the Underground."

"No one has explained to me what that is."

He sighed, leaning back on his ankles as he crouched. "It's a collection of spies. It's no place for you."

"You think I'm incompetent?"

"I don't much care if you are or not. You don't belong there. And if Haneul is trying to train you for it, that means he's training others behind my back as well. I want you to find out and tell me."

I processed his words. "So you want me to be your spy?"

A smile curled on his lips.

"Haneul's in too deep to realize what he's doing," Kangdae said. "He's trying to lick an old wound. He'll only end up biting himself in the ass."

"Then why don't you order him to stop?"

Kangdae's eyes drifted to the side of the lake again. "I can't give that order. I can only stop what he's doing with your help."

I shook my head. He wasn't making any sense. Wasn't he the leader? Couldn't he give any order he wanted? Couldn't he order one of his other men to do this?

"I'll make it worth your while," he continued. "You want your brother back, don't you?"

I paused.

"We can rescue your brother," Kangdae said in response to my silence. "And I'll give you whatever else you may need once he's free. What is it you want? Imported clothing? Food? Your own shop in town for an income? Name it."

My fingers curled under the water, the possibilities overwhelming me. Trade in information about Haneul to get Kiwan? Could I betray Haneul after all he had done for me? Was this a test?

I never even thought about what I would do after getting Kiwan back. We would be fugitives. We couldn't go back to the way things were. Any dreams I had of a regular life had dissolved in front of me the day Saejun came back to take Kiwan off in chains.

"I don't want anything," I finally said. "Only my brother's freedom."

"I'll give you more than that if you refuse the Underground. I'll allow you the first mission. But after that mission, you need to tell Haneul that you no longer wish to be part of his pack."

103

Suddenly the water felt colder. Haneul had been kind to me. He trained me, he fed me, he even forgave me for stabbing him. He brought me to the Rebellion in the first place.

But... he was also using me. Using me for information on Saejun. Would he discard me as soon as he was finished getting information?

And didn't I come here in order to get Kiwan back in the first place?

My desires were conflicting. Haneul was offering me a chance of ultimate revenge against the emperor. Kangdae was offering me Kiwan.

Which was more important?

"What do you want me to report?" I asked.

I wasn't going to agree, but I was going to keep my options open.

The whites of Kangdae's eyes glistened in the moonlight as the darkness swarmed around his body.

"Tell me everything Haneul may be keeping from me," Kangdae said. He chuckled as he rose back to his full height. "Well, look at that. I finally found a use for you."

CHAPTER 14

HAVE YOU EVER

"I refuse," I said, stepping back and crossing my arms against my chest.

Haneul shrugged. "Too late. I've already made the arrangements."

When Haneul announced that I was joining the mission, I was proud to finally have his approval. I thought he was recognizing me as an equal.

That was before he told me the details.

"I won't dress like a whore," I said.

"That's a terrible word for it," he said, sighing. "*Hostess* is a much better term."

"That doesn't change the job description."

"You won't be a real hostess. You'll be collecting information. All you have to do is walk upright, serve drinks, and eavesdrop on every piece of scum in the place."

"You forgot that I also need to avoid wandering hands," I added.

Haneul smirked. "You've been trained well enough in the art of avoidance."

"Mainly from sleeping in the same hut as you."

Geonho walked in with the pile of robes stacked as high as his nose. There were blue and green silks with gold embroidery, a white undergown, and a jeweled veil. Haneul took each piece and explained how to put them on.

"You know a lot about women's clothing," I said when he was finished.

His eyebrow bounced. "I have my experiences with it."

Geonho frowned. "Yes, and I've been on the other end of that."

"I only made you wear it once," Haneul said to Geonho. "You were stunning."

"You could have at least waited until the men had left the camp."

"I needed second opinions."

Geonho huffed. I held the fabric up to his skin, imagining him dressed in it.

"Stop thinking about it!" he scolded me, blushing.

"Get dressed and come out," Haneul said to me over his shoulder, escorting Geonho out of the hut.

I did my best to arrange the layers of clothing as Haneul said, but it was rather confusing. I never had formal wear. I had work robes. That was all my family ever had. As a child, I dreamed of owning this kind of fabric for myself, yet I fully accepted that it was never meant to be.

Yet here I was, dressed in the finest clothes I had ever seen.

I traced the silk with my fingertips, the fabric soft and rich.

"What is it you want? Name it."

I shook Kangdae's words out of my head. Money and clothes weren't important. Kiwan was. Revenge against the emperor was. I didn't have time for such beautiful things. Beautiful things were for other people.

Resolving not to get attached, I stepped out of the hut and went to meet Haneul, gathering my skirts in my hands so they wouldn't touch the ground. A shadow crossed my path, stopping to cock his head to the side.

"Is this your side business?" Kangdae asked, the corners of his mouth curling to hide a smirk.

"Haneul's idea," I explained. "I'd rather swallow fire."

His eyebrow slowly lifted, looking over the gown and then back up into my eyes.

"Almost presentable," he said flatly.

"What do you mean, almo-"

He stepped forward, grabbing the waist of my skirt and straightening it. His ragged fingers tugged on the top and sleeves, then he pulled at the ribbon, undoing it completely. He tied it another way, the folds of the bow laying flat against my rib cage. He stepped behind me, his fingers suddenly running through my hair and pulling it back. There were a few small tugs as his hands worked through my hair. I didn't say a word. I could only stand there as his fingers grazed my scalp, his touch warm and comforting despite his usual attitude towards me.

After a few moments, he stepped away, looking at me from the side. I reached back to feel a long braid.

"You fashioned my hair?" I asked.

He shrugged, running his tongue through his cheek.

"You did that so quickly."

"I've had practice," he said. He looked me over once more. "You look far more presentable now. More suited for a man to have tempting thoughts about you."

His gaze was strong as he said it, his eyes lingering a heartbeat too long.

"Remember our deal," Kangdae said, turning his head away. "Don't get sidetracked by men with large purses."

I frowned. "I have no intentions of being distracted by anyone."

"Good. Keep your focus, and I'll give you anything you want."

I swallowed and nodded, trying to hold my expression still. Without another word, Kangdae left.

I approached the hut where Geonho, Intak, and Haneul were speaking with a few of the others. Geonho's jaw slacked. He nudged the other two and pointed at me. Intak only wrinkled his nose, looking more annoyed than impressed. Haneul, however, lit up like the night sky with a full moon. His teeth showed, his eyebrows raised.

"Well, well, well," Haneul chattered, coming closer. "And here I thought I'd have to help you dress."

"No chance in hell," I replied.

He leaned over to look at me more, his face blanching at the sight of my hair. His fingers came up and touched the braid gently, his eyebrows matting together.

"Did… did Kangdae do this?" he asked.

I nodded. "He said I was unpresentable and felt the need to fix all my offenses."

He didn't respond. He was completely focused on the braid, his fingers curling around it. Something flashed across his eyes. Something like sorrow.

He cleared his throat and stepped away. "I suppose it's my turn to get ready. We both have important parts to play tonight."

***

Haneul instructed me to wait by the horse stables. The smell of manure and sweaty horses didn't suit my attire, and it brought me back to the reality that nothing in my possession could be kept.

Maybe not even my place in the Rebellion.

What would they do with me in the end? In the beginning that hadn't mattered, but as time went on, I was realizing that my place here was temporary. I wanted Kiwan more than anything, but after that - after I had what I wanted - then what?

Would Haneul toss me aside? Kangdae would. Saejun already had.

I needed to watch out for myself. Only myself. Before I trusted Haneul too much.

"You practice your frown more than your smile, sweetheart."

I turned to the sound of Haneul's voice, not prepared to see his new look. His robes were much richer than they usually were - blue and silver silk with gold embroidery. There were red bands at his waist and wrists that somehow accented the natural pink in his lips. It reminded me of the first night we met, when I had nearly stabbed him in the chest.

He smiled. "Hard not to stare, isn't it?"

I turned my head away, blinking. "They're only garments."

He stepped in close behind me, leaning into my ear. "Yes, but the better I wear them, the more tempted you'll be to see what's *under* them."

I threw my head back to glare at him even though my heart was pounding. He chuckled and took the veil out of my hand.

"Don't forget to wear this," he said. "I don't want anyone knowing what that pretty face looks like. Not if you're going to be part of my Underground."

He pinned the veil across my face, tracing his fingers against my jaw. He then brought out his horse and saddled it, the rest of the men coming in to do the same. They made their comments about my appearance as they came in.

"What's this? Are we escorting a princess?"

"Wow, you look like a real professional hostess. Don't hurt me. I meant it as a compliment."

"Isn't that the same dress Geonho wore that one time? I wonder if we could pay him to wear it again?"

"Enough," Haneul said, coming up beside me. "Saddle up and get ready to go to the Red House. Remember my orders."

He held out his hand for me, hoisting me up on his horse. He then climbed on behind me, pressing his chest into my back and wrapping his arm around my waist. I shifted in the saddle.

"You don't have to sit this close," I noted.

He chuckled. "You're my hostess. The public should see me close to you. I don't want to ruin my reputation."

"What reputation?"

Haneul kicked the horse to get it moving.

"I'm known as a popular businessman in the city," he said. "Some say I'm in the black market, and others say I'm in textiles. Neither is true, obviously."

"You're a con-artist then?"

"Anyone working for or against the government is some kind of con-artist, really. It helps me collect information on the emperor. I know everything he's doing. When. Where. How. Who. It's my best asset. So stick close and pay attention."

He gave me the overview again. Haneul, myself, and a few of the others were to enter into the Red House, while a few more men stayed on the outside. I would serve alongside the other *hostesses* while he and the others spoke with the men.

It was a simple mission. One that didn't involve any violence or extreme risk.

I knew he was testing me. He wanted to see if I could obey orders. The problem was, I now had two sets of orders to follow: his and Kangdae's.

The ride was longer than I wanted. Haneul had the horse in a full gallop at the start of it, but between the constant sharp movements of the horse and my nerves, I couldn't handle it for long. I gripped onto Haneul's arm, asking him to slow down. He obliged, letting the horse walk for a few kilometers. I leaned over, clenching my stomach.

The Rebellion wasn't home. I knew that. But something about leaving the campsite and heading back into town made me want to throw myself off the horse and run back.

"Relax," Haneul purred in my ear. "I won't let anything happen to you."

I dropped my head, annoyed that I wanted to believe him.

His arm wrapped around my stomach, and he leaned down to drop his head on my shoulder. His breath tickled my neck, his nose nuzzling against it.

"What are you doing?" I asked, pulling back.

"Practicing. Have you ever been like this with a man before?"

I started to push him away, but he clicked his tongue and pulled me back.

"You have to stay close to me if you want to live, sweetheart," he said. "I want to know your background with men, especially now that you're my hostess."

"I'm not your whore."

"I bet you're the true love type of girl," he replied, ignoring me. "One that would sacrifice everything for a man."

"Don't insult my intelligence."

"I'm not. I admire the dream."

"That type of dream is a waste of time."

He unwrapped his arm from my torso and took my hand. Warmth and comfort came out of his fingertips as he stroked my knuckles.

"It sounds like you believed in it once," he said. "Have you ever been in love before?"

I looked at him for a brief moment, then turned my head away. He pulled my chin back until I faced him again, small traces of sympathy in his eyes.

"Don't worry, sweetheart. I'll make sure you get a happy ending." His lips pursed. "It may not, however, be the happy ending you want."

His fingers were firm as they held mine.

The lights of the city lanterns peaked over the side of the capital walls. I swallowed, trying to keep down my pounding heart and shaking nerves.

"Are you ready, Jaehwa?" Haneul whispered in my ear, his arm wandering back to my waist and constricting me against him. "Because after this… anyone with any importance is going to know you as *mine*."

CHAPTER 15

THE PACK

I had never heard Haneul's name before that night we met in the bar. Maybe I had been in the wrong circles.

Because in the thick of a brothel, everyone knew his name.

As we walked in the door, all heads turned and all mouths grinned. We were swarmed by both men and women, clawing for his attention regarding both business and pleasure.

"Haneul! How's trading these days?" one of the men said, dressed in fabric as lavish as Haneul's. "You disappeared on us. Good to see you healthy."

"Haneul, what do you think of the wares from the Western Province? I think the devils are trying to cheat us."

"It's been too long, old friend! Come have drinks with us before the night's over."

The women were even more obsessed with his arrival than the businessmen. Despite my obvious presence, they draped themselves across his arms, escorting him deeper into the House.

I had never stepped foot in a brothel before, but I automatically hated it. The scent of jasmine, cinnamon, and heavy liquor drenched the air, accompanied by drunken laughter and loud chattering. Women sat on the laps of obvious strangers, with no apprehension or reservation. They laughed and cooed at each other, making my stomach turn in both disgust and morbid curiosity. What would it be like to feel a man's genuine caress in such a way?

I could still feel Haneul's presence against my back from our horse ride together, which seemed to mean nothing now that he was surrounded by rich women.

A hand reached out for my arm and pulled me close, Haneul's smile coming into sight.

"Keep your eyes on me, sweetheart," he said in my ear.

The other women took a step back at his gesture, looking at me as if they had just noticed my existence. Their faces mixed in confusion, annoyance, and disappointment. Served them right.

"Where is Kana?" Haneul asked the other girls.

They looked at each other.

"I'll get her for you," one of them said.

"No need," he returned. "I'd like to meet with her privately."

His hand wrapped around my waist, signaling that *private* didn't mean *alone*.

One of the girls led us past a couple of rooms, towards the back of the house. She knocked in a pattern - double, single, triple. After a moment, the door opened and a woman drenched in golden silk stepped out. She was perhaps in her thirties, but her straight posture and pursed lips showed a woman who had been in her field for quite some time. She smiled.

"Sok Haneul," she said with a voice like pure honey. "What a pleasant surprise. I see you haven't lost your style… or physique."

"Wouldn't dream of it," he replied. "Is it a good time to speak?"

She looked at me, then dipped her head back to look at him. "For you? Of course."

The door was shut behind us, no one else in the room.

"Did you bring me a gift?" the woman asked, pinching my chin in between her fingers.

"She's a gift to myself," Haneul replied, plucking away the woman's hand. "But I want her to be one of yours for the night."

The woman giggled, her laugh sounding like river water rushing over stones as she sat on her cushioned chair, her robes draping open in all the tempting places. "No offense, Han, but she hardly looks like a decent whore."

I automatically wrinkled my nose at the word.

"Don't look so disgusted, dear," the woman said. "It's a decent living for some of us."

"She won't be part of the House," Haneul replied. "I have a special use for her: Kim Saejun."

The woman laughed, a hand fluttering to her collarbone. "That old, wet blanket? Why would you ever put a beautiful girl in his company? Every time he comes in, it's like talking with a tombstone. A gorgeous tombstone, mind you, but a good shine doesn't change a cold rock."

My stomach sank. Saejun came to the Red House?

"Not as his hostess," Haneul corrected. "We're collecting information. When was the last time he was here?"

"A month or two ago."

"What did he talk about?"

"His men were talking about taxes they collected from the north side. A few dead bodies. Something about executions for the murderers."

Executions for murderers. Kiwan.

"When is the next execution?" Haneul asked.

"Six weeks," she replied, patting the back of her hand to her mouth as she yawned. "About a dozen murderers, they said. A few citizens that didn't pay taxes. Even a thieving child, maybe ten or eleven in years. No mercy these days, eh?"

I shook my head in disbelief. Saejun wouldn't execute a child.

… But maybe Captain Kim would.

"Well enough," Haneul said. "I appreciate the information, Kana."

The woman twirled her hand in acknowledgment.

"Do you mind if my pet makes a few rounds?" he asked.

He gripped me by the waist again, pulling me close. I didn't push him away.

"If she wants to play for a day, I don't mind," the woman said. "As long as she doesn't drive away any customers."

His grip on me tightened as he turned his nose towards me, his lips unbearably close to mine. "I'll keep her in line."

117

It's just a game, I told myself, turning my head down. *You have to remember that all of this is a game to him.*

Kana stood from her chair, stepping into his space. "And what will you do to keep me in line, Han?"

He chuckled darkly and pulled a small purse from his robe. He brought it in close to her breasts, and she finished the route by tucking the purse between them.

"Always a pleasure, dear," she said.

"Same to you," Haneul replied.

Kana left the room, an extra swing in her hips. I nudged Haneul as he stared.

"Mind telling me what that was about?" I asked.

"I already told you. Be a good hostess and go eavesdrop on the men in the room," he said. "Don't talk to them. Don't even look at them for too long. I don't want them taking an interest in you. Just serve the drinks and come back to your master when you've finished. If you're a good pet, I'll give you a treat."

He left the room before I could scold him for talking to me like a dog. When I followed him out, Kana came to greet us, holding a platter of small glasses filled to the brim with sour alcohol.

"Walk around and hand a glass to any man with his hand raised," she said. "Sway your hips a little to double the sales."

I took the tray, mentally refusing hip swaying.

Overall, the men at the Red House were boring and obnoxious. They raised glasses, cheering and making loud drunken promises about making money and buying land outside of the country. If the emperor heard of such talk, they would have been put to death immediately. Even

118

talking about a life outside the borders was treason. You lived here and you died here. That was the only option.

But honestly, it was hard to tell the difference between living and dying after awhile.

"I hear Captain Kim's been giving the treasury some trouble," one of the men said, taking a glass from my tray.

"Aye, he's a pain in the ass, that one. His men would sell him for a sick sheep if they weren't so damn afraid of him."

The second man winked at me as he took his drink. I ducked my head and pulled back, trying not to kick him in the face for the way he stared at my chest.

"He's the devil to work for and a demon to go against," the man continued. "I feel sorry for the suckers under his command. They live in hell no matter what they do."

I grit my teeth as I walked away. He felt sorry for those under Saejun's command? Saejun was hard, but he was caring about those under his authority.

No, wait. That was Saejun. Not Captain Kim. The past and present were two different places. Saejun and Captain Kim were two different people.

Why was that so hard to remember?

A quarter of my shift passed, but there was nothing of any interest. My feet were starting to hurt. All-day combat training I could handle. An evening of serving men drinks and I wanted to die.

"Is my pet tired of playing?"

I turned to Haneul sitting behind me, arm draped against the teal and purple sofa he had claimed as his own. He flirted a grin before licking his lips and pulling on my arm, bringing me sideways onto his lap. His rough hands grazed my sides and pulled me in closer, his breath making contact with my neck. Fire shot through my spine, the sensation overwhelming.

"What the hell are you doing?" I asked, pulling back.

"Nuh-uh-uh. Remember the game, sweetheart."

He pulled me back in his embrace, letting his hands wander around my back. He was a physical type of person to begin with, I knew that. But his energy had never been truly sexual. It was playful and manipulative at times - a means to an end. And in small pockets, it was affectionate, like he knew I had been starved of it for a long time.

But sitting in his lap in front of a crowd was a completely different feeling. I didn't know how to respond. It was supposed to be fake, but the heat at his fingertips had even me confused. I looked down at his lips, wondering how far he would take the act. I was starting to wonder how far I'd let him take it.

"I won't hurt you," he chuckled. "Lean in a bit more… like that. Put your arms around me. Now, tell me what you found out."

"Taxes have gone up in the north."

He shrugged. "Doesn't affect me much."

"No one likes working with or dealing with Saejun."

"Not news. Everybody hates him."

"A member of the emperor's court is cheating on his wife with someone here."

"That's what these places are made for." He scowled. "You'll need to do better than this."

"How can I when I'm not allowed to talk to anyone?"

Haneul's head dropped to the side, his eyes drifting around the room. His gaze stopped. His smile widened.

"Don't worry, sweetheart," he said, rubbing my cheek with his fingertips. "Your golden opportunity has arrived. The man I've been *dying* to show you off to just walked in the door."

"Who?" I asked, distracted by his fingers on my skin.

He grinned ear to ear. "Captain Kim Saejun. He's here."

CHAPTER 16

REUNION

E verything turned white the moment I saw him.

Saejun shed the outer layer of the emperor's red cloak, handing it to the hostesses of the House. They bowed, the two men beside him talking as they also took off their cloaks. Saejun's main robes showed the riches of his accomplishments with their deep blues and teals. The silk cloth with delicate white embroidery was a stark contrast to his stoney expression.

The light in the House was stronger than in my home, and even from across the room I could now see how much time had aged him. His eyes were deeper set, even though they were still clear. His shoulders were higher and stronger, the silky fabric curving around his muscles like water. I couldn't help but stare, remembering those days training in the lavender fields. He had changed, but he still looked so much like I remembered. It made my stomach ache, desiring a way back to the past.

From across the room, his eyes met mine.

I turned away, ready to jump from Haneul's lap and run, but Haneul's fingers dug into my thighs to hold me still as his smile widened.

"Don't run away now," he said. "It's about to get fun."

"Haneul…" I pleaded, "if he sees me, he'll kill me."

Haneul smiled. "Will he? I'd love to watch."

"What?"

My heart pounded as I caught the glimmer in Haneul's eyes. He kept the stare until I could read exactly what he was thinking.

Haneul didn't want me to collect information. This was the real reason he brought me here.

This was the bastard's plan all along.

"Captain Kim," Haneul said over my shoulder with a large smile. "How long has it been since our last meeting? Three months? Four? The seasons have certainly changed since I saw you last."

Even though I was wearing a veil, I didn't have the guts to turn and look at him.

"Sok Haneul," Saejun returned, his voice vibrating deep in my ears. "I was hoping we'd never meet again."

Haneul shrugged. "Fate feels otherwise, I guess. She keeps bringing us together, over and over again. Please, have a seat."

Haneul gestured to the chair next to him. I ducked my head down, trying not to face Saejun as the fabric of his robes rustled beside us.

Haneul's fingers kneaded into my waist as he brought an arm around me, the other hand coming up to twirl stray strands of my hair in his fingers. My heart pounded in so many different ways that I thought it might burst.

"Still a regular, I see," Haneul said. "Are there any women here you recommend?"

Saejun grunted. "I only take part in the alcohol."

"Fascinating. There are dozens of women here ready to lay beneath you, and you choose the wine. I dare say you haven't learned how to live at the top yet."

"Ha. The top and the bottom are a matter of perspective, I suppose."

"Let me get you a drink." Haneul nudged me. "Sweetheart, why don't you serve the Captain and his men, eh?"

His fingers pressed into my skin in a warning.

This bastard...

I tried not to let my breath shake as I exhaled, standing up from his lap and grabbing a tray of drinks from one of the other hostesses. I brought the tray over, looking at the floor as much as possible.

"Appreciate it, beautiful," one of them said as he took the drink from my tray. "Stick around. I might be thirsty again later."

"That one is off limits," Haneul interjected playfully. "She's been with me for the last month. I finally put in the signatures for her."

I gripped the sides of the tray as Saejun's other man took his drink.

"Business is well, then?" Saejun asked Haneul. "The black markets must be filling a lot of orders."

Haneul chuckled. "We've been over this, Captain. I have no black market dealings. You must be parched from all those circles you run in. Jaehwa, sweetheart, give Captain Kim his drink."

Saejun's hand froze as he reached for the drink, and in spite of myself, I followed his hand to meet the eyes behind them.

Saejun's eyes dilated as he looked at me, his forehead shifting back.

Haneul clicked his tongue. "I said she was off limits, Captain Kim. Must you stare like that?"

My breath stopped as I stepped back. Saejun didn't take his eyes off me, the corners of his eyelids narrowing.

"She has beautiful eyes, yes?" Haneul continued, taking the drink from my tray and handing it to Saejun himself. "I thought so too. She's also surprisingly strong for a woman, despite her fragile frame. She was practically starving to death when I found her."

Saejun's tongue rolled over his lips before he brought the cup to them, not taking his eyes off me. He swallowed, his jaw ticking.

"How much did you pay for her?" Saejun snarled.

"Ah, let's see." Haneul leaned against the arm of his chair, taking a drink for himself. "She really wasn't worth much when I first found her. I think I paid two hundred."

I glared at him. It was bad enough being called a whore. It was even worse being called a cheap one.

Saejun's hand tightened around his glass. "I'll pay you two thousand to release her to me."

"Two thousand?" Haneul said, laughing. "I've invested nearly as much in her. Hardly gives me enough to replace her."

"Ten thousand then," Saejun countered.

He kept his focus on me, barely blinking. His stare froze me to the floor.

Haneul downed his drink. "It seems that you've taken quite an interest in my pet. I like the sound of your money, but have to admit, I'm apprehensive. I rather enjoy playing with her. I like all the little yips and whines she makes."

Saejun jumped from his seat and grabbed Haneul's collar, taking him down to the floor. The women behind their seats gasped and ran to the side as everyone turned their heads. Haneul's hands raised beside his head in surrender as he chuckled.

"Is the great Captain Kim wanting to fight me for a whore? I suppose even the noblest of men have their weaknesses."

Saejun's hands tightened around Haneul's throat. "Don't you dare call her that!" he barked. "She's not —"

He stopped himself, looking around the room. He looked back to his men, who had their heads cocked to the side, eyebrows raised.

Saejun turned back to Haneul. "She's not a whore. She's a wanted fugitive."

He released Haneul and jumped towards me, ripping the veil from my face. I glared back at him as he stared, a familiar look of disappointment in his eyes.

But I wasn't the little girl he was training anymore.

I threw the tray in his face and ran. I heard a few frustrated grunts behind me, but paid no attention as I ran towards the exit.

I ran out into the streets, avoiding the stares of the gentlemen hanging around outside. There weren't many people out this time of night, making me an easy target with my bright gown.

I ran to the park towards the middle of the city, holding my skirts so not to trip over them. There was a large bridge over the river that went through the town, and I sped part way down it, stopping to catch my breath.

I turned back, hoping for Haneul. I got Saejun instead.

He stopped at the edge of the bridge, anger pouring off his shoulders as he panted. Running to the other side of the bridge was a straight shot, but I knew Saejun could outrun me if I tried it.

So I jumped.

The river wasn't deep, but I managed to jump from the bridge and into the water, absorbing the impact without hurting my legs. The current was strong, however, and I had to fight to keep from being pushed around by it. I tore down the side of the river, jumping onto the streets and into another side of town. Thanks to Haneul's training at the lake next to camp, it wasn't difficult to run in wet clothes.

The shops in the market were shutting down for the night, but there were still plenty of people in this part of town. They didn't appreciate it when I stripped off my robes in the middle of the street, but I didn't have the time to be modest. I removed my outer robes and tied them like a belt around my waist. It made it far easier to run, and Haneul wouldn't kill me for losing the robes.

…Wherever he was.

The crowd started to dissolve the more I went through the city, until I reached a nearly deserted place on the darker side. Running down an empty street, I came to a dead end. When I turned around to go back, I came face to face with the person I had been running from.

Saejun's nostrils flared. I turned to face him, steadying my breath.

"A whore, Jaehwa?" he growled, panting as he approached. "You escaped to become a goddamn whore?"

I gritted my teeth. "You gave me no choice."

"That was never allowed to be an option!" He stepped towards me. "You're coming back with me. You can come willingly, or I can drag you."

I stepped back and pulled my heel up. Just like he taught me.

"Go to hell," I replied.

He stepped forward to charge. A crash deafened us both as wooden barrels of wine smashed between us, with chicken cages and random stacks of garbage piling on after. There was a familiar arm around my waist, pulling me up by rope onto the rooftop behind us.

Haneul's grin came into view from the side, his arms bringing me in close to him as he faced Saejun.

"I already told you that she's mine, Captain," he said. "I wish you the best of luck if you want to take her from me."

Saejun jumped over the broken barrels towards us, but stopped at the wall. There was no way for him to reach us. That didn't change the determination in his eyes, however.

"You won't have her, Sok," Saejun replied. "Not you."

Haneul shrugged. "And yet... I do."

Haneul's lips came to my cheek, the faint kiss making my knees weak.

"Let's go home, sweetheart," Haneul said, loud enough for Saejun to hear.

I swallowed, emotions fluttering from all angles. But there was one emotion that held fast — stronger than all of the others.

I looked Saejun straight in the eyes as I responded. "Yes… Master."

I turned my back on Saejun and walked away, satisfied to finally show him how it felt.

CHAPTER 17

FAMILY SECRETS

"Why did you do it?" Haneul whispered in my ear.

He hadn't said a word until we were halfway back to camp. I had been too lost in muddled emotions to bother starting any type of conversation myself.

"I could ask you the same question," I replied. "You knew he'd be there."

"I had a hunch."

"And you were practically foaming at the mouth when you were right. You're satisfied? Putting my life on the line like that?"

"I told you to trust me. And if you're going to call me *Master*, I'd prefer you did it because you mean it, not simply to piss Captain Kim off." He chuckled darkly. "Although, I admit, it was the highlight of my night."

I hated the sound of *Master*. I hated the idea of submitting to anyone. If I had chosen a lifestyle of submission to authority, Kiwan and I wouldn't be alive. But Haneul risked himself for me by bringing me into the Rebellion.

He took care of me more than anyone; feeding me, training me, encouraging me, and even forgiving me.

I swallowed.

Saejun did all the same things when we were younger... and look where we ended up.

"I trust your instruction," I admitted. "But I don't trust your kindness."

"I don't want you to trust my kindness. I want you to trust me with your life. I want you alive, Jaehwa. Do you not believe that?"

I didn't answer.

Haneul cleared his throat. "Also, there's another matter."

I turned my ear towards him to indicate that I was listening.

"If Kangdae finds out that there are women on the outside working for me, he'll pull my mission," he said. "I need you to keep this to yourself. This is my order as your master."

"Am I supposed to obey without asking questions?"

He chuckled. "You can ask, but I can't guarantee an answer."

"There were women in the Rebellion at one point, weren't there?"

"Yes."

"So why is Kangdae against it now?"

He hesitated. "Kangdae doesn't want history to repeat itself. That's where we don't see eye to eye. Kangdae wants to run from it. I want to face it head-on."

"Didn't you once say you were the reason there were no women at camp?"

He gave a long sigh. "I am."

The arrogant air around him vanished, replaced by something heavy and melancholy. I couldn't bring myself to ask any more questions as we trotted further through the forest towards camp.

The shadows were always endless, but late past midnight, they swallowed the earth even more. The moon disappeared completely, leaving us with only darkness and the sounds of the horse's hooves and Haneul's gentle breath. His elbows brushed across my sides as he pulled on the horse reins, taking us further into the forest. The gentle rocking of the horse started to put me to sleep. I leaned against Haneul for most of the ride back, his shoulder supporting me the entire way. To my surprise, he didn't give me a single snarky remark about it.

He waited for that until *after* we got back to the camp.

"Alright, let's take off your clothes and go to bed," he said, sliding off the horse first.

I nearly fell over. "Excuse me?"

He chuckled, helping me down. "Your clothes need to be dried, and you're falling asleep. So change and return your robes to Geonho to get them properly dried. I have a spare robe for you. Come on."

After putting the horse in the stables, Haneul led me back to our shared hut, handing me a fresh robe to change into. I expected him to walk out and leave me to undress, but instead, he started stripping.

"What are you doing?" I asked, turning my head away.

"What? I need to return my robes as well. Does it bother you? It wouldn't bother the rest of my men."

"I'm not one of your men. I'm a woman."

He smirked triumphantly, stepping outside. "You said it, sweetheart. Not me."

Bastard.

I changed, then stepped out of the hut so Haneul could do the same. He folded the garments and handed them to me in a pile, telling me to return them to Geonho.

As I walked, I wondered what to tell Kangdae. If I told Kangdae about the women at the brothel, he would pull Haneul's plan to weaken the emperor. If I kept it a secret, Kangdae wouldn't help me get my brother back.

What information could I give him that would keep me on both sides?

My stomach dropped when I realized I didn't have time to come up with an answer. Kangdae was headed straight for me.

I kneaded the robes as he came closer.

"Kangdae —"

"Yeojin…" he said. "You came back."

His arms stretched out, and he embraced me in a hug once again. The robes fell to the ground as he squeezed me against him.

"I had a horrible dream," he said. "You stupid girl… selfish sister…"

He started to slump on me again, the trance fading.

Sister? Yeojin… was Kangdae's sister?

"What was your dream?" I asked him, hoping for some clue.

He muttered and slurred something unintelligible. I shuddered as he answered, his lips unintentionally pressing against the flesh of my shoulder.

"This is… interesting," a voice said behind Kangdae.

I looked up to see an apathetic Dolshik.

"It's not what it looks like," I said.

He raised an eyebrow. "It looks like Kangdae is sleepwalking again."

I paused. "Perhaps it's exactly what it looks like, then."

"Don't worry," Dolshik said, rolling his eyes. "I had no assumptions that Kangdae was meeting you secretly. He's not the type."

I thought about Kangdae meeting me at the lake when I was completely naked... but kept my mouth shut.

Dolshik stepped forward and pulled Kangdae off of me, and that was enough to set Kangdae in motion again towards his hut. He stumbled twenty paces, then collapsed on the ground. Dolshik sighed, walking over and picking him up, throwing him over his shoulder like Kangdae was a recent kill.

I picked the robes up off the ground and followed.

Dolshik threw Kangdae back into his hut, tucking the blankets under Kangdae's chin like a child. He turned around and pulled me out of the hut, then stared at me for a long moment. I held up the robes to explain why I was walking about so late.

"The mission was successful?" Dolshik asked.

"I suppose so."

I wasn't sure what the mission actually *was*, if I was honest.

Dolshik took the robes, making a face at the damp clothing. "At least Geonho doesn't have to dress like a woman anymore. I guess that's one good thing about a woman being here."

"Is a woman so disgusting to all of you?" I asked, reaching my limit. "I work in your gardens. I train every day with the men. The mission was successful. Doesn't that prove my competence?"

"Your competence doesn't matter."

"You sound like Kangdae. Why are you all against me being here?"

Dolshik took a deep breath, squinting one eye.

"Answer me this," he said. "Would you let a child fight in the army?"

"Of course not," I replied, annoyed at the random change in subject.

"Why not? Aren't they capable?"

I scoffed. "They might be capable, but they should be protected, not enlisted."

Dolshik stared.

My mouth gaped. "That's not the same thing!"

"Have you ever seen a man lose the woman he loves?"

I shook my head at him, confused. "What?"

"You don't know our history, do you?" Dolshik asked.

I admitted that I had never asked.

"The Rebellion was created by Kangdae's father. There were plenty of groups against the previous emperor, but they failed miserably. To avoid failing like the others, Kangdae's father recruited anyone and everyone willing to go against the emperor. Men or women, any age or status. Believe it or not, this caused more problems than advantages. Affairs, jealous fights, entitlements due to family backgrounds."

"So he decided to kick women out to make sure everyone played nice?"

"I wish it was as easy as that." Dolshik looked up at the sky, running his tongue against his teeth. "Kangdae's mother was part of the Rebellion as well. She was caught for conspiracy and the emperor decided to make her an example for all citizens to submit. He had her beheaded… while Kangdae and his father watched."

My body turned to lead.

"Kangdae's father blamed himself, and in his self-pity, he went insane. He made sloppy military decisions out of vengefulness and grief. He could never recover from the loss of Kangdae's mother. And in the end, it killed him."

I didn't respond, the information processing. At my long silence, Dolshik took the robes from my arms.

"I'll return these," Dolshik said. "You can return to your hut."

He left. I stood still as thoughts bounced around in my head, trying to make sense of what I heard.

Kangdae's mother and father… such tragic endings. And what about his sister, Yeojin? What tragedy did she befall that Kangdae would say her name in his sleep? Was that the reason no women were allowed in the Rebellion?

It made sense, and yet, something wasn't connecting.

"I'm the reason for the rule, aren't I?"

Even though Kangdae's mother was executed, Haneul said he was the reason for the no women rule. Something else had happened.

…What did Haneul do?

CHAPTER 18

RECRUITS

Haneul announced that a celebration would be held in the evening, and Dolshik grumbled all day during preparations. I offered my help, not out of generosity, but because I needed something to distract me from all the events from the day before. Dolshik sent me to the gardens to collect whatever small vegetables were available, deciding to prepare a variety of side dishes and stew.

Regardless of the task in front of me, I replayed the previous day over and over again in my head. Kangdae's sleepwalking, Dolshik's explanations, Haneul's mysterious past, and - most of all - Saejun.

The Saejun I knew would have never set foot in a brothel. Saejun was honorable. Old-fashioned. Loved by everyone and a role model for those who depended on him.

But Captain Kim wasn't. Captain Kim was stone-faced and spoken badly about. He was feared and taunted.

How could Saejun change so much in only five years?

I recalled the moment in the brothel when he tore my veil from my face, genuine disappointment and anger mingled in his dark eyes.

"Don't you dare call her that…"

He was so quick to grab Haneul's throat at the word *whore*, but then he used it himself when we were alone.

"You escaped to become a goddamn whore?"

My stomach sank as I smoothed the soil beneath my hands. I had never seen Saejun so quick to anger. He was always so patient and diplomatic…

But he wasn't Saejun anymore. He wasn't. I knew it. I repeated it. Nothing I said to myself, however, dimmed the memory of the farmer's son who wanted to change the world… or how I always believed he would.

"You didn't come to me."

I looked up to the new voice. Kangdae chewed on his cheek, leaning against one of the trees near the gardens.

"I didn't need to. You're always lurking around somewhere," I replied. "At least I'm dressed this time."

He dipped his head as he smiled and stepped forward.

"Did you get the information I wanted?" he asked.

I stared at him for a long time, debating what to say. I had thought about it for awhile, and now I had to find the nerve to actually give Kangdae my answer.

"Why should I?" I replied.

Kangdae raised an eyebrow. "You don't want your brother?"

"How do I know you'll deliver?" I asked, standing up and brushing the dirt from my knees. "Haneul takes care of me. He's shown me what he can do for me. All you've done is made an empty promise. How do I know you can be trusted?"

He cocked his head to the side in thought, seemingly amused. "The only reason Haneul provides for you is because I approve it. Anything you have is because of me."

I tried not to clench my hands. Haneul could read my emotions when I did it. Kangdae could have been just as smart.

"Prove it," I challenged.

He chuckled, stepping closer. "I'm not bargaining with you, woman. You can either trust me and give me the information I want, or I can make it miserable for you."

"You're not exactly making it lavish as we speak."

His lip twitched. "I can make it worse."

I dropped my head down, looking at the dirt under my nails. "What will you do with the information?"

"That's my business."

"Why do you need me to work for you when there are at least fifty other men that can give you what you want?"

"That's also my business."

I grunted. "You're not convincing me."

"I'm not trying to convince you," he said, shrugging. "It's a simple trade. Information on Haneul's dealings in exchange for your brother. I thought it would be an easy decision. That's your reason for being here, isn't it? Or did you think this was a permanent arrangement?"

I chewed my lip, not answering.

He sighed, shaking his head as he turned to walk away. "What a waste of time. To come so far only to end up with nothing in the end."

I grabbed his sleeve.

"Wait," I said.

He turned his eyes down at my hand and then looked at me. He waited.

If I was going to be kicked out eventually, I at least wanted something to go back to. The truth was, I didn't know if Haneul would keep me either. If both of them were going to get rid of me...

"What do you want to know?" I asked.

Kangdae's lips pulled to the side in a smirk.

"Tell me about the mission," he said. "All of it."

***

Everyone came to the celebration that night, half of them not knowing why we were celebrating, but appreciating the drinks and food nonetheless. I didn't understand the reason for the celebration either. All I did during the mission was show up and make Saejun angry.

Haneul seemed far too happy about that.

There was double the usual amount of deer meat, along with extra rice, and some vegetables that were usually reserved. The alcohol was high quality, bought in from the city thanks to Dolshik's recent supply run.

"Our people are still in prison," one of the men next to me muttered. "I'm not sure why we're celebrating at a time like this."

Haneul plopped down between me and the grumbling man. "Because high spirits make for better strategies. Disheartened slobs are useless to me."

He heartily bit into some meat before shoving the plate at me.

"So what's the plan, then?" the man asked.

Haneul shook his head dismissively. "We'll get them out. I have my methods."

Yeah. Me.

The question was, what did he want me to do, exactly?

The men cheered and drank, becoming more and more unbearable as the night went on. Sometimes they made me laugh, but other times they made me shake my head in disappointment. I was used to male nonsense from growing up with a younger brother and Saejun, but this was that feeling multiplied by fifty.

The only person not drinking was Kangdae. He kept to his tea, sipping it in between the men's jokes. He smiled and enjoyed himself, something I rarely saw him do in the time I had been there. It was the first time I had heard him laugh in good spirits, mercilessly teasing his subordinates.

"I think in another life, I would have been a shoe maker," one of the drunken men said dreamily.

"They would use your face for the leather," Kangdae replied with a childish smile.

I watched him in fascination, appreciating this relaxed side of him. Refusing to consume alcohol, he stayed cool and quick-witted, yet not as loud or dramatic as the rest of the men.

But, to be fair, no one was louder or more dramatic than Haneul.

"Ah, you should have seen his face!" Haneul said, coming to his feet as the men around him watched.

He pulled his shoulders back, strutting forward, looking around the tables of men with his nose in the air. He arched his eyebrows as he pulled off the outer layer of his coat and threw it to the man behind him.

He was pretending to be Saejun.

My eyes went down to my cup.

"Captain of the Guards to his Lord Emperor!" Haneul mocked. "Honorable and just hero of the capital! Authority above all men! Biceps of the gods!"

The men laughed and jeered as Haneul continued to reenact yesterday night for his men. He went through everything, from his own playful banter to Saejun attacking him, and finally - to my annoyance - the moment I called him Master.

The men "oh"ed at the last part.

I frowned, looking around. Kangdae's eyes met mine as he brought his cup to his lips. The look was interrupted by Haneul's swaying, drunken figure.

"You've really grown on me, sweetheart," Haneul said, smashing my face between his hands. "I can't wait to put you to work."

I wriggled out of his hold.

Haneul went to talk with the others. I went back to my rice, mindlessly picking up the stray grains with my chopsticks. To my surprise, Intak sat down next to me, crossing his legs.

"Are you planning to give me a hard time even now?" I asked with a sigh.

Intak pursed his lips and reached for the small bowl of kimchi in front of him. "Congratulations on your first successful mission."

He stuffed the kimchi in his mouth, not looking at me. He chewed slowly, as if he had to create words from scratch before speaking.

"It will only get harder from here," he said after swallowing. "If you truly consider our master as your own, I hope you keep to his orders. For your own sake. And for his."

With a long look at Haneul, he dropped his chopsticks on the table and left.

***

The night continued, and most of the men lost themselves to their cups of alcohol by midnight. Most of them fell asleep on the floor of the dining hall, except for Kangdae, who stood from his seat and left back to his hut without a word.

"This is exactly why I didn't want to celebrate," Dolshik muttered, picking up the dishes. "I'm never going to get this smell out of my dining hall."

"The men seemed to enjoy themselves," Geonho replied, trying not to trip over the intoxicated bodies as he picked up the cups. "Besides, when was the last time we celebrated like this?"

Dolshik's jaw ticked. "Not sure if there's anything worth celebrating in our particular situation. We're all far too close to death or imprisonment to be cheery."

"We need to work on your optimism," Geonho said, frowning.

Haneul grabbed my arm, helping me up off the floor. He hadn't drank as much as the others, but it hadn't stopped him from acting just as drunk. Now that the men were asleep, however, he was back to his regular energy. The only difference was now he had an extra arrogant smile plastered to his face.

"Come with me, sweetheart," he said. "I have something for you."

Ignoring Dolshik's complaints about taking his help, Haneul took me to the training room. He left me at the entrance and lit a few candles ceremoniously. When half the room was filled with a warm glow, he turned back to me.

"What's all this?" I asked.

"Romantic, isn't it?"

I rolled my eyes. "Quit your nonsense. What's really going on?"

He smiled. "I have a gift for you."

He stepped over to the side of the room, pulling a box out from one of the shelves. He came back to me and lifted the lid. There was a small dagger in the box, the handle worn, but the blade glistening. Its shine was captivating even though it had obviously been used for battle.

"This dagger has been part of my family for some time," he said, pulling it out of the box. He set the box down and flicked the blade around his fingers a few times. He then opened my hand and placed it gently inside.

"Now," he said, "you're part of my family, too."

He closed my hand around the handle.

My breath caught in my throat. "Haneul…"

"Nuh," Haneul tutted. "*Master*, remember?"

I tightened my hand around the handle, the dagger comfortably fitting it.

"This is a sign of my trust in you," Haneul said. "Because calling me Master is your sign of trust in me."

I suddenly felt sick to my stomach. "Han — Mas — I can't accept this. What if I betray you?"

He smirked, reaching up to tuck a strand of hair behind my ear. "You probably will. I've been betrayed many times. I'll just have to trust that when you do betray me, something valuable will come of it. Until then, something valuable can be produced from our trust."

I looked down at the blade again, unable to look him in the eye.

"This dagger is a lot like you," he continued, touching his hand to my arm. "It's small and worn down, but in the worst of situations, it provides a bit of hope."

There was only sincerity in his voice. I looked up into his eyes to make sure what I was hearing was real. He glowed as he looked at me, a pride in his face I hadn't seen before.

"You, Jaehwa, are exactly what I've been needing to bring down Kim Saejun and weaken the emperor's defenses. I've been training dozens of people for years, and now, I have the final piece I've been needing all this time."

Bring down Saejun? The words hit me suddenly. With the dagger in my hand, I realized…

Was Haneul planning to kill him?

My stomach sank. Haneul brought his hands to my shoulders and squeezed them, forcing me to look at him.

He grinned.

"Welcome to the Underground, sweetheart."

CHAPTER 19

SCATTERED

"Go with him," Haneul commanded.

I frowned, watching Intak help load the horse saddles with supplies. He turned his head to narrow his eyes at me, holding his glare as he walked to the next horse.

"He'll kill me," I replied.

"From what I remember, *you* left him to die. Not the other way around."

I folded my arms. "Why aren't you coming?"

"Because the leader and the second-in-command don't go into missions together. If things go south, there would be no one to lead my men."

I frowned, curling my lip at Intak.

"When you made me part of the Underground, I didn't realize that *he* would be my leader," I said. "I would have rejected the position had I known."

Haneul shrugged. "Do you have other options?"

I glanced back towards the middle of camp, thinking of Kangdae.

He wasn't there to see me off, of course. He didn't approve of me going on the mission in any form, and it took a full night of Haneul convincing him to allow it. Whether or not this compromised his promise to help me get my brother, I didn't know.

"All you'll be doing is collecting information on the layout of the prison," Haneul said. "Watch how the guards move. Take note of any weaknesses in the structures. Pick up any details that might be helpful. Intak will be there to guide you. Obey him."

Intak cocked his head at the side to look at me. I gave a slight nod with a dirty look.

The prison was quite a distance from the camp, and we'd have to camp out in the forests for a few days to collect information. That would mean three or four days under Intak's command. If I could do that, I could do anything.

"Don't do anything foolish," Haneul added, turning around to leave. "If I lose you…"

The muscles in his face twitched, as if they couldn't decide on which emotion to pick.

"Come back to your master alive," he finally said. "That's an order."

He walked away before I could respond.

When I turned back, Intak was standing right in front of me. I jumped.

"I expect the same amount of obedience that you give Haneul," Intak said. "Don't forget that I'm your superior."

I rolled my eyes. "I'm not calling you *master.*"

His lips puckered. "I don't want that title. Not from you. Simply keep quiet and follow orders if you want to stay alive."

He hopped on his horse and trotted towards the forest, motioning for us to follow. Haneul had lent me his own horse, which was a relief. I was familiar with Goyanggi's abilities and quirks, and it also meant that there wouldn't be any strange men snuggled up behind me as we traveled.

Only Haneul was allowed to do that.

There were nearly a dozen men that went with us. There was a medic, there were some that were good at stealth, and there were a handful of strong combat fighters. It wasn't meant to be a dangerous mission, but anything could happen when the government was against you.

I didn't speak to anyone as we rode, even though I trained with most of them. Part of it was because silence was helpful in keeping away enemies. The other part was that I didn't want to be friends with any of them.

I wasn't staying. Why bother?

But then again... where were Kiwan and I going to go after this?

We spent hours riding towards the prison, the sun making its way from one end of the sky to the other as we rode.

"We're almost at the first checkpoint," Intak said, stopping his horse at a riverside. "Let the horses drink again."

The men stopped and led their horses to the water, taking some for themselves. I hopped off my horse and led it to the water. He stared at me.

"Come on, Goyanggi," I coaxed. "Drink."

He wagged his head back and forth.

I tugged at his mouthpiece. "Just one drink. Come on."

He didn't budge.

Intak approached, leaning his hand on the horse. "Don't you know the saying about horses and water? If he doesn't want to drink, he won't."

"But he'll get sick if he doesn't,"

"Then use your head to solve the problem. Stop using force for everything."

He opened the saddle bag and fed the horse a treat. After gobbling the treat, Goyanggi stepped forward and dipped his head in the water.

"Our entire existence revolves around strategy," Intak commented, watching Goyanggi drink. "There's an angle to everything. You just have to find the right opportunity. And if there isn't one, you make it."

I cocked my head to the side, staring at him. "Why did you join the Rebellion?"

He scratched his nose with a single finger. "Why do you ask?"

"I'm curious."

He sighed. "Haneul found me, same as you. But the circumstances were a little different. I used to fight him in the Moonlight Duels."

"Moonlight Duels?"

"Street fights," he replied. "Illegal gambling. Winner take all. Haneul was a regular. He was a street fighter when he was a teenager. I met him at least two or three times a month. Then, he disappeared. A few months later, he randomly showed up and told me he had a job for me if I was willing to take it. So here I am."

149

"So you've known him a long time."

"I've known him longer than anyone here, and I respect him based on what I know. That's the only reason I don't plan to leave you here, as much as I'd like to."

I frowned at him. "You really think I'm incompetent, don't you?"

He looked me over for a long moment. "No... I think you're too competent and under-experienced. That's even more dangerous."

"Intak!" a voice cried out from the other side. "Ambush!"

There was shouting and metal hitting metal before I saw anything. In a flash, the horses had scattered, except for Goyanggi. I grabbed his reins before he could get away, pulling him back despite the clamor.

The dozen men with us were now scattered with their swords drawn, attacking a new group of men. They all blurred together. I wasn't able to identify any of them.

Intak pulled his sword and stepped in front of me, trapping me between him and the horse.

"There's too many," he growled. "Why are there so many?"

One of the attackers put a sword through one of our men, then charged Intak. Intak raised his sword and met him.

I wrapped the horse's reins around a nearby tree limb, determined to keep some mode of transportation for escape. I removed the dagger Haneul gave me from my belt and raised my heel.

Intak stabbed his sword straight through his opponent, then spun to face me.

"Get out of here, Jaehwa!"

"I'm not leaving -"

"That's a command!" he threw back. "Tell Haneul—"

An enemy soldier came up behind Intak and raised his sword. I shoved Intak out of the way, slamming my dagger into the man's chest. He dropped his sword and screamed, reaching for my throat. I pulled back and pulled the dagger out, then elbowed him across the face. Intak's sword went through his throat, and he dropped to the ground.

Intak grabbed my arm and pulled me back to the horse.

"Twelve to two," he said.

"What?"

"Tell Haneul *twelve to two*. Now! Go!"

He jerked me forward, his face stern, but his eyes pleading. He turned back to face the enemies in front of him.

Watching our men get slaughtered, I knew I had no choice.

I jumped on the horse and dug in my heels, only looking over my shoulder once. There had to be fifty men against us.

Fifty against twelve.

Would they survive it?

***

I raced back to camp. It was too far, however, and I was forced to stop and give the horse a rest. I allowed him to get water and feed for a bit, my heart pounding and my stomach clenching.

I had no one. I was completely and totally alone in the forest, with the sun setting in the distance. I wanted to cry, but I couldn't. Everyone behind me... they all could have been dead.

I dragged myself back on the horse, but he didn't budge.

"Come on, boy. Don't give up now. I need you."

The horse shook his head, signaling his exhaustion. He had been running all day with few breaks. There was no way to get a horse to gallop if he didn't want to. What could I do? The horse didn't want to run. I couldn't give him a treat... it wouldn't have had the same effect it did at the river. There was no strategy. There was no chance.

The men were dying. I had no time.

"You leave me no choice," I scolded.

I pulled him into the forest, tying him to a tree root next to a spring so he could drink. With a few treats, and the promise to return, I took the saddle bag and threw it over my back.

And I ran.

CHAPTER 20

GHOSTS

S weat poured down every inch of my body by the time
I reached the camp. My feet were on fire, my head
pounding, my throat parched.

"Haneul!" I yelled through my dry throat. "Master!
Where are you!"

I felt myself falling, but I didn't hit the ground. Two
hands grabbed me before I could.

"Jaehwa!" Geonho's face blurred in front of me.
"Jaehwa! What happened?"

"Twelve to two," I said automatically. "Twelve...
two. Master..."

Geonho yelled for Haneul, and my vision blurred
even more.

"Stay with me, Jaehwa," Geonho said. "Stay with me."

I felt Haneul's arms around me before I heard his
voice.

"Jaehwa!" he shouted. "Shit, what happened to you?
Did you *run* here?"

"Twelve to two," I repeated. "Intak... twelve to two."

"Shit," Haneul replied, pulling me up into his arms. I felt myself being carried, but I couldn't even object. Everything in me ached: my body, my heart, my mind. It was all crashing together, turning me to lead.

In moments, I was in the medical hut, water being poured down my throat. It felt like life even though it tasted like dirt.

Haneul's face came into view. Did I have my eyes shut this entire time? I couldn't remember.

"Are you injured?" he asked.

His hands wandered my body, checking my bones and skin. The touch comforted me, bringing me back to my senses.

"There were fifty men…" I said. "…ambush… the others…"

Haneul's hand came to my forehead. "It's alright. You're alright. I'm with you."

I shuddered underneath his touch, but somehow, it settled my nerves. I tried to breathe deeper. Haneul barked some orders to the others while he started to pull apart my clothes.

"You're overheating," he said, as if reading my confusion. "Let's get you cooled. Where did —"

He stopped, pulling the small dagger from my belt. I blinked, suddenly realizing how much blood was on the blade.

I had stabbed a man. I put a knife in his chest and he screamed in terror right before Intak killed him.

I could still hear that scream.

I turned away from Haneul to vomit from the memory. Haneul's hand came to my back, rubbing it.

He didn't say anything condescending, nothing teasing, nothing funny. I was grateful.

"What's the commotion?" a new voice rang out.

I fell back against the mat, looking up.

Kangdae stepped forward, motioning for someone to clean up my mess. He did it casually, as if he had done it a thousand times before.

"Twelve to two," Haneul said.

"Shit," Kangdae replied.

"What does it mean?" I asked weakly.

Haneul's hand came back to my forehead. "It means that there are too many to fight, so the men have scattered from a group of twelve into pairs of two in order to survive. It… it doesn't…"

Haneul's hands shook.

Kangdae cleared his throat. "Haneul, attend to the men. They need you now. Take the medics."

"But what about the men here that need treatment?"

"I'll take care of them," Kangdae replied. He pulled up his sleeves as he walked across the room, dropping to his knees beside a table of herbs.

Haneul paused, watching Kangdae.

"Stop hesitating," Kangdae said, not looking up.

Haneul turned to me, asking me about the location of the men. I gave him all the information I could, including where to find his horse. He nodded, a small smile on his lips.

"Be a good pet," he whispered. "Wait for your master to come home."

He leaned down, kissing the top of my forehead. He squeezed my hand, then stood and bolted out of the hut. My fingers retracted, digging into my palm.

Please don't go…

I looked over to the side of the room, where Intak had been every time I was in this hut. His ghost was there, but he wasn't.

What if he…? No, he couldn't die. Not when I had lived. There was no reason for him to protect me to the point of death. I had given him no reason to.

"Easy," Kangdae said, bringing a wet cloth to my forehead. "Breathe this."

He put a sachet of herbs under my nose as I inhaled. Dried lavender.

It reminded me so much of home. My real one. My home with my father, mother, Kiwan, and Saejun. My muscles relaxed, but my heart ached, tears escaping my eyes before I could stop them.

Kangdae's hand came to my forehead. It was softer than Haneul's, his fingertips cooler and more delicate.

"You'll be fine," he assured me.

I swallowed. "I'm not worried about me."

"It will be alright," he added. "You did good."

I turned my head, unsure that the compliment I heard was real. He didn't respond. He didn't even look at me.

He made multiple mixes of herbs and teas, cooly telling Geonho how to distribute it to the other men in the hut with us. Geonho had a cheerful bedside manner, but I couldn't say the same about Kangdae. Though, he wasn't cruel. His face was calm and collected, no emotion leaking from any corner. But something about him there next to me was soothing, not intimidating like usual.

I watched him, trying to get some sort of glimpse of who he really was. I had never seen him look after the men in such a way, but he obviously knew what he was doing.

"How long will you stare at me like that?" Kangdae asked, not looking up.

I averted my eyes. "I'm sorry. You know a lot about medicine. I didn't realize."

He shrugged. "I was the lead medic for the Rebellion when it was under my father's command. When he died, I became the leader of the Rebellion."

"That explains the ointment you gave me."

He smirked. "Finally put that together, did you?"

His tone was serious, but his eyes were playful. I rested against the mat, wondering about all the thoughts behind those eyes.

"How old were you when you became leader?" I asked.

"Nineteen."

So Kangdae had lost both his parents by nineteen? My own father left when I was thirteen. My mother died two years ago. Both Kangdae and I had become parentless at the same age. With that in mind, Kangdae suddenly didn't look intimidating anymore. He looked strong.

"Get some rest," he said softly. "Worrying about them won't keep them alive. Restore your strength."

My body ached but my mind was wide awake. Part of the Rebellion had been captured and imprisoned. Another part had been ambushed.

And I… I was resting peacefully with nothing but sore muscles.

My first chance to use my training, and I ran away.

"I don't think I can sleep," I said, the guilt overtaking me.

Kangdae looked over, his eyes softening.

"Stop worrying," he said. "The men are in Haneul's care now. And you… you're in mine."

CHAPTER 21

SLEEPOVER

Haneul had been gone for three days.

Despite lack of sleep and scarcely eating, I obeyed without complaint when Kangdae asked me to do tasks around the camp. He had me bring him herbs for those in the medic hut, collect vegetables from the garden, clean the men's clothes, and send messages to the remaining members at the camp... everything short of helping Dolshik and Geonho in the kitchen. Mainly because Dolshik forbade it.

I tried to throw myself into Kangdae's chores to keep my mind off Haneul and the other men, but every time someone came back to camp, my heart pounded.

What if Haneul was ambushed like the others? What if he didn't return? He wouldn't die, would he? He couldn't die. I could never forgive him if he did. I could never forgive myself if he did.

"Focus on your work, woman."

I turned my head up from the garden, looking Kangdae in the eye. He nodded to the dirt I had piled into a strange mound next to the vegetables. I guess I hadn't been paying attention. Sheepishly, I flattened it.

He leaned down, grabbing my dirty hands and pulling me up to my feet. He looked down at my fingers and sighed.

"You need to sleep," he said.

I shook my head. "I can't."

His eyes searched mine for a moment, pressing his lips together. "You're that loyal to him?"

It took me a moment to realize what he meant. I didn't know how to answer the question, though.

"Are you so attached that you need him to sleep?" he asked.

"It's not that."

"Then what?"

He waited for an answer. I clenched my teeth, wishing I wasn't so weak… but I was too tired to lie about it anymore.

"I hear the screaming when I shut my eyes," I said.

I tried to stiffen my body to keep myself from shaking. Kangdae's hand on mine suddenly softened. He gently rubbed the dirt off my fingers.

"Don't sleep in the medic hut tonight," he said. "Go to your own hut. You need to sleep somewhere you feel safe."

"I don't feel safe without Haneul."

The words surprised me as they left my mouth. It didn't, however, seem to surprise Kangdae. He sighed again.

"You're a pain in the ass, woman. You know that?"

I forced a smile, hands still trembling. "Yes… I know."

Kangdae looked at my hands for a long moment, then turned his head to the side.

"He'll return," Kangdae assured me. "Until then, I'm watching over you."

***

I was able to stomach dinner, but the rice didn't settle well. After a long walk around camp to clear my thoughts, I went back to Haneul's hut. I pulled back the door slowly, hoping everything had been a dream, and that in reality he would be waiting inside for me.

He wasn't.

His scent was still in the hut - that strange mix of iron, wood, and stolen cologne. I sat on top of my bed mat and held my knees. The men wouldn't touch me, I knew that, but not having Haneul to block the entrance made the hut feel too large and empty for only me.

"Wait for your master to come home…"

The kiss he left on my forehead felt genuine, but it didn't feel romantic. Did he have any genuine feelings towards me? Or did he just want me in his mission to bring down Saejun?

The door of the hut opened, and my heart shot to my throat… then dropped into my knees.

It wasn't Haneul.

"You're still awake," Kangdae said flatly.

I blinked. "Why…"

"You're going to get ill if you don't sleep," he said. "Then you'll be even more useless to me."

I looked at Haneul's bed for a moment before turning my eyes back to my knees.

"I'll do my best," I replied in a half-whisper.

He sighed, closing the hut door behind him. He removed his outer robe and laid it beside Haneul's bed, then leaned over and adjusted the blankets.

"What are you —"

"Stop talking."

He grunted to himself as he finished sorting the blankets, then slipped his feet under them. He leaned back, trying to adjust the wooden pillow. With a final grunt, he went still, staring at the ceiling.

It was quiet.

"Stop worrying about him," Kangdae eventually said. "He's skilled at what he does."

"I'm not worried," I lied.

"You're not in love with him, are you?"

I frowned. "No. I care about him as my master."

"Cute," Kangdae replied, chuckling darkly. "But you're a woman and he's a man, and you spend every night in the same hut together. These mats aren't that far apart. You can't tell me that nothing has happened between you."

"The only physical thing that happens between us happens in the training center, when he beats the hell out of us during training," I snapped. "There's nothing else. There has never been anything else."

I don't know why I was so adamant about Kangdae understanding that there was nothing between Haneul and myself, but I wanted him to stop assuming I was the woman he thought I was.

Even though, in all honesty, Haneul's touch had been anything but disciplinary when he had me in his lap at the Red House. The way he touched me in front of everyone as if I was his... it was difficult to forget.

"Keep it that way," Kangdae replied, lethargic. "Remember that Haneul is training you for his own purposes. Don't get his intentions confused with love. Trust me. That's not what it is."

I scrunched my nose. "I had no assumptions."

"You should find yourself a nice little boy in the city. One with a good, honorable job. A carpenter or blacksmith, maybe. Have kids. Raise a family. Sell wares in the marketplace."

"…then watch my husband work himself to death as my children starve? That's the life you want me to build?"

He sat up and turned to me, eyes narrowing.

I looked him in the eye as I spoke. "As long as the emperor holds his power over us, I can't feel at peace with having a family."

"It's been this way for decades. If you refuse the few pleasures in life there are, then you'll miss out on life completely."

"What about you then? Why don't you have a family?"

"Because my job is to look after the men who lost theirs."

"But not the women."

He leaned in towards me until his face was only an arm's distance away from mine.

"My job isn't to discipline the women," he said. "It's to discipline the men. The ones who need reminders that the women and children are the reason we risk our lives to bring down the emperor."

I mulled over the words, along with what Dolshik had asked me so long ago.

"Would you allow a child to fight in an army?"

When I thought about it, there was a softness some-where in the shadows of Kangdae's eyes… Maybe it was my imagination.

"If a woman wants to fight," I replied, "if she's willing to give her life for a cause, why would you stop it?"

He sighed through his nose. With a swoop of his wrist he took my hand in his, looking down at my fingers. My pulse quickened at the sudden affectionate touch.

"Because a woman's hands are meant to hold life," he said. "Not to be covered in blood."

He held my hand for a brief moment as his eyes met mine again. I was afraid to do anything else besides hold his gaze, his gentle touch a stark contrast to the hard lines in his face.

He looked away and dropped my hand, going back to his side of the mat. He laid back down, adjusting the blanket under his chin.

"If you hear the screaming again, wake me," he said.

He turned over on his side, leaving me to sleep.

***

Night passed and I felt drowsy, but I could only doze. Where was Haneul? Why were they taking so long? When would he come?

Kangdae was fast asleep, unbothered. I envied his peace. I suffered with the same questions over and over until my brain felt like it was bleeding. But part of me wanted to stay awake, just in case Haneul returned.

Shit. I really was his pet.

I internally sighed, annoyed with my defeat. I never imagined submitting to anyone, but when it came to Haneul, I couldn't control my own feelings.

"You trust me, Jaehwa. You're foolish enough to trust me with your life."

But how could I trust him when he was using me to possibly kill Saejun?

"Yeojin…"

I turned to Kangdae's voice. He was still asleep, but he was crumpled in bed, his knees halfway in his chest. I approached the side of his mat, watching the blanket shudder against his shoulder. I sat next to him, wiping away the damp strands of hair clamped on his forehead.

"Forgive me…" he whispered.

I leaned over him, rubbing his shoulder in an attempt to soothe him. He continued to shudder, and I searched for words that might break his spell.

I couldn't speak as Yeojin. But I could speak as a sister to a brother.

"I miss you too," I whispered. "But I'm alright. I've found a place where I don't suffer like I used to. I'm stronger now. I'm more at peace. And when the time is right… we'll be together again. I promise."

I promise… Kiwan.

With a few more shudders, Kangdae went still. His breathing was still too shallow, but it gradually deepened. As the night went on, I stroked his hair and his back, trying to leave him with any peace I could give.

After all, it was because of Kangdae and Haneul that I had any peace at all. It was only fair that I returned the favor.

***

I woke up to the sound of birds. For a brief moment, the earth was still and at peace, the sun feeling like gentle light instead of a harsh reality.

Then I opened my eyes.

Kangdae was laying against me, his body pressed against mine.

And he was staring right at me.

I rolled off the mat onto the floor. I sat up, Kangdae still blankly staring at me.

"Sleep well?" he asked, cocking his head to the side with a faint smirk.

I didn't answer.

He sighed, rolling onto his back and looking at the ceiling. "And here I thought you wanted Haneul all this time. Were you trying to get me alone?"

I stood up. "I wasn't trying to sleep with you."

"And yet you did."

"I didn't *sleep with* you. I fell asleep."

"On top of me."

My stomach dropped.

"I had to roll you off my chest," he continued. "And get your knee out of… places."

He motioned between his legs. I shut my eyes, mentally choking myself.

"You have your own bed over there, yet somehow ended up on top of me," he continued. "Is this how you sleep with Haneul? Is that the normal position?"

I grit my teeth. "I wouldn't have even been so close to you if you hadn't —"

I stopped. Kangdae raised an eyebrow at me, waiting.

As much as I wanted to bring up his nightmares and sleepwalking, as much as I wanted the upper hand at something, I couldn't bring myself to say the words out loud.

It hurt too much to lose a sibling.

"If I hadn't what?" he asked.

I clicked my tongue. "If you hadn't been snoring so loudly."

He sighed again and sat up, rubbing his forehead. "I don't snore."

He stood from the mat, walking over to reassemble his robes. I adjusted my own and straightened up my hair, putting it back in a braid.

"Will Haneul return soon?" I asked, trying to break the awkward silence.

"Maybe," Kangdae replied.

I swallowed. "You don't think they…"

"No."

I dropped my head, hoping that Kangdae was right.

After dressing, Kangdae waved for me to follow him to the dining area for breakfast. When we arrived, I had to rub my eyes.

I wanted to cry.

Haneul.

I ran over to him, stopping a few feet away just in case I was seeing things.

"Master?" I asked.

Haneul's eyes raised to mine. He winced and laughed at the same time.

"Miss me, pet?" he asked flatly.

"I was so worried!" I dropped on my knees next to him. "I thought they captured you. I thought you were…"

He patted my head, not looking at me. "Hush. I don't die. Don't whine so much."

"I'm happy you're safe, Haneul," I said. "I don't know what I would have done…"

I trailed off as Haneul's eyes darkened towards Kangdae stepping up behind me.

"You would have found another foot of the bed to sleep in," Haneul said bitterly, taking a drink from his cup.

"You didn't wake us?" Kangdae asked.

"I thought you might both need the rest."

Kangdae's face became even more somber than it already was. "You have bad news."

Haneul nodded, shooting back the rest of his drink. Whether it was alcohol or not, it was hard to tell.

"We found the men who went missing," Haneul said. "Some of them were alive. Some are missing a few limbs. Some…"

He stopped.

"We'll compensate them," Kangdae said. "Who didn't make it?"

Haneul swallowed.

"Intak," he finally said. "Intak's dead."

CHAPTER 22

MEMORIALS

There were no bodies. Only a sunset service.

"We buried the men where they were," Haneul had told Kangdae. "It seemed right."

Now, with the evening glow overhead, Haneul looked as if he had aged ten years in three days. His eyes were heavy and glossed over, his skin gray. I had never seen him so lifeless. I had never seen him in so much pain.

I hated it. It weighed my heart down to see him like that.

Everyone gathered at the edge of the river near the camp training grounds, hands crossed in front of them and heads bowed. The wind was smooth and warm, trying to soothe the troubled souls in the field as Haneul lit candles on five small wooden boats.

Five candles for five bodies.

Four men with severed limbs.

Three injured and ill from the battle. Alive, they said, only because Intak had sacrificed himself for them.

And me… with nothing but the remnants of sore muscles.

I bowed my head in shame.

There was complete silence as the small boats of single candles drifted out on the water. We watched the boats take to the current and float away. As they started to fade out of sight, I lifted my eyes to look at Haneul. The set of his jaw was firmer than I had ever seen, his eyes darker than the shadows. His breath was deep and controlled.

Too controlled.

Haneul's eyes shot over to me, then turned to the ground. He pulled his shoulders back and stepped away from the crowd. I stepped forward to follow him, but Kangdae put out a hand in front of me.

"Let him grieve," Kangdae said.

I opened my mouth to speak, but could think of nothing to say. Instead, I only watched Haneul disappear into the forest.

We stood in silence, looking out on the water until both the candles and the sky ran out of light. The men left in small groups, until only Kangdae and I were left. I didn't feel like I had the right to leave before everyone else.

Not again.

"You would have been one of those candles if you had stayed," Kangdae said, breaking the silence. "I trained my men to protect. They did just that."

I grit my teeth together, tears stinging my eyes.

"You want me to sit silently from a distance as the others die?" I muttered.

He turned to me, his eyes soft but serious.

"Yes," he said. "I want you as far away from us as possible. I won't watch a sword go through you."

His eyes flickered in pain as he turned his head away.

It was the same pain I saw when he called me Yeojin.

Without realizing what I was doing, my hand reached for his and squeezed it.

"If a sword goes through me," I replied, "it was because I wanted to fight beside you."

His eyes drifted to our hands together. He shook his head and pulled away.

"It's too dangerous for you here," he said.

"It's dangerous for me everywhere."

He rubbed his face, sighing through his hand. "You don't belong here."

"You've said that before."

"That's enough, Jaehwa!"

I stepped back at the sharp sound of my name coming from his mouth. Kangdae's eyes exploded with rage, his fists clenched at his sides.

"Do you think fifty men were sitting around drinking makgeolli out of boredom and decided to attack a random string of horses? It was a planned ambush. And whoever came for us once will come again. You included."

He shook his head to himself again.

"You can't stay here," he said. "Not anymore."

My mouth went dry as it dropped open. "I won't leave. Not now. I have nowhere -"

"I'm sending you to a safe house. Someplace away from us."

"You can't -"

"I can and I will." He stepped forward, looking down into my eyes as he towered over me. "I told you not to accept the Underground. I told you to reject Haneul. Now he's gotten it in his head —"

He huffed, not finishing his sentence.

"I won't let Haneul continue with his path," Kang-dae said, looking back towards the river. "Otherwise, he'll be the next candle I have to light."

He walked away before I could say anything else. I wanted to go after him, but there was nothing I could say now. Not on the day of a memorial for our fallen men.

Not today.

***

Night crawled on, but Haneul didn't return to the hut. When it had passed midnight, I began to worry, so I dressed to go out and look for him. He wasn't in the training room, or on the training grounds, so the next obvious place was the dining area.

If I had blinked wrong, I would have missed him.

He was huddled in the corner of the dining hall, drinking straight out of a jug of makgeolli. He slammed it down on the table, staring at the ceiling. As I stepped forward, I could hear his ragged breaths, stuck between anger and grief.

"Master?"

He turned his head, pain and intoxication pooling in his eyes.

"My pet…" he slurred. "Did you miss your master?"

I stepped in closer, the stench of the alcohol burning my nose. His lips fell open into a smile that quickly morphed into a grimace.

"Intak… the bastard. Who the hell is going to take my place?" He laughed to himself bitterly. "I can't wait to kick his ass in the afterlife."

His face twisted. So did my heart.

"I'm sorry, Master," I said, bowing. "I failed you again."

He turned his head up. "You followed your commander's orders. If you hadn't, you'd be dead as well."

His hand reached out for mine and clasped it. He brought it to his forehead, leaning against it like a sick child with a fever.

"What can I do?" I asked.

He looked up into my eyes and laid his head back against the wall, his hand still in mine.

"Comfort me," he whispered.

I watched him for a breathless moment, trying to decipher his meaning. Not knowing any other method, I leaned down, doing the only thing I could think of: I hugged him.

He took the hug with a drunken chuckle, then pulled me down into his lap. I shifted against him as he wrapped his arms around me. It was just like the Red House. The same energy. The same burning sensation against my skin as he touched me. The same playful look in his eyes as if I was the only one he could see.

"You shouldn't be so obedient, Jaehwa," he said, putting his head on my shoulder. "When a man asks for comfort, he usually wants something... specific."

I shifted, heart pounding as his hand slid up my arm.

"I'm glad you're safe," he continued. "I'm glad you survived. I know your brother would be too."

I gripped onto Haneul's robe, the mention of my brother putting a knot in my stomach.

Haneul leaned back, looking at me. "Maybe Kangdae was right. Maybe I shouldn't have brought a woman here. If I lose you too — "

I shook my head. "It's not a mistake. I know the risks. Whatever happened to Kangdae's mother or sister—"

I stopped, biting my lip. Why had that slipped out?

Haneul's eyebrows matted. "Kangdae's sister? Who told you that Kangdae had a sister?"

I didn't answer.

"Jaehwa," he commanded, voice stern.

"No one." I sighed. "Kangdae's been sleepwalking. He calls me Yeojin when he sees me in his trance. That's her name, isn't it?"

"Yes… that's her name." Haneul swallowed, the last bit of light fading from his eyes. "But she wasn't Kangdae's sister. Yeojin was *my* sister."

My mouth gaped open, but no words came out. Haneul traced his calloused thumb against my bottom lip as he spoke.

"Kangdae found us when we were teenagers," he continued. "My baby sister and I used to fight in the Moonlight Duels, taking dozens of weak suckers for their money. He found us and told his father, the leader of the Rebellion at the time. Once his father saw us fight, he took us in. We were together for years, Kangdae, Yeojin, and I. They were close… but she was *my* blood."

The air in my lungs turned to gravel. "What happened to her?"

He swallowed, throwing his head back and shutting his eyes.

"She didn't listen to her master… and she barked too much."

He brought my hand up to his heart. I felt it pound under my fingers as he inhaled to speak again.

"My sister was one of us," Haneul said. "She trained with us, she trained other women on the outside, and she was one of the best damn fighters there was. Better than me, probably."

He opened his eyes to look at the ceiling.

"But she ignored my commands. She put herself on the frontlines, up against the emperor's guards. Kangdae went in to pull her back, but he didn't make it in time. He did everything he knew to save her... but it was over. After that, he reinforced his father's rule once and for all, with no exceptions. No women in the Rebellion. No women on the frontlines."

He leaned forward, resting his head on my shoulder. His breath shattered, his fingers clasping around mine.

"If he dies, it's not my fault. Repeat that every day until you believe it."

How many times had Haneul said those words for himself?

"Haneul..."

"You need to go, Jaehwa," he whispered in my ear, clasping my hand tighter against his chest as his heart started to beat faster. "I've lost too much, and you... you're far too close."

I met his eyes, full of pain and grief. The spark of them had gone out completely. I wanted Haneul back. I wanted to give him the same comfort he had given me so many times. I wanted to show him how much his care had meant to me.

And I wanted him to keep holding me. I wanted him to continue to treat me as his own.

"If it comforts you..." I whispered back, "I won't stop you."

He sucked on his bottom lip, his breath quickening. His fingers traced my cheek. He then suddenly stopped, turning his head away with a grunt.

"You're tempting," he said, "but we both know it's not me you're wanting. If I make you mine, it'll be because I'm the only one you're thinking about."

I pulled back, shoulders hunching. "What are you talking about?"

He gave an empty smirk. "Kim Saejun. Your teacher. Your first love. The man you pretend not to think about."

I felt all the blood rush to my face. His hands came to my back, fingertips pressing against my spine to make me look at him once more.

"I could make you mine," he said. "I'd love to watch Kim lose his sanity knowing I had you."

His fingers gripped into my sides. His eyes maneuvered around my body, finally landing on my face as he leaned his head back. I couldn't move, entranced by the pain deep in his eyes.

"But I won't take you," he said. "Not now. You're what I need for the future. You're the key to avenge my sister, and now, Intak. You're the key to our victory. That's why you need to obey your master, Jaehwa. You can't go to him. You can't go back, despite your feelings."

"Go back?"

"To Kim Saejun."

I looked away. "Why would I? He'll kill me if I ever get close to him."

He laughed, deep and confident. "He won't kill you."

"What makes you so sure?"

His lips pulled back in a drunken smile, teeth showing as he traced his hands against my thighs.

"Because, sweetheart… Kim Saejun is still madly in love with you."

CHAPTER 23

BETRAYAL

"When did you all get so weak?" Haneul yelled. "Again!"

We all did the sword drill again, my muscles violently shaking. I had nearly thrown up twice from the previous ten drills that had lasted most of the evening. Haneul hadn't given us any breaks like he usually did. He didn't give any criticisms or methods to improve. He only barked when we did something wrong, telling us to do it again. Over and over. For days.

He had barely even spoken to me after the memorial service, now two weeks ago. Every day he left early in the morning and came back late at night. The only time I heard him speak was during training.

But he was only talking. He wasn't listening to anyone anymore.

"Hold your stance!" he commanded. "A hundred more upper strikes! I don't want to see any swords go below your ears, or I'll rip them off myself."

I did my best to keep my arms up, swinging high for the sword head strike drills. The long sword was nearly impossible to hold after four hundred strikes, and I could feel it slipping through my hands.

I wasn't good with weapons. Saejun never trained me with weapons.

"You are the weapon, Jaehwa," Saejun had always said. *"The sword is never the element between you and death. You are."*

Remembering his voice in that moment made me lose my focus. I noticed too late when the sword slipped from my sweaty grip, hitting the floor with a clang.

Everyone turned to me.

Including Haneul.

The fire in his eyes knocked the little strength that was left in my knees. I fell to the ground along with my sword. I reached out to grab it and pull it back before Haneul could come to scold me again, but it was too late. The moment I saw his feet, his hand wrapped around my wrist and yanked me to face him. He dug his fingers in to keep his grip from slipping down my sweat-drenched arms. His gaze was strong as he looked down on me, gritting his teeth like he was about to open his mouth and swallow me whole.

"Again," he commanded me. "From the beginning."

My fingers trembled, the urge to vomit coming up again. "Mas—"

"Do you think the enemy will go easy on you?" he spat. "Do you think they'll give you the time to pick up your sword?"

He pressed two of his fingers into my throat.

"They'll slit you open in a second," he continued, "wasting all the time I've put into you. I'm not going to let you be a waste of my time! Understand?"

Waste of time? He had never been so harsh with his words. Haneul was the one person who had never treated me as worthless.

But looking into his cold eyes, I realized... Haneul was gone.

"*Enough*."

Everyone turned to the doorway, stepping back as Kangdae entered. It was the first time I had ever seen him step foot in the training room. His eyes were focused, his jaw set and shoulders square. At the most, I had only ever seen Kangdae irritated. Now, it looked like he could destroy the entire room in a single blow.

Haneul turned from me to face him, confusion flashing in his bloodshot eyes.

"Why are you here?" he asked.

Kangdae brought his finger to his nose, scratching it. He didn't speak, but the tension in the room said more than words.

Haneul released my wrist. "Water break."

I didn't move, still stunned at everything Haneul had just said. Kangdae came to me, taking my hand in his and looking down at my wrist that was now red from Haneul's grip. He rubbed his thumb over the marks.

"Is this a new training technique?" Kangdae asked over his shoulder.

Haneul huffed. "She needs to be as tough as the men to be in this war."

"I'd agree if you were treating the men like men, instead of like dogs." Kangdae turned away, putting himself between Haneul and me. "You're going too far."

"My training has always been intense," Haneul replied. "You never disapproved before."

"Because your methods always promised success. This promises failure." Kangdae stepped forward to meet Haneul, crossing his arms. "Also, that was before you went behind my back and trained people you weren't supposed to."

Haneul whipped his head to me, his eyes hitting me so hard that I had to look down.

"Don't look at her," Kangdae continued. "You knew I would find out eventually. And you also knew I wouldn't let it last."

Haneul chewed on his lip. There was a long moment of silence before he spoke again. "You're pulling my operation?"

Kangdae nodded.

"Do you have any idea what you're doing?" Haneul spat back.

"Our numbers are too low. We can't go up against them like this. We need recruitments. You need a second."

Haneul sighed and shook his head in defiance. "I don't need numbers."

"You risk the men still standing then? You're going blind, Haneul. You've lost all your sense."

"I have the sense that I need."

"You have the sense for revenge. Not for winning."

Haneul bit his lip again, smirking. He let out a strangled growl and stomped his foot, roughly running his hand through his hair. "We're so close, Kangdae!"

"Close to being wiped out!" Kangdae threw back. "My job is to keep the focus of this group. Your job is to train them for their missions, not throw them into losing battles."

"All my men are prepared to die for this cause."

"Then the cause will continue to be a problem. We fight for a solution, not a cause."

Kangdae kept a straight face as Haneul's turned a darker shade of red. Kangdae stepped forward into Haneul's space. His voice dropped so low that I almost didn't hear him.

"If you're willing to put *my* men's lives on the line for your revenge," he said, "I'll have to rethink your position. Understand me?"

Haneul stepped back, his fists closed as his side. The veins in his arms nearly broke the skin. Kangdae left the training center, not looking back.

I stepped forward, reaching a hand out to Haneul's arm.

"Master…"

He pulled back. "You told him, didn't you?"

My hand dropped. "I —"

"Just couldn't obey your master, could you?"

I looked down at my hands. "I came for my brother. You wanted to feed me to Saejun. I wanted someone on my side when you decided I wasn't necessary anymore."

He laughed ironically. "I was never going to let Captain Kim have you. But now… maybe it doesn't matter who you go to. Do you want to go to Saejun? Or Kangdae? So be it."

"Haneul…"

He stepped back. "Go."

He didn't blink as he stared at me. I deserved his anger. I knew that. He had given me a command and I broke it.

Maybe it was best to be obedient this time.

I bowed and stepped out of the training center, my heart shattering behind me.

***

I waited for Haneul to return to the hut that night, but he didn't. He probably didn't want to see me. He told me to leave, right?

Did he mean the training center… or the Rebellion?

There was a high chance he wouldn't let me back under his command. I had lost his trust. I told Kangdae about Kana, about the Red House, and about his possible plans. I didn't spare any information. I was afraid that Haneul would dump me eventually, especially after he had revealed my identity to Saejun that night.

But now, Kangdae was going to pull Haneul's entire plan. His entire strategy against the emperor.

"I'm going to start a revolution," Haneul had said on the night of the memorial, drunk out of his mind. "I won't let any woman be unarmed and gutted like my sister was. I'll train up these women to fight for themselves. Starting with you."

He had so much faith in me. That faith was gone now.

My heart stopped as the hut door swung open. But it wasn't Haneul.

Kangdae's face was hard and flat, the deep lines in it enhanced by the candle glow. I swallowed.

"I'm leaving?" I asked, already knowing the answer.

He gave a single nod. I stood to pack.

I took only what I came with: my own clothes. Everything else belonged to Haneul and Kangdae.

And there was one thing I definitely couldn't take with me.

I took the dagger Haneul gave me and placed it on his bed. Kangdae's eyes fell on it, but he didn't say anything. He only nodded for me to follow, putting a finger to his lips.

Kangdae had a horse already saddled. He helped me up onto it, then nestled in close behind me in the same manner Haneul used to. His arm reached around, holding me close to his chest as we trotted out of the camp. I tried to ignore the sinking feeling in my gut as we passed the entrance. It took all my willpower not to turn around and look back. It would only hurt more.

Kangdae didn't speak as we traveled. I wasn't sure if it was for stealth, or if it was his usual silent nature. The silence wasn't uncomfortable, however. He kept a firm grip on the reins, steadying me in his arms as we rode deeper into the forests.

It wasn't until we were on the other side of the forests that he spoke.

"You did the right thing," Kangdae said in my ear.

I shook my head. "I betrayed him."

"No. You protected him. Haneul is lost in his vengeance. With Intak gone, even more so now. Rage is the type of blindness that leads to your own destruction."

"Will you really pull his operation?"

No answer.

"You know what he's trying to do, don't you? He wants —"

"I know what he wants. I know he's capable of it."

"Then what are you afraid of?"

There was a pause before he answered.

"I'm afraid that women like you will have their throats slit. And I'm afraid men like me will have to watch."

CHAPTER 24

SAFEHOUSE

I t was the dark part before the dawn by the time we arrived at the safehouse.

It wasn't lavish or something that stood out. It was just a regular inn; two stories, wide and inviting. It was close to the same feeling as my own home, which - for some reason - I didn't miss.

Instead, I missed musty-smelling huts and the sound of the river through the forest.

Kangdae dismounted and raised his arms towards me to help me off the horse. In the brief moment that he held me in his arms while helping me down, I wanted to latch onto him and beg him to take me back.

But there wasn't anything there for me anymore. I was an outcast.

The inn on the inside was warm but empty. Dozens of candles scattered across the floor and shelves, the glow bringing a sense of peace. There were pillows on the ground, unoccupied, as the guests were probably sound asleep in their rooms.

Kangdae stepped up to the front desk, leaning against it. He didn't say anything to the woman with her back turned against him. He waited until she turned, then smiled. She jumped, throwing her hands up and then clutching her chest. He smiled.

"Kangdae!" she cried. "You come at me like a ghost! Child, why you sneakin'?"

He laughed. The woman caught me in her eye.

"Ohh, I see," she said, nodding. "Never took you for the type."

He shook his head. "I'm not the type. I'm here for checkpoint."

Her shoulders slumped. "Is that all? Ah! And here I thoughts you'd be in the middle of a romantic escapade."

"There's no escapades," Kangdae replied. "Romantic or otherwise."

He glanced back at me, a small bit of mischief in his eyes.

"Why are you harassing the boy, Daeun? Your fantasies are bad for business."

A man entered from the side room, his large shoulders taking up half the doorframe. Half-hidden behind his wild beard was a wide smile as he came to Kangdae and bowed. There was a slight limp in his step.

"You lost, son?" the man asked.

"No," Kangdae replied. "But the moon is high and the wolves are hungry."

The man's smile straightened and he nodded.

"Of course," the man said. "You're welcome here for as long as you like. Who's the gal?"

Kangdae turned to me, his head cocking to the side. "Haven't decided yet."

I raised an eyebrow at him pointedly.

The man chuckled. "In any case, your room is clear. Take it."

Kangdae bowed his head in acknowledgment. "How's the leg?"

The man tapped his thigh with his fist. "As good as it'll ever be. I'm grateful it's still there. I'd be left to the guards' mercy if it hadn't been for you. You still medicining these days?"

"I gave it up. but I might go back into it under the right circumstances." He paused. "Let me take her to the room. Then I'll take a look at you."

The man nodded, his hand raised towards the stairs. Kangdae motioned for me to follow him up the stairs and to a room at the end of the hallway. It wasn't anything but a couple of bed mats and some candles. Kangdae lit one of them.

"It's not a luxury inn," he said.

"I wouldn't know," I replied, sitting cross-legged on one of the mats.

Kangdae looked out the window, the last bit of moonlight catching his eyes. He turned back to me, then walked over to my mat, crouching down on one knee and speaking softly.

"Tell no one who you are, or what you know. You're safe here, but only if you follow these rules. The couple that runs the inn knows more than they seem. Trust them. They're with me."

I nodded, not looking at him.

"I'll send for more clothes if you want them," he offered.

I shook my head. "I don't."

He sighed through his nose. "Tell Samsoon and Daeun what you need, then. I'll give it to you."

"Anything?"

He nodded.

I turned to face him, holding his gaze as best I could. "Tell me about her."

He raised an eyebrow. "Who?"

"Yeojin," I replied. "Haneul told me his story. I want to hear yours."

The color in his face faded. He turned away, shaking his head. "There's nothing to tell."

"He told me you tried to save her. You did everything you could. Yet you sleepwalk at night, saying her name."

He dropped his head to his chest.

"You haven't forgiven yourself, have you?" I asked.

"It has nothing to do with you."

"Of course it does!" I threw back, coming to my feet. "She's the reason you hated me from the beginning. She's the reason you won't let me stay. She's the reason you won't let me fight. It has everything to do with me."

Kangdae was silent for a long moment as he rose to his feet. I stared at his hands as he rubbed his fingertips together.

"You loved her," I said.

Kangdae sadly smiled. "Yes... but not as a man loves a woman. I loved her as my own sister. I watched her grow up. I trained with her. I was proud of her."

He chewed his lip, licking it.

"And then she bled to death in my arms," he continued. "I couldn't do anything to save her. She was just a child. Haneul lost his sister because of me."

I shook my head, touching the side of his arm. "She disobeyed Haneul. She made her own decisions."

"Which is why I make mine now. No women in the Rebellion. That is the rule. That will always be the rule."

"But a woman is still capable —"

"I know it," Kangdae growled, his eyes flaring. "I know what they're capable of. But do you know how many women I've seen slit open? How many I've watched die? All of them were fighters - all competent - all willing to die for the cause. And they *did.* They died and we had to find the courage to fight for our cause without them... when they were the only reason we were fighting for the cause in the first place."

"But if —"

"My father lost his mind when my mother was executed," he said, cutting me off. "He died from his rage against the emperor, leading dozens of our men to their deaths in his pain. The same will happen to Haneul if I don't stop this now. I let his sister die. I won't let him die too."

He leaned forward, his hands cupping my face in soft desperation. The man who held me tenderly in his dreams was now awake... and I had never been so equally terrified and mesmerized.

"And you..." he started, his voice softening, "you shouldn't live this kind of life. You should fall in love with someone who can protect you. Someone who doesn't have arrows aimed at his back. Someone who won't get your throat slit."

"Kangdae..."

"I couldn't save either of my parents. I couldn't save Yeojin. I couldn't save the women on the frontlines. And… I… I can't save you."

My breath stilled, the heart of the Leader of the Rebellion suddenly unfolded in front of me like a blossomed flower.

"Do you understand now?" he asked. "Is it enough?"

I wanted to cry. Not for myself, but for him. There was nothing I could say to him… not when his eyes held so much pain.

I nodded.

His hands slowly released me, dropping to his sides. "Sleep, then. You'll be safe here."

He stood, turning for the door.

"Will I see any of you again?" I asked, tears blurring my vision.

He turned back.

"Do you still hear the screaming?" he asked.

I smiled and shook my head. "Not since that night you stayed with me."

He nodded, a faint smile tugging at the corner of his lips.

"If you hear the screaming," he said, "I'll come find you. Wherever you are, I won't be too far behind."

CHAPTER 25

CUSTODY

I waited five days, but no one came for me.

Part of me wanted Haneul to come... but why would he? He wouldn't forgive me. His plans to take over the emperor were now wasted because of my slip of the tongue. I had only done it to secure my brother's rescue. In the end, however, I didn't have my brother or the chance to bring down the emperor.

I'd lost everything and more.

But, in some way, Kangdae was right. Haneul was losing himself. If I hadn't said anything, maybe he would be lost completely. Maybe he already was. Losing Intak brought out a lot of pain and anger in him that I'd never seen before. I always trusted Haneul, whether I liked it or not. But now... I didn't know if I could. He had become unstable. The flirtatious, carefree Haneul had been replaced with a vengeful master.

Would the old Haneul ever return?

My hosts at the inn were pleasant, at least. They taught me a few basic things to help them around the inn. Daeun had made it a mission to teach me to cook,

191

and in three days she taught me better than my own mother. There was a slight ache every time I stepped into the kitchen, realizing that I never had enough time to learn much of anything from Mother. Her and Kiwan were always in the fields or in the city working, leaving me to figure out everything alone.

Except for all the things that Saejun taught me.

I remembered the face he used to make whenever he ate my cooking, puckering slightly at the bitter flavor, but smiling as if I was the best cook in the world. That was his way, since he knew how insecure I was about homemaking. It wasn't until years later that I realized he was doing that to encourage me.

That was when I fell in love with him.

The one thing he was never dishonest about, however, was my fighting skills. He didn't pretend that I was great when I wasn't, and he pushed me harder and harder every day. I never asked where he had learned to fight, but he was one of the most naturally talented fighters I had ever seen.

Even now, the only person I could think of that fought on the same level as Saejun was Haneul.

"Because, Sweetheart… Kim Saejun is still madly in love with you."

"What makes you think that?"

"He fought for your honor, when he was supposed to kill you for your rebellion. He hasn't forgotten the past… same as you."

Did Saejun really love me? Or was Haneul playing with my mind for his own purposes?

No, it didn't matter. Whether or not Saejun loved me, it didn't make a difference. He was the enemy now.

I continued to help out at the inn by cooking, sweeping, and washing blankets. Samsoon and Daeun even mentioned in passing that I would make a great addition to the inn, but when night settled and I was alone, I couldn't imagine it. A regular job with a regular purpose seemed so… empty.

There was something in me that wanted more. No matter how reckless it was.

***

On the sixth night, I couldn't stay in the walls of my room any longer. Kangdae hadn't sent any word, and Haneul hadn't come for me. I wanted to know what Kangdae had decided. I wanted to know if Haneul was getting better or worse. And most importantly, my brother was still in shackles, ready for the execution block.

How could I sit still?

With the moon full, I climbed out of the window of the inn and dropped to the ground without a sound. I couldn't ask Samsoon and Daeun for permission to leave. They would surely refuse and secure me tighter to the inn.

But I wasn't made for cleaning.

I slinked off towards the city, determined to find out more information on the Rebellion and their current status. There was only one place I could think of that might have an answer.

The Red House.

The summer breeze was humid, and it stuck to the beads of sweat dripping down my back. Quietly I followed the road from the safehouse to the city, keeping an eye out for anything out of the ordinary.

After Intak's death, I couldn't be too cautious.

"You really think I'm incompetent, don't you?"

"No... I think you're too competent and under-experienced. That's even more dangerous."

I replayed Intak's last words to me in my head. There were many things about him that I disliked: his arrogance, his bluntness, his attitude. But... he wasn't always wrong.

I tried to decipher the meaning of his last words while utilizing every stealth technique I had learned from Haneul and Intak to sneak into the city. I was drenched in sweat, but the feeling was more comforting than disgusting. It reminded me of training back at camp. A camp I'd never see again.

I followed the city road to the bridge. It was the same bridge I had jumped off of to escape from Saejun. That seemed like a lifetime ago now.

Once I reached the bridge, I could see the glowing lights of the Red House. I wished I had a veil. Not that it mattered. If Saejun or Haneul were there, they would be able to see right through it.

My heart fluttered, wondering if either one of them would be there.

Approaching the entrance, laughter and drunken cheering poured into my ears before I had even made it all the way inside. A few heads turned when I walked in, but no one took notice for long. I wasn't wearing the same lavish clothes I had on when I was in Haneul's company.

I was nobody.

I scanned the room, holding my breath. But there was no Haneul. Also, no Saejun.

My stomach sank. What if I never saw Haneul again? Would he care? Did he hate me that much?

And Saejun…?

No. I couldn't see him again. Saejun of the fields was dead. There was only Captain Kim now.

I pushed through the crowds of people, heading towards the back room. Remembering the secret knock, I lifted my hand to give it myself.

"Hey!" a female voice cried on the other side of the door before I could knock. "What do you think you're doing?"

I stopped.

"Eye for an eye," a familiar male voice calmly replied.

I knew that voice…

There was a gasp. Then a cry.

Thud.

I swung open the door. Dolshik turned his head to me, flicking the dagger in his wrist that was now dripping in blood. My eyes fell to the body next to his feet, dressed in a beautiful gown… that was open in all the tempting places.

I held down the bile in my stomach. Dolshik's heavy boots pounded against the ground as he stepped over the body, his eyes fixed on me.

"You came at a bad time," he said, flicking the dagger again.

I didn't reply. Instead, I ran.

I ran back out the door, back over the bridge. I checked over my shoulder for Dolshik, but he wasn't in sight. I slowed down for a moment, legs shaking from what I had seen.

Dolshik killed Kana. But why?

I stepped forward to sprint back to the safehouse, but I was forced to the ground before I could even take a step. A boot came to the back of my knee, folding it, and sending me sprawling to the ground. A pair of hands came from behind, twisting my hands behind my back.

"I said I would drag you," a voice commanded in my ear.

That voice I could never mistake for another.

I turned to look over my shoulder, Saejun's cold eyes burning into me.

"No running this time," he said, more of a threat than a statement.

I glared at him.

He lifted me to my feet, holding both my hands behind my back as he locked me in his arms to face him. His eyes looked down on me, pride swelling up in the corners.

"Where's your *master*?" he taunted.

I clenched my jaw.

Footsteps came behind me, and for a brief moment I hoped it was Haneul himself to answer the question. But it was only Dolshik.

Dolshik looked between Saejun and me, raising an eyebrow.

"Did you do what I asked?" Saejun asked, still looking at me.

"It's taken care of," Dolshik replied.

I looked into Saejun's dark, heavy eyes as the words settled.

"You?" I asked. "You ordered Dolshik to…"

He nodded. His hands gripped mine behind my back as he leaned closer to my ear.

"I know where you've been…" he whispered. "And you're not going back."

CHAPTER 26

HOSTAGE

"Stop moving," Saejun commanded. "If you fall off, I'll drag you behind the horse all the way there."

Saejun's arms caged me in tighter as he gripped the reins. This wasn't the first time I had ridden horseback with him. Father taught Kiwan, Saejun, and me how to ride when we were kids.

But Father didn't teach me how to ride a horse while my arms were bound against my back.

"Where are you taking me?" I demanded.

"Away from *them*."

I clenched my jaw. "Why do you have a spy in the Rebellion?"

"Why should I answer that?" he replied. "You've al-ready created your own answers and won't listen to anything I tell you."

He knew. He knew about Kangdae and Haneul. He knew where I had been and what I had been doing. And if Dolshik told him anything, he knew that my goal was to get Kiwan back. The question was, what was he doing with this information? Was he the reason for the ambush? Was he the reason half the men had been captured? Was he the reason Intak had been killed? Dolshik certainly had no reservations about killing Kana, and he didn't seem concerned when he left me in Saejun's custody to return to the Rebellion's camp.

"Wherever you are, I won't be far behind..."

I shut my eyes, praying that Kangdae's words were true.

I asked Saejun a dozen more questions, which he also didn't answer. I was forced to give up, deciding to save my energy for an escape instead.

Following the paved roads, we crossed a strip of the forest towards the largest structure in the kingdom: the palace.

The palace of the emperor fanned out in front of us, high on the hill in the moonlight. I had never seen it so close, but the shadows suited it. It was dark, with little light for the living.

We didn't go to the palace, however. Our path curved around the side, to a fortress half its size. The wooden gates creaked open, and the guards bowed as Saejun's horse trotted through. The blood-red robes of the emperor's guards stood out even in the darkness. The gates creaked shut, locking us in.

The grounds were dismal at best. From what I could see in the shadows, there would be nothing to see in the light. It was only long stretches of bare ground surrounded by stone walls. The men stared at us as we trotted towards the center of the prison grounds, stopping before the long stretch of training ground.

"Stick close or you'll end up in a lot of hurt," Saejun mumbled in my ear.

He swung me over the side of the horse and lowered me down to the ground, coming down right after. One of the men handed Saejun a lantern and took the horse as Saejun gripped the ropes behind my back. He began to drag me through the grounds as I twisted in his grip.

"Let me walk alone," I said.

"It's too late for dignity," he replied.

"What are you going to do? Kill me? Like you do with children and people who dodge their taxes?"

He scoffed. "I should have known you'd pick up ru-mors while hanging around the whores."

We arrived at a house near the training grounds, painted in bright teal and red, with a pair of lion statues guarding the entrance.

"You're not taking me to prison?" I asked. "What is this place?"

"My house."

He motioned for a guard about forty paces from us. How the guard could see the signal in the dark, I didn't know. These guards had trained eyes, that was sure.

The guard bowed when he approached.

"Yes, Captain?"

"I want you to tell the others that I have brought in a... personal hostess. She is not to leave my quarters. Should anyone approach her, they will be punished."

The guard visibly swallowed and bowed. "Yes, Captain."

"Also," Saejun added, looking at me through the corner of his eye, "should she leave my quarters, kill her."

My breath caught in my throat, shattering as I swallowed.

"Yes, Captain," the guard said for the third time, leaving.

Saejun's grip tightened. He swung the door open and shoved me inside. When he shut the door behind us, I turned to kick him in the face. He grabbed my foot in midair and twisted it, sending me to the ground. My hip slammed against the wooden floor, echoing in pain at impact, my bound hands doing nothing to break the impact of the fall.

He sighed. "Did Haneul train you to do that? It was quite easy to catch."

I sat up, scowling at him. "You taught me that."

He chuckled, shaking his head. "I never taught you to kick above the chest. Ribs, groin, and knees, remember?"

I thrust my heel forward to take out his knee, but he leaned to the side, dodging it.

"Stand up," he commanded, walking back towards the entrance.

I rose to my feet as he untied his sword from his belt and hung it in its placeholder on the wall, next to a whip. He then took off his outer robe and hung it next to that, turning to face me. He lit a lantern, and it filled the room with a dim light.

I could see the rest of the room now. It wasn't as arrogant as I had anticipated, but the smell of heavy exotic perfume made the sitting pillows and wooden table seem more expensive. Other than that, however, there was nothing else in the room to be impressed by. Ironic considering how much Saejun loved showing off his new power.

"You'll stay here," Saejun said, stepping in closer. "These are my personal quarters. No one will bother you here. Not if they want to stay alive."

"You're just going to hold me hostage here, then?" I asked. "Leave me bound up and in your bedroom?"

"Isn't that your new job anyways?"

I clenched my teeth. "If you touch me, I'll *let* them kill me."

His jaw tightened as he leaned over to the table, picking up a dagger. He unsheathed it, stepping towards me again.

"What are you going to do now?" I asked, backing up. "Slit me open if I don't get in your bed?"

"Shut up!" he barked. "I don't want you in anyone's bed! Understand?"

He bit his lip as he drew closer, adjusting his grip on the dagger. He reached behind me and grabbed the ropes behind my back, then cut through them. My throbbing wrists fell to the sides. He put the dagger in his belt.

"You can move about my house freely," he said. "But don't leave it. I can't do anything for you if you step outside."

"You expect me to comply?"

"You don't have another choice," he said. "You belong to me now. I can send Haneul the ten thousand to make it official, if you want."

I punched him in the stomach. He took it, barely wincing. His eyes laughed as he looked at me, and I wanted to rip them out of his skull.

He walked over to pick up the lamp, nodding his head in the direction of the hallway.

"I'll take you to your room," he said.

"My room?"

He turned to face me. "What? Do you want to stay in mine?"

"Drop dead."

He smirked. "I didn't think so."

He led me to a small and empty room that had a pile of blankets and a table littered with brightly colored bottles covered in dust. He lowered the lamp onto the table next to the bottles, the light creating a purple and red hue across the walls.

"I'll be in the room across the hall if you need me," he said.

I folded my arms. "You don't think I'll slit your throat in your sleep?"

"If you were going to, you would do it. Not threaten me with it."

"I'm not a little girl anymore," I threw back, annoyed with his indifference. "I'm not weak and helpless. I've been trained to kill, same as you. You really think I won't do it?"

"Fine then."

He grabbed my hand and forced his dagger into it, then brought the blade to his throat.

"Slit it," he dared. "Do it now while you have the chance."

His eyes didn't waver from mine as my hands shook against the knife. The tip dented his skin at the base of his throat, nearly piercing it.

I heard the screaming.

I slammed my eyes shut and shook my head, trying to get the sound out. Saejun released my hands and the knife dropped to the ground. I stumbled back, resting against the table behind me.

"You're not a killer, Jaehwa," he said, his shoulders dropping. "I know you. You could never live with yourself if you took life instead of giving it."

I shut my eyes again, trying to keep myself from throwing up.

"Even if you lost your mind and killed me," he continued, "you wouldn't make it out of this prison alive. If you're going to come up with an escape plan, come up with a better one."

I swallowed the nausea back down my throat. "I don't need an escape plan. They'll come for me."

He stepped in towards me, his robes dancing across my feet. The flames from the lantern danced in his eyes, the purple and red hues along with it.

"If they want to take you back," he said, "they have to get through me first. And trust me… I won't let anyone take you from me that easily."

CHAPTER 27

LATE

"Come to breakfast."

The words rang hard in my ear, jolting me from sleep. I sat up and swung my arm out. Saejun caught it, smiling.

"You still punch people in your sleep, I see," he teased.

His hand was soft against mine. I pulled out of his grip and turned my head away from him.

"Sleep well?" he asked.

I didn't answer.

He tapped on the wall next to my head. "I'm guessing you were watching the guard changes, seeing as how you're propped up next to the window. Smart, but not enough. Come to breakfast."

He stepped away, waiting in the doorway.

"I'm not hungry," I muttered.

"Get up and eat," he said. "If you're going to fight me, you'll need the strength."

He stepped away. After a few moments, I followed.

The table was set with half a dozen side dishes and the smell of cabbage stew. Saejun gestured to the seat across from him, and I took it. He began to eat, bringing the bowl of soup to his mouth.

I sat across from him, looking down at the table. A knot twisted in my stomach. This is how Saejun ate? All the time while Mother starved to death?

I looked down at the dishes, unable to touch them. "You eat like a king."

"It's decent compensation, considering everyone wants to kill me."

"Are you comforted knowing that you eat like this, while you left us to die?"

He put down his chopsticks. "I didn't leave anyone to die, Jaehwa. Considering a moment ago I had to force you to breakfast."

"Those are two different things and you know it!" I threw back. "You spent the last five years not giving a damn about us, and now you want to offer me food and pretend that you care?"

He sighed and rubbed his face with his hands. "I should have known that our first breakfast together in five years would end in a fight."

"What do you want me to do, Saejun? Cry with happiness to see you again? You left us without a word. I waited for you, and — "

I stopped, swallowing my true feelings. I wouldn't make myself a fool by telling him how long I had waited for him to return.

He swirled his soup bowl. "I wanted to come back to you… but I couldn't."

"Why would you? You're treated better than the emperor. Of course you'd leave us to starve once you found success."

He slammed the bowl down. "You don't know what I went through, Jaehwa! Don't preach to me! Yes, I left. You don't have to forgive me. But if you think for one moment that I deserted you to line my own stomach and pockets, then you never knew me at all."

My hands shook. "I knew a generous nobody named Saejun. I don't know the infamous, greedy Captain Kim."

He stared at me for a long moment, as if he was trying to read every line in my face. I turned my head down so he couldn't. He wasn't allowed to know me anymore.

"I never changed," he whispered. "I just had to change who everyone thought I was."

I didn't answer him. The smell of the stew was as strong as the silence between us. He took a few more sips from his bowl, and a mouthful of rice. He swallowed, tapping the table with his chopsticks.

"I knew everything about you," he continued. "I knew the type of person you were. The type of person you'd always be. I guess it was stupid to believe you felt the same way about me."

He stood from his seat and walked over to the doorway putting on his belt and adjusting his sword. Without glancing back, he left the house, slamming the door behind him.

***

Ten days.

That was how long I had been trapped in Saejun's house, and it was how long I had until Kiwan's execution. Even in the entire time I had been here, I never had a chance to even look at where they were keeping him.

Saejun had barely spoken to me since our first breakfast together. He kept his distance, but not in a cold way. He came home, had dinner set, and we ate together in silence. Even in silence, his aura was calm and, at times, warm. He was never cruel or unkind. I watched him each meal, looking for the Captain Kim that everyone feared. The one I hated.

But I couldn't find him.

The longer I stayed with him, the more I saw Saejun. The one who had always spoken to me directly, but took care of me from afar. My Saejun, however, wouldn't have put Kiwan up for execution.

I picked up a rose bottle of perfume on the table in my room. For the first time I had the courage to open it and take in its scent, a mix of rose petals and dark wood. I heard Saejun's footsteps, but I didn't look up when he came to my door.

"Why did you collect these?" I asked, putting the rose perfume back on the table.

He hesitated. "They reminded me of home. Of you."

I met his eyes. He was dressed in the emperor's robes, his shoulders back and head high like a soldier, but his eyes were soft and affectionate. How could Captain Kim hold both personas so well?

"The light purple one is my favorite," he said, pointing to it. He hesitated. "I need to go to work now. I'll see you at dinner."

He stepped away, and I eventually heard the door shut after him. I picked up the light purple bottle, opening the lid.

Lavender. It was lavender.

***

I wasn't hungry, but dinnertime had long passed and Saejun hadn't returned at his usual time. I wasn't waiting for him, of course, but I wasn't enjoying my time locked in his home alone either. I had watched the guards for days now, memorizing their shift changes in accordance with Saejun's work schedule. They normally switched directly after sunset - after Saejun came home for dinner - but Saejun hadn't come home and they had already switched. The moon was rising and Saejun wasn't home yet.

I went to the window, wringing my robes. Where was he? Was he in trouble?

A man screamed.

I ran to the door, throwing it open. Was it Saejun?

It wasn't.

There was a group of four men, about fifty paces from Saejun's door. Two were on the ground wrestling, while the other two stood on the sides, laughing.

"You son of a bitch!" one of the men on the ground yelled. "You broke my arm."

The man let out another cry, rolling to his side in pain. By the sound of his voice, he was young. His opponent stood, receiving a pat on the shoulder by the two men standing.

"That was worth the money!" one of them said, applauding. His voice sounded vaguely familiar.

I leaned in to try and get a good look at his face, but he turned it away to lean over his comrade with the broken arm.

"That'll make you think twice before acting better than everyone else, won't it?" the man said. "You should know your place now."

Gritting my teeth, I took a step forward at familiar words I was tired of hearing. But after a few steps, I stopped. It wasn't my place to defend a guard. They'd kill me if I came closer. I should let the bastards kill each other if they wanted.

But something gripped my heart to see the youngest on the ground in pain like that. He was still so… human.

The gloating man straightened, and one of the others tapped on his shoulder. He pointed in my direction. The winner of the fight looked over his shoulder, eyes meeting mine.

I stepped back.

"I'll show you submission…"

It was the guard from my house arrest.

"Well, well. Look who it is," he taunted, approaching the house. "The woman that caused my demotion. It looks like Fate has blessed me tonight more than once."

I tried to keep my face as calm as possible. "I don't know about Fate, but I'll bless you with a broken face if you step any closer to Saejun's house."

He chuckled, now only a few paces from the door. "Name dropping now? You're only a whore, woman. That's the only value you'll ever hold."

I jumped back and went to shut the door, but he was quick on it, throwing it back open. His eyes raked over me, and he licked his lower lip before biting it.

"What kind of services are you providing?" he asked. "I might be interested."

I prepared my hands into fists. "I'm *not*. And *I'm* not."

He clicked his tongue in disappointment. "You're just supposed to obey, beautiful, not object."

He stepped forward into the house, his shoes slamming against the floor. I stepped back. He rubbed his bottom lip with his thumb. I crept my right foot back.

"Why don't we pick up where we left off last time, hmm?" he asked.

I smiled. "Sure."

I kicked him full force in the stomach, stepping in to palm strike him to the chest. He stumbled out of the doorway, and I tried to shut the door in front of him, attempting to lock it. The door busted open before I could, and I was sent sprawling to the ground. He towered over me, pulling his knife from his belt. He pointed it at me.

"That was a mistake, whore," he said. "I was going to be nice to you... but I think I've changed my mind."

He held his knife horizontally and climbed on top of me, pressing the blade against my throat. With his other hand, he reached for my robe. I knocked away the hand holding the knife, bucking him off of me. I went to slide through his legs and away from him, but he grabbed my hair and pulled me back. His arm wrapped around my neck, cutting off my air. I tried to elbow him, but he only grunted and took the hit. Everything was starting to go black.

Then suddenly, he released.

I gasped for air, looking over my shoulder.

Saejun's silhouette caught my eye seconds before the guard was thrown out of the doorway. Saejun reached for the whip he kept on his wall, following after.

"You dare come into my home?" Saejun yelled, the sound of the whip cracking through the air.

There was a scream.

"Gambling after hours?" Saejun continued, the whipping sound cracking again. "Initiating fights among the ranks? Trespassing into your commander's home?"

I crawled forward to watch Saejun as he towered over the guard, who was now holding his face while coming to his knees.

"Captain, I —"

Saejun whipped him again. The veins in Saejun's neck and hand jutted from his skin as he continued to whip the guard, who screamed in agony after each crack. I shuttered while watching him, rubbing my throat.

"Chilbok," Saejun said, holding out the whip. "Is your right arm still good?"

The guard with the broken arm shuffled forward, bowing. Even from where I sat, I could see how pale he was from the pain.

"Yes, Captain," the kid said through forced breath.

"Good." Saejun forced the whip into the kid's good hand. "First, you'll give Kyungsuk fifteen lashes for his disobedience to me. After you see the medic, whip him every day until your arm fully heals."

Kyungsuk came to his knees. "Please, Captain —"

"Don't you dare ask for forgiveness!" Saejun barked. "You've lost the right."

Saejun called over a few more men, then gave them orders as the kid with the broken arm continued to whip

Kyungsuk. Saejun stepped away, coming back into the house and shutting the door behind him.

He came to me, dropping to his knees and touching my shoulders gently. "Are you alright? Did he…"

The concern in his eyes was genuine and overwhelming. I trembled, still holding onto my neck. When I failed to answer, he took me into his arms and held me close to him. I should have fought back, but… I couldn't.

"I'm terrible, aren't I?" he asked into my hair. "I can't protect you, no matter how close or far I keep you from me."

I leaned against his shoulder, his familiar scent stronger than it had ever been. His arms around me were strong and safe; the same arms that held me as a teenager when I cried, when I had nightmares, and when I was afraid the world was ending.

"Don't be late again," I whispered.

His arms around me tightened. "I've already come too late for you before. I won't live with that regret again."

CHAPTER 28

TRUSTWORTHY

"Come with me. I want to show you something."

Saejun's eyes were soft and gentle as he stood in my bedroom doorway. He wasn't giving a command, but instead, extending an invitation.

He had been kind to me for the last two days, as if whipping my attacker and holding me in his arms had erased the betrayal of the last five years and the fact that my brother was going to be executed in seven days. He acted as if there was nothing but an inconvenient pause between today and the day he left us to die five years ago.

I mentally scolded myself for letting him hold me. It was a weak moment that I didn't want to give him again. I didn't want to forgive him so easily. We suffered so much after he left. I suffered. How could he go unpunished for everything? How could he be set free when I was still hurting so much?

I turned away.

"You're losing your spirit," Saejun continued. "Come with me. I can't stand you locked up like this."

"You had no problems locking Kiwan up."

He sighed through his nose. "*You* didn't murder anyone."

"How do you know I didn't?" I replied, turning back to meet his eyes and challenge him.

He stared at me for a long moment, then smiled and shook his head. "Because I know you. Also, because Dolshik told me. Come on. Unless you want to be locked up in your room for a lifetime."

I stood to follow him. It would have been stupid to give up the chance to walk around the prison freely and gather more information.

Keeping me close to him, he took me through the prison grounds, the guards making minimal eye contact with us before turning their heads away. The news of Kyungsuk's lashings had everyone on their best behavior.

Saejun took me to the watchtower and led me up the stairs.

"You always liked the stars at night," he said. "I think you'll like this place."

I stopped halfway up the stairs. "Why are you doing this?"

He stopped a few stairs above me, turning back. "Doing what?"

"Treating me like this. You have lavish breakfasts prepared every morning. You punish your men if they get too close to me. You remember every detail of the past and…"

I trailed off. He stepped down into my space, leaning down towards my ear.

"You're not that naive, Jaehwa," he said. "I know you're not."

214

I turned to his gaze, as powerful and bold as his words. With a breath, he leaned back and continued up the stairs.

We came to the top of the tower, to a secluded outlook post. I could see everything from here, from the entire expanse of the prison grounds to the fields on the other side of the wall. The city had a faint glow from where I stood, despite how far away it was; and on the other side of the city were the forests, barely anything more than shadows.

But in those shadows was the Rebellion. My heart ached to be part of those shadows once more.

"Look up," Saejun whispered.

I turned to him for a moment, the moonlight catching the playful pieces of his eyes. I quickly turned away then tilted my head back, looking at the array of lights glimmering in the dark skies. The sky was stretched thin, but the light was seeping through. I smiled. It was a small reminder that there was always hope.

Saejun laughed. "You're exactly as I remember. It comforts me."

He stepped forward, taking my hands in his. I wanted to pull away. I should have. But the warmth in his fingers kept me from moving. His touch was protective. Gentle. Familiar.

For a moment, I was home again.

"What are you going to do with me?" I asked, looking at our hands together. "You want me to just sit and wait for you to come home every day, saying nothing on the day of my brother's execution?"

He shook his head. "I want you safe. Away from Haneul. Away from groups plotting against the emperor. Away from anything that puts you in danger."

"Do you think I'm safe with you?"

He chewed his lip, obviously hearing the skepticism in my voice. He pulled a hand away from mine and ran it through his hair, staring at the ground for a moment before shutting his eyes.

"I'm sending you to the northern kingdom," he said.

My mouth gaped. "You're... you can't do that! They'll kill me if I try to escape out of the borders."

He opened his eyes. "Not if I'm the one to do it."

I let go of his other hand, stepping back. "Are you insane? Do you really think I'll allow you to send me off to a kingdom of strangers? Do you think I'll abandon my family?"

"You need to. To survive."

"I don't want to survive!" I yelled, fists clenching. "I want my family! I want to fight beside the people I care about most! And you want me to disappear? You want to exile me?"

"I want you alive, goddammit!"

His breath shuddered. With a clench in his jaw, he turned his eyes away, scanning the black horizon.

"I won't go," I said. "I won't abandon my family."

"Kiwan can't be saved. Only you can."

"So you want to play my savior? When you've done nothing for us in the last five years?"

"So everything I did for you in the years before that has suddenly vanished?" he threw back. "All the sacrifices I made after your father left and you couldn't even put a spoonful of rice between your mother and brother? Everything I gave you, Jaehwa... You don't remember any of it?"

My eyes fluttered, tears starting to rise behind them. I stepped back as Saejun's shoulders tensed.

He slowly exhaled through his nose. "What will it take for you to trust me?"

"That's not possible."

I raised my head towards the sky again. Silence passed between us as I stared at the stars.

"Fine," Saejun said. "I'll take you to see him."

My heart fluttered. "You mean…?"

"Come on."

Saejun took me down from the tower and across the yard, into the dark spaces of the main prison. It was too far from the house for me to see from my window, and it was difficult to get to.

He opened the main door of the prison, his arm coming to my side and pulling me close. I was about to step away, until the prisoners started shouting.

"New flesh," one of them hissed.

"Put her in the cell with me, Captain. I can help you punish her."

"Did you get us a new gift?"

I shuddered, allowing Saejun to keep me close.

At the end of the line of cells, Saejun turned and nodded to the cell next to him. In the cell was a kid in shredded clothes, his knees bent into his chest. His eyes were shut as he leaned his head against the wall.

It took me a long moment to recognize him.

"Kiwan!" I called, my knees weak.

His head shot up, turning towards the sound of my voice. His jaw slacked before he unfolded his knees.

"Jaehwa!" he called back, getting up on his knees and crawling to meet me.

217

I ran my hand over his face through the bars. He had the same large eyes, the same small and sharp nose. His long hair was matted and gritty under my fingertips, but it didn't matter. There was still some life in his eyes and that was the most important thing.

"You're so thin," I said.

He tried to smile, his icy hands gripping mine. "Prisoners aren't exactly fed well. But I'm okay, Sis. I'm okay."

I turned back to Saejun. "How could you leave him like this!"

Saejun's face stayed cold and empty. "It's standard for all murderers."

"You still think I did it, do you?" Kiwan asked, shoulders dropping.

"Not *think*," Saejun replied. "I *know* you did."

"Kiwan wouldn't hurt anyone," I interjected. "You know that."

Saejun stared at Kiwan. "I thought that too. Unfortunately, in my line of work you see things you wish you hadn't."

I stood to face him. "In your line of work, you see things that aren't there. Your kind feeds on the innocent."

Saejun's nostrils flared. He raised his hand, pointing behind his back towards the long row of prisoners. "Do they look innocent to you, Jaehwa? Do their words sound like the cries of innocent people? Yes, the innocent suffer. I do everything in my power to make sure that doesn't happen, but that doesn't change the fact that the guilty still exist. They exist and I have to punish them in order to protect the innocent."

He pointed to my brother. "He's no different. I *watched* him murder three of my men. You think I wanted to believe it? You think I wanted to put him in here? After everything? And worse! The worst part is knowing that I trained him to do it! If I never taught him to fight, my men would be alive and there wouldn't be blood on his hands!"

He huffed, his chest sinking down with his shoulders. His dark eyes shattered into a thousand pieces.

I looked away.

"But I promised myself..." Saejun continued, "I promised I'd always be just. Even if it killed me. I can't walk away from that."

"Why not?" I snarled. "You walk away from everything else."

His face darkened. He reached out and yanked me towards him, picking me up and throwing me over his shoulder. Kiwan yelled my name before it was lost in the sound of the prisoners' crude comments and cheers. Saejun paid no mind to them or me as he marched out of the main prison. I hit his back, struggling to get out of his grip, but he didn't even flinch as he walked towards his property.

He flung the door of his house open, dropping me on the ground as he turned to slam the door. He removed his belt, then his outer robe.

"I really didn't want to do this," he growled. "But if it's what it takes..."

I jumped to my feet, bolting back for the door. He grabbed my wrist and pulled me back, pushing me against the wall as he ripped open the top of his robe. I screamed and pulled my leg up to knee him. He knocked it out of the way, taking hold of my wrists again.

219

"Look!" he commanded. "Look at me, Jaehwa!"

I grit my teeth before standing up straight, opening my mouth to scream again.

I didn't.

All the air left my lungs as soon as I looked at him.

The top of his robe was fully open, showing me everything from his collarbone to his waist. I had seen him bare like this when we had trained in the lavender fields... but it wasn't like I remembered. Dark lines stretched across his skin, some thicker and more ragged than others. His once pale and smooth skin was now covered in scars and burn marks, the flesh torn and scabbed from what looked like a thousand battles.

"There's a difference between walking away," he whispered, "and not being able to return."

He dropped my hands and took a single step back. His scars and scabs shifted with his muscles as he took shallow breaths. I reached up and mindlessly touched his chest, running my fingers over the scabs to make sure it wasn't a trick of my eyes.

"Saejun... where... when did this happen?"

He gently wrapped his fingers around my wrists and held them, not answering.

"Saejun?"

"It was after I was accepted into the Emperor's guard," he whispered back. "There are certain... welcoming ceremonies for newcomers."

"Why did they hurt you?"

"Because they could. And I knew they would come after other things more precious than my skin if they knew what - or who - mattered to me."

I went silent. He held our hands together, staring into my eyes.

"Do you think the people that left you didn't think about you?" he asked. "That they didn't miss you? That they didn't want to see you again?" His hands tightened around mine. "Did you honestly think I felt *nothing*?"

His body was dangerously close to mine, breaking down my defenses in ways I hated. He raised his hand towards my face, but stopped. His fingers clenched and he stepped back even further, adjusting his robe to hide his skin once again.

"I couldn't come back to you," he continued, "until I knew it was safe to. Then Kiwan... And then Haneul..."

He chewed his lip again, seeming to search for his words that were getting more and more jumbled.

"I can't leave you with them," he finally said.

By the glare in his eyes, I could hear the second part of that sentence.

I won't leave you with Haneul.

"What are you going to do to the Rebellion?" I asked, voice starting to weaken. "Why do you have a spy? To destroy them? Is that why you took me away from them?"

A smile pushed through his lips and he laughed, shaking his head. I clenched my fists, annoyed at his reaction to a serious question.

"If I wanted to destroy them, I could have done it a long time ago," he said. "Haven't you heard the phrase, *the enemy of my enemy is my ally*?"

I paused, trying to understand. "What?"

"The problem, of course, is that my ally can never know that they're my ally."

I squinted. "What are you saying?"

Saejun leaned in towards my ear, his warm breath flooding my senses.

"Honestly, Jaehwa… how do you think they eat so well?"

He stepped back. With a single glance, he walked to his room, leaving me with a thousand more questions than answers.

CHAPTER 29

SNAKES

They would execute him in two days.

Kiwan was in his cell, nearly starving, just waiting for his head to be chopped off by sword in a matter of hours. And here I was, in Saejun's home, only a few dozen feet from him.

I couldn't let him die. I was too close.

Mother was dead. I held her hand as I watched the light leave her eyes. And Father... no. I wouldn't forgive him. If I forgave him, I would have to accept that he was dead and never coming back for us.

I wasn't strong enough for that.

His dark, warm eyes flashed through my mind for a moment. The smell of the mines. The sound of his laughter when I beat him at games of gonggi. The way he sang off-key and danced off-beat...

No. I couldn't remember him now. If I lost my focus, I would lose Kiwan.

The flag of the emperor flew over the prisoners' cells, signaling the coming execution. Each snap of the flag in the wind wound my heart up tighter a little more, a little more, and a little more... until it completely snapped.

I waited until Saejun slept, until the darkest part of night. I couldn't slip out the front door or my bedroom window, but the main room had a larger window I could squeeze through. With every stealth technique Haneul had taught me, I moved down the hallway past Saejun's door and into the main room. In pure darkness, I felt my way to the window, opening it and slipping through.

I slid onto the ground, laying flat, waiting for any indication that Saejun had woken up. I kept a close eye on the guards as they stood to their posts, remembering that if any of them saw me they'd kill me per Saejun's command.

After a moment of silence, I crawled away from the house on my elbows, the dirt shifting ever so slightly under my toes. I had no shoes - it was easier to control my sound that way - so the dirt dug into my flesh. I kept my eyes on the guards, pausing every few moments to make them doubt their senses if their eyes caught any movements.

The only things close to Saejun's house were the open training field and the main hall. If I could get to the walls of the main hall and crouch low enough, the men in there wouldn't see me. The prison was a straight shot from the hall, maybe five hundred feet.

I waited until the guards had turned to each other in conversation, then sprinted across the training ground to the hall. Adrenaline took over, but I couldn't give into it. There was a sharp pain of fear in my stomach as I dropped to the ground next to the hall, checking to see if the guards at the gate had seen me.

They were still talking.

With a quiet breath of relief, I crawled under the windows, still keeping my eyes on the guards. If I could sprint quickly down the main path to the prison, I could —

A woman laughed.

I raised my head to the corner of the window, taking care not to be fully visible. Through the window, I saw a group of guards and a half-dozen hostesses. They were drinking and laughing, playing in their own personal brothel. Some women even walked in and out of the main hall without any fear, stepping out into the night as if they owned the stars. The guards paid no attention to them.

I had seen unfamiliar shadows walk in the night before, but I was never able to identify them. I thought they were guards released from duty or some type of servants. They were hostesses? Saejun actually allowed hostesses in the prison?

And what was more frustrating was the fact that they had more freedom than I did. They walked in the night while I crawled on the earth.

"You can join them if you want."

I spun around to the voice, meeting eye to knee with a shadow. I immediately went to sweep out its leg, and the shadow stumbled. It had me by the arm before I could run.

I knew the fingers.

Saejun spun me around to look at him, and even though the moon wasn't out and the darkness was heavy, I could see the whites of his disappointed eyes and the frown on his face.

"I told you to come up with a better escape plan," he said.

He slid his hand down to my wrists, gripping tight and putting them behind my back as he guided me back to the house.

"Wouldn't you be better off with me dead anyways?" I replied, somehow angry and defeated at the same time.

He stopped. "Do you think I would have gone through all this trouble if that were true?"

He pulled me back into the house.

"My guards would have killed you if they caught you," he said. "Didn't you think —"

"By *your* orders," I replied. "You told them to kill me if I left the house."

He pointed back to the hall. "If I didn't, you'd be dragged into that hall right now with the rest of the whores. I had to separate you from them so my men wouldn't take you for themselves."

I clenched my teeth. "You could stop them from coming at all."

Something gripped my stomach as I said it. The idea of Saejun surrounded by women… women who were willing…

"They're gifts from the Emperor," he said flatly, hissing out the word *gifts* like a swear word. "I couldn't ban them if I wanted to."

My body suddenly ached, the frustration and exhaustion overwhelming.

"Do you really care if I'm dead or not?" I whispered.

With only the lighting from a single lantern, I couldn't tell if he was surprised or angry. By the tone of his voice when he answered, maybe both.

"You think set up a way for you to escape this hellhole of a country because I had nothing better to do with my time?" he spat.

"For five years, you did nothing —"

"I had no power!" he said, cutting me off. He stepped forward, taking my face in his hands. "I'm so sorry about your mother, Jaehwa. I'm sorry. I couldn't do anything. It took me three and a half years to get to my position. By then, she had —"

"What about after?" I asked, throwing off his hands. "For the last year and a half -"

"- for the last year and a half I've been bribing Kiwan's boss to pay him extra, and he wasted it!"

He stopped, taking a long breath.

"I thought of all people, Kiwan would take care of you," he continued. "Then, a few months or so before I arrested him, I saw you in the market." He swallowed, looking at me from head to toe. "You were so thin. So was Kiwan. I couldn't understand it… until I found the gambling ring inside the Red House. I spent weeks going to that disgusting place to find a way to get him out."

Suddenly, I remembered what Kana said about Saejun.

That old wet blanket? Why would you ever put a beautiful girl in his company? Every time he comes in, it's like talking with a tombstone.

"Kiwan isn't your innocent little brother anymore," Saejun said. "He's a compulsive gambler. He owes a lot of people a lot of things, and he probably did long before

227

I even got to him. When I found out that he was a regular customer at the Red House, I went to find him." He paused. "When I did, he —"

"Stop. Stop!" I said, covering my eyes and dropping my head. It was too much information, truth or not. It was silent for a moment, until Saejun's warm hands came to my shoulders.

"Maybe I'm not innocent," he said, "nobody is. But I don't want to be blamed for his mistakes anymore. You need to see Kiwan for who he really is. I want you to see me for who I've always been."

Intak's voice rang through my ears.

"Don't play with the snakes, princess. You're not experienced to know which ones are harmless and which ones have venom."

Suddenly, the scar he left on my arm ached. I glanced at it before looking Saejun in the eyes.

"You sent the ambush against the Rebellion," I said. "You have so much blood on your hands —"

He laughed. I stopped.

"I didn't send the ambush," he said. "Kana did."

I blinked, not understanding. "What do you mean?"

"A woman like Kana doesn't get into her business based on morality. I don't know if you've noticed, but the emperor has a high reward for the heads of the Rebellion."

I was starting to get nauseous. "So you had Dolshik…"

He gave a sharp nod. "If I allowed her to go free, then eventually you… eventually the Rebellion would have been slaughtered."

My knees started to slack. Saejun reached out to hold me up, looking at me with concern. When I looked back, I couldn't decide who I saw.

"Who are you?" I asked, voice cracking.

He smiled, his warm hands squeezing my shoulders gently. "I am who I've always been."

"No." I shook my head at him, my last bit of resistance dissolving. "Saejun is dead."

He grabbed my hand and put it against his chest, his heartbeat pounding against it.

"I'm very much alive," he said close to my ear. "Even more now that you're with me."

His fingertips traced my jaw, the touch burning my skin. Snaking his other arm around my waist, he pulled me closer, his hair brushing against my cheek. When he leaned in, I pulled back.

"Don't…" I said, softer than I wanted.

His fingers dug into my back.

"Why?" he growled. "Because I'm not him?"

There was a string of pain mixed in with the anger in his voice. Part of me wanted to explain my real relationship to Haneul… but the other part of me didn't know the answer either.

"It has nothing to do with him," I said honestly. "It has to do with you. In all the time we spent together, you never acted like this. You never said these types of things or touched…like this…"

I stumbled through the words as his fingers ran through my hair.

"That was before I lived in a world where there are no chances for last words," he said.

The lantern caught his eyes - eyes that were so harsh and deep in the daylight. But as he stood close to me, I saw the deep pain in them; the exhaustion, the determination, and the fear.

I saw Saejun.

"I have to be more dangerous than the wicked to survive," he said. "One day, they'll find my weaknesses and tear me apart. Before that time comes, I want to show you how I feel. How I've always felt."

He leaned in again. I shut my eyes.

Knock, knock, knock.

Saejun's breath pulled back, and I opened my eyes again as he released me.

Saejun threw the door open. "What the hell —"

A wave of heat hit us as the door opened. The room filled with light.

Fire. Everything was on fire.

CHAPTER 30

WEAKNESSES

"Get the fire out!" Saejun ordered, stepping out of his house and into the chaos.

Guards ran back and forth with buckets of water, trying to contain the uncontrollable flames, their knuckles dragging close to the ground from the weight of the water in the buckets. The fire spread from the main hall, to the guards quarters, and to the prison building; the twisting flames licking the sky as the flags of the emperor dissolved in the fire.

Kiwan.

I bolted out the door, but Saejun yanked me back to his side. He locked me in his embrace.

"Let me go!" I spat in his face.

"Why?" he yelled back. "So you can run to your death? Not happening. You're going to the northern kingdom. Tonight."

He pulled me forward, rushing us both towards the exit. The heat and bright flames overloaded my senses, making it hard for me to do anything but comply. As we reached the other side of the gates - which were now un-manned - and down the path towards the city, I pulled back so hard that Saejun turned on his heel.

"I can't leave him!" I screamed. "He's my brother!"

"He was mine too!"

Saejun's eyes glossed over as he caught his breath.

"Don't act like he meant nothing to me," he growled. "I raised him as my own brother after your fa-ther left. I poured everything I had into both of you."

He attempted to pull me further down the path.

"Until you found a better offer," I threw back. "Maybe if I was the richest bastard in the country with an endless supply of whores, I would let my brother die too."

He spun back and gripped my wrists, his eyes flash-ing brighter than the flames behind us.

"Do you want to know how they died, Jaehwa? Do you want to know how Kiwan killed them?"

I shook my head, leaning back as he leaned forward. "No. You keep your lies —"

"They were gutted in front of their own children. Ambushed at the town square on their day off. I saw eve-rything from the bridge. By the time I got there, Kiwan and his friends were stringing them up by their necks in the trees. It was planned. By someone who had a lot of damn practice."

My knees buckled. "You're lying."

"I wish I was," he said, his grip slacking. "Kiwan killed the only men who were fighting with me. The ones who saved my life when the superiors tried to burn the flesh off my body for sport. They were the ones fighting for the sake of their children. Children who now have their fathers' blood smeared on their clothing."

I looked back at the flames, the smoke billowing in the skies like a dark, reverse waterfall. Nausea overtook me as I imagined Kiwan's dead body burned among the ashes.

"If he dies," I said, shaking, "I have no one left."

Saejun locked his jaw, his eyes desperate.

"And if you die," he replied, "I don't either."

He pulled me farther from the flames, into the fields on the other side of the gates. I tried to pull back, but he knew every move before I made it, blocking my attempts to escape.

"Idiot, stop fighting me!" he said.

"I'm not going anywhere with you!"

He locked me between his arms, forcing me to look up at him. "You're not going anywhere *without* me. I won't let you go so easily."

"I believe that's my line," a third voice said behind us.

I knew that cocky tone anywhere.

Saejun spun me around, throwing me behind his back. He held his arm up, putting a block between me and the person I thought I'd never see again.

Haneul.

Haneul looked at Saejun's arm between us and shrugged his shoulders as he shifted his weight to one side. There wasn't an ounce of tension in his body, but there was a keenness in his eyes that was sharper than I'd ever seen.

"I should have known…" Saejun started.

"I told you, Captain Kim," Haneul returned. "Fate keeps bringing us together, over and over again."

"You. You started the fire."

Haneul grinned, showing his teeth.

"I came to get my pet back," Haneul said. "I don't like other men touching my things. Don't you know that?"

Saejun's hand rested on the hilt of his sword.

"Saejun, don't," I begged.

"I told you, Jaehwa. I won't let anyone take you from me." He started to unsheathe his sword. "Go now if you know what's good for you, Sok."

Haneul chuckled. "Why should I walk away? Jaehwa doesn't want to go with you. *I'm* her master."

"I don't care if you are the emperor himself," Saejun replied. "I won't allow her to go to you."

Haneul sighed. "Then I guess I can no longer be a gentleman."

He pulled out his own sword and jumped to meet Saejun's blade. The blades crashed together, the sound vibrating through the night air.

"Don't!" I yelled.

But it was too late.

Haneul kicked Saejun in the chest, sending him back. Saejun stepped back in immediately, swinging his sword up to bring it back down on Haneul's head. Haneul dodged and sliced sideways, cutting Saejun in the arm.

My stomach seized.

Blood dripped down his arm. He stepped back in to meet Haneul's advances, wincing as the blades continued to crash together.

"Your girl taught me everything I wanted to know, Kim," Haneul taunted. "She was very hospitable. She was willing to show me — well — everything."

His lips twitched at the last word. Saejun grunted and swung his blade, nearly cutting Haneul across the face. Haneul ducked and swept his leg, and Saejun tumbled to the ground. Before Haneul could pounce, Saejun kicked him square in the gut, sending him back. Haneul hissed and fell back. While Haneul was down, Saejun came to his feet again and charged. Haneul caught his foot and tripped him. Saejun stumbled, giving Haneul enough time to come back to his feet.

I can't watch either of them die. Please...

They both stood, swords ready, Saejun now wielding his weapon in his left hand. The cut Haneul gave him must have caused enough damage to leave Saejun unable to use his dominant arm. He didn't look uneasy in his stance, but he didn't look comfortable either.

Blood was dripping from Haneul's nose, but the wild look in his eyes showed that he felt nothing about it. He lunged for Saejun again, cutting him across the shoulder. Saejun's robe hung sloppily from his body, blood seeping into the fabric.

And I was frozen... watching a nightmare where I could neither move nor speak.

"She came to me so easily, Kim," Haneul said, his words dripping as dark as the blood on his face. "How does it feel to know that she'll keep coming to me, over and over again?"

Saejun's eyes darkened as he gripped his sword. "I'll shut you up for good."

Haneul switched his sword from his right to his left, spinning it with ease. "I look forward to it."

Saejun lunged. Haneul reached into his robe...

...and Saejun hit the ground, his sword flying to my feet.

Haneul hovered above him, a sword in one hand pointed at Saejun's throat, a dagger ready in the other. Blood dripped from the dagger, matching the new stain on Saejun's side.

"You're too easy to read now, Kim. I'm almost disappointed it was so easy."

Haneul recoiled his sword like a python.

"Almost," he said again.

"No! Haneul, please!"

I dropped to my knees between them, blocking Saejun. Haneul's sword pointed at my chest, ready to run me through.

But he only smiled.

"I knew you had a weak spot for him," he whispered. His eyes shimmered as the moonlight reflected off his teeth. "It's a pity I can't allow that."

He put the dagger in his belt and grabbed me by the collar, yanking me to my feet and forcing me hard against his chest, while the cold tongue of his blade dug into my throat. His other arm locked around my torso, trapping my arms. Saejun came to his feet.

"Back off, Captain," Haneul said, pressing the blade harder into my skin. "Or I slit her open right in front of you. Just like you did to my sister."

Saejun's fingers twitched, his eyes widening as he caught his breath.

I swallowed, all my fears confirmed. I couldn't pretend to be shocked or betrayed. Everything had been obvious from the beginning: the reason Haneul brought me into the Rebellion, the reason for his plans, the reason he hated Saejun.

It had been obvious. I had ignored all of it.

Saejun stepped forward.

"Stay there," I told him.

He'll kill you… Don't die because of me…

Saejun stopped, eyes burning as red as the flames behind him.

"Survive," I said as Haneul's blade dug into my collarbone. "Don't sacrifice your mission for me."

Haneul chuckled into my ear. "Which side are you on, sweetheart?"

Saejun's shoulders fell as he brought his head back. He straightened, the muscles in his neck tightening. There was a cold determination in his eyes. A deadly promise.

"This isn't over," he said.

"I wouldn't dream of ending it now," Haneul replied. "Not when I have the one thing that will rip you apart."

"I have to be more dangerous than the wicked to survive. One day, they'll find my weaknesses and tear me apart."

Me. I was Saejun's weakness… and Haneul knew it this entire time. That's why he took me to the Rebellion. That's why he agreed to train me.

"Don't get Haneul's intentions confused with love. Trust me. That's not what it is."

237

Kangdae. He must have known Haneul's heart as well. He knew Haneul's darkness better than anyone. And it was part of the reason he sent me away… wasn't it?

"If there's a single cut on her body, Sok, I'll hear of it," Saejun growled. "And I'll rip the skin off your body piece by piece."

Haneul gave an ear-splitting whistle, and the sound of hooves followed close behind. He stepped us back until the hooves stopped behind us. He nudged me to mount Goyanggi, and I wished it was a happier reunion.

I looked at Saejun, clenching my teeth and giving the best reassuring smile I could.

Survive. Please survive. I hate you… but I don't want to lose you.

I climbed on the horse, Haneul close behind me. He trapped me in his arms and grabbed the reins.

"I hope you come for me, Captain," Haneul said to Saejun. "I really do."

He kicked his heels into the horse and it took off, leaving Saejun in the moonlight and shadows of the flames. Looking over my shoulder, I felt the same ache in my chest the day that Saejun had left me all those years ago.

Haneul… this bastard…

I elbowed him hard in the ribs. When he doubled over, I tried to slide off the horse, but Haneul trapped me back in his arms and pulled me back.

"Is that any way to treat your rescuer?" he asked.

"I'm getting my brother. I don't care if I have to cut through—"

"No need for all that, sweetheart. He's on his way to camp now."

"What?"

"Your wish has been granted," he said, tightening his hands on the reins. "We freed the men from the prison… and your brother is waiting for you back home."

CHAPTER 31

ASSUMPTIONS

I couldn't hold my brother tight enough.

"Honestly," Kiwan said, tapping my arms. "I'm fine. Stop strangling me."

"I thought I lost you," I said, trying not to cry again.

Kiwan pried my fingers off from his neck and held my hands proudly. "I would have found a way to survive. I wouldn't have let Saejun win."

A pang of guilt hit my chest and I tried to push it aside. I didn't want to care. I wanted to say that Saejun deserved it. But there was still so much of the old Saejun in Captain Kim. If I had seen it sooner...

I turned to Haneul, who was passionately embracing the comrades he had saved from prison. He patted their shoulders and smiled warmly, a stark contrast to the man who had put a sword to my throat only a short time ago.

"I say this is a cause for a massive celebration!" Haneul said, turning away from his men and walking towards Geonho. He didn't acknowledge me.

Geonho groaned. "You want me to prepare by myself?"

"Where's Dolshik?" I asked.

"Out getting supplies," Geonho returned. "He should be back tomorrow."

I stayed silent. I could have revealed that Dolshik was playing both sides, but there was something holding me back. There were too many missing pieces and I wasn't ready to give information away so easily. Not this time.

And maybe... Dolshik could confirm whether or not Saejun was alive.

I rubbed the raw skin on my collarbone.

"If there's a single cut on her body, Sok, I'll hear of it. And I'll rip the skin off your body piece by piece."

Saejun meant his words. He would have let Kiwan die, but he would have torn Haneul apart to keep me safe. Even in his anger, Saejun never let me come to harm while I was under his imprisonment.

But Haneul...

Haneul gave instructions to Geonho, smiling and waving his arms in excitement. He was back to his old self, despite the extra darkness around his eyes. But as he teased Geonho, it was like nothing had changed since the first time I had met him. As if Intak hadn't been killed. As if I hadn't betrayed him. As if he hadn't put a sword to my throat.

"Back off, Captain, or I slit her open right in front of you. Just like you did to my sister."

Would he have slit it?

"I'll help you, Geonho," I volunteered, suddenly not wanting to be alone. "It's the least I can do."

Haneul looked at me for the first time since we had returned, his lips and eyes flat.

I turned to Kiwan and embraced him once more. "I'll be right back."

He grunted. "I'm not going anywhere. Stop suffocating me."

I pulled back, nodding. He must have been hungry after so many days in prison. That's why he wasn't being himself.

Avoiding Haneul's gaze, I followed Geonho into the kitchen. I helped him set up for the evening, collecting bottles of alcohol and prepping food. Geonho was a better cook than I had given him credit for, and he was a decent teacher as well. He tasked me with the stew as he prepared some potatoes.

"Keep stirring," he said over his shoulder. "Don't let it stick to the bottom."

I obeyed, the smell of the deer and rice together becoming more and more familiar.

… It was the same smell as Saejun's house.

"I've missed this smell," I said casually. "Is this type of deer popular in the forest?"

"Dolshik gets it from a supplier."

"The supplier must be expensive. This deer tastes as good as the emperor's."

I paused and looked at Geonho. He didn't make eye contact with me, his ears turning pink.

"Do you know Dolshik's supplier?" I asked firmly.

Geonho scratched his head. "N-not really."

He stepped back and knocked against the jars of makgeolli, cursing as he scrambled to keep them from falling.

I stopped stirring. "You know, don't you?"

Geonho went still, looking at his feet.

I tried to find words to express my confusion. "How... why... are you...?"

With his arms open in surrender, he stepped closer to lower his voice. "I just do what I'm told. I have no fighting skills, and this is my only way to stay alive."

"Why? Why would... *your supplier*... support you like this?"

"I never asked, honestly," Geonho said, shrugging. "All I know is our supplier doesn't want to see the people suffer, as much as the rest of us."

I swallowed, trying to process the information.

"Will you say anything?" Geonho asked. "If you do... Haneul might..."

He didn't finish the sentence, but I could guess it. If there was anything Haneul hated more than Saejun, it was taking charity from him.

"Soup!" Geonho yelped, jumping over to the pot and stirring.

My head was spinning. "I think I need a moment."

I stepped out, inhaling the night air as deeply as possible. Why did it feel so hard to breathe?

I'm sorry, Saejun. I'm so sorry.

Wandering along the path, I stopped to lean by a tree and catch my breath, even though I hadn't been doing anything more than walking.

Someone sighed behind me. "All this trouble, and you still look miserable."

I turned to face Kangdae, wearing his dark robes and arrogant glow. All my thoughts went numb.

"You didn't come to me," he said.

243

I half-smiled. "I knew you'd be lurking somewhere."

He smirked, his eyes twinkling.

"You came for me?" I asked.

He scratched his nose. "No. Haneul did."

"But you allowed it."

"I protect what belongs to me."

I cocked my head to the side, heart pounding. It took him a long time to look at me, but when he did, I couldn't look away.

"Do I?" I asked. "Belong to you?"

"I told you…" he said, stepping closer. "Wherever you are, I won't be far behind."

I searched his face for a moment, the dark shadows I used to see in them suddenly disappearing. With a stride, I wrapped my arms around his neck, holding him tight. He didn't move, but after a moment, his fingers traced my back. I wasn't going to let go until he fully embraced me.

Which, eventually, he did.

"Thank you, Kangdae," I whispered. "Thank you for being my guardian all this time."

He patted my shoulders then pulled away. His fingers traced my arms for a moment, but then quickly dropped, and he stepped back completely.

"What happened to the Captain?" he asked.

I shook my head, trying not to show my real feelings. "I don't know. Tell me… did he really kill Haneul's sister?"

There was a flash of something in his eyes before he looked away.

"Yes," he finally said.

"And you didn't want revenge?"

"I told you. My father died from his quest for vengeance. I wasn't going to follow the same path. Besides, I can't even blame the son of a bitch. Yeojin went against orders and tried to ambush him. I can't say I would have done any differently if I was him."

"That sounds… heartless."

"The acceptance of reality usually does."

I stepped forward again, putting my hand on his chest, over his heartbeat.

"If you've accepted reality," I said, "why are you still sleepwalking?"

He looked down at my hand and took a deep breath. His hand came to mine.

"Because accepting reality and forgetting the past are two different things," he said.

I slowly dropped my hand intertwined with his, nodding. "I know exactly what you mean."

***

I walked back to the dining hall with Kangdae, to a celebration that put all celebrations to shame. Most of the missing men had been restored back to the camp, and there was a new liveliness that hadn't been there since the day I arrived. Haneul was clapping wildly and telling jokes, while the others shoveled rice and soup into their mouths.

Kangdae left me to sit with my brother at the table. I caught Haneul's eye across the room. He was sitting with his recused men instead of with me tonight, but his eyes kept wandering to mine. He was completely expressionless, masking his thoughts. I couldn't help but think about the night of the memorial, when we were alone in this room together. I had offered myself to him. The touch of his hands across my skin had completely intoxicated me, and believing that he actually cared for me, I let down my guard.

I was a damn fool.

I turned back to Kiwan, laughing at the way he ate with such vigor.

"You're going to get sick," I said. "Slow down."

"I forgot what real food even smelled like," he said, shoving more rice in his mouth.

"All the sacrifices I made after your father left and you couldn't even a spoonful of rice between your mother and brother? Everything I gave you... You don't remember any of it?"

I shook Saejun's voice out of my head, but it didn't change the fact that all of this was his provision. Maybe he was exactly who he said he was. But if that was the case...

Haneul called for attention, and the room went silent in a single breath. His solemn face melted to silk as he raised his glass in a toast.

"To our brave men," Haneul said. "To the ones we gained, regained... and to the ones we lost."

Haneul looked at his drink and winced, then threw it back. The men cheered and did the same, and the night continued with drinking, storytelling, and jeering. Haneul didn't talk to me the entire night, but I had nothing to say to him. Instead, I spent my time with Kiwan and Geonho, and at times, I made eye contact with Kangdae and smiled. He returned the gesture.

The night ended around dawn, the men deciding on different places to sleep.

"Your brother can sleep in the training center with the others until proper arrangements are made," Haneul said.

I held onto Kiwan's arm. "But I want to stay with him."

"Who said he was staying at all?" a third voice rang out.

Kangdae joined the conversation, his face suddenly cold.

"What do you mean?" I asked. "You're not going to separate us now after everything."

He raised an eyebrow. "Can't I? Don't I have the right to determine what happens in my camp?"

I would have thought he was joking… but Kangdae didn't joke. Not with me.

"Well, what do you want to do with him?" Haneul asked Kangdae. "He's not one of us."

"Technically, neither of them are," Kangdae replied. "At least, not officially."

His eyes met mine for a moment, then dropped.

"Are there requirements?" Kiwan asked, stepping forward.

"Yes," Kangdae said. "I have to be interested."

Kiwan's face broke into a smile. "Oh? Well, I think you should be very interested in me."

"Is that so?" Kangdae cocked his head to the side, scratching his nose. "Tell me why."

Kiwan's eyes sparkled. "Because… I've killed over a dozen of the emperor's guards."

CHAPTER 32

SIDES

The world crashed around me.

"I thought it was three?" Kangdae asked.

Kiwan's eyebrow twitched as he smiled. "He only caught me for the three."

"Fascinating…" Kangdae said, scratching his nose again and looking at me.

Words turned into garbled sounds as my thoughts muddled together. Kiwan - my baby brother, my only living family - was a murderer.

"*It was planned. By someone who had a lot of damn practice.*"

Saejun's words echoed so hard in my head that I wanted to vomit.

A hand grabbed my shoulder.

"You alright?" Haneul asked.

I stepped back from his hand, no longer feeling any warmth from it… hating that I used to feel any warmth from it at all.

"No," I said. "No, I'm not alright."

I stumbled away, holding my stomach as I left towards the gardens. My hands shook as my blood froze.

"*I don't want to be blamed for his mistakes anymore. You need to see Kiwan for who he really is. I want you to see me for who I've always been.*"

…Why? Why was Saejun right?

"Jaehwa?"

The shell of my brother came into view, a deeper shadow around the edges of his shoulders, and a shift in his eyes that made the darkness stronger than before. Was it the twilight? Or were his eyes always that dark?

He crouched down and patted my back. When did I sit down?

"You alright?" he asked. "Don't worry. Kangdae said we could stay. He said it might not be permanent, but if I can —"

"You killed them?" I asked. "You really…"

His eyes dropped to the ground. His tongue roamed his cheek, his response taking longer than it should have. He then stood, towering over me with a coldness in him I had never noticed before.

"They were going to come for us sooner or later," he said. "I put a stop to it before they could."

"And that justifies it?" I spat, coming to my feet. "Kiwan! You stooped to their level!"

"I was fighting back!' he yelled. "This is war, Jaehwa. The emperor has taken everything from us. Father's gone. Mother's dead. Our neighbors all starved to death. I buried two of my best friends myself after they were sliced open by men under Saejun's command. What do you want me to do? Sit down and talk with him over tea?"

249

"Saejun saved us. Multiple times. If it wasn't for him, we would have starved to death -"

"And when he left to become one of *them*, mother did," he growled back. "Or did you forget that he left us to die?"

"He wanted to change things for the better—"

"So did father. They were both idiots." He stepped back, glancing at the sky. "The past is gone, Jaehwa. Saejun isn't our ally anymore."

He laughed, the sound twisted and hollow.

"God, what did he say to make you so stupid?" he asked. "I've never seen you so pathetic."

I whipped my hand across his face. He barely acknowledged it, licking his bottom lip. My eyes burned as much as my hand.

"I don't care who you think you are," I said. "After everything… you don't get to run your mouth with such disrespect."

He scoffed, rolling his eyes. "What should I do then? Let you defend him? Does he have you under his thumb now, too? Honestly, were you just pretending to be a whore, or did you— ah!"

Haneul came from behind and twisted Kiwan's arm behind his back before he could finish the sentence. Haneul then dipped down to his ear, his voice low and warning.

"In my camp," he said, "we don't disrespect the women we share blood with, especially not the ones who risked their lives repeatedly to save us. Remember that. My discipline is not something you want to experience."

Haneul released him and shoved him sideways.

"Show respect to your sister," he continued, pointing to me. "If I catch you speaking to her like that again, I won't take it lightly."

Kiwan looked between us. He bowed slightly to Haneul, but turned away from me without a second glance. I shuddered as Haneul's hands came to my shoulders.

"Haneul… he really killed them."

His hand grazed against my cheek. "How did you think war worked, sweetheart? There's always a chance you have to risk the lives of the ones you love, whether because they fight with you or because they fight against you."

I shoved him away, anger bursting through my chest. "Is that your motto, then? Were you going to slit me open so you could have the satisfaction of revenge?"

"Jaehwa—"

"You. You were going to use me to kill him." I balled my fists, tears of anger and frustration dropping to the ground. "You were using me for nothing else but to reach your goal."

"Didn't you come to us to do the same?" he whispered back.

My fists dropped at my sides. I shook my head. "I should have never come to you. I should have never looked for you."

Silence passed as more tears fell without my consent.

Haneul stared at me, not blinking. "Yes, I wanted to kill him. Yes, I planned to use you to do it. But no… I was never going to sacrifice you."

"Then why didn't you kill him yourself? You had the chance."

251

He gave a weak smile, then dropped it. "Maybe because letting him think you're mine is a more painful punishment for him than death."

I clenched my teeth.

"But mostly, because Kangdae was right." He ran his fingers through his hair. "That night when we met in the forest and I realized that you fought like him, I saw a way to revenge and I got too thirsty for my own good. So I trained you. I made you one of us. I put everything I had into you because you were the missing piece I needed to bring Kim down. But…"

He stopped.

"But what?" I asked.

"Then… you were gone. And I didn't know what to do anymore."

I scoffed. "Because your tool was gone?"

"No. Because you weren't there when I came home, and it drove me crazy."

He stepped forward, wiping my tears away with his thumbs. I didn't look at him as he did.

"I damn near lost my mind when you went to the safehouse without a word," he whispered. "I thought I had lost you completely."

"You told me to go."

"I meant back to the hut! I didn't expect you to leave camp. Not after how much work you went through to get here. With how much you endured to be part of us. You belong here, Jaehwa. With us."

He pulled something from his belt, taking my wrist and placing the object in my hand.

It was the dagger I left on his bed.

"You're still part of my family," he said.

My hand gripped the handle. I raised my eyes to his, looking at him through my tears.

"I don't know if I want to be anymore," I replied.

Footsteps rustled behind us. We turned to look at their owner.

Dolshik.

"News just came from the city," he said, glancing at me.

I turned my head away, wiping my tears and stepping back so he could speak. He raised an eyebrow at me, seeming to catch my intentions to stay silent.

"It must be big if you're coming to look for me at this hour," Haneul replied. "Out with it."

Dolshik glanced at me again, then back at Haneul. "Captain Kim Saejun has been held responsible for the destruction of the prison and for abandoning his men. They're executing him tomorrow at sundown."

CHAPTER 33

GUARDED

I rushed to Kangdae's hut and threw open the door. He turned his head, narrowing one eye as Haneul came in behind my.

"Did I say you could enter?" Kangdae asked.

Haneul grabbed my arms and pulled me back.

"Sorry, Boss," he said, his fingers digging into my flesh. "I'll take her back —"

"He's going to die because of me!" I cried, chest burning. "I can't let that happen!"

Kangdae paused, then laughed through his nose. "This scenario seems familiar."

"Kangdae, please. Saejun protected me. He saved —"

"— and what should I do about it? Send my men back to save their captor? Does that make sense?"

My knees weakened. He was right. The Rebellion had done so much already. Kangdae had guarded me. Haneul strengthened me. They had even saved Kiwan without a real reason to. I couldn't ask them for more.

It was time I stopped taking from them.

"You promised me anything I wanted if I gave you information," I said. "Clothes, a job, a house in the city. Remember?"

"Yes, but I didn't promise to —"

"I want to leave the Rebellion."

Kangdae stopped, his lips parting. His eyes glossed over, as if he didn't understand what I said.

"What?" he asked.

"Release me," I said. "I've done nothing for you since I came here. So let me go. I'll never set foot in this camp again. You don't have to be responsible for me any longer."

Kangdae's mouth clamped shut, his eyes narrowing. There was a span of two breaths before he opened his mouth again.

"Haneul," he said. "Step outside."

Haneul's grip on my arm slowly unfurled, and he met my eyes only for a moment before swallowing and stepping out of the hut. Silence passed as Kangdae rubbed his fingers together in thought. My heart pounded, waiting for his response.

"If I let you go," he said, finally, "you'll go after him."

"It's not your responsibility if I do. You didn't want me here in the first place. So just release me and —"

He stepped into my space, the heat from his body coming off in waves of warning. His jaw was set hard, but his eyes were like silk, his breath still.

"I told you," he growled. "I protect what belongs to me."

I swallowed, trying to find my voice again. "Am I yours? I was the one you sent away."

"No. You were the one I watched from a distance."

He held my gaze until it felt like his breath was burning through me. I turned my head away, my rapid heartbeat making me dizzy.

"Only a little while ago you called me your guardian," he said, voice low. "Do you expect your guardian to let you go and run towards your death? You think I would allow that twice?"

Twice? Kangdae never let me...

No. Not me. Yeojin.

"Then tell me," I replied, "should I live with the regret of not saving someone when I had the chance?"

He reached for my hand. He looked down at my fingers, as if inspecting my fingernails, then shut his eyes as he stroked my fingers with his.

"You want to torture me," he whispered. "Don't you?"

He opened his eyes, but I couldn't read the expression in them.

"You can hate me for a lifetime, but I won't release you," he said. "Not until I know I protected you with everything I had."

Still clasping my hand, he brought me in towards him. He brought both my hands to his lips, pressing a soft kiss against the back of each one. He lingered there for a moment, his breath fanning my skin; the warmth of his body contradicting the chill of his power.

Then, he stepped back, the silk in his eyes turning to cold oil.

"Haneul," he commanded.

Haneul stepped back in, his face set in cold submission. "Yes, Boss?"

"Take Jaehwa back to the hut and watch her. Until further notice, she's no longer our ally. She's our enemy."

***

Haneul pulled me into our shared hut, not bothering to listen to my protests.

"Haneul, wait —"

"Stop," he commanded, taking me by the wrist and throwing me down on the mat. "You heard Kangdae's command."

I came to my knees, trying to hold back my frustrated tears. "Haneul, please. I'm begging you."

Tears started to stream down my face as I laid my hands out in front of me in a deep bow.

"Don't do that," he commanded.

I lifted my head up. "Had I known my brother was guilty of his crimes, I never would have come here. Saejun would still be Captain. He wouldn't have abandoned his men to save me. His head is on a chopping block tomorrow and it's all my fault."

"You expect me of all people to care about the life of Kim Saejun? What makes you think I'd give a damn about him?"

I sniffled. "Because you know how much he means to me."

He went silent, turning his head away. I stood to my feet, stepping towards him and grabbing the collar of his robe in desperation.

"Please. I'll do anything."

He stared at me, cold. Then he curled his lip. "Anything?"

His rough fingers ran my hair behind my ear, then traced the line of my jaw. As his finger traced below my lip, I swallowed.

"Yes," I replied.

He leaned forward. His hand came to my waist, pulling me in, his body tight against mine. I could smell his breath - heavy, yet sweet - as he looked down at my lips then back to my eyes. As he cocked his head to the side, I closed my eyes and surrendered, waiting for him to take over.

"Stupid," he said, pinching my nose. "I trained you to fight. Not surrender. And I'm not the type to take bodies as business dealings."

I let go of my breath as he released me and walked across the room.

"You want him that badly?" Haneul hissed, refusing to look at me.

I stared at my feet. "I just want him alive, Haneul."

"That makes one of us."

"Haneul —"

"Quiet!" he barked, eyes turning red. "Don't beg me to let you go to him! That's one thing I won't accept. I'm not going to lose you too!"

His lips trembled as he said it. He ran his fingers through his hair, gripping hard onto his scalp. Grunting, he ripped his sword from his waist and threw it to the side.

"I saved your brother's life. I came for you. I walked away from killing that Kim bastard myself when you stepped in front of my sword. How much more do you want from me, huh? How greedy are you?"

I shook my head at him. He didn't understand. He didn't understand at all.

Yes, Saejun was my first love. There was a part of me that would always love him.

But Saejun had also protected the Rebellion. He fed them supplies from the emperor's personal reserves. He avenged Intak by having Kana killed. He had the same goals as we did. He was on our side.

But I couldn't tell Haneul any of that. He wouldn't believe me now. And if he found out Dolshik was part of it, Haneul would probably kill him.

I had no options now… and I had no one to blame but myself.

"Yes, I was greedy," I admitted. "I always have been. My greed gave me something to fight for. It kept me alive. But my greed has been a burden on you since the beginning. I've never given you anything in return for what you gave me. So let me go. Let me go so I don't burden you anymore."

He stepped forward, roughly pinching my chin and forcing me to look at him.

"I already told you," he said. "I won't allow you to be a waste of my time. *I'm* your master, Jaehwa. Whether we're enemies or allies, I'm not going to let you find another one."

He let go, stepping back and staring down at me.

"If he dies, it's not your fault," he said, the familiar words hitting my ears once again. "You will never have the chance to save him… because *my* greed won't let you go."

***

259

Dawn came quickly. Neither Haneul nor I slept.

Haneul stood to dress, watching me from the corner of his eye, but saying nothing. I couldn't say anything myself, knowing that any plea I made would only be a waste of energy. I couldn't ask Haneul for anything more. I couldn't ask for anyone's help now.

"Haneul! Come quickly!"

Geonho's panicked voice came from the other side of the hut. Haneul jumped to the door, opening it.

"What is it?" he asked.

"A message from Dolshik," Geonho said, trying to catch his breath. "The emperor's guards have found the camp. We're surrounded."

CHAPTER 34

SECOND

"Let's go."

Haneul grabbed my arm, dragging me to the dining hall. Kangdae was already there, as well as some of the others in high command. And they were all surrounding... Dolshik?

"There aren't many of them," Dolshik said, his arm resting on his knee nonchalantly. "The fires weakened their defenses. But they're pissed."

"How many?" Kangdae asked.

"Twenty to thirty."

"And our men are still weak and hungover."

Haneul stepped forward, dragging me with him. Dolshik caught my eye for a moment before looking at Haneul.

"How bad is it?" Haneul asked.

"Bad enough," Kangdae replied. "We'll need to look far more competent than we actually are."

"Luckily," Dolshik said, "it looks like their goal isn't to attack, but to wait for us to come out. They're still weak from being attacked themselves."

Haneul sighed. "Backup?"

"Sent for."

"Response?"

Dolshik nodded.

"Have Geonho summon the others," Haneul said. "Everyone who isn't in the medic hut should meet in the training room. We'll need to send out a few scouts as well to keep an eye on them."

"The Underground is taking care of it," Dolshik replied.

The Underground…?

Haneul turned to me, eyeing me thoughtfully. He shook his head to himself, then turned back to Kangdae.

"Thoughts, Boss?"

Kangdae licked his bottom lip. "Get information. Prepare to look bigger than we are."

Haneul nodded at me. "And what about her?"

Kangdae glanced at me for a moment, then looked back at Dolshik.

"Watch over the prisoner," he commanded Dolshik.

Dolshik snickered. "Not in my job description."

"As the Underground's second in command, it's your job to watch over the members," Kangdae said. "Enemy or otherwise."

Dolshik's lip curled.

The Underground's… second?

As Haneul stepped forward, I stepped in front of him.

"Let me fight with you," I said.

He paused, taking an unusually long deep breath. His face was unreadable, but the determination in his eyes wavered. Regardless, he jerked his head to the side in rejection.

"Even as our ally, you're not allowed on the front-lines."

"I'm sober and trained."

"You're emotionally drained and unstable."

"Haneul —"

He grabbed my shoulders. Kangdae stepped out behind him and walked towards the door.

"I already told you," Haneul said, lowering his voice, "I'm as greedy as you are. And when it comes to my greed, you can't win."

"Then what do you expect me to do?"

He reached a hand out, patting the top of my head, his fingers trickling through my hair. With a lingering gaze, his lips pulled back softly in an exhausted smile.

"Wait for your master," he whispered.

He stepped in and kissed my forehead as he had once before - same as the last time he had said it - but this time, his touch was raw; a mix of possession and an apology.

I grabbed his arm before he stepped back, trying to spit out my words before I lost the courage.

"Even if you won't let me out, I'll still protect you," I promised. "That's what a pet does, isn't it? Protect her master from the threat?"

His eyes glowed as he looked at me, pain and pride surging through them.

"Jaehwa..." he whispered.

"Let's go," Kangdae said behind him. He didn't look at me when he said it.

Haneul ran a thumb against my cheek, stepping back to leave me to Dolshik. I watched as his and Kangdae's shadows disappeared into the camp.

"Touching," Dolshik said flatly.

"Shut it," I snapped. "Before I tell them who you are."

"You won't tell them."

"And why wouldn't I?"

He cocked his head to the side. "Don't you want to save Saejun?"

I squared my shoulders at him, narrowing my eyes. He stood up, smiling as if he owned me.

"Whose side are you on?" I asked.

He stepped forward, folding his hands behind his back. "I'm on the Rebellion's side. My responsibility is to keep it alive in any way I'm able. Remember how I said that Kangdae's mother was executed?"

I nodded.

"She was Kangdae's mother… and my aunt."

My jaw dropped. "How was I here for months without anyone telling me that you're cousins?"

He shrugged. "Our family doesn't talk much."

"No kidding. And I heard correctly? You're also the second leader of the Underground?"

"It's Kangdae's attempt to keep Haneul in check." He stroked his chin, looking back at the door. "But I think Kangdae has been suspicious of me. That's why he kept you here - to tell him the things I didn't. It actually helped me more than it hurt me, so I'm not worried about it."

I grabbed the side of my head. "You're… you're playing on three different sides?"

He smirked.

"How?"

"Easy. Talk as little as possible. People will always take the smallest bit of truth and create their own lies from it. But you're missing the point. The point is, I'm the leader of the Underground at the moment."

"And?"

"And you're a member of the Underground."

His lips pulled to the side again. I waited for an explanation, but Dolshik only continued to stare at me.

"I still don't know what that is," I said bitterly. "I haven't had any duties as part of that group."

"Oh, but you have. Who do you think gave Saejun your safehouse location?"

He smiled, this time showing his teeth.

"I needed someone on the inside," he continued. "Someone to study who the emperor's guards were and what they did. You seemed like the perfect option. Someone Saejun wouldn't harm. Someone he would trust."

My eyes dropped to my hands. Even Dolshik knew that Saejun had faith in me, yet all this time, I never had any faith in him.

Not until it was too late.

"I'm not required to look after him," Dolshik said with a sigh, "but he kept us alive for the last few years. I should return the favor. Also, he could be useful later. The question is, whose side are you on? The Rebellion? Or your own?"

I swallowed, trying to cool the emotions bubbling inside me. Living for myself had kept my brother and I alive, but only barely. I had never thrived. It wasn't until I found the Rebellion that I found the strength to be something more than I was.

"Even if the Rebellion considers me the enemy," I said, "I will always think of them as family."

"So what will you do, little traitor?" he teased. "Will you obey your master's command to stay... or will you disobey in order to save him?"

I laughed ironically, folding my arms and cocking my head at Dolshik in the same cocky manner he had with me.

"All this time... and you don't know the answer?"

CHAPTER 35

THE SLIP

"Why are you just sitting there?" I asked. "We need to go."

Dolshik didn't look up. He continued to sharpen his sword, eyes focused on his work as he scraped the metal against a rock.

"It won't be much longer until sundown," I said. "Are we going to save him or not? I swear to the gods, Dolshik, if you don't —"

"Shut up." He checked the blade before shaking his head in disapproval. He scraped it against the rock again. "Wait."

"Wait for what?"

He looked up from his work to smirk. "Wait for the right moment."

"I think *immediately* is the right moment."

"And that's why you'll never be in a place of power. You'd rather run your mouth and follow your own ideas then look at the best way to control the situation."

I folded my arms. "I'm giving my honest assessment of the situation. You have a problem with honesty?"

He laughed. "I have a problem with you thinking that honesty is a good tactic. You're built on reactions. Yeojin was the same way. That's what got her killed."

Geonho burst through the door, holding his chest and panting.

"Dolshik!" Geonho cried, his words forced through shallow breaths. "The Underground in the South. They've been — *huff*— they've been captured!"

Dolshik raised his head with a flat expression, nothing revealing his feelings except for a glimmer of mischievousness in his eyes.

"Are you sure?" he asked.

Geonho nodded frantically.

Dolshik pulled his blade from the rock and glanced at it for a brief moment before placing it in his scabbard. He nodded to Geonho.

"Prepare the horses," he commanded.

Geonho nodded again and disappeared outside.

Dolshik smiled and scratched his chin. He gave a dramatic sigh. "What to do? I've been entrusted with a prisoner, but those under my command need my help. I can't very well leave them to die to protect our enemy… can I?"

He rolled his neck around to loosen it, smiling.

"You planned this, didn't you?" I asked. "There are no guards surrounding the camp, is there?"

He shrugged. "I didn't get this far by my handsome face alone, you know. Here, you're going to need this."

He held his arm out, a familiar dagger in his hand. The metal shined with a dark light now, weighing my heart down.

"You know this dagger was hers, don't you?" he asked.

"Who?"

"Yeojin."

There was no trace of irony in his eyes and he held it out for me.

"Haneul wouldn't have given this to you - on more than one occasion, I might add - if he didn't have faith in you," Dolshik continued. "He sees the past in you, maybe. But I also think he sees a promising future. Don't let him down."

I hesitated. With a long breath, I reached out and took it, the grip warm and familiar. I hid it in my robe, close to my heart.

"I won't," I replied with a whisper.

Dolshik took me by the arm, dragging me towards the stables. The camp was mostly empty, save for a couple of medics and their sick patients. As we reached the stables, a face I had nearly forgotten about in the chaos appeared in front of me, scowling in hollow concern.

My wayward little brother.

"Where are you taking her?" he asked Dolshik, more of a threat than a question.

"Nowhere you can follow," Dolshik replied flatly.

He stepped to the side to pass Kiwan, but Kiwan only stepped in the way again.

"If it's about the emperor's men, take me with you," Kiwan said. "Leave Jaehwa here. I can help you destroy them."

Dolshik sighed. "That's the problem. You think I'm out to destroy. Step aside."

Kiwan fastened to his spot, eyes narrowed. I searched for any emotion in his face - anything besides the desire to prove himself - but found nothing.

It wasn't there. It never had been.

"Leave, Kiwan," I commanded.

Both of them turned towards me.

"You have your freedom now," I said. "So don't waste it. I'd like to pretend you're doing this to protect me, but you're not. I can see it in your eyes right now. You're only thinking of yourself."

He looked surprised. "Jaehwa? What are you —"

"I don't have one good memory of you," I said, trying to hold my nerves. "I don't remember you protecting me. I don't remember you encouraging me. I don't remember you comforting me. Saejun did that.

"I've realized…" I continued, "I erased all the good memories I had of Father because he spent so much time with you, trying to turn you into a good man that would take care of our family when he was gone. And I was so angry at him… because he failed."

Kiwan's eyes hit the ground for a moment before he looked back up.

I took a deep breath before continuing. "I loved you with everything I had, hoping someday you'd show some sort of compassion towards your only sister. I thought that us being the last living family would make you change… but it didn't. You still have no idea what family means, and I'm tired of trying to teach it to you."

"What are you trying to say?" he asked, still emotionless.

"I'm saying you're a shit brother."

Dolshik scratched the back of his ear as Kiwan looked between us.

"I honestly believed you didn't kill those guards," I said. "I didn't think you would go that far. It was my last hope. But you're still out for yourself."

Kiwan then took a single step back, laughing. "What do you want me to do then? Give up and support your ideas of morality? You and Father are the same, you know that? Always preaching to others, while never having the backbone to actually get something done yourself. And even when you try, you mess it up. You're too caught up in ideals to face reality."

"You know," Dolshik said, his voice flat. "You say a lot of words for an idiot."

Kiwan's anger transferred to Dolshik, a look of defiance in his eyes. "You want to try me, then? Trust me, I have no trouble letting my blade do the talking."

He reached for the sword at his side, and unsheathed it, pointing it at Dolshik's throat. Dolshik's eyes widened for a brief moment, then settled into a perturbed grimace.

Clunk.

Kiwan fell to the ground, unconscious.

It took me a moment to register Kiwan's unconscious body sprawled across the dirt, and another moment to register Geonho standing behind him with a long plank of wood in his hands.

He stared at Kiwan's motionless body, eyes wide.

Dolshik chuckled. "I didn't know you had it in you, Geonho."

Geonho shook his head frantically. "I don't. I'm quite nauseous right now, actually. Did I kill him?"

271

Dolshik looked at Kiwan's body and put two fingers under his nose. He shook his head, stepping over Kiwan and pulling me along with him.

"He's fine," Dolshik said. "Take him to the medic hut and tie him up. We'll deal with him later. We have people to rescue."

I didn't bother glancing back at Kiwan as I walked to the stables with Dolshik. There wasn't a good way to say goodbye to him, so I decided not to.

He would wake up. Maybe someday, in more ways than one.

***

"There are guards on the west side that change stations when the bells ring. The east guards change halfway between the bells. The southern guards change soon after that. And the northern guards change every time the bells ring twice."

Dolshik soaked up the information I gave him in the best way he could: with considerable distaste.

"Can you offer me something other than that?" he asked. "Hardly seems like enough information to get in."

I grunted. "I'm not sure how to get in otherwise. There are only two gates, one in the north and in the south. Saejun only brought me in and out of the northern one. I'm not positive on the location of the second."

Dolshik sighed. "You were *almost* useful."

Dolshik, myself, met with the "captured" Underground members and hid among the trees of the forest, watching the guards change. The sun was starting to lower, not quite sunset, but getting far closer than I liked.

"Murderers get three months," I said. "Saejun had less than a day."

Dolshik hummed. "Saejun shamed the name of the emperor. We're lucky we got this much time."

Hold on, Saejun. Don't die. Not like this.

"I'd love to storm the prison, but it doesn't seem wise at this junction," Dolshik said. "You have a different idea? You watched from the inside. What can you tell me?"

I shook my head. All I could ever see from Saejun's house were the useless things outside the dusty windows. There wasn't much else that was of any real value. No one went in or out without the filthy eyes of the guards on them.

Wait... Except...

I turned towards Dolshik. "I have an idea. It's going to require your persuasion skills."

CHAPTER 36

RESCUED

"I should have brought Geonho."

Dolshik curled his nose at my robes adorned with red and gold embroidery. I smiled confidently as I attached the veil to my ear.

"I won't let them catch me," I said.

"They'll see how... *inexperienced* you are."

"My job is to make sure they don't see me at all. A boring hostess is better than an experienced one when your goal is to be a shadow."

"Don't get yourself killed."

I nodded solemnly. "Too many people would be affected if I did."

Dolshik cocked an eyebrow. "Thinking highly of yourself, are you?"

"No," I said, turning to walk towards the gate. "I'm done thinking of myself at all."

I walked down the forest path, taking the main path in a way that made me look as if I was coming from the city road. My heart hummed in my chest, not daring to pound. If the adrenaline took over, it would be the end of me.

As I reached the gate, the guards held their hands out to stop me. One stepped forward.

"Your business?" the man asked.

I nodded politely. "I'm from the Red House, sirs. A present for those damaged in the fire."

The men looked at each other. "Did Kana send you?"

I looked them in the eye, holding my hands still. "We have new management now."

I didn't know if they knew Kana was dead, but best to keep it simple.

"You're alone?" they asked.

"Last night was one of our busiest, or else I would have come with the others yesterday."

The men stopped to look at each other for a moment.

"I suppose today is a good day to celebrate with extra company," one of them eventually said.

"The main hall is straight forward, towards the tower," the other told me. "You can't miss it."

I bowed again, stepping through the gate.

I can't... but I will.

I walked the familiar path, the burnt structures standing charred and ragged against the sky. Haneul had burned the main prison, but there were still parts of the prison untouched by the fire. Saejun's house was still standing, but my gut told me that he wasn't there.

Where would they keep the captain on the day of his execution?

I eventually went with my gut, taking the path towards the waving flag of the emperor. It might as well have been a sign for death.

Eyes wandered in my direction, but didn't stay long, the execution preparations taking up too much of the guards' attention. They ran from one place to another, a spring in their steps despite the destruction around them.

The death of Captain Kim Saejun was a celebrated occasion among the ranks of the emperor. Evil always celebrated when good was being destroyed.

"I never changed... I just had to change who everyone thought I was."

Saejun was the same man he had always been. I realized that now. He was darker and more formidable, yes; but he had to be fearless, ruthless, and unwavering to live in this place. He never lost his principles or priorities. He fought for himself so he could, in turn, fight for others.

Unlike me.

"You fight like fire. I need you to fight like water."

I finally understood what Haneul meant that day. Fire was chaotic. Fire didn't relent. Fire struck fear in people's chests. Looking at the skeletons of the buildings around me, I understood: fire only knew how to destroy.

But water could bend. Water understood its surroundings. Water never gave up its strength or its serenity. And in the end, water gave life.

The hum of my heart stopped as I reached the entrance of the cell. There was only one guard, but it was one guard I was not happy to see: Kyungsuk, the devil who tried to force himself on me with a knife. How could he stand so tall with the whipping lashes against his chest and face?

My biggest problem wasn't getting past him. It was not killing him as soon as I got close enough.

I stepped forward, bowing politely. "I've been sent for the prisoner. A gift from the Red House."

Kyungsuk laughed, raising his eyebrows. "Why should a man be treated so well on his way to the execution block?"

"Shouldn't the executed get one last pleasure before his death?" I asked. I cocked my head to the side. "If you like what you see, I can offer you the same services."

My skin crawled as I said it. I was glad there was a veil to conceal how my lips curled to hold back my own vomit.

He licked his bottom lip before biting it. "You're speaking my language, miss."

I know I am, you perverted snake.

He opened the door, allowing me inside.

"A gift for you, *Saejun*," he called.

He was practically laughing as he said Saejun's name, happy to drop the formal surname of the emperor. In all honesty, Saejun looked nothing like a captain in his state. He was on his knees in the middle of the cell, his hands tied behind his back. Not that he could escape - there were no windows in his cell and no exits besides the one behind Kyungsuk.

He looked up. He blinked when he saw me, his forehead shifting back.

"Maybe now we'll see the noble captain crumble into humanity like all the rest of us," Kyungsuk teased. "Even facing death do you still want to act like the moral god among us?"

He shoved me forward.

"Show me what you got, woman," he said, leaning against the cell door. "Make sure I can see everything."

I nodded, meeting Saejun's gaze. "Get ready."

His eyes flickered.

I stepped forward and crouched in front of him. Saejun swallowed. He didn't take his eyes off me as I ran my hand through his hair and down his jaw, stroking his bottom lip with my thumb. With a hand clamped on his neck, I stepped behind him, leaning down and pressing my body against his back. He straightened, his feet shifting awkwardly under him. I ran my hands down his chest from behind, leaning in to inhale his scent for maybe the last time. The way his breath quickened, I could tell that he noticed.

As my hands ran down his arms and towards his back, I pulled Haneul's dagger from under my robe. I cut the rope with it, then tapped the handle against Saejun's palm. He gripped it, the veins in his arms strong as venom.

"Get to the good stuff, lady," Kyungsuk said, sighing. "Why don't you take off that veil and show me what you can do with that pretty little mouth of yours?"

"Oh, but sir…" I returned, sitting back on my heels. "I'm much better with my hands."

I barely finished the sentence before Saejun was on his feet, across the room, holding Kyungsuk by the throat against the cell wall. The man gurgled, his eyes going wide in terror. I saw him struggle for a brief moment before his eyes rolled back into his head. Saejun dropped his body to the ground, pulling the dagger out of his heart.

Saejun turned to me, and I tried to ignore the dead body on the side of the room. At least Kyungsuk hadn't screamed.

"You came for me?" Saejun asked. "Do you know how dangerous —"

"I want you alive, goddammit."

I smiled behind my veil, hoping he could see it in my eyes.

"You saved me so many times," I continued. "I'm returning the favor. After this, we can go our separate ways and forget each other."

He shook his head, eyes soft as his shoulders dropped. "Then leave me here. Because I'd rather die than forget you."

I nodded to the door. "Shut up and get out, stupid."

We went to the entrance. He leaned up against the wall, looking out the window to the guards outside.

"There are six immediate guards we have to watch for," I said. "Two are about twenty feet from this building, in the east. Two in the west. One north, one south. After that, there are another dozen waiting by the exit."

"And all of them would love to put a sword through me, I'm sure."

"Is there only one way out of here?"

He nodded. "Just the front door."

I started to strip off my clothes. Saejun stopped, swallowing again.

"Jaehwa… what are you…"

"Shut up."

I stripped off my red and gold embroidered robes to reveal another set of blue and violet robes I had been wearing underneath.

Saejun gawked. "What on—"

I threw him the red and gold robe, smiling. He looked down at it, raising an eyebrow. I nodded at the fabric, then to him.

"It's time to play dress up," I said.

CHAPTER 37

ACT

"I'm sure you look beautiful," I teased over my shoulder.

"I don't want to hear it."

Saejun finished dressing and gave me permission to turn around. I bit back my laugh. The intimidating captain of the emperor's guards was now transformed into an awkward, muscular hostess. His red robe barely stretched across his shoulders, the length brushing his rough shins. He scrunched his nose as he put on the veil.

"If we live," he said, "never speak of this again."

I stepped forward and straightened out his robes, not saying a word as I made him more presentable. I thought of when Kangdae had done the same for me, the memory weighing on my mind. My heart ached leaving him and Haneul as I did.

Saejun grabbed my hands, his eyes searching mine. I spoke before he had the chance to.

"I'm sorry," I whispered.

He shrugged. "I've been in worse situations."

"No. I mean for not trusting you."

He pressed his lips together in an innocent smile. "Don't apologize yet. Live through this to tell me properly."

He leaned over and picked up Kyungsuk's sword, handing Haneul's bloodied dagger back to me. I gripped the handle and nodded, squeezing his hand as we approached the door.

We strolled through the prison grounds, assuming the role of hostesses. Eyes followed us, some lingering too long. No doubt that Saejun was bringing attention, since he was rather tall and it was hard to hide his strong shoulders.

"Where are you going?" a voice asked behind us.

Three hostesses stopped us, no expressions behind their veils.

"The hall is this way," the tallest said. "Come with us."

The tallest led the way while the others waited for us to follow. I glanced at Saejun for a suggestion, but then noticed the guards around us. There were at least six at the front gate, and gaining their attention would set the whole camp on alert. I nodded to Saejun to follow. I could tell by the flicker in his eyes that he wasn't happy about it, but he complied all the same.

The hostesses led the way to the hall, which somehow hadn't burnt to the ground. It didn't look as lavish as it had when I had peeked in the window a few nights before, but the men were just as drunk and the women just as affectionate. I swallowed my heartbeat, mentally preparing to continue my act. It would be no different than the night I pretended to be Haneul's hostess. Except Haneul wouldn't be the one with his hands on me. These men... they wouldn't show any restraint.

I walked in, the stench of alcohol overpowering my senses. There were eight men and six hostesses. Eight windows. Two doors.

The men glanced in my direction, and my heart stopped as they looked at Saejun. They were quickly distracted, however, by more alcohol. The girls behind us ushered us towards the drunkards, taking their places in their laps. Saejun and I went for the drinks, handing them to the men as they were distracted with their current company.

"If I believed in a god, I'd say he was on our side!" one of them drunkenly yelled as the other cheered in agreement.

"Who'll be the new captain?" another asked.

"Who cares? No one could be worse than Kim. The dog gave me thirty lashes for having some fun with the locals. Harmless! They only faked pain to make him feel sorry for them. He didn't even believe my side of the story. I tell you, he can burn for all I care."

One raised his glass. "For all those extra drills for staying up past curfew."

"For throwing us in the frozen river after having a good time with the women in town."

"For the end of Captain Kim."

The men cheered and drank down their alcohol. All except for one kid in the back, stroking a bandaged arm.

"Captain Kim was a better man than any of you," he snarled.

The men stopped and turned to him.

"Say again, Chilbok?"

"I said he's a better man than any of you," the kid said again, defiant. "He was honorable. Your morality is as dirty as your fingernails."

They laughed, one of the men taking a large drink before speaking. "Is Captain Kim your hero, kid? What exactly is so great about him? Did he teach you to piss standing up? Or feed you from his own tits?"

The men were rolling in drunken laughter. Saejun held his cool, eyes narrowing.

"Maybe he taught you how to get between a woman's legs, is that it?" the man continued. "Nah, nevermind. Captain Virgin Kim never even touched a girl properly. If you want lessons, kid, watch here."

He grabbed my wrist, pulling me into his lap. His hands were as rough as his breath. Out of reflex, I elbowed him across the face and jumped back. He fell from his seat, blinking at the ceiling for a dazed moment.

The men laughed even louder as before.

"Great lesson!" they jeered. "Good job, Master Teacher!"

His face turned red. I stepped back further as he rose to his feet.

"Damn bitch!" he yelled. "You'll pay for that."

He charged. Saejun stepped in front and kicked the man straight to the groin before grabbing him by the neck and slamming him into the ground. The whole hall hushed and stared, the mood shifting from drunken cheers to tense silence.

"Hey…" one of them said. "She looks familiar…"

My heart flipped, realizing my veil had fallen.

"Ain't she Saejun's whore?" another asked.

"Then the tall one…"

Saejun stepped between me and the others, sword drawn. I reached for my knife. The men had stumbled to their feet, aware of the situation, but still incredibly drunk. At least the Rebellion had the intelligence to keep some of their men sober for battle. These men were useless without a leader.

The hostesses had fled to the corner, whimpering. The men started closing in on us. Saejun ripped the veil from his face and charged. I followed.

They lunged for Saejun first. I stepped in to the side to fend off two of them. One attempted to strike me with his blade, but missed the mark completely, making it easy to sidestep him and kick him across the face. The second was maybe only half as drunk and had no weapon, but he punched me hard in the gut, knocking the air out of me. I wheezed, trying to take in air before slamming my knee into his stomach and bringing down my elbow against the back of his neck. I coughed, his previous blow making my head reel.

Another stepped in, grabbing me by the hair. I grabbed his hands and dropped to the ground, throwing him off balance. He took out my legs on the way down, wrapping an arm around my neck. Then he screamed, releasing.

I jumped up, seeing my rescuer: the kid with the broken arm. He pulled back his bloodied sword, pointing it towards the door.

"This way!" he yelled, nodding to us.

We followed silently, Saejun pressed close to my side. Since his robes were already red, I couldn't see if there was any blood, but I prayed there wasn't.

"They'll figure out you're gone if they haven't already, Captain," the kid said.

"Chilbok — " Saejun started.

"We'll get you to the South gate. It's less guarded now that -"

"No. It'll get you killed."

The kid raised his broken arm. "I'm dead either way. It might as well be for something worthwhile."

My stomach squeezed in pain. How did men like this accept death, and men like Kiwan live a lucky life of dishonesty?

"Not like this," I said. "Give us a plan that saves as many men as possible. Any other route is unacceptable."

The kid smiled, nodding at Saejun. "You sound like him."

The corner of Saejun's lips pulled to the side. I nodded at him.

"Of course," I said. "He's my teacher."

Saejun's eyes sparkled with pride.

"Alright then," the kid said, looking between us. "What do you suggest?"

Saejun stared at me, the gears of his mind working behind his eyes.

"Awaiting orders, Captain," I encouraged.

He cocked an eyebrow at me. "Can you handle that?"

"If it keeps us all alive, then I can submit. Sometimes to defeat the snakes, you have to run with the pack."

His lips twitched as if he was going to smile but changed his mind.

"In that case," he said, "listen closely."

***

Saejun reattached his veil, sighing. "I refuse to make this a habit."

"Red is a good color for you," I teased.

His eyes dropped, and I realized my mistake. Red was a color Saejun had been trapped in for far too long.

"I understand why you did it," I said softly. "I understand all of it now."

He didn't respond, his eyes meeting mine.

"Saejun… if…"

Words failed me. He stepped forward and brought a hand to my cheek, his coarse thumb rubbing against it. I lost my breath, his gentle touch taking away my thoughts and fears all at the same time.

"You know how I feel about you, don't you?" he asked.

I looked into his dark eyes, his feelings as clear as daylight. I knew. It wasn't so different from how I felt about him. But whether or not those feelings were something we could pursue in the future were another matter. All I knew was that I wanted to keep him alive. Men like him were in short supply. And if there was anyone who could change the world, it was him. For everything he did for me… this was the least I could do.

I nodded.

"Then that's all that matters to me," he said with a hollow smile. "Let's go. We're running out of time."

"Do you think Chilbok —"

"He'll be okay."

"But his arm…"

"Healing. Don't worry. His attitude will keep him alive. Now, it's your turn. You think you can handle your job?"

I nodded.

"Remember, no reaction. Not until it's time. Promise?"

I thought for a moment and nodded again. He reached down and squeezed my hand. I used the other to pat the dagger next to my chest.

I tried to keep a casual pace walking down the courtyard. The men ran around in the distance, as if they were still trying to grasp the full situation. No doubt one of the hostesses had reported the scene and the guards would be searching for Saejun now.

We made it halfway to the South Gate before getting stopped.

"You two!" one of the guards called.

We turned.

"Why are you out here?" he asked, approaching. "You should be with the others."

I put a hand to my chest, letting out a terrified moan.

"Oh, we barely made it out alive!" I cried. "We took the back door when the fighting started! It was terrifying!"

He eyed us.

"Is that so…?" he asked, sounding unconvinced. "And you didn't see anything?"

"We barely made it out!" I repeated.

The man turned to Saejun. "And you?"

I stepped in. "She's mute, Sir. Hasn't said a word since her birth."

Saejun stared back at the guard, and I held my breath until the guard clicked his tongue.

"Well, let's get you back to the others, shall we?" he asked. "It's quite dangerous to be out here."

"Oh, thank you, Sir."

I met Saejun's eyes and then followed.

"The other hostesses gave their accounts," he continued. "They said it was caused by two women, one who was a man dressed as a woman."

"Really?" I asked, feigning surprise. "A man dressed as woman? Scandalous!"

"And our previous commander has been reported missing."

"Commander? What commander?"

"The one sentenced to die this evening. You'd know him if you saw him, I'm sure."

"How terrifying! You'll keep me safe, won't you, Sir?"

I grabbed his arm, squeezing his bicep. The man slowed his walk, looking down at my hands on his arm.

"Of course, Miss… catching criminals is part of my job."

He yanked me forward and wrapped his arm around my neck, the pit of his elbow clamping around my throat. He drew his sword, pointing straight at Saejun.

"You really think I can't see you behind a veil?" he spat at Saejun. "Reveal yourself."

Saejun slowly raised his hands to his veil, removing it and raising his hands in surrender. He glanced at me, repeating his order through his eyes.

No reaction.

But I want to put my elbow through him.

No reaction, Jaehwa.

"Let her go," Saejun commanded, hands still raised. "It's me you want."

"Has the great captain a weak spot for her? That's quite interesting. That explains why you never let the rest of us near her. What if I do this?"

He kissed me on the cheek. I struggled, but heard Saejun's order echo.

No reaction.

"Do that again…" Saejun warned, "and I'll put a sword through you."

I couldn't tell if it was part of the act or a real threat.

A few other guards rushed forward, taking Saejun by the arms. He struggled for a moment, his eyes still fixed on me. One of the guards punched him across the face, the other bringing him down to his knees. A third stood with his sword ready.

I started to bring my arm up to claw my attacker.

Not yet.

I grit my teeth, holding still.

"What should we do with them?" one of the guards asked.

"Execution is set for the next bell strike."

"Forget it. Let's just end him now. He doesn't deserve the honor of the block anyways."

"Expose his neck then," the guard behind me said. "How about it, princess? You want to watch the great Captain Kim get executed?"

He brought me forward. I dragged my feet.

Saejun looked at me for a split second before his face was forced towards the ground. Two men held his neck down, while the other readied his sword. The one behind me still had his elbow deep in my neck. I turned my head towards his wrist, creating a pocket for air.

One...

"Long live Captain Kim!" one of them jeered.

Two...

"We'll be called heroes for getting rid of you," another said.

And...

"Say hello to the devil for me," the third said.

Three.

The guard raised his sword. I raised my hands, yanking down on my captor's arm and throwing my elbow into his nose. He yowled and released, and I jumped forward, pulling out my knife.

"Not if I kill him first!" I yelled.

I plunged the knife in Saejun's throat.

CHAPTER 38

SAVIOR

Saejun's blood-curdling scream echoed through every inch of the fortress.

The men stopped, stunned. Saejun's body dropped to the ground. The sight and sound nearly made me vomit. I tried to hide my shaking hands as I held the knife in front of me.

"You wanted him dead, right?" I asked. "Is that enough?"

I glanced at the fortress walls.

Steady...

Coming out of their shock, the guards took a step back.

"Who are you?" asked the one who had held me by the throat moments ago.

"Someone who's seen enough of your kind rule people in fear. But fear runs out eventually, same as power."

I checked the wall again.

"Does anyone want to be next?" I asked.

They started to step forward. I could probably take them, but that wasn't the best option.

"You're really going to fight all of us by yourself, woman?" one of them asked.

Shadows formed on the walls.

"No," I replied, smiling.

I kicked the ground twice.

Saejun's foot whipped under two of the men's legs, sending them to the ground. He sprung back to his feet, taking both their swords and pointing it at their throats.

"Show your hands!" he commanded.

They raised their hands in surrender, and I stood to face the third whom I had elbowed in the face. He held his bloody nose.

"There goes your promotions," I said with a sneer.

The guard in front of us blinked and then snickered. "You think you'll escape?"

"Yes."

"Oh?" He laughed at our confidence. "There are dozens of guards looking for you both now. What makes you think you can fight them all?"

"We won't," Saejun said, nodding to the walls. "They will."

The guard looked up, his jaw slacking. At least fifteen men were on the fortress wall, bow and arrows pulled back, aiming straight towards our attackers.

"What the devil…?"

"Never underestimate the power of your enemies," Saejun said. "I taught you that, didn't I?"

The guard looked between us. Saying nothing, he brought his hands up in surrender.

"Come on," Saejun commanded.

He nodded towards the wall, swords still pointed at the guards. We sprinted to it. The men didn't bother to chase us, but one of them screamed orders to the others. It was too late, though. The men on our side had dropped ropes from the wall for us to climb up and escape. Saejun dropped his swords and pulled me onto his back. I wrapped my arms around his neck. He hissed as his hands dug into the rope, pulling both of us up.

"Come on, Captain," I cheered in his ear. "Don't die in a dress. That'll be too hard for me not to bring up in the afterlife."

His hiss turned to a strained laugh.

When we reached the top, two men pulled us up. Chilbok stood between them, smiling.

"You called?" the kid asked. "Man, I thought they actually killed you with that scream. Good signal."

"Get moving," Saejun said. "They're coming. I hope you're ready for a revolution."

"Yes, Sir!" everyone replied in unison.

They threw the ropes on the other side of the wall, sliding down. The first set of men went down the ropes and pulled their bow and arrows and swords, ready on defense while Saejun and I dropped with the second set. We headed towards the forest.

"Dolshik said he would wait over here," I said. "Follow me."

Saejun ripped off his hostess robe, taking a sword from one of the others. I glanced at his arm, the gash Haneul had given him still fresh and undressed.

It reminded me of the cut across Intak's chest. And now Intak was —

"Faster," Saejun said. "It won't be long before —"

There was a scream.

I glanced back, but Saejun grabbed my arm and pulled me deeper into the forest. I couldn't look over my shoulder, but I could hear footsteps behind me. Whether it was friend or foe, I couldn't tell.

"This way!" I said, seeing the landmark.

But Dolshik wasn't there.

"Keep going!" Saejun commanded, seeing my confusion.

We continued to run until we reached a river in the forest, stopping for only a second to analyze the depth and strength of the water. Before I could form an entire thought, however, guards burst from the trees and sur-rounded us. We stood back to back, taking in our newest attackers.

Their men rushed ours, and we could only respond as fists and legs flooded our vision. I slashed my dagger towards anything red that came near me, keeping my dis-tance from anyone with a sword.

Why hadn't I asked for one?

It wasn't necessary, however. My dagger ripped the enemies' arms and sides, weakening them enough for Saejun to jump in to finish them off. As many went down, more came from the trees - some being our backup and some our enemies - and we were forced to cross the river and keep going.

"There's a path to the east," Saejun said. "We can reach it if —"

A guard jumped from the trees, swinging before I had a chance to duck out of the way. Saejun jumped in front of me, taking a cut to his side. He returned his own sword just as strong, and pushed the guard farther from me. I tried to step in, but the way Saejun circled him blocked me from getting into the fight. Maybe on purpose.

Saejun grunted as he switched his sword to his weak arm, the same way he had before losing the fight to Haneul. The guard stepped in and prepared to strike, but he never had the chance. He was slammed in the side by a blur, and when he hit the ground, the force that knocked him down put a sword through him.

Chilbok.

"You have the *best* timing," I said.

The kid smiled and nodded, then motioned for us to follow.

We ran through the forest, to a dirt pathway surrounded by thick trees and high jagged rocks. I stopped to catch my breath, looking around for reinforcements.

"Dolshik was supposed to be here," I said.

Saejun huffed to catch his breath. "If they found him, he would have fled. He's probably still here somewhere. We can fin— ugh—"

Saejun grabbed his side, the blood dripping through his fingers. I grabbed his arm as he started to sink to the ground in pain.

"I'm fine," he said. "It's not critical."

"It's critical enough," I said.

"We need a plan," Chilbok cut in.

I could hear voices in the distance. The guards were coming, and my two allies here were broken in ways that would get them killed on the battlefield. I looked at my surroundings. The path was narrow, and the trees outside of the path were hard to get around. With the jagged rocks, there weren't many places…

Wait.

I caught sight of a large boulder at the top, large enough to block the path if I could unhinge it. It was our only option.

"You two go," I said, pointing to the boulder. "I'm going to block the path."

They both looked up. Chilbok seemed hopeful. Saejun's eyes went dark.

"We're not leaving you behind," he said.

"You don't have a choice. I risked everything to save you. You owe it to me to live."

He paused for a moment, his eyes darting back to the forest as the voices got louder.

"They'll kill you if they —"

"They won't," I said. "I'll be up there. They won't be. You need to go."

He hesitated. I knew that he would die for me - or with me - if he could. But I couldn't allow it. If there was anyone to lead the kingdom out of suffering, it was Saejun.

"*...Because the cow herder and the weaver neglected their responsibilities, their town suffered. Should being in love mean letting the people around you suffer?*"

I approached him, holding a steady gaze as he looked at me in desperation; the determined farmer's son as protective as he had always been.

"In the past, I loved you," I said. "I hope in the next life, I can love you again."

I grabbed him by the neck and kissed him hard on the mouth... both my confession and my goodbye.

I didn't dare look him in the eye as I pulled away and jumped up the pile of rocks. By the time I had reached the top, Saejun and Chilbok were gone. I felt my heart ease despite the hole in it.

I set to work on the boulder, nudging it back and forth. It wasn't stable, making it easy to roll, but it was much heavier than I had anticipated. Gathering every bit of anger, pain, frustration, and determination in me, I shoved it. It lurched forward, but didn't go completely over.

And now the guards were in the path. If they got further, Saejun and Chilbok were as good as dead.

I shoved it again, unable to hold back a scream as my muscles and chest heaved with it. The guards looked up right before the boulder and other rocks crashed down on them. I didn't stop to see if they got back up again.

It was a straight shot down the rocks to the other side, and I had to risk it. I scrambled for footholds, but there were none. I slipped from the side and hit the ground, rolling my ankle and crushing my arm underneath me. The pain was stronger than any words I could have cursed, and I opened my mouth in a silent scream as pain rushed to my head and nearly knocked me out.

After a moment, I scrambled to my feet, limping through the pain. My eyes blurred as it became harder to breathe. Holding my lungs and grunting, I went further into the forest. If I could get back to the path, I could meet Saejun on the other side.

My feet gave out under me, the world spinning. I tried to get back up, but my ankle refused to hold me, and my muscles shuddered from moving the boulder.

You can't be weak, Jaehwa. You can't.

I tried again, stumbling forward and bouncing off trees as my head spun. I hated being so broken, so vulnerable, so weak, so…

…so *human*.

I hated it in the past, and I hated it now. Everyone around me was so strong, so fearless, so impenetrable. But as the faces of Saejun, Haneul, and Kangdae flooded my thoughts, I realized all the people I had tried to be an equal to were just as weak and human as I was. The difference was they ran in packs. They weren't strong and impenetrable by themselves. And I couldn't be either.

Pain shot through my head right before I hit the ground.

I was brought to my knees, my hands forced behind my back. When my eyes focused, I saw three men, swords drawn.

"Far enough," one of them said. "We can spare you if you tell us where he is."

I held my gaze, not allowing him to see how hard it was for my eyes to focus on his face.

"Last chance," the guard warned, pointing the tip of his blade at my throat.

I had fought so hard to live, but I accepted my death, no regret in my mind. I met his gaze, holding it as much as I could for my last words.

"Drop dead," I said. "Both you and the emperor."

Haneul would avenge me. Kangdae would bring down the emperor. Saejun would change the world.

I thought of their faces, remembering the kindness and encouragement each one of them had shown me.

But there was one face I wanted to see one last time.

I shut my eyes, imagining him.

One last time.

THE END - FATE I

There was a whistle.

I opened my eyes to see a man jump down from the trees and land in front of me. He swung his sword, cutting the guards back. I ripped from the grip of my holders, side-kicking one guard and then elbowing the other in the face.

I pulled my dagger and stabbed the closest attacker in the shoulder. As I jumped in to knock him across the face, I was able to catch a glimpse of who had saved me.

Dolshik?

A sword swung at my face. I rolled back, coming back to my feet, but winced as pain shot through my weak leg. I stood ready to attack, my opponent holding his sword ready.

"You've brought a dagger to a sword fight," the man said, circling me. "Pity. I wanted a real challenge."

A sword pressed against his throat before he could step closer.

"Fight me then," a voice said behind him.

I nearly dropped to the ground in relief.

Saejun held his sword against my opponent's throat, ready to slit it. The man dropped his sword and raised his hands in surrender. Saejun commanded him to his knees, and the guard shook as he obeyed.

"You tell them that the former Captain hasn't forgotten his enemies," Saejun commanded. "Understand?"

The man nodded nervously, and Saejun motioned for him to go. The man sprinted back into the forest. The guards who were still standing followed. The rest remained on the ground in permanent sleep.

Dolshik stepped over one of the bodies, approaching us.

"Good timing," I breathed out.

Dolshik pulled his lips to the side in a slight smile. "You're welcome."

"Are you alright?" Saejun asked, stepping in and holding my face between his hands.

I relaxed at his touch and nodded. In a moment, I was in his embrace, holding him tighter than I ever had.

Dolshik put away his sword. "What's the plan?"

Saejun's thumb rubbed against my cheek as he looked around the forest. "Not sure. I can't go back. The only place I can go is forward." He turned back to Dolshik. "Sorry to say, I've lost my ability to give the Rebellion any resources for now. I'll have to find another way."

"You'll still support the Rebellion?" I asked. "Even now?"

"Even if I can't bring down the emperor myself, I can assist those who can. My power is gone. My abilities aren't."

My heart sank into my stomach. Saejun had a group of men ready to follow him into battle for a revolution. They needed him as a leader.

Which meant… he wouldn't be beside me.

"Where will you go?" I asked, almost whispering.

He sighed, his hands dropping to my shoulders. "South? West? Somewhere they can't find us."

"But I —"

Dolshik cleared his throat. "Time to get moving. Both of you."

Saejun dropped his hands to hold mine. I squeezed them.

"I don't want to lose you again," I blurted out.

He smiled, innocent and proud. "Idiot. When I said *us*, I was including you. You think I came all this way just to let you go?"

His eyes sparkled. I became light-headed, unable to hold back a smile.

"I hate to ruin the romance," Dolshik said, "but people are trying to kill us. Jaehwa, are you going with Saejun or coming back to the Rebellion?"

I thought of Haneul and Kangdae, their faces warming my heart and filling me with deep gratitude. But I knew the hole in my heart would be too deep without Saejun. I interlaced my hands in his, leaning my head on his shoulder.

"Haneul will ask for you," Dolshik said.

I chewed my lip. "I know. But I can't do anything for him anymore. My place is with a new resistance."

I looked up at Saejun. He smiled.

"So be it," Dolshik replied, shrugging.

Saejun nodded and we made our way out of the forest, my hand tightly laced in his.

***

Through a connection in town, Saejun got horses for us and his men to ride to the southern part of the kingdom. There was a small group of ex-guards with us - Chilbok included - all bashed, bandaged, and worn down from the fight.

Night had long fallen by the time we arrived at an inn, the innkeeper supplying space for all of us. He gave Saejun and myself a room on the top floor, alone. We had already been separated for far too long. We didn't want to be separated again.

Saejun rested himself by the window, looking up at the stars as I straightened out our beds for the evening. He had been silent for a long time, and I had struggled to find something to say to him on the ride to the inn. I didn't know what to say at all. There was so much I wanted to tell him, but I didn't know how to start.

"I'm sorry," I finally said, breaking the long silence.

He turned to look at me. "For what?"

"Everything you worked for. It's gone because of me."

He laughed. "Everything I had was because of you. It's fair that you took it away."

"What do you mean?"

"I thought of you every day. You and your family, starving to death because of the iron hand of the emperor. It motivated me. It kept me alive."

I leaned back against the wall, shifting my weight to my good ankle. "I'm sorry I doubted you."

"I'm sorry I gave you reason to."

I grunted and rolled my eyes. "Stop being so damn nice, Saejun. I almost prefer Captain Kim. He didn't apologize so much."

He leaned his head back against the wall and propped his arm on his knee.

"Is that who you want me to be, Jaehwa?" he asked.

I didn't answer, my heart pounding as his eyes dropped to my feet then crawled up my body to meet my gaze once again.

"Did you mean it?" he asked. "When you said that you loved me?"

My hands shook in anxiety and relief. "Yes. That's why it was so hard to forgive you for leaving."

"Have you forgiven me?"

"Yes… because that's also part of love."

"Then do you love me now?"

I licked my lips, partially because they had dried, and partially because I needed to build the strength to answer the question. But breath had left my lungs, and I couldn't bring myself to say anything.

"I loved you, Jaehwa," he said, the moonlight hitting his eyes as he leaned against the wall. "And I never stopped. You know that, don't you?"

For a few breathless moments, he did nothing but watch me. Then he rose to his feet, his heavy footsteps echoing in the room as he strode over to my side. He didn't even blink as he towered over me, his hand reaching out to cradle my chin in his fingers.

His eyes searched mine. All I could do was swallow.

"What am I to you?" he whispered.

Lavender fields. Training until sundown. Looking at the stars at midnight.

Family. Security. Love.

"Home," I whispered back.

He leaned in closer. His hands slid onto my waist, soft for only a moment before gripping hard. I straightened my back against the wall as he met my gaze, waiting for the answer to a question he was asking with only his eyes.

I nodded.

He pressed his lips firmly against mine. His first kiss was loving. The second, possessive. And every kiss after, dominating.

He held me against the wall, his hands kneading my sides. My hands rested against his chest while I tasted his lips, his torso rising and falling with each kiss, one after the other. He pulled me away from the wall, only to wrap his arms around me and clasp me tight against him, breaking away from my lips to trail his kisses up my jaw.

He stopped at my cheek and then leaned against my ear as he caught his breath, the sensation making my skin burn. I had to shut my eyes from how dizzy he made me.

"I can't tell you how long I've wanted to touch you," he hummed in my ear, fingers tracing my sides. His lips latched onto my neck under my ear in harsh kisses as he continued to speak. "When we were young… when you were across the room from me… when you walked away with *him*… I swear, Jaehwa, from this day forward, I will never let you call another man *master*."

His strong kisses trailed down my neck until he came to my shoulder. He stopped, resting his forehead against it.

"Nothing happened," I replied in a whisper, my eyes still shut. "Nothing happened between Haneul and me. Even he knew I wanted you."

Saejun tightened his grip on my sides, before sighing with relief. "Honestly, I could accept you being happy with another man if you were alive and well, but I couldn't handle you being dead because of me."

"I survived because you taught me to fight."

He lifted his head and ran his fingers through my hair, pecking my lips one more time.

"Now we fight together," he said. "Until the day I die, Jaehwa, I will fight the enemies of this life with you."

***

It wasn't long before Saejun and I went into hiding, along with the other men that had sworn their loyalty to him. In a matter of months Saejun and I were married, and despite the elements against us, we decided to start a family the year after that. Even with the evil surrounding us, and the struggles pressing on us from all sides, we found fulfillment and motivation to fight because of our family.

As far as I knew, Kiwan stayed under Haneul's command. My relationship with my brother remained strained, and he rarely contacted me. I eventually forgave him, tired of wearing the weight of my useless expectations. He couldn't meet my hopes as a brother, but he was only human, and I accepted that our relationship could never be what I wanted. But he sent messages every once in a while, including the news that he would take Intak's place as Haneul's successor. If Haneul had decided that Kiwan was good enough to be his successor, then there was hope that my brother was becoming someone of honor.

I expected Haneul to come for me, but he never did. According to Dolshik, he had his hands full training up the Rebellion, using Saejun's absence as his opportunity to weaken the emperor. He still had no idea that Saejun had been his supplier for so long. Dolshik intended to keep it that way.

When I asked Dolshik if Haneul had said anything about me, he said that Haneul only muttered that he knew I'd leave eventually. His demeanor softened back to the old Haneul - the Haneul before the death of Intak - but his determination was still as strong as ever.

I kept his memories close to me, praying that victory would be his in the end.

I didn't hear much about Kangdae, but Dolshik assured me that Kangdae was well. He had gone back to practicing medicine, and on top of his regular duties, he spent his time recruiting and training medics for the Rebellion. Dolshik was annoyed because one of those medics was Geonho, meaning Dolshik had lost his kitchen gopher.

Saejun and I created our own resistance group - the Guardians - a group formed to protect and assist anti-emperor groups like the Rebellion. We supplied food, weapons, and training to multiple groups in the kingdom. Slowly, we saw a force rise against the emperor. One that would be hard to fight against.

I didn't know if we'd see the kingdom's freedom in our lifetime, but when I looked at Saejun and our three strong children, I knew that redemption was coming.

It was only a matter of time.

THE END - FATE II

There was a scream.

I opened my eyes, the man in front of me no longer holding his sword, but instead, trying to dislodge a knife from his chest.

The other two behind him were struck by throwing knives as well. While they tried to pull the knives from their bodies, I elbowed my holders and slashed them with my own knife. They backed away, pulling their swords to strike.

But they didn't reach me.

A shadow dropped in front of me. I raised my arm to strike it… but stopped.

"Thank you for finding my pet, gentlemen. She escaped the fence."

Haneul glanced over his shoulder at me and smirked, then turned back to the opponents in front of him. He thrust a sword through them both while a group of men came from the trees to his aid. Haneul's allies soon outnumbered his enemies, and before I could grasp the entire situation, the enemy had been chased from the clearing into the forest.

Haneul kept his sword drawn, his eyes burning through me as blood dripped from his blade. Stepping forward, he wrapped his other arm around my waist and pulled me tight against him.

"You awful woman," he growled. "How can you run off and die for another man? You're *my* property, remember?"

There wasn't a twinge of irony in his eyes when he said it. He leaned his forehead against mine.

"Let's go home," he whispered.

I smiled and nodded.

Haneul whistled for Goyanggi and I settled into the saddle. We rode back to camp together, his body tight against mine. I nestled back on his shoulder, smiling.

He came for me. Despite everything, he came.

I suddenly straightened. "Haneul, it's Dolshik. He—"

"We passed each other on the way here," Haneul interrupted. "He'll return after completing his task. You, on the other hand, are coming home with me *right now.*"

He whispered the last of his sentence in my ear as he held me close.

Dolshik's task… he had made it his task to save Saejun. I had to have faith that he would. My heart panged at the thought of never seeing Saejun again, but I couldn't go back to the past. Not now.

I had found the place I belonged.

***

It was nightfall by the time we reached camp. The men were excited to have me back, even though Kangdae was furious that I left without permission

"Do you have any idea what might have happened?" Kangdae scolded. "Of all the stupid —"

309

"I'll be the one to punish her," Haneul interrupted, his eyes sparkling. "I'm her master, after all."

Kangdae looked between us, his eyes scrunching with his nose.

"As you wish," he muttered before walking away.

I shifted my weight to my good leg. Haneul's eyes wandered down to my feet.

"You're hurt," he said. "Serves you right for leaving me. Come on. Let's get it dressed."

He grabbed my wrist and pulled me onto his back.

"What are you doing?" I asked, trying to get down. "I can walk."

"Just enjoy the ride, sweetheart. I don't do this for everybody."

He carried me to the training room, dropping me on the ground like a sack of rice once we got inside. He shut the door, then walked towards the corner of the room, collecting his medical supplies.

"You could have taken me to the medic hut," I hissed, rubbing my side.

"You haven't earned the luxury. You disobeyed my orders on multiple occasions. I shouldn't even allow you back in here."

I didn't answer, watching him as he pulled out bandages. He sat at my feet and wrapped my ankle. His hands were strong but smooth, his long fingers gently caressing the skin around my feet. My heart started to pound in my ears, remembering the sensual way he touched me in the Red House and the night he was drunk.

If I was honest... I enjoyed the way he touched me. Even back then.

When he had finished dressing my leg, he nodded to my knife and held out his hand. I handed it to him. He looked it over.

"I never taught you how to clean it," he said. "Did I?"

His eyes met mine, playful glitter tucked away in the corners of his serious expression. He sat cross-legged, pulling out a cloth to wipe it.

"You've been using it well," he said. "Even though you said you didn't want to be part of my family."

I folded my arms. "I didn't know how to feel about a man who was using me for his vengeance."

"To be fair, I didn't know how to feel about a woman who was using me for my generosity."

Silence passed between us as he flicked the blade in his hand.

"He's alive then?" he asked.

It took me a moment to realize who he meant. I nodded.

"I don't want to keep chasing you, you know."

"What do you mean?"

He looked at his reflection in the metal, silent. After a moment he answered.

"I want you to belong to me," he said. "Only me."

My heart pounded even faster than before. He stood and put the blade on the table behind us.

"I can't make you mine unless you want to be," he said, circling me. "So answer me. Will you go to Captain Kim? Make your choice."

I looked at the ground, thinking. There was something in my heart that would always belong to Saejun. He made me who I was. He taught me to fight. He fought for me. And thankfully, his heart was still as strong as I remembered.

But the flame I once held had now dimmed into a warm, nostalgic glow.

"It takes too much energy to be in love with the past," I replied, coming to my feet to meet Haneul face to face. "I'm content knowing that he's still the man I grew up with, fighting for the same things he always fought for. But I can't fight beside him any longer. I have a new master now."

I smiled. Haneul stepped in, his face dangerously close to mine.

"Then as your master, I should punish you for disobeying a direct order to stay."

I leaned in. "I look forward to it."

He smiled, pulling back. "So how should I punish you? Extra training? No, you might enjoy that too much. Cleaning the training room? No, not difficult enough." He cocked his head to the side, looking at me from head to toe. "I think I have an idea. It's not often I have you this… vulnerable."

I swallowed. He grazed his tongue against his lip.

"Fight me," he said.

I raised my eyebrows. "What?"

He chuckled. "Fight me. It's your favorite thing to do, isn't it? Let's see how you do with a busted foot. I obviously didn't train you hard enough."

I couldn't beat Haneul when I was fully well. He knew that. What was he doing?

"The terms?" I asked.

"Same. Head, chest, gut."

He showed his teeth in a wide smile, taking his stance.

"3… 2… start!"

He rushed me, but I dodged out of the way before he could land a punch. As I stepped to the side, I kicked him in the stomach.

"Gut," I sang as my ankle ached from the impact.

His eyebrow bounced before he stepped forward to roundhouse me low, sweeping my leg out from under me. I fell to the ground and he was quickly on top of me, pinning my wrists to the ground. He leaned down and pressed his lips against my temple.

"Head," he whispered.

I froze. He chuckled darkly, then leaned down again and pecked my collarbone.

"Chest," he said.

He slid a bit further and pressed his lips against the robes on my stomach.

"Gut," he finished.

With his knees on both sides of my hips, he stared down at me. His grip on my wrists softened.

"It honestly doesn't matter what you decide, Jaehwa. I won't let go of you."

His fingers caressed my palms. My breath quickened by the sensual way he touched the lines in my hands.

"Why?" I managed to ask.

He sighed, looking off to the side. "I don't know. You're stubborn. Reckless. Noisy and thick-headed. You can fight, but you're one of my worst soldiers —"

"Are you trying to convince me to stay or not?" I asked, frowning. "It's hard to tell."

He leaned down until his hair brushed against my cheek as he grazed his lips down my neck.

"I'm not convincing you of anything," he replied. "I'm *telling* you. You're not leaving. I'm not done with you yet."

He leaned forward more, his breath fanning my lips.

"I don't think I'll ever be done with you," he whispered.

Then his lips were fast against mine. His hand slithered under my waist to press my hips against his as he put his full weight against me and kissed me deeper. His rhythm was sensual, but sporadic, as if he wanted full control of the kiss without permission. I surrendered, allowing him full control.

If I was honest, I felt safest when Haneul was in control.

His kisses slowed, but didn't stop. His tongue grazed my lips, making me arch my back in surprise. He didn't go further, even though his fingers against my lower back told me that he wanted to.

With a few strong, deep kisses he parted from my lips. He laid his forehead against mine, breathing heavily.

"I don't care who your first love was," he whispered. "From now on, I'm going to be the only man who touches you."

He brought my wrist to his lips, kissing down to my elbow. Then he sat back, pulling me into his lap. He looked up into my eyes, smiling with pride and seduction.

"Give yourself to me, Jaehwa," he said. "Not only as a soldier, but as a woman. You know that I'll take care of you… better than anyone else."

I smiled. "I know you will… Master."

Craving his lips, I leaned down and kissed him again, allowing my heart to find its new home in his arms.

***

Eventually, Haneul's thirst for vengeance slowly dissolved, morphing into motivation. He spent his time pouring all his energy into me and his men to train us to go up against the emperor. With his head clear of the greed for blood, he was even stronger. His forces multiplied triple-fold in the course of a few years.

He — reluctantly — kept Kangdae's command of only men in his armies. He never forgot his dream of a clan of female fighters, however, especially after Haneul and I were married and had two daughters.

Kiwan was allowed to stay in camp, and Haneul took him in as his own brother, forcing the darkness out of him as he had with me. It took a few years, but eventually Kiwan grew into a better man, even though he still struggled with his selfishness. Kiwan was strong under Haneul's command, and eventually took Intak's place as Haneul's successor.

My relationship with my brother never became what I dreamed, but as Haneul's wife and assistant instructor, Kiwan - at the very least - came to treat me with respect due to my station. And he couldn't help but love his nieces, thankfully treating them better than he had me.

Word from Dolshik came that Saejun was alive, creating his own group to help resistance forces like the Rebellion to weaken the emperor. He still continued to supply many things for the Rebellion through Dolshik, but I never breathed a word to Haneul about Dolshik's connection. My heart still warmed when I thought of Saejun, and I prayed for his victory and happiness.

Kangdae had gone back to studying medicine, and on top of his regular duties, he recruited medics in the Rebellion. Dolshik was annoyed because one of those medics was Geonho, meaning that Dolshik was now without a kitchen gopher.

Kangdae stayed the same: unrelenting, focused, and protective. He became one of my dearest friends... even though he would never admit that our friendship meant a lot to him too.

Slowly, the citizens of our country began to rebel, and it felt like a civil war was close on the horizon. I didn't know if we'd see freedom in our lifetime, but when I looked down at my two strong little girls, I knew that redemption was coming.

It was only a matter of time.

THE END - FATE III

Battle cries pierced my ears.

The forest filled with swordsmen with their swords drawn, ready for battle. There were at least thirty men, some familiar faces and some unfamiliar.

But one stood out among the rest.

"This is what an ambush feels like, gentlemen," Kangdae said as he stepped forward. "Tell me, how does it feel?"

Fear flashed across the faces of our enemies. The men in front of me dropped their swords immediately in surrender, and reluctantly the others with them did the same. They dropped to their knees and put their hands above their heads.

Kangdae rolled his eyes. "Typical. At least *my* men fight to their deaths."

He glared at the men holding my arms, and they released me, as if by force. They stepped back, hands above their heads as Kangdae's men surrounded them. Kangdae then turned his eyes to me and motioned for me to come to him. I raced over, unable to hold in my smile.

His lips pulled to the side. "Don't be so cocky, woman. You're in trouble. Let's go."

Kangdae waved to his men to finish their jobs. Whether it was to execute the men or release them, I didn't know. Kangdae had hoisted me on his horse and led us out of the forest by the time anything was done.

I looked for Haneul, but he wasn't there, and I realized that Kangdae must have ordered him to stay behind in order to protect the Rebellion. After all, Kangdae rarely stepped off the campsite grounds and left the men at camp.

Come to think of it, the only times I remembered him leaving camp… was for me.

"Kangdae," I said, suddenly remembering. "It's Dolshik. He's — "

"I know," Kangdae replied. "He and the others are fine. Dolshik said he had a mission to complete and that he would return afterwards. Don't worry."

I slumped forward and sighed. I knew Dolshik's task was to rescue Saejun. I had to have faith that Dolshik would do as he intended. My heart weighed heavy in my chest, wondering if I would ever see Saejun again… but if he was alive, that's all that mattered. The past was gone, and we couldn't return to it.

Now, I had a new home.

***

It was nightfall by the time we reached the forests surrounding camp. I expected to go straight to Haneul to be reprimanded for my behavior, but Kangdae turned the horse down a path that led away from the campgrounds instead.

"Where are we going?" I asked.

"To discuss some things," he replied flatly.

He took me past the camp and towards the training grounds by the lake. When we reached the end of the path that was too narrow for the horse to get through, Kangdae slid from the horse and held out his arms to help me down. His strong grip made me think of the time he had carried me through the forest a lifetime ago. From that, and the way he rescued me earlier in the day, I knew that if Kangdae had ever chosen to fight, he could have.

But Kangdae wasn't a fighter. He was a guardian angel.

"You came for me?" I asked.

"Don't get used to it."

I followed him through the forest, taking care to not put too much weight on my bad ankle.

"Why not send Haneul?" I asked.

"I ordered him to stay behind. I didn't know what he would have done if you and Captain Kim were together."

"And what would you have done?"

He pressed his tongue in his cheek. "Nothing."

"Don't you hate him as well? You don't want revenge?"

He shook his head. "At one time I did. I saw Saejun cut Yeojin's throat. But I also saw her draw her weapon first. He didn't kill out of cold blood. He killed her out of self-defense. And also, because he lives, so do my men."

I paused. "You mean … you knew the whole time?"

"I had a feeling. I was always curious how Dolshik supplied so much. So I had him followed a few times.

That's when I realized that sometimes enemies and allies are too close to the same thing."

Silence passed between us, the breeze whipping through his hair. He stopped as we reached the open field, then turned back to look at me.

"But I don't care about Saejun," he said. "I don't care about Haneul right now, either. I care about you. You have your brother. That was the objective. Our working relationship is finished. What do you want now?"

I thought about it, my mind going blank. Instead of answering, I walked forward, making my way towards the lake in the middle of the field.

"Do you want to stay?" Kangdae asked as I passed him.

"You won't let me fight."

"Not on the frontlines. But I can find another use for you."

"Will you pay me for it?"

I turned my head over my shoulder to smile cheekily at him. He smiled in return, making my stomach flutter.

"I have one condition if you stay," he said. "Don't sleep in Haneul's hut anymore."

"And where should I - ah!"

My ankle folded. I yelped as I hit the ground, knee first. Hissing, I brushed off the twigs and leaves sticking to my leg as my ankle ached in mockery.

Kangdae sighed before coming up behind me and scooping me into his arms. I clasped his neck. His arms snaked under my knees and around my back.

"What are you —"

"Stop talking," he said, shaking me. "Or I'll leave you here."

A hint of a smile peeked from the corner of his mouth.

He carried me all the way to the lake. My fingers brushed his skin, my arms tightening around his neck as he took me over the bumpy terrain. My heart started racing as I became aware of how my skin felt against his, making it harder to breathe the more he held me.

I promised myself that I would let go of this feeling the first time I had felt it... but I loved it too much.

"You do this on purpose, don't you?" he asked. "Hurting yourself so I carry you."

"I never asked you to. You volunteered. Quickly, I might add."

He grunted. I leaned towards his ear.

"Maybe *you* like it?" I whispered.

He turned, eyebrow raised. His eyes trailed from my eyes to my toes, slowly, as if memorizing every inch of me.

"Are you some kind of pervert?" I teased.

"I already told you," he said, his eyes dark, "everyone is some sort of pervert. And also... I told you to stop talking."

He tossed me from his arms into the lake. I screamed as I hit the water and went under. I screamed again when I came back to the surface.

"You snake!" I cursed while coming to my feet and splashing him.

He tried to dodge the water, laughing. It was the first time I had heard him laugh so clearly. He bit his lip and crouched down, challenging me to come after him.

I accepted.

I lunged out of the lake, taking care of my weak ankle as I charged him. He stepped sideways, avoiding my advance. I turned around, only to meet him face to face. He grabbed the fabric at my waist and yanked me forward, his arms clamping around my torso and trapping me.

I glared at him. "I should have known that you'd fight dir—"

His lips pressed hard against mine, silencing me. With a strong, single kiss, he knocked all the words from my head. He pulled back, his most arrogant smile on display.

"If you think *that* was playing dirty," he said in my ear, "then you don't know what you're in for."

He slowly released me, stepping back as I looked at him in wild confusion. He wasn't bothered by it, and he didn't answer any of my unspoken questions. He only traced his thumb against his bottom lip, glancing at the water.

"The night I found you here…" he said. "That was the first time I saw you not as an intruder, but as a woman."

He smiled sweetly at me, reaching up to move my wet hair out of my face.

"Because I was naked?" I teased.

He frowned and pinched my arm. "Because you were real. Vulnerable. All the thick walls you built around yourself were gone. You didn't have that look on your face as if you had something to prove."

"But you told me to prove myself."

"I did. But you don't have to do that anymore." He stepped into my space. "I already know that I want you."

His arm snaked around my waist once again and he held me close against him, the heat of his body overpowering the chill of my damp clothes. There was something powerful and somehow possessive in his eyes; the same look he always had when he was determined to protect me.

That's what he had always done, wasn't it? From the Rebellion, from Haneul, from myself, and from death… Kangdae had always protected me.

"Kangdae…" I whispered.

He dipped down to my face again. I closed my eyes, but he didn't kiss me.

"Stay with me," he breathed against my lips.

I nodded.

"I want to hear you say it. I won't ask twice."

I opened my eyes to look at his lips, so close to mine.

"I want… I want to stay with you."

I leaned in to close the kiss. He accepted it. He used one hand on my back to hold me close, while the other hand lifted my chin to his mouth so he could pour long, slow kisses against my lips. Each kiss was somehow slower and stronger than the last, as if he wanted to take his time. He then broke away, leaving only the lingering sensation of his cool breath.

"I don't understand this," I admitted, breaking the silence. "You were always so distant."

"I thought you wanted Haneul. But the more he lost himself, the more I wanted to protect you. When I took you to the safehouse, I realized I wanted you away from him not only because he was losing himself... but because I didn't want him to have you."

"We barely know each other," I said, as his hands held tight to my waist.

"I know you. As I've protected you, I've learned who you are." He leaned into my ear. "Now, I'll show you who I am. Can you handle it?"

I froze, unable to answer. He leaned down and brushed his lips against the nape of my neck, giving me faint kisses so slow and calculated that it became torture. I gripped his shoulders, signaling my impatience. His lips came to my ear, chuckling darkly.

"What's wrong, my darling?" he asked, the new pet name sending lightning up my spine. "I may not treat you like a man... but I know exactly how to treat you as a woman."

His arms came around my back to hold me close as I shuddered from both the cold of the summer night and from the heat of his touch.

"You may want to fight to the death," he said, "but my goal is to give you life. As a medic, as a man, and as the owner of the Rebellion."

I rolled my eyes as I smiled. "Do you really think you could ever own me?"

He smiled dangerously.

"No," he said, "but I'm going to have fun trying."

***

After a night of talking and drying off, Kangdae took me back to camp. Haneul wasn't thrilled that I left, and Kangdae wasn't thrilled that he let me escape in the first place.

Kangdae gave me my own place next to the training center, which gave me some much-needed breathing space. He allowed me to train with the men, but didn't allow me to go on the frontlines. Ever. My training wasn't in vain, however, since I ended up working as Haneul's assistant instructor a few years later.

Kiwan stayed in camp as well, and Haneul took him in as his own brother, forcing the darkness out of him as he had with me. It took a few years, but eventually Kiwan grew into a better man, even though he still struggled with his selfishness. Kiwan was strong under Haneul's command, and eventually took Intak's place as Haneul's successor.

My relationship with my brother never became what I dreamed, but as Kangdae's woman and Haneul's assistant instructor, my brother came to give me proper respect due to my station.

Haneul's desire for vengeance began to fade, and he poured all his energy into me and his men for the right reasons. With his head clear of greed for blood, he was even stronger. His forces multiplied triple-fold in the course of five years, and reluctantly he kept Kangdae's command of only men in his armies. But he didn't forget his dream of a female army... and I knew deep down that eventually Kangdae wouldn't be able to hold him back.

Word from Dolshik came that Saejun was still alive, and had created his own group to help resistance forces like the Rebellion to weaken the emperor. He still continued to supply many things for the Rebellion through Dolshik, but Kangdae never seemed threatened by it. As I watched him, it seemed that Kangdae was - at times - returning the favor to Saejun. My heart still warmed when I thought of Saejun, and I prayed for his victory and happiness.

Kangdae went back to studying medicine, and on top of his regular duties, he recruited medics for both the Rebellion and the group Saejun created. Dolshik was annoyed because one of those medics was Geonho. Dolshik had lost his kitchen gopher, but Geonho was a fantastic medic and worthy of his station.

Kangdae and I built a deep relationship together, at a slow pace with no pressure. We both had wounds to heal, and we took the time to let those scars fade before getting into anything complicated. He wasn't an emotional man, but he was caring and deep; which I saw daily after we were married and had a son and daughter.

Slowly, the citizens of the emperor began to rebel, and it felt like a civil war was close on the horizon. I didn't know if we'd see freedom in our lifetime, but when I looked down at my two little ones, I knew that redemption was coming.

It was only a matter of time.

SCENES FROM HIS
POINT OF VIEW

Don't like any of the endings? Well then, write your own! At the end of the book there are blank pages for you to create whatever ending you want.

For further inspiration, or to spend more time with your favorite leading man, here are some scenes from the point of view of Saejun, Haneul, and Kangdae. Get to know them better by seeing the story through their eyes.

HIS POV - SAEJUN
PAST ESCAPES

M y stomach twisted. How many years had it been since I stepped on this soil?

The scent of lavender and dust flooded my senses, bringing up memories I had long forgotten. But nothing here was as I remembered. The desolation was more than I even imagined, the fields bare and the river dry. The smell of the lavender fields in the distance was the only indication that I was in the right place.

Guilt squeezed my gut.

"Captain?"

I shook my thoughts out, turning back to my men.

"Stand down," I said. "I'll be doing this arrest personally."

My men didn't question it, even though they should have. I never made an arrest myself. I always let my men do it, only showing off my power when it was absolutely necessary. If they saw my power too often, they'd find the weakness in it.

But this... this arrest was personal.

I knocked.

"Who is it?"

I swallowed at the sound of a soft voice I hadn't heard in so long. The door inched open, a pair of deep, beautiful eyes greeting me.

Jaehwa.

I hadn't stood this close to her in five years, and it took everything in me not to wrap my arms around her and tell her how much I missed her. She looked at me - blank, like a stranger - until she glanced at my robes. Her lips parted in astonishment.

"...Saejun?" she asked in a whisper.

That voice...

Someone cleared their throat behind me, and I remembered my new reputation. If I didn't keep my facade as Captain Kim, all the torture I endured for years would be a waste.

"Where is he?" I asked, toughening up my voice.

"Who?" she asked.

I stepped forward, standing as tall as I could even though everything in me was shattering. This home was just as I remembered, as if time had preserved it to torture me for leaving. The only difference was that there was no warmth in this place anymore. It was the same, yet somehow, a skeleton of what it once was.

Or maybe I was describing myself.

"Saejun?" Jaehwa asked again.

She looked over her shoulder at the men who followed me in. They looked at her like a pack of wolves in heat. Even with their fill of the emperor's hostesses, they assumed they could take without asking.

But this time, they had to answer to me.

I sent them a warning glance. They took my signal and stayed at their posts. Jaehwa stepped towards me.

"Kiwan. Where is he?" I asked before she could speak.

She clenched her jaw the way she always did when she was scared and angry at the same time. I had to keep myself from smiling at the familiar mannerism.

"Why are you here for him?" she asked boldly. "You have no right to be here."

I tried to shoot her a warning glance.

Don't give my men an excuse to hurt you, Jaehwa.

"He's under arrest," I replied. "For the murder of —"

I swiveled my head to the sound of footsteps behind us.

"What's all the noise?"

Kiwan stepped into the room. Hot blood exploded in my veins when I saw his nonchalant expression. His eyes shot open when he saw me. He made a break for the door, but I lunged and hit him so hard in the jaw that he fell to the floor instead. My men picked him up off the ground, dragging him towards the door as his head spun.

"What do you think you're doing?" Jaehwa asked, grabbing my robe and pulling me back.

I shrugged her hand off. "Your brother is a murderer and a traitor. He'll be executed in three months' time for his crimes."

I'm sorry.

While her eyes glanced around the room in confusion, I stepped out before my men could see our past. If they knew what she meant to me...

"You can't take him!" she suddenly shrieked.

My men grabbed her and pulled her back. It took everything in me not to rip their hands off her.

"It's too late," I said.

"He's all I have left, Saejun! You know that!"

I turned back, gritting my teeth.

330

No... You still have me. You'll always have me, Jaehwa.

I stepped back towards her, wishing I could say everything that had been on my mind for the last five years. How much I had wanted to see her. How much I wanted to hold her. How much I had dreamed of building a life together with her.

But I had made my decisions. I couldn't go back now. If I tried, the deaths of my two closest friends would be in vain. I had to bring their murderer to justice.

Even if that person was the man I always imagined to be my brother-in-law.

I came in close and put my fingers under her chin, forcing those deep eyes to look at me one last time.

"Stop fighting against me," I said. "You won't win."

If I let you win, you'll never be safe.

She sneered at me. "Get out of my house."

"I hate to say this, but this house no longer belongs to you. This house was in your brother's name. It has now defaulted to the emperor."

"Saejun —"

"You can live here for the time being, but you can be thrown out at any time. These are the emperor's orders."

I tried to step away again, only to have her throw more curses at me.

"Who the hell do you think you are?" she spat. "You become captain of the guards, disappear for five years, and then show up at my door to take my brother and home away from me? What right do you have to come back here?"

I tried to ignore her. I couldn't show weakness.

"Put her under house arrest," I told my men. "Secure the first floor."

I stepped halfway out the door before she called my name again. She was crying out to me in half-fury and half-desperation. It shattered me. But she was going to give away my weaknesses, putting her own life in danger. I couldn't allow that.

"That…" I said, turning to face her, "is the last time I'll allow you to say my name and live."

I shut the door behind me before I was expected to keep my promise.

My men had shoved Kiwan to his knees, and he only looked at me with a smirk.

"You and your men came to take me to prison?" he asked, grin widening. "Huh. It feels like there are a few men missing?"

His eyebrow twitched in mockery. I punched him in the face again.

"Keep your dirty mouth shut," I said as he dropped his head towards the ground. "Or I'll rip your tongue out before the execution."

His head rolled back, the smile still somehow plastered to his face. "I would expect no less from the monster of the emperor."

He smiled as blood starting to seep from his nose. I kneeled to meet him, to look into his twisted eyes.

"Trust me," I said, "after the things you've done, you're going to *wish* I was a monster. A monster only destroys from instinct, but a man… a man is far more to be feared."

I came back to my feet and signaled for the men to move out, then turned my head over my shoulder at the second-story windows.

Get out, Jaehwa. Jump from the windows like I taught you. Then make a life for yourself... one where I can't hurt you anymore.

REUNION

There were others. I was sure of it.

Kiwan was part of a gambling ring within the Red House. If there were more men ready to kill as Kiwan had, I needed to find them. What better place to launder money than a place where people thirsted for all the world's sins?

I had been coming to this horrible hellhole for months now. I wasn't sure if it was more of a hellhole because of the evil in it, or because of how tempted I was to submit to it. A man could only be alone for so long. He couldn't live in memories forever.

As time went on, the act of Captain Kim became harder and harder to separate from Saejun of the fields. If Captain Kim overtook Saejun, then my mission to relieve the kingdom of her turmoil would fail. If Saejun overtook Captain Kim, then they were both dead.

There was no balance. There were only acts necessary for survival.

Hyunki and Seulong had taught me that. They kept me alive and taught me how to become Captain Kim in honor of my family and the kingdom. They treated my wounds - wounds that should have killed me twice over

- and put their faith in me for a better world for their children.

And now their children were without fathers. I should have been there. Would Kiwan have attacked me if I was in the square with them, as I was supposed to be? Maybe not. If I had been there, they would both still be alive.

They kept me alive, and in turn, I got them killed.

I wasn't letting my guard down again.

My men never objected to a trip to the Red House, but I only took two men with me this time. Any more than that became babysitting. They were practically salivating when we reached the door, and I couldn't even hate them for it.

Ever since I had seen Jaehwa again, I became lost in my own fantasies. I could have taken her for myself; kept her beside me to never leave again. I wanted to protect her and provide for her again. I was torn between Saejun and Captain Kim: one man who loved her dearly, and the other who had the power to bring any desire to reality.

That power… how could one person live with it and not lose his morality?

The hostesses of the Red House took our outer robes and I searched the room for any new faces.

Instead, I found a very familiar face. One I hated seeing.

Sok Haneul.

There was nothing I liked about Sok. He was too arrogant to be a beggar, and too immoral to be a soldier. Every time I had to deal with this place, he was there. I was sure he had some connection to the gambling ring.

He was always there just in time to deter me from my mission.

And tonight was no exception.

"Captain Kim," he said with a smile and a woman in his lap. "How long has it been since we last met?"

"Sok Haneul," I returned. "I was hoping we'd never meet again."

He shrugged, his hands wandering around the waist of his woman. "It seems Fate feels otherwise. She keeps bringing us together, over and over again."

I lifted an eyebrow. Maybe one day Fate would be so kind as to let me take Sok Haneul down.

"Please," he said. "Have a seat."

I motioned to my men to accept the invitation. Better to keep your enemies close. Maybe if I could stay near, Sok would slip some information about the ring.

"Still a regular, I see," he said, still enamored with the woman on his lap. "Are there any women you recommend?"

Like he didn't have women begging for him as it was.

I grimaced. "Ask my men. I only take part in the alcohol."

"Fascinating. There are dozens of women here ready to lay beneath you, and you choose crushed grapes. I dare say you haven't learned how to live at the top yet."

At the top? I knew what was there: dirty dealings, crooked soldiers, and women who would never truly love you as you were.

"The top and the bottom are a matter of perspective, I suppose," I said.

His lips curled to the side, more than usual. "Let me get you a drink."

As his woman left his side he turned his head towards me, his eyes taunting. He knew something I didn't, and he knew I wanted to know. That was the game we played here. I was sick of it. I didn't come this far to have the scum of the kingdom hold his head over me.

His eyes shifted from me to my men.

"That one is off-limits," he warned them. "She's been with me for the last month. Finally put in the signatures for her."

I rolled my eyes. "Business is well, then? The black markets must be filling a lot of orders."

His woman came to me, extending her tray of drinks. I contemplated whether or not it may be poisoned, but knew that he was too clever to kill anyone here.

"We've been over this, Captain. I have no black market dealings. You must be parched from all those circles you run in. Jaehwa, sweetheart, give Captain Kim his drink."

I froze.

What did he say?

My head shot up to the woman in front of me, her eyes piercing through my skull like a spear.

I heard it correctly.

No... Jaehwa.

"She has beautiful eyes, yes?" Sok asked. "I thought so too. She's also surprisingly strong, despite her fragile frame. She was practically starving to death when I found her."

I took the cup, forcing down every instinct to grab Jaehwa and run. But my men were watching, as was Sok. I couldn't be Saejun.

I had to be Captain Kim.

"How much did you pay for her?" I asked.

"She really wasn't worth much when I found her. I think I paid two hundred."

Not worth much? This son of a —

"I'll pay you two thousand to release her to me," I replied.

"Two thousand?" the bastard asked, laughing. "Hardly enough to replace her."

"Ten thousand."

I wouldn't let him have her. I wouldn't let anyone have her. Not in that way. She was far too valuable for that kind of dirty trade. I kept my gaze on her, trying to tell her that I would get her out of this mess. She didn't respond. She only looked at me like I was a stranger.

Maybe I was.

"It seems that you've taken an interest in my pet," Sok said with a dramatic sigh. "I like the sound of your money, but I have to admit, I'm apprehensive. I rather enjoy playing with her. I like all the little yips and whines she makes."

Before I could think straight, I had jumped from my chair and grabbed him by the collar. I threw him to the ground. All he bothered to do in return was smile.

"Is the great Captain Kim wanting to fight me for a whore?" he said with my hands around his throat.

"Don't you dare call her that!" I snapped. "She's not—"

337

I stopped myself. My men were watching, and they would question why I was acting this way. They would know my weakness.

"She's not a whore," I said, trying to steel my nerves. "She's a wanted fugitive."

I stepped over to her and pulled the veil from her face, praying to the gods that it wasn't her.

It was.

Not you, Jaehwa... anyone but you.

She threw the tray in my face, rushing to the door. Before I could go after her, I was pulled back, Sok stepping in front of me with that twisted grin on his face.

"As her owner, you need to go through me first," he said calmly.

I grabbed him by the neck, leaning into his ear and lowering my voice so only he could hear. "If you touch her, I'll slit your throat."

He chuckled, not a twinge of fear in him. "Will you? Tell me, Captain Kim... just what does your student mean to you?"

He held my gaze.

He knew.

The bastard knew who she was.

I threw him down, rushing out the door. If my men caught her, she was dead. I had to be the one to find her.

I rushed down the streets, trying to find her. Why the hell would she go to him? Dolshik said that she was under his care in the Rebellion. I trusted him with her. There would be no reason for Sok to have her unless...

I grit my teeth, the realization hitting me.

Sok Haneul wasn't a black market dealer or part of the gambling ring.

He was part of the Rebellion.

SAFEHOUSE

"Why didn't you tell me Sok Haneul was part of the Rebellion?" I demanded.

Dolshik shrugged with his eyes. "Is he?"

We stared at each other for a long moment. I knew he wasn't going to confirm it, but I was half-tempted to beat it out of him.

"You said no names," he replied eventually. "Liabilities, remember?"

Yes, we made that agreement. I didn't know any names of the members within the Rebellion. The only reason Dolshik had told me about Jaehwa is because I had been searching for her since she had escaped the arrest. It would have led me to them eventually, and once Dolshik put the pieces together, he released her location to me so I would keep my nose out of their camp.

But with Sok Haneul - the way he had his hands on her that night - I suddenly hated every decision I ever made.

"You should have called me a damn fool for it," I huffed.

"My job is to deliver your supplies to the Rebellion. You said you wouldn't be involved otherwise. No names equals no traces. I have to think of my group's safety as well, you know."

I swallowed down my agitation. "Yes… I suppose that was our agreement."

He paused, waiting for me to say something else. I couldn't form sentences at this point. I could only reimagine Sok's lips against Jaehwa's cheek again and again... and me cutting them off his damn face.

"What do you plan to do?"

I shook my head. "To the Rebellion? Nothing."

To Sok? Anything was possible.

"Does she really belong to him?" I asked. Dolshik shrugged. "She pretends to defy him, but in the end, she always submits."

My fingers burned. She spent so long trying to survive, and now she had no one, and he... But how could I blame her? How could I be angry?

I was. I shouldn't have been, but I was.

"Did you call me out here for her?" he asked, bored.

"No," I finally said, refocusing my attention. "I heard there was an ambush. I have information on who may have gone after the Rebellion."

"It wasn't you?"

"I wouldn't feed you and kill you at the same time. That's expensive."

"Who would then?"

"Desperate people in need of a lot of money."

We exchanged glances a second time.

"What do you suggest?" he asked.

I raised an eyebrow. "I can't bring them to justice on my side. You'll need to do it on yours. I'll give you the names. You take care of them. My supplies will continue per our agreement. But in exchange, I want something."

His lips twitched. "The girl?"

I shouldn't have been so possessive of her. I had been gone for too long and she wasn't mine anymore. Maybe she never was. But even after all this time... I wanted her beside me. It was the one thing both sides of me - the powerless Saejun and the powerful Captain Kim - completely agreed on.

I had to take her from him. By any means necessary.

I nodded.

He watched me for a long moment. Too long. There was something calculating in it, but I didn't have the energy to care. I needed to get Jaehwa away from there. I didn't care about the consequences.

He swung his head to the side, looking over his shoulder. "I may happen to know where she is now. Someplace not too difficult to find her. But…"

He stopped for a moment.

"But?" I echoed.

He exhaled through his teeth. "I don't know if Haneul will let go of her so easily. And I don't know if she'll come to you the way you want."

He met my eyes again, waiting for my response.

I left Jaehwa alone for too long. I expected every type of resistance from her. She hated me. I could see it in her eyes at the Red House. I was a stranger to her, someone who meant nothing.

But to me… she was everything.

"That's my problem to deal with," I replied. "Do you want the names or not?"

After a moment, he gave a single nod.

I'm coming for you, Jaehwa. I won't let anyone else possess you.

Not now. Not ever.

TRUSTWORTHY

"Honestly, Jaehwa… how do you think they eat so well?"

She looked at me in terror. I huffed, half-growling at her tunnel vision. She really saw nothing past her wayward brother, grasping for the family she wanted that could never be. Nevermind that I was standing right in front of her. Nevermind what I had sacrificed for her.

The mist in her eyes seemed to clear, and she looked at me with a thousand questions I didn't want to answer. I didn't want to explain myself anymore. I didn't want her to question me. I wanted her to trust me. I wanted her to trust me the way she had when I was her teacher.

But I wasn't her teacher anymore. I wasn't anything to her anymore.

I walked away before my anger took over. Captain Kim had a temper, one that Saejun had a hard time controlling. And I was having a hard enough time controlling myself around Jaehwa these days.

I went to my room, shutting the door and pacing the floor. I was tempted to go out in the training fields and run laps, the adrenaline rushing through my blood. Instead, I did push-ups, fighting with my thoughts.

How could she not understand what I was trying to do? She had been there since the beginning. I told her everything. I never held back from her, lied to her, or hid myself from her. I was there when her father left for his death. I was there when she cried herself to sleep as a teenager. I trained her and Kiwan every day until I couldn't even stand.

I had always been there.

But she wasn't there when I had my skin burned by my superiors. She wasn't there when they beat me until I nearly died. She wasn't there when I risked my life to help those I wasn't supposed to be helping... including her precious *master*.

She didn't know me. If there was anyone in this world who was supposed to know me, it was her. If there was anyone to see through this Captain Kim charade it was her.

I needed her to see me. Everyone else who had seen the real me was now dead.

Without her, I was nothing but Captain Kim.

I stopped doing push-ups, my hands shaking. I collapsed and rolled to my back, ignoring the salt on my lips as sweat beaded down my face. My robe draped open, showing me my scars.

Had I lost my mind? Why did I show her these? What was it going to do? All she would do is feel sorry for me, at the most. She wasn't suddenly going to change her feelings about Kiwan or anything else for that matter because I had shown her my suffering. It probably satisfied her.

She would hate me until the day she died. That was our fate.

But... her hands on my chest were so warm. It was the touch of the girl I knew five years ago, not the touch of someone who hated my existence.

And I knew if I had let her touch me any more... I wouldn't have been able to hold myself back.

***

The evening passed, and I did everything I could to stop my thoughts.

I wanted to go to her. Despite everything, I still wanted to go to her.

She didn't see me for who I was... but I couldn't stop seeing her. No matter how much she hated me, I couldn't forget my first love, even after all this time.

I stepped out, sliding her bedroom door open. I expected her to be awake, but she was deep in sleep. I couldn't help but smile. She treated me like a monster, but slept like I was her guardian.

My eyes wandered to the bottles on the table. Perfume bottles I had collected that reminded me of her. Did she still dream of being a perfume maker? Maybe not. But the smells and colors reminded me of that girl that used to light up whenever she passed the market, and before I knew it, I had collected a dozen of them. I collected memories of her in the same way, keeping them close even though I knew they would eventually shatter.

She slept soundly on her mat, not in the window like she had been. I knelt next to her. I trained her to sleep lightly, to be alert for any sound, but here she was, disobeying my orders.

I smiled.

Do you trust me enough to sleep like this, Jaehwa?

"Jun..." she whispered in her sleep.

The breath in my lungs shook. I lowered myself to her side, laying on my back and looking at the ceiling in the same way we used to stare at the stars when we were kids.

"I'm here," I whispered back.

She hummed. "Mother's out late again. I'm scared."

I tried not to laugh. For a moment I felt sixteen again, looking after the careless girl who muttered nonsense in her sleep.

"I'll stay until she comes back," I said.

She snuggled up to my side, and I lost all my resolve. I brought her in more, smiling at the familiarity as she draped an arm over my chest. I placed my hand gently on hers, rubbing her skin with my thumb.

She did this when we were young, after her father left. She felt abandoned; afraid that everyone would leave as he did. What she never understood was that her father left because he wanted to save his family, not leave it. His family meant everything to him, and coming home every day to watch them starve made him feel like a failure. He left to find a new life to take them to.

And when he didn't come back... I knew it wasn't because he didn't want to.

Maybe I was more like her father than I thought. Both of us wanted to find a better life for our families, yet neither of us could return to them, no matter how badly we wanted to.

"Jaehwa... listen to me," I said, trying not to break her dream.

She whimpered with a deep sigh. I knew she wouldn't remember this conversation in the morning. She never did in the past, either.

"That night... That night they came for me... I was going to ask you to marry me," I said. "I couldn't imagine a life without you."

She didn't answer. I continued.

"But we aren't who we once were… and I know you hate me. If you find someone who makes you happy, then I hope you go to him."

When she didn't respond, I leaned over and kissed her forehead for the last time.

Maybe in another life, I could hold her like this forever. But in this life, all I had was this moment. I couldn't give her anything more. I had already given her everything, and it wasn't enough.

I leaned into her ear, hoping out of anything, she would remember what I said next.

"Just remember…" I whispered, "no matter who you go to… remember that I loved you first."

RESCUED

I gripped my sword, turning to find the path to the city.

He wouldn't have her. That Sok bastard wouldn't touch Jaehwa again if I had anything to do with it. I hadn't survived so long just to give her up. I had to find a horse. If I was quick, I could follow them to the —

"Captain."

I turned at the harsh sound of my title. Behind me stood a group of men - the ones who had no love for me. Kyungsuk was among them. I had no doubt that he was the one to say my title with such disdain. To be honest, I didn't know why I hadn't killed him. I regretted my own mercy as soon as I saw the smile on his face.

"Where are the others?" I asked him.

He held my gaze, a glimmer of darkness settling in them.

"Why do you ask?" he replied. "Especially when your idea of leadership is to grab your whore and run, leaving your men to their deaths."

The others grumbled in surprise.

"Don't twist my actions," I said. "That was not my intention."

"Wasn't it? Just what were your intentions then, Captain?"

The men stared at me for my response. In normal circumstances, I could lie without a pause. But my mind was blank - horrifically and dangerously blank.

"You abandoned your station and your men," Kyungsuk said with a twisted grin. "I wonder what the emperor would say to that?"

The men around me glared.

I tried to detour the conversation. "Get back to the prison. Make sure —"

"It's too late, Captain Kim," Kyungsuk said, waving his hand at me. "I already know what you've been doing."

He grinned at me again, continuing when I didn't respond.

"You know," he said, "the emperor would not be pleased to know that his captain of the guards is no more than a spy for the enemy."

A spy? I wasn't a spy. I was an… accomplice.

"Arrest the former Captain," Kyungsuk said, waving his hands to the others. "Show him the same courtesy he's shown us."

I raised my sword, pain surging through my bleeding arm as I did. As the blood dripped to the ground, I met

Kyungsuk's eyes, the whites of them blazing like the fires of hell.

We both knew I was as good as dead.

***

My bones and body ached, but it was nothing compared to my spirit.

I had lost.

In the end, Captain Kim couldn't save Saejun. Or anyone else for that matter.

I could accept my death. In all honesty, I had made it further than I ever dreamed. I never imagined that I would have survived long enough to become Captain, distribute the emperor's resources to his enemies, and say goodbye to the woman I had loved most.

It was enough. The emperor couldn't evade his enemies forever, and Jaehwa was tucked away in safety to live the rest of her life with purpose.

Maybe my death would satisfy her. In her eyes, I was the enemy anyways.

But my first act as a phantom was to find Sok and haunt him in his sleep. Even in death, I wouldn't let him own her.

"I've been sent for the prisoner," I heard a voice say.

I laughed to myself. I must have been losing my mind. I could actually hear Jaehwa's voice now.

The cell door creaked open. I didn't bother to look up.

"A gift for you, *Saejun*," Kyungsuk said.

Yep. I definitely should have killed him. It was my one regret.

Soft footsteps came forward, and I looked up into the eyes of my *gift*. I kept blinking, wondering why my mind was playing so many tricks on me. First, it was Jaehwa's voice. Now it was her eyes.

"Maybe now we'll see the noble captain crumble into humanity like the rest of us," Kyungsuk goaded. "When facing death do you still want to act like the moral god among us?"

My throat constricted as the woman turned back to face me. Whoever she was, she looked too much like my past to fight against. I had no will left in me. If I was to die, at least I could pretend for a moment that someone loved me, even if it was a hostess in a cell moments before my death.

"Get ready," the woman said.

The little growl at the end of her word... only Jaehwa did that. Another woman couldn't copy that. Could they?

She crouched in front of me, her delicate fingers running deep into my hair. The sensation made everything in my neck vibrate, and I breathed out slowly to try and savor it. Her fingers traced down my face and around my jaw, coming to my lips. As she traced the bottom of my lip with her finger, I felt it tremble.

It couldn't be...

This was her touch. The terrified, strong-willed touch of Jaehwa.

She came to me...?

Her hand clamped hard on my neck as she stood up, circling behind me.

Definitely Jaehwa. I taught her that neck clamp.

I shifted as she pressed hard against my back, running her hands up my chest from behind. It was impossible for me to concentrate, her touch stirring emotions in me I had been fighting against for years.

I wanted her to keep touching me. Even if it killed me, I wanted her to keep touching me.

My wrists became loose, and when metal hit my skin, I understood what she was doing. I gripped the handle of whatever she had handed me - a weighted dagger, it felt like - and got ready for the opportune moment to fulfill my last wish.

"Get to the good stuff, lady," Kyungsuk said, stepping in closer to us. "Why don't you take off that viel and show me what you can do with that pretty little mouth of yours?"

One more step, you son of a —

"Oh, but sir," Jaehwa said behind me softly. "I'm much better with my hands."

Kyungsuk took one step forward. I jumped to my feet and slammed the dagger into his chest. His hatred for me burned into my eyes one last time before he went limp. I dropped his body on the floor.

I turned back to Jaehwa as she stood to meet me.

My relief turned to anger. "You came for me? Do you know how dangerous —"

"I want you alive, goddammit."

Her eyes sparkled behind her veil as she threw my own words back at me, and all my anger washed out of me.

She was smiling at me. I thought she would never smile at me again.

I sighed in relief. All this time, I thought that Saejun had been wiped away completely; that there was no love left for me. I thought I'd die and it wouldn't matter to a soul.

But here she was, proving me wrong.

She saw Saejun.

I wasn't completely lost.

Even if I died today, I could die knowing that the woman I loved more than anyone still cared about me.

That was enough.

Saejun's Ending

"In our past life, I loved you... I hope in my next life, I can love you again."

The words rang hard in every fiber of my being as we rode south. Captain Kim wasn't hated in this part of the country as much as at the capital, and I could use my connections to keep my remaining men safe. Jaehwa had barely spoken the entire trip down, no matter how I tried to start conversations to distract myself from her body so close to mine.

Her words and her kiss right before rushing to her death to save me...

I was ashamed I had even listened to her orders to leave her. I should have stayed with her even if it meant death. If it wasn't for Dolshik showing up when he did, we all would have been dead.

I thanked the gods for their foresight. I praised Fate for her kindness. In the midst of my bad decisions, the woman I had loved most had returned to me. Twice. And I would never let her leave me again.

We arrived at the inn and split up the spare rooms. I didn't ask for any permission from anyone to spend my night alone with Jaehwa. We had practically lived together before the Rebellion had even known her name, and there were too many loose ends for us to tie.

But how to start…?

Jaehwa insisted on making our beds for the night, and sensing her discomfort in facing me, I stepped back to give her some space. I sat in the window, looking up at the sky, hoping the stars would guide my words. I couldn't think of any.

"I'm sorry," Jaehwa said shyly.

I looked at her frown, cocking my head to the side. "Why?"

"You lost everything you worked for because of me."

I laughed, relieved. "Everything I had was because of you. Why do you think I worked so hard? Imagining you and your family at the hands of the emperor… it motivated me. It kept me alive."

She leaned against the wall, dipping her eyes to her feet and then back up at me. She had no idea what that stare of hers was doing to me across the room.

"I'm sorry I doubted you," she said.

"I'm sorry I gave you reason to."

She bit her lip in frustration, shaking her head. "Stop being so damn nice, Saejun. I almost prefer Captain Kim. He didn't apologize so much."

I felt my blood steel in my veins. Is that what she truly wanted…? The man who used his power to take whatever he wanted?

I could do that. It would be quite easy.

"Is that who you want me to be?" I asked.

Suddenly she went silent, holding my gaze like a mouse about to get eaten by a snake. I never knew I wanted her to look at me like that until that moment.

"Did you mean it?" I asked. "When you said that you loved me?"

She folded her hands in front of her, not looking at me. "Yes. That's why I couldn't forgive you for leaving."

My heart pounded in my throat. "Have you forgiven me?"

"Yes… because that's also part of love."

"Do you love me now?"

She stared at her feet, not answering. But if I was honest, I didn't care about her answer.

"I loved you, Jaehwa," I confessed. "I loved you then and I never stopped. You know that, don't you?"

She stared at me, Those eyes… I had seen them in my dreams so many times, and here they were in front of me, begging me to tell her everything in my heart.

I couldn't control myself this time.

I stood to meet her, keeping her between me and the wall. When I slipped my finger under her chin and pulled her forward to meet me, she stared at me with a mix of fear and desire.

But did she see Captain Kim or Saejun?

"What am I to you?" I asked.

She didn't speak right away, her eyes dropping to my lips and then back to my eyes.

"Home," she whispered.

I slipped my hands to her waist, gripping her and pulling myself closer. She didn't resist, her hands crawling up my arms. Her breath shallowed right before she nodded in permission.

I pressed my lips to hers, afraid the dream would break. When it didn't, I kissed her harder, wondering where the boundary of reality and fantasy lived.

She put her hands on my chest as I pushed her harder into the wall with my kisses, showing her every desire for her I had ever had. She kissed me back with just as much passion, the taste of her breath sweeter than I had ever dreamed.

I broke the kiss, pressing against her as I leaned into her ear.

"I wanted to touch you so many times," I whispered, kissing down her neck. "When we were young... when you slept down the hall... when you walked away with *him*... I swear, Jaehwa, from this day forward, I will never let you call another man *master*."

I kissed down to her collarbone, resting my forehead on her shoulder. She was everything I had imagined and better. The smell of her skin, the taste of it...

... it would have been worth dying for.

"Nothing happened between us," Jaehwa breathed out. "Even Haneul knew... I wanted you."

I couldn't hold back my smile as I held her, the taste of her skin still tingling on my lips.

She wanted me. What's more is she saw me as I truly was. Captain Kim had not erased me from her life, and that would leave me with all the peace I needed to face the grave.

After all, the grave was going to be the only thing that took me from her this time.

HIS POV - HANEUL PROPERTY

We were being followed.

I knew it wasn't Saejun's men. They had lost our trail this morning.

It was a shame, honestly. I wished that Saejun was more dedicated to finding me. I wanted him to. I wanted him to come challenge me on my own soil. But there was nothing to encourage him to risk it.

I needed to find something… something that could lure him to my territory. Something valuable that would drive him to lose his common sense. But what? He was already the demon of the kingdom. He had no living family, no friends, and no assets. He loved nothing… which meant I couldn't take anything from him.

Not yet, anyways.

So… who was this little spy following us now?

Anyone who ventured this far into the forest was vengeful or suicidal. By the amateur way this creature was tracking us, I assumed he was the first of the two. But he was noisy. Perhaps it was a small, stupid child trying to get a glimpse at the Rebellion.

Honestly, what was the point of striking fear into people's hearts if it made them want to find you?

I guess it was just something I'd have to endure. Popularity was such a burden.

"Take Goyanggi," I whispered to one of my men, handing him the reins. He didn't ask any questions as I turned around to go back into the forest alone. This wouldn't take long.

It had been such a long time since I had played a good game of cat and mouse. My fingers twitched as I tried to force down my smile.

The pursuer's footsteps were steady, making him easy to trace. He should have changed up his rhythm. It wasn't much of a challenge, to be honest.

I hid among the trees, waiting.

And then... I saw her.

She was the one after us, all right. Her quick pace and the way she looked around was a sure sign of trailing. She was fast but easy to follow. She seemed familiar. Where I had I—

I tried not to laugh outright. The girl with the stick? Bold little thing.

Who was she, anyways?

She was far too thin, meaning she wasn't from the Red House or any government houses. Who were the poorest people in the city? The travelers? Farmers? Homeless?

Why would any of those people be out searching for us?

I decided to ask.

Cutting her off between the trees, I rushed forward and took her to the ground, pulling my sword and aiming it at her throat.

Her eyes glistened in beautiful confusion.

"This is a dangerous place for you, sweetheart," I said. "Haven't you heard the rumors? I went through an awful lot of trouble to spread them."

She looked at my blade and narrowed her eyes, not appreciating my wit as much as she should have.

"Are you part of the Rebellion?" she asked.

She had a strong, firm voice, yet it was somehow hollow. Her shoulders were too high, her back too curved. Even in the darkness, I could see the nervous twitch of her fingers. It made me smile. I loved it when they were nervous.

"Why would you risk your life looking for the Rebellion?" I asked.

Especially when you're terrified?

"If you're not part of the Rebellion, I have no reason to tell you."

Ohh, a game. I liked her enthusiasm.

"I have no reason to tell you whether or not I'm part of the Rebellion," I returned.

"Then I'll find someone else."

"And who said I'd let you live?" I asked, wondering if she'd tremble.

She didn't. She only smirked at me. "Who said I was asking for permission?"

She swept my legs, and I hit the ground.

A takedown? Where did she learn? The only people trained with takedowns like that one were —

This woman. I couldn't let her get away.

Whether she liked it not, she was now mine.

INVITATIONS

He loved her. Any fool could see it.

When I found my pet in the forest I knew immediately that Captain Kim had been the one to train her. Her fighting style was the same as Kim's, same as the new emperor's royal guards. There was no other place for her to learn those takedown techniques. Kim brought them with him when he became captain.

Just from that alone I knew she was the link I needed to something in his past.

And I was right.

Jaehwa was more than a student to Captain Kim. She was a deep and precious memory, preserved in his mind like a family jewel. The moment he put his hands around my throat, I saw it.

He thought I had been inside her... and he was going to strangle me for it.

And she? She wasn't much different from him. In my lap at the Red House she emitted a curious, welcoming energy every time I touched her. She responded to me. She acted like she was mine. Yet, as soon as he walked in, she went cold. Distant. Avoiding my fingers like poison. She wasn't scared for her life - she was reckless and stubborn even in the face of death - so there was only one other explanation.

"You escaped to become a goddamn whore?"

The way he said it... he wasn't going to kill her. He was keeping her alive. Secretly, it seemed. Oh well. It made no difference to me either way.

I had something precious to him. I had something I could control him with.

"Have you ever been in love before?"

She never answered my question, but I knew the answer now. These two had a much deeper bond than teacher and student. The possessiveness of a teacher and the possessiveness of a man were two different intensities. He loved her once, and he loved her still.

But... if she loved him in return, she could betray me at any time.

I couldn't allow it. I couldn't allow Jaehwa to go to him. I couldn't lose everything now.

After our return from the Red House, a party was thrown to celebrate our win. Now, the men were laying in the dining hall in drunken stupor, and I happily let them sleep, making a mental note to beat the alcohol out of them tomorrow afternoon.

Jaehwa sat among them, not drunk, but her thoughts obviously clouding her head in a way that was stronger than alcohol. I had to put a stop to it. I had to seal our relationship. She trusted me. She called me *master.* But she still wasn't mine.

Not yet.

"Come," I said, taking her arm. "I have something for you."

She silently followed me to the training room, and I left her at the entrance to light the room with a few candles. Their glow gave me other ideas on how to seal our relationship - ones of a more intimate nature - but I pressed them down. Jaehwa was not the romantic type. She had struggled too long to survive to hand over her body and heart so easily.

I had to use another way to win her... despite my temptation to find the heart in her that once loved a man.

"What is this?" she asked, breaking my inappropriate thoughts.

I turned back to her and gave my best smile. "Isn't it romantic?"

"Quit your nonsense. What's going on?"

"I have a gift for you."

I swallowed my heartbeat as I went to the shelves on the other side of the room. I hadn't touched this box in almost a year, the memories from it twisting my guts as soon as my fingers stroked the bamboo.

"Take her body. There are more in the forest, I'm sure. Find them and gut them. Then hang all their dead bodies in the town gallows. Let everyone see the result of going up against me."

"But Captain Kim —"

"Do it or I'll hang your bodies instead."

They took two more of my men that night. I couldn't give any commands, to save or to stop them. I was trapped in place. All I could do was look at the body of my sister next to Captain Kim's feet.

Kangdae had to step in and order a distraction, giving him a chance to grab her body before Kim's men could fulfill his order. But it was too late. My baby sister was gone.

But I wasn't.

Forgive me for giving away your most precious possession, Yeojin… but he can't have her.

I won't let him.

SLEEPOVER

Thirteen years.

That's how long I'd been fighting.

360

I got into my first fight when I was twelve. Yeojin was ten. At the time, the emperor allowed his men to collect girls under fifteen for the trade. When they came for her, I hid her in a well, refusing to let them take her.

I got my arm dislocated and my nose broken that day.

After that, I looked for a way to get stronger. I looked for a way for Yeojin to become a fighter if something happened to me. Our parents were long dead, and our uncle would sell us both if he had the chance.

Then we found the Midnight Duels.

It was the fastest way to learn to fight, and anything I learned I took back to Yeojin. Out of everyone, I learned the quickest. I worked the hardest. I naturally became a leader among the men at the Duels. I was a force. Even if men fought me - even if they hated me - they always ended up following me.

Intak was one of them.

He was wild but strong. He learned my ways the quickest, even if he had the biggest attitude. I knew that if there was anyone who would sacrifice himself for our men, it would be him.

And he did.

As the combat leader of the Rebellion, I had prepared for every kind of battle. Every kind of fight. Every outcome.

But there was nothing to prepare a man for burying the sliced up pieces of his friend with his own hands.

He wouldn't be dead if it weren't for me.

I shook the thought out. It was a foothold for self-pity. Self-pity equaled death here. I pushed it down; down until it felt like my guts were rotting.

The trip back to camp through the forest felt more like a desert. My thoughts were disconnected. My men had to repeat their questions, and I wasn't sure I had answered any of them.

There were only two thoughts.

One: Captain Kim would pay for his crimes.

And two: Jaehwa was almost another body.

She was supposed to be my vengeance, but she was becoming something else. What was she? Why was I thinking of her safety when my men were dead?

I had gone through every possible suffering. I watched my sister die by Kim's hands. I even stole the surname Sok so he would know that we were equals. Who cared about the emperor's chosen favorites? I wasn't going to let Kim have a higher status than me. I wasn't going to let him hold anything over my head. No. He was going to suffer by my hands. He was going to learn what it was like to lose what he loved most.

And somewhere in my plan of taking what mattered to him… Jaehwa was beginning to mean something to me.

Intak… my friend, my successor, my second. I should have been furious to the point of insanity. I should have stormed the emperor's palace in rage. But I couldn't feel anything. Everything in me had gone completely numb. All I could think about was Jaehwa.

She was alive. I needed her to remind me that I was, too.

Every night she slept next to me and I never crossed the line. I refused to get attached. But tonight… I needed her to touch me. I needed her warmth. I needed her to breathe life back in me in ways only a woman could.

There was warmth in her. She hid it from me, but when she thought I wasn't looking, she let her guard down. When she begged for her brother, I saw a woman who loved her sibling as much as I had. When she stared at her breakfast in the morning, I saw a woman lost in memories of her family. When she fought, I saw her determination to prove herself to the man she once loved.

I wanted to find those broken pieces in her. I wanted her to give them to me willingly.

And I... I wanted to hand mine over to her now. I wanted her to soothe the jagged edges. I would do the same. I already promised to do the same.

Tonight I needed a cure. She was the only hope I had.

I stumbled into camp, mindlessly releasing Goyanggi to Geonho before heading to my hut. It was early morning. She'd be asleep. I told her to wait for me, but I knew she'd be asleep. It was okay. As long as she was alive, it was okay.

But whether or not she would give herself to me...

I pulled back the door of the hut, only to have my heart dissolve in my stomach.

She was asleep... in Kangdae's arms.

I blinked to make sure I wasn't dreaming. He was still there, his arms around her as she draped over his chest.

This woman... had she even waited for me? I had slept next to her for weeks, never daring to touch her because of how valuable she was to me... and yet, after three days, here she was...

I closed the door and walked away.

363

I was foolish to think I could make her mine. What was I thinking? She was a tool to destroy the emperor. To bring down Kim. Nothing else.

She couldn't mean anything else to me.

Not when I meant so little to her.

SAFEHOUSE

"Where is she?"

I stormed the dining hall. Kangdae wasn't in his hut, so there was only one other place for him to be: sipping tea at the dining table like a heartless bastard.

And he was.

He looked up at me, with no hint of annoyance or guilt in his face, frustrating me even more. He should have been as angry as I was. Instead, he went behind my back and made things worse.

Was I a joke to him? Was Intak? Was Yeojin?

I stepped in front of him, my shadow doing nothing to intimidate him. He brought his tea to his lips, then sipped, taking far too long to answer my question.

"Gone," he finally said.

"Where?"

"Away from you."

He raised his head to meet my gaze, waiting for me to challenge him.

"How could you —"

"You're losing your mind."

I shook my head at him. "You don't have the right to take her from me."

"In this state, you'll put her in more danger —"

"She's mine!"

My lungs strangled me as I said it. I had to take a dozen breaths to fill my chest with air.

He took another long sip.

"Is she your woman," he eventually asked, "or is she your weapon?"

He waited for my answer, but I knew it was a trick.

"Neither," I replied. "You wouldn't allow it."

He chuckled and came to his feet. "You're right. I wouldn't. Both a woman and a weapon cost too much."

"But she belongs to me. All of my men —"

"She's not a man. And you don't treat her like one. You let her sleep in your hut —"

"To protect her."

"You wouldn't do that for a soldier. You never have, male or female."

I didn't answer.

"You give her your food portions," he continued. "You train her privately. You discipline her the most. You either love her… or you love what you can do with her."

There was a long pause. Only because punching my employer in the face would have too many consequences.

"She's not Yeojin," he said flatly.

I clenched my fists. "Don't insult me. I never thought of her that way."

"Yes…" He dragged out the word. "You don't treat her like a sister, I suppose. I don't believe she sees you as a brother, either. I've seen the way she tries to impress you. Pushing herself until she breaks, looking for your approval. Watching your every move. Looking for you when you're not around. You noticed it too, didn't you?"

Yes, I noticed. I noticed the determination in her eyes whenever I gave her a challenge. I noticed the way she tried to prove herself to me until she was ill. I noticed the way she prepared my bed before nightfall, and the way she cared for the sick men at camp alongside Geonho. I noticed the light fade in her eyes at night, looking up at the stars and asking them if she was good enough.

I noticed everything about her.

"You can't take her from me," I said again.

He only stared at me. "I can return her when I think you're ready. Until then, if you take one step off this campsite, I'll release you."

He walked away. I knew he meant his words, and I couldn't say anything else. For now.

There were at least six places he could have hidden her, and I couldn't reach any of them easily. Even if I went to find her, she would have left long before I got there. She would never let someone hold her captive. She was too afraid of being weak.

It was something we had in common.

"If it comforts you... I won't stop you..."

That night was still so vivid to me. Even drowning in pain and alcohol, I still remembered everything. The way she felt under my fingers, the shape of her waist in my hands, the smell of her hair. The woman who was afraid to be anything but serious - the girl looking for a way to ease her pain - was completely willing to give herself up to me at that moment in order to comfort me.

And I understood... I understood why he loved her.

I stepped out, looking up at the stars, wondering if she could see them now too.

"You're enough," I said to her, knowing she would never hear me. "To me, you have always been enough."

GUARDED

"Haneul," Kangdae commanded. "Step outside."

His tone was solemn, but he looked calm as always. He wasn't going to release her. I knew that.

And if he did, I'd drag her back.

I nodded and stepped out, leaving them to talk. I had nothing to say to her now, anyways.

I came for her. I risked my life for her and her brother. I risked getting cut down by the same man that cut down my sister. And when I had the chance to run him through - to complete the mission I had been working towards for the last three years - she stood in front of me and begged me to surrender.

And like an idiot, I did.

And now she was begging again for him. She wanted us to let her go? To fight for her *true love*? To hell with her. Didn't she think of us at all? Didn't she think of m—

"Haneul," Kangdae commanded again.

I walked back into the hut, not looking at her. I didn't want to feel anything towards her.

"Yes, Boss?"

"Take Jaehwa back to the hut and watch her. From now on she's no longer our ally. She's our enemy."

Jaehwa's jaw slacked as she looked at me in confusion. It pissed me off. She had the nerve to be surprised? After everything?

I nodded. "Understood."

I leaned forward and grabbed her arm, dragging her out of Kangdae's hut and heading back to ours. She yelled something, but I wasn't paying attention. I was too frustrated to care anymore.

When we reached the hut, I threw her inside. She collapsed on the bed, tears streaming down her face. I turned my head away. It would turn my heart soft to look at her as she was now.

"Haneul, please, I'm begging you —"

She bowed deeply to me, her forehead against the ground. The first time she had ever shown that kind of respect to me.

And it was for *him*.

"Don't do that," I growled.

"Had I known my brother was guilty, I never would have come here," she sobbed. "Saejun's head is on a chopping block and it's all my fault."

I clenched my teeth. "What makes you think I give a damn about him?"

Tears ran down her face, her eyes glistening in desperation.

"Because… you know how much he means to me."

I scoffed and looked away again. Was I supposed to care about her feelings? Why? Because of my feelings towards her? Did she know how I felt this entire time?

"Please," she said, coming to her feet.

She stepped forward, coming in close and gripping my robe. There wasn't any space between us, her body against mine. It was so much like the night she stabbed me in the leg; when she cried desperately against my chest, asking me to understand her and to help her.

That was the night I decided she was mine.

But she never agreed to it, did she? She wanted to be his. It would always be him between us.

"Please," she begged again. "I'll do anything."

That did it.

Clenching my teeth harder, I ran my hand through her hair, then caressed the soft skin against her jaw. Her lips trembled. I traced my fingertips around the edges, thinking of all the different ways I could still her mouth.

"Anything?" I echoed.

A breath passed.

"Yes," she replied.

When she shut her eyes, I knew she understood my meaning. It took everything in me to hold back. This was the second time she was willing to give herself to me.

But… she was still thinking of him.

I could have forced him out of her. Dominate her until I erased his memory. But that wasn't how I wanted it between us. I wanted her to give herself to me because she felt the same way about me as I did for her. I couldn't take her like this. Not when she was desperate, vulnerable, and thinking of him.

I loved her too much for that.

I pinched her nose instead.

"Stupid," I said. "I taught you to fight, not surrender. And I don't take bodies for business dealings."

I walked away before I could change my mind.

I could hear both her breath and heart shatter as I turned my back on her. But I wasn't caving. Not this time.

She was mine.

She couldn't go to him. Not until she understood what she meant to me. She could hate me until the day she died if she wanted. At least she would remember me.

On the way to the prison, I imagined how I would tell her my feelings towards her, but I couldn't tell her now. She wasn't in the state of mind to accept it. But someday I was going to show her what I felt. Someday, she would understand it.

Someday, I would make her completely mine.

HANEUL'S ENDING

I couldn't stand it anymore.

I was tired of this woman. I was tired of her running towards danger. I was tired of her not obeying orders. Most of all, I was tired of her thinking about *him.*

"*Isn't that what a pet does? Protect her master from the threat?*"

Jaehwa didn't know the power of those words. When I came back to camp, finding her gone, I thought that would be the last thing she ever said to me.

Since Dolshik had left with her this time, I had an excuse to take my men to go get her back. But this was the last time I was going to allow her to leave. She would know my feelings before the night ended.

I would make her mine. I didn't care what it cost anymore.

After rescuing her from her near death, I dragged her back to camp, dropping her disobedient ass on the training room floor. She hissed at me.

"You could have taken me to the medic hut," Jaehwa said, sitting on the floor and rubbing her backside.

She was probably sore from fighting, but I didn't care. It was her punishment for disobeying my orders. But her ankle was bad, and if I didn't wrap it, she'd ruin it further. She was reckless like that.

I tried not to smile. Why was I so attracted to reckless?

"You haven't earned the luxury," I returned. "You disobeyed my orders. Multiple times. I shouldn't allow you back in my camp, let alone this training room."

She went silent, shifting uncomfortably on the floor. I went to the bandage cabinet, pulling out a wrap for her leg. She started to fuss, but I gave her my best death glare and she went silent again.

I wrapped her ankle in silence. The soft skin on her legs made my fingertips itch. I wanted to touch her more. All the way up to —

That's when I noticed the dagger at her side. There was blood on it. I nodded to it, and she handed it to me. She didn't gag this time from it. Good. She was getting stronger.

There were so many memories from this knife. A blend of Yeojin's memories, and now Jaehwa's.

The two women that meant the most to me.

"I never taught you how to clean it, did I?" I asked. I took out my cleaner and started to wipe it down as she watched. "You've been doing well with it, even though you refused to be part of my family."

"I didn't know how to feel about a man who was using me for revenge," she said.

"I didn't know how to feel about a woman using me for my generosity."

She met my gaze, strong and unwavering. She was bold. I had to give her that. Probably the boldest woman

371

I'd met in a long time. Bold enough to leave camp when-ever it suited her. But I didn't want to chase her again.

"He's alive then?" I asked.

She picked up my meaning and nodded.

I sighed. "I don't want to keep chasing you, you know."

"What do you mean?"

I inspected the cleaned dagger in my hand. "I want you to belong to me. Only me."

I put the dagger down on the table, coming back to face her.

"I can't make you mine," I said, "unless you want to be. So answer me. Will you go to him again?"

She looked around the room for a moment, coming to her feet. She stood a foot or two away, the color of her eyes capturing me.

"It takes too much energy to be in love with the past," she replied. "I can't fight beside him any longer. I have a new master now."

I tried not to smile.

"Then as your master, I should punish you for diso-beying a direct order."

She leaned in, tempting me. "I look forward to it."

I pulled back a little, wanting to tease her more.

"So how should I punish you?" I asked coyly. "Extra training? You might enjoy that too much. Cleaning the training room? Not difficult enough. Hmm…"

I looked her over from head to toe, an idea striking me.

"I think I know," I said. "It's not often I have you this… vulnerable."

She swallowed. That's when I knew I had her.

There was no Captain Kim this time. It was just us. Us and the empty training room, where my men would never come without my orders.

"Fight me," I said.

Her face dropped, obviously not expecting my order. "What?"

"Fight me," I said again. "It's your favorite thing to do, isn't it? Let's see how you do with a busted foot. Come on."

"The terms?" she asked.

"Same as always. Head, chest, gut."

Get ready, Jaehwa. You're mine now.

I counted. "3…2…start!"

I ran towards her, and she stepped back and kicked me in the side. It was impressive with a busted ankle, but it wasn't enough. I swept her, sending her to the ground in a moment. I then mounted her, pinning her hands to the floor.

I leaned over and kissed her temple.

"Head," I said.

She laid still, her eyes wide and breath becoming shallow. I leaned down more, pressing my lips against her collarbone.

"Chest," I said.

When she said nothing, I kissed her stomach.

"Gut," I said.

I watched her as she lay under me. This is where she belonged. She belonged with me. She didn't belong with anyone else.

"It honestly doesn't matter what you decide," I said. "I won't let go of you. I'm not done with you yet."

I leaned down over her, stopping short of her lips. Her fingers clenched as she looked up at me, a look in her eyes that was daring me to do what I was thinking.

"I don't think I'll ever be done with you," I whispered.

I kissed her, rough and uninhibited, the way I should have kissed her the dozens of times she slept next to me. Her body molded so well to mine, better than all my fantasies; her kiss warm and sweet. My tongue grazed her lips. She didn't stop me. Instead, she pressed into it.

She wanted me. I could feel it.

I wanted to go further, but instead, I stopped the kiss, victorious.

"I don't care who your first love was," I said, looking into her eyes. "I'm going to be the only man who touches you."

She smiled as I kissed up her arm, as if it were an agreement to my terms. She would never go back to Captain Kim. She would never leave my side. She would never belong to another man.

And most of all, I would never be without her.

I needed her. I needed her to challenge me and make me stronger, to hold me and heal my wounds. If I had that, I could make it. If I had that, I wouldn't need anything else.

HIS POV - Kangdae
PURPOSE

How did I get here?

I couldn't remember wandering off into the forest, but that's where I woke up.

How annoying.

It must have been the dreams again. Dolshik mentioned that I sleep-walked. That was the only thing that would explain why I repeatedly woke up in various places. I highly doubted that Dolshik was carrying me around camp and leaving me in weird places as a prank, even though his warped sense of humor made me question it a few times.

Sleep-walking… One day I was going to walk off into the enemy's hands if I didn't cure this. But I didn't know how to cure it.

A medic who couldn't cure his own illness. Ironic.

Since I was awake, I decided to walk around to make it look like I came out here on purpose. I had done the same thing when I ran into Jaehwa.

"It looks like you've run out of options…"

She was beyond stubborn, with an endless amount of willpower. But whatever training Haneul was doing in the middle of the forest that night, it had broken her completely. I had never seen her so defeated.

That empty look in her eyes… it made the medic in me want to heal her. It made the man in me want to protect her.

And that's why she needed to leave.

I couldn't have a soft spot or else it would jeopardize my men. The last time I had a soft spot for a woman, my judgment clouded. I couldn't do my job as a leader effectively. And in the end, it led to her death. I wouldn't allow Jaehwa the same fate. It was better to treat her as an enemy than to get her slaughtered.

I looked down at my hands. I couldn't have more blood on them. They were already drenched as it was.

My job in the Rebellion had always been simple: protect life. As a Rebellion member, as a medic, and as a leader.

I wouldn't change my mission.

But the woman…

I went to the lake, hoping to clear my head of her, but irony was my best company.

As if I had summoned her with my thoughts, she appeared in front of me at the lake. She was bathing; wisps of moonlight reflecting off forbidden patches of her skin. My mind was screaming to look away, but I couldn't. The water was too deep and the sky too dark to see anything but her shadows and her shoulders, but it was enough to make my mind hum. She was dipping low in the water, looking up at the sky in empty hopelessness.

It was the same broken aura she had when I found her in the forest.

Before I knew what I was doing, I leaned against a nearby tree and watched her stare emptily into the sky.

She had a vulnerability to her now; something she would cover and hide once she stepped back into camp.

Whatever. Why did I care about that anyways? I barely knew anything about her. More importantly, I knew it was dangerous to get attached. Father taught me that. Watching him lose his mind over Mother was painful for all of us. And Yeojin… I never knew how I felt about her. I loved her deeply as a sister - just as I loved Haneul as a brother - but there were pockets where I thought of her as something more. I always stopped those thoughts, however, before I could fully explore them. Why label your feelings when something could never be?

Even in her death, I couldn't reflect on how I truly felt. Why bother loving the dead?

"Show yourself," a frail voice commanded.

I smirked. Haneul was right. Her body betrayed her intentions. She acted tough, but she was probably more broken than the rest of us. How could I allow her to walk onto the frontlines when the only person who couldn't see her true feelings was herself?

"I said show yourself," she said, a little stronger this time.

I stepped forward. "Is that what you really want?"

She dipped lower in the water, her face going whiter than the moonlight.

"How long have you been there?" she asked. "Are you some sort of pervert?"

She was staying in a camp of all men, sleeping in a hut with a total stranger, and *I* was the pervert?

Well… I *was* watching her bathe.

"Everyone's some sort of pervert," I replied.

The more I stepped forward, the deeper she dipped down. I couldn't help but feel powerful. It was impossible for her to talk back to me when she was completely exposed.

"Do you often sneak out here?" I asked.

"If I did, I wouldn't tell you."

"I own you. You need to tell me everything."

Because if I don't own you, you're dead.

"Property of Kangdae?" she asked. "Isn't that Haneul's line?"

Something stirred in my blood when she referred to herself as my property - while naked, nonetheless - but it quickly ran cold at the sound of Haneul's name.

This bastard... he never understood our mission.

"I own Haneul," I replied. "He can't own you without my permission."

She tried to harden her face into something defiant, but failed. "Didn't you give him permission to do anything he wants with me?"

I swallowed. She sounded accepting of that situation. Maybe she was easier to... *persuade* than I anticipated.

Whatever. Not my business.

But... I could bring her into my business... couldn't I?

Suddenly, a brilliant idea struck me.

"Within reason," I replied. "But I own you both."

And I could make sure my unpredictable second in command became predictable. Haneul had been slipping mentally since Yeojin's death. He wasn't getting sloppy, per se, but he was getting more aggressive, the same way my father did before he lost his mind completely. When

Haneul brought Jaehwa into camp, he was far too happy about it. I couldn't have a soft spot for Jaehwa, but Haneul undoubtedly did. I could use that to keep him in line. Because if I didn't, I would lose him to the darkness I saw building within him.

But the woman... she could help me defeat the darkness in him.

Jaehwa... You just became quite useful to me.

HAVE YOU EVER

I knew Dolshik was lying to me about something. I just couldn't figure out what. Or why.

"What are your orders?" Dolshik asked, nonchalant as always.

I moved the pebbles around the table, clumping them in threes. There was no way to surround the emperor's prison in a useful way, and I wasn't going to lose more men in a hasty battle plan.

"Don't advance," I said. "We still need to collect more information."

I need more information on them... and you.

He gave a mild nod. "And what about our men hiding in the city? Should I give them orders to weaken the emperor's men, as before?"

"No. Tell them to wait."

"The forest troops?"

I sighed. "Hold."

"You seem distracted today."

"I need sleep. You keep asking questions."

He clicked his tongue. There was silence.

"Very well," he said. "Would you prefer a report?"

379

"That's another question. Stop asking them."

"Haneul is taking Jaehwa to the Red House."

My head shot up, blood rushing through me. "Why?"

"Intelligence."

I snorted. "Debatable."

What information could Haneul want from the Red House? I knew he visited there every once in a while to keep appearances, but taking Jaehwa... that was different.

That was something I didn't approve of.

"I think he's following a lead," Dolshik said. "I wouldn't get so worked up over it."

"I'm not worked up."

"You're crushing rocks with your hand."

I looked down at the pebbles in my hand, now half-ground into dust. I dropped them on the table and sighed again.

"Where is he?"

***

"Do you have clearance for this?" I asked Haneul.

He wagged his head back and forth, like a puppy holding a rag. "Didn't think it was necessary. You never required it before."

I looked over my shoulder at Geonho and Intak, who were pretending not to listen.

"That was before the woman," I replied.

He frowned. "You think I won't protect her?"

"You keep putting her in danger."

"She's not in danger. She's with me."

"That's the most dangerous situation there is, if you ask me."

He smirked, irritation puckering in the corners of his lips. "It's only to collect information and to introduce her to a mission. There's very little danger. She'll pretend to be a hostess -"

I couldn't help but laugh. "A hostess? She would slit throats before wrapping her arms around them."

"Maybe. But I can teach her to do both."

His gaze held mine, challenging me. I let the bastard get away with too much - I knew that - but I couldn't put up harsh boundaries with him like I did with the others.

I looked down at my hands.

"Don't take it too far," was all I could say.

I stepped out before he could say something witty. I didn't have the energy for it. I couldn't argue with him either. He was cocky, but he got the job done. And he was reliable despite our differences in leadership. I could only force my way when appropriate. I held back more orders more than necessary when it came to Haneul.

After all, it wasn't his lack of orders that got Yeojin killed. It was...

I shook the thought out of my head. I couldn't think about the past now. I had to take care of the forest troops out west, and our allies towards the kingdom prison at—

I stopped.

I blinked. Was I having a vision? A mental breakdown? Because for some reason, I was seeing a ghost. I tried to shake the image of a female ghost out of my sight, but it stayed.

The ghost was real.

Jaehwa.

She was dressed in a robe of blue and green with embroidered gold, her hair wild around her shoulders. Her gown was lopsided and sloppy. I tried not to laugh outright.

Could she even be part of regular society after leaving us?

"Is this your side business?" I asked as she came near.

She looked up at me, her bright eyes complemented by the colors in her dress. She frowned with pale pink lips.

"Haneul's idea," she said. "I'd rather swallow fire."

Would the Red House even accept her like this? Probably not. She was too rough. Her beauty was neither cute nor sexy, but something raw and natural. Like the woman I saw in the lake so many nights ago.

She was too good for the Red House, honestly.

"Almost presentable," I teased.

Before she could run her mouth at me, I reached out and straightened her clothes. It was obvious she had no idea how to properly assemble them. Not that I was an expert, but Mother was rigid about appearances. I applied what I knew, straightening out Jaehwa's bows and retying them, adjusting her seams, and anything else she had clumsily put together. She said nothing as I did it, her tongue finally silenced. But I could feel her breath quicken under my fingers as I touched her, and it sent me into a flurry of thoughts that distracted me from my task.

As for her hair... I only knew one way to do it: the same way I did mother's hair each morning before she died. The way Yeojin begged for me to do her hair both when my mother was alive, and for months after my mother was executed. I think it was Yeojin's way of helping me through it. I couldn't cry when the emperor killed my mother. Father was too far gone for me to be the weaker of us two.

I pulled Jaehwa's hair back into the familiar braid, her hair heavy and stubborn in my hands. But there was something that soothed me as I braided her hair, nostalgia tickling the corners of my mind.

I stepped back. Jaehwa reached for her hair.

"You fashioned my hair?" she asked.

I looked her over. She wasn't any different from moments ago - not really - but touching her had created a burning sensation in my hands that I couldn't shake off, and it was somehow warping my vision.

"Now you look presentable," I said. "More suited for a man to have tempting thoughts about you."

She said nothing and swallowed. It took me a moment to realize I was staring.

"Remember our deal," I said. "Don't get distracted by men with large purses."

Or by government officials with wandering hands.

"I had no intentions."

"Good. Keep your focus and you can have anything you want."

I walked away before she could respond, and before my eyes could drink in much more of her.

I regretted making her better to look at, but better my fingers to do it than Haneul's. After all, I didnt feel anything for her. And Haneul… Haneul wasn't allowed to.

SLEEPOVER

She tossed and turned like the world was torturing her in her sleep.

I knew the feeling.

It had been days since Haneul left to find the others, and Jaehwa hadn't slept soundly since, despite the amount of chores I made her do. I could tell she was sore, weak, and drained... words she would hate to hear if I ever said them aloud.

This woman... as if being weak was the worst thing to call another human being. Foolish, selfish, greedy, insane, evil... those were adjectives people should worry about. Not weak. Weakness had limits. Boundaries. A place to rest. But this woman had no limits, no boundaries, and no rest. She refused to back down. Refused to accept what was in front of her.

Yeojin was the same way. And there was only one way to describe her now.

Dead.

If Jaehwa couldn't accept her limitations and weaknesses, she would end up the same way.

Dolshik had been giving her orders around camp recently, and I allowed it. For now.

"Where is she?" I asked Dolshik, who was unpacking the last of a current trade.

He paused before answering. "The gardens. Why?"

"Just checking."

He looked me over for a long moment, until I was irritated about it.

"You've been keeping a close watch on her," he said.

"Your point?"

He shrugged. "Just an observation."

There was a glint of presumption in his eyes.

"I keep watch on everyone," I said, stepping in closer. "Remember that."

He said nothing, but gave a small curl of his lip as he nodded.

I turned back towards the gardens, passing by Haneul's hut on the way. Damn him. He had been gone too long. There was no doubt that there would be casualties from the ambush, and part of me wondered if he had found himself in trouble by going out to find them. If he didn't survive, then what? I'd have the blood of his entire family on my hands. He was an unruly bastard, but he was the best fighter I ever had.

And what's more… he was the closest friend I had. Not that I'd tell him. He was cocky enough.

Also, if he didn't make it, what was I going to do about the woman?

I reached the gardens, stopping when I saw her. She was working alright, but her eyes were glazed over as she mindlessly shoveled dirt into a pile. I shook my head. I supposed she couldn't stop thinking of him. This obsession was going to swallow her whole.

Something in me couldn't bear to watch her get consumed by the darkness.

She didn't even hear me as I approached her.

"Focus on your work, woman," I said.

She looked up at me, seemingly snapping out of her daze. I reached down and pulled her up to her feet, looking at her dirtied hands.

"The blood on your mother's hands is because of me. The fault is mine. I should have been the man to

decorate her fingers in gold. If I had, she would still be alive... her hands healing the wounds in both of us."

I shook my father's words out of my head. Why was I thinking about that now?

"You need to sleep," I told Jaehwa.

She shook her head. "I can't."

I clenched my teeth. How deep was she in her feelings for Haneul that she couldn't sleep unless he was next to her? All those nights next to him... just how far did their relationship go?

"You're that loyal to him?" I asked. "Are you so attached that you need him to sleep?"

It came out angier than I wanted. Why did it bother me anyways? It had nothing to do with me. She could stay sleepless for all I cared. It's not like we —

"It's not that," she said, her voice oddly cracking.

"Then what?"

Her hands shook in mine, then steadied. I caught her wild gaze before she turned her head down.

"I hear the screaming when I shut my eyes," she whispered.

I took in a long breath, looking down at her hands again. I could almost see the blood on them.

The fault is mine...

I cleaned the dirt from her fingers as if it would erase the memory. But I knew better than anyone that blood on your hands couldn't be erased.

"Don't sleep in the medic hut," I commanded. "Sleep somewhere you feel safe."

"I don't feel safe without Haneul."

I bit my tongue. I expected that reaction, but hearing it still set my chest on fire. As if I hadn't been here.

As if I hadn't tended to her for the last three days. As if I hadn't watched her every night at dinner since the day she came here.

But none of that mattered. Compared to Haneul, I was a ghost. It was what I had wanted… yet at the same time, what I hated most.

"You're a pain in the ass, woman."

Her weak smile filled my eyes until there was nothing else.

"Yes," she whispered. "I know."

***

"That's the last of it," I said, handing Geonho the flask of medicine. "Make sure he drinks it twice more before sunrise."

Geonho nodded, taking the flask and holding it to his chest. "Are you alright, Boss?"

I rubbed my aching eyes. "I'm fine."

"You haven't been sleeping."

"I've been working."

"You're going to get ill. Then we won't have any medics."

I folded my hands under my chin, annoyed at his logic.

"The men here are stable," he continued. "Let me look after them tonight. If there's any trouble, I'll come for you."

He gave me a light smile and walked away, and I didn't have the energy to argue with him.

I wandered out of the medic hut, looking around camp. It was cold and empty, like it had been when I was a child. Like the day after my mother had been executed.

Like the day after Yeojin's death. Nights as still as this - nights filled with the anticipation of death - how could anyone sleep?

And the woman… was she sleeping?

No. She wouldn't sleep. She would be awake in her hut, looking where he slept, thinking about things she never said or did…

I knew because that's what I did with Yeojin. So many times.

The terrible thing was that I was relieved Haneul wasn't there next to her to hear what she had to say.

But someone needed to be beside her tonight.

And tonight… I think I needed someone next to me, too.

SAFEHOUSE

I slid down the stairs, trying not to look over my shoulder at Jaehwa's room.

I shouldn't have been hesitating. I needed to get back to camp. Haneul was supposed to be the mobile leader. I was the stationary one. I needed to protect my men and make sure that moron wasn't trying to get himself killed.

But here I was, thinking about turning around and going back up the stairs of the inn… holding Jaehwa until she stopped asking questions.

"Will I see any of you again?"

"Wherever you are, I won't be too far behind."

Why had I said that? I had been trying to get rid of her since the beginning. I still didn't want her close to us. She would get herself killed in our company.

But those tears in her eyes… the way she looked at me as if I meant something to her…

God, I wanted to see that again.

No. No time for that.

"Anything I should worry about?" Samsoon asked as I met him at the bottom of the stairs.

I licked my dry lips and shook my head. "She'll probably try to escape or rebel against you. She does that. Keep her busy and she'll stay out of trouble. Now, let me see your leg."

He sat in one of the chairs and lifted his robes to show me the scar running from his knee to his ankle. He didn't flinch when I touched it, which was a good sign.

"Does it still hurt?" I asked.

"Only when the weather's bad. I don't think it could have healed any better. The scar still looks nasty, though. It's hard to believe it was so long ago."

"You used the remedy I gave you?"

He nodded. "Painful as the devil, but heals like an angel."

I lost my train of thought, remembering that I used the same ointment on Jaehwa's shoulder after carrying her out of the forest. She was nearly bare when I put the ointment on her. I didn't think about it at the time - I had seen plenty of naked women as a medic - but now I was thinking about it in ways that were not professional.

Samsoon tapped my forehead. "You haven't heard a word I said, have you? Are you worried about her?"

I rubbed my face like it would wipe thoughts of her out of my head. "I have to think of my men first."

"Aye, you have many people to care for. It's hard to decide who to put at the top of the list, isn't it?"

"Chain responsibility," I said. "At the top, you take care of the ones directly below you. Then they take care

389

of those below them. Those people take care of the ones at the bottom. I can't go straight to those who aren't directly in my care."

Even if I wanted.

I tried not to look back at the stairs.

"There's nothing wrong with a little rearrangement," Samsoon said. "It makes more room. Besides, I've never seen you at the top, Kangdae. You always put yourself at the bottom - sacrificing everything for the well-being of those around you."

I didn't answer.

"You have your father's wisdom in you, and your mother's compassion," he continued. "That's what makes you such a damn good leader. I'd follow you to war again if you asked."

I chuckled to myself. "I wish you could fight with me, but I'm afraid the war I'm fighting now is meant to be fought alone."

He looked me over, a hint of understanding. "Are you winning or losing?"

I finally broke, looking over my shoulder as if she was going to be standing there behind me.

"Hard to tell," I replied. "But for the first time in a long time... I've found a new strength that keeps me fighting."

***

The moon hung high over the lake. I leaned against the tree, the same way I had when Jaehwa was bathing. I pictured her there still - that blank, vulnerable look in her eyes. That same vulnerable look when I left her at the safehouse.

Those eyes… they haunted me more now that they weren't here.

Rustle.

I wondered what she was doing at the inn. I knew the chores there wouldn't hold her long. She was a fighter, and not training was probably killing her. Not to mention her brother…

Rustle. Rustle.

… I made a promise to save him. Not that I really wanted to. No man was as innocent as they seemed. If Kim Saejun had taken him into custody, he was guilty of something.

That was the odd thing about Captain Kim. He was merciless, but he had a strange habit of only punishing the guilty. I had never seen him punish the innocent. I had him followed enough to know.

Rustle.

"Good god, Geonho, will you stop making so much noise?"

I looked over my shoulder at him. He shyly folded his hands in front of himself and stepped out from the trees he was trying to hide in. I raised an eyebrow at him. He hunched his shoulders in embarrassment.

"What are you doing?" I asked.

"Dolshik told me not to disturb you while you're sleepwalking."

I huffed. "I wasn't sleepwalking. I just couldn't sleep."

He trotted forward. "What's wrong?"

"I have a lot to think about."

He paused. "Do you miss her?"

He seemed proud of himself for asking. I smacked his cheek, wiping the smug look off his face.

"She's better off elsewhere."

He rubbed his cheek and frowned. "*She* might be better off, but you don't seem to be."

I sighed, aggravated at his talking. He continued to do it anyway.

"You should send word to her, at least," he continued. "She might miss you too."

I couldn't help but laugh. "She doesn't miss me. She misses fighting, maybe. She misses rebelling against me. She misses her mas—"

I stopped myself. I wasn't about to call Haneul her *master*.

"You know…" Geonho started, "I don't think she has feelings for Haneul in the way that you think. She's alone and he takes care of her. She doesn't have a family and he made her part of one. They might sleep together, but they - you know - don't *sleep* together."

I rubbed my forehead. "Stop talking."

He went silent for a long time, tapping his foot on the ground.

Tap… tap, tap, tap… tap, taptaptap…

"Stop talking with your feet too!" I commanded.

He opened his mouth to say something but shut it as soon as the shadow of another person stepped in behind us.

The shadow bowed. He was a contact of mine - an outsider of the Rebellion I used as a spy.

"What news have you?" I asked.

"The girl has escaped," the shadow replied.

I chuckled. "Figures."

"She's been taken."

My smile dropped. "Say that again?"

"She's in Kim Saejun's custody. He's taken her to the prison."

Geonho started to panic, but I raised a hand to silence him.

"What else do you know?" I asked my contact.

He blinked and took a breath. "You may not like what I have to say. It's about Dolshik. We found his supplier."

WEAKNESSES

Haneul would come back with her.

I should have been relieved. Our men were being rescued, as was Jaehwa.

As for whatever was going to happen to Kim Saejun, well, I had no control over that now. I wasn't going to get involved with it. I should have ordered his execution. After all, he slit Yeojin's throat and killed quite a few of our men while he was in his position.

But at the same time, he was our supplier.

My twisted curiosity was the only thing holding me back from giving the order to kill him.

Why would he work with Dolshik to keep us alive?

"We followed Jaehwa to the Red House," my contact had said. "She left in a rush and ended up in Captain Kim's company. Dolshik met them, but there seemed to be no conflict between them. Dolshik left her with Captain Kim."

"Is she alive?" I had asked.

"As far as we can tell. She might have been a trade, or he might be leaving her in his custody to gather information. Or both."

Yes… he had done things like that before. I wouldn't have put it past him.

I had ordered my contact's silence, waiting for the right moment to tell Haneul that Jaehwa was in the prison. With his slippery mental state, I had to wait until I could control him well enough, otherwise, he'd get himself and everyone else killed. Telling him a few days before the planned rescue for our men was enough. His mind had started to calm by then; and telling him that she was in Kim's custody somehow cleared his wild eyes.

He was sharper than before. I could tell that. I just hoped whatever feelings he had for her wouldn't cloud his judgment. I didn't want him to have the blood of someone he loved on his hands like I did.

Love… could any of us live in this kind of life with such a risky emotion? My father couldn't. What if history repeated itself? Would it be worth it?

Footsteps interrupted my thoughts. I looked over my shoulder to see my dear cousin, a blank stare his only return.

"Welcome back, Dolshik," I said flatly.

He nodded.

"Why did you take so long to return this time?" I asked.

"I found our little leak that led to the ambush. I decided to rectify the situation myself. There were a few loose ends I had to tie as well."

Yes, including sending Jaehwa off with Captain Kim.

"Without telling me?" I asked.

"I found out when I was already in the city. I had no time to track down pigeons and send them. I had to act fast. As the Underground's second, I assumed I had your trust in the matter."

We stared at each other while I tried to find my words.

"You have my trust," I said. "Do you think I'm a fool to give it to you?"

He searched my face for a moment. I could see the flicker of understanding in his eyes.

"My loyalty is to the Rebellion," he said. "Until the day I die, Kangdae. I owe your parents far too much to forget my place."

Pain flashed in his eyes and I knew he was thinking of his own mother - my mother's sister - who abandoned him and ran off with some Rebellion soldier before we had forbidden women from our camps.

I remembered the way my mother took him in as her own for years.

I remembered the night he crawled to camp, stabbed and half-dead to tell us she had been captured.

And I remembered the first man he ever killed the day he tried to save her from the execution block.

Seeing that pain in him still, I knew he had no betrayal in him. He would do whatever it took to preserve us... even if it meant accepting Kim Saejun.

For now, I could do the same.

I nodded. "Just checking."

"Where are the others?"

"Rescue mission. They should be back soon."

"You mean…?"

I nodded.

He stood still for a long time then bowed. "If there's nothing else."

As he walked away, I almost stopped him to ask one more question.

Why did you sacrifice her to him… when you knew how much she meant to us?

…How much she was starting to mean to me?

As he walked away, I chewed my lip, a sudden dangerous realization hitting me.

She meant more to me than I wanted. Far more.

It was dangerous to love… that's why I never decided my true feelings towards Yeojin. But when it came to Jaehwa, they were pretty clear.

Even though I knew them… I could never tell her.

All I could do was protect her with everything I had.

And I would.

KANGDAE'S ENDING

"Where are we going?"

Jaehwa's eyes darted back to camp as our horse passed it. I wasn't going to stop and give Haneul any chances to claim her. Not until I made myself known first.

"To discuss some things," I replied.

I led the horse towards the lake where I had first seen Jaehwa bathe… all those moons ago when I had started to question all the things I never questioned before. The horse couldn't make it through the narrow path, however, and we were forced to stop and dismount before continuing. I helped Jaehwa off, wondering if she was going to keep pretending that her ankle wasn't hurting her. It was swollen. I could see that from where I stood. But she walked ahead, trying to lessen the limp in her step. I stayed close behind, just in case.

"You came for me?" she asked. "I thought you didn't care."

"Don't get used to it," I replied.

"Why didn't you send Haneul?"

"I didn't know what he would have done if you had been with Captain Kim."

"What would you have done?"

There were plenty of things I would have liked to do. It was difficult to choose between asking him why he was keeping my men alive, or slitting his throat for killing my friends.

Maybe neither would have satisfied me.

"Nothing," I finally said.

She cocked her head to the side. "Don't you want revenge as well?"

I shook my head. "Maybe at one time. But he didn't kill Yeojin out of cold blood. He killed her out of self-defence. Also, because he lives, so do my men."

She stopped, eyes wide. "You mean... you knew the whole time?"

I laughed to myself. That's right. She knew about Dolshik and Kim, too. She was stupid not to tell me about it once she returned to camp. I would have to reprimand her for that later.

"I had a feeling," I replied. "I was always curious how Dolshik supplied so much. So I had him followed. That's when I realized that sometimes enemies and allies are too close to the same thing."

She looked at me as if she wanted to say something, but closed her mouth instead. She must have had a lot on her mind if she was keeping her mouth shut. The only time she was silent was when the weight of the world was heavier than the words in her mouth.

"I don't care about Captain Kim," I said, understanding that she wasn't going to tell me what she was thinking. "I care about you. You have your brother. Our working relationship is over. What do you want now?"

My heart skipped a beat as I asked. If she had a goal, she would leave. She was too pig-headed for me to get in the way of that. But I wasn't ready to hear her say she was leaving.

I could tell thoughts were spinning in her mind, but she only looked to the ground as she walked past me.

"Do you want to stay?" I asked hopefully.

"You won't let me fight," she replied with a huff.

"Not on the frontlines, no. But I can find another use for you."

She turned her head over her shoulder and looked at me sideways with those large, bright eyes.

"Will you pay me for it?" she teased.

Then she smiled at me - that coy, powerful smile I had seen her use a few times but never directed towards me. There was something challenging in it. Something I wanted to win against.

"I have one condition if you stay," I said, walking to meet her. "Don't sleep in Haneul's hut anymore."

She stepped away, not letting me catch up to her. "And where do you suggest I — ah!"

She fell to the ground, hissing and reaching back for her ankle. I could tell how much it was hurting her, despite her straight face. I was tired of this woman not being honest with me. The vulnerable woman bathing in the lake was the one I wanted to see.

I bent over and swept her into my arms. She grabbed hold of my neck, her eyes wide and nails scraping my skin.

She blinked. "What are you —"

"Stop talking," I said flatly. "Or I'll leave you here."

She pressed her lips together and I continued forward with her in my arms.

I carried her all the way to the lake, my arms starting to ache by the time we arrived. It reminded me of the last time I found her in the forest, carrying her back to my hut and putting medicine on her wounds.

Now, it was time for her to medicate mine.

"You do this on purpose, don't you?" I asked. "Hurting yourself so I carry you?"

"I never asked you to," she objected. "You volunteered. Quickly, I might add."

I scoffed and rolled my eyes. She leaned in, her breath against my ear.

"Maybe you like it," she whispered.

A chill went through me. This was definitely a challenge. She was testing my authority and my self-control. Little did she know, I only had one of the two.

"Are you some kind of pervert?" she asked, catching me staring at her.

She gave a triumphant smile. I needed to wipe it off her face.

"I already told you," I said, leaning in. "Everyone is some kind of pervert. And also... I told you to stop talking."

I dropped her into the lake. She screamed and spat, thrashing around like a cat, stringing my name with curse words. It made me laugh to see her come undone so quickly. She climbed out of the lake and charged me, but with a twisted ankle, she wasn't powerful enough to overtake me.

When she charged, I locked her in my arms in an embrace. She seemed too aggravated from losing to notice.

She glared at me. "I should have known you'd fight dir—"

I cut her off with a kiss. Her lips froze against mine, but I didn't care. The point was, I was the winner. When I pulled back, her mouth was as wide as her eyes. I laughed.

"If you think that was playing dirty," I said, "then you don't know what you're in for."

She stayed silent, allowing me to step back and express myself.

"The first time I found you here," I said, looking at the lake, "was the first time I didn't see you as an intruder, but as a woman."

I reached up and moved the wet hair sticking to her face, her skin teasing my fingertips.

"Because I was naked?" she asked bitterly.

I pinched her, irritated. "Because you were real. You were vulnerable. All the walls you had built around yourself were gone, and I could see the real you. You didn't have that look on your face saying that you had something to prove."

"You told me to prove myself."

I nodded. "I know. I did. But you don't have to do that anymore. I already know that I want you."

I wrapped my arms around her, pulling her close.

"Kangdae…" she breathed out.

Hearing my name on her lips… I was going to lose it.

"Stay," I breathed against her lips.

She nodded.

"I want to hear you say it," I commanded. "I won't say it twice."

She opened her eyes and looked down at my lips, entranced. "I want to stay with you."

She then kissed me, sealing the agreement. I kissed her back, her hands resting on my biceps as I pulled her closer and kissed her more. I reached up, tipping her mouth to mine so she couldn't pull away as I slowed the kiss.

I reluctantly broke from her lips, leaning my head against hers, and taking in this new sensation I had no clue what to do with. I was starting to understand why this feeling was so addicting to people. I was starting to understand how it could make a man go crazy.

"I don't understand," she said. "We barely know each other."

"I know you," I replied. "As I've protected you, I've learned who you are. Now… I want to show you who I am. Can you handle it?"

She said nothing, but the softness in her eyes told me everything I needed to know. She knew my pain. She knew my struggles. She knew the ghosts that haunted me. But she wasn't afraid of those things. She accepted them. And with time, and her next to me, maybe I could one day overcome them.

She was mine. That was the greatest source of strength I could ask for.

WRITE YOUR OWN ENDING!

Not satisfied with any of the three endings of this book? Have a great idea of your own? Write your ending to The Rebellion here!

WRITE YOUR OWN ENDING HERE

WRITE YOUR OWN ENDING HERE

A CHOOSE THE ENDING NOVEL

THE REBELLION

DEIDREA DEWITT

Like the book? Leave a review!

Your reviews help make my books better.

Speaking of which,
I'd like to share my next book with you...

Turn the page for an excerpt from

GODS OF THE SEA

A Choose the Ending Novel

Coming Soon

I leaned over the rail like a child at Christmas.

"Which one is my husband, do you think?" I asked Lina enthusiastically.

I searched the room, looking for a gentleman who might peak my interest. Thankfully, the most unattractive men had women on their arms, meaning I was safe from their claws. My eyes wandered around the room, stopping at a man on the side of the room standing towards the balcony. His broad shoulders stood stronger than anyone else's in the room, his eyes and hair darker than the night settled behind him. He raised wine to his lips, and something in my chest fluttered as he swallowed. He was certainly a sight to look at, and I didn't mind it.

His head raised. His gaze met mine and he looked at me in a way that stole my breath. But not from romantic notions. It was more like looking into the eyes of the devil.

"Stop gawking," Lina said. "Your father is waiting."

"Of course," I replied, nodding. "But what's a party without a proper entrance?"

She rolled her eyes. I only laughed at her lack of appreciation for dramatics.

I stood at the top of the staircase, placing my hand delicately on the banister. Pulling back my shoulders, I straightened and cleared my throat ever so gently. Even though the sound was no louder than a breeze, it stopped everyone in the room. They turned to look up the staircase at me.

The room was quiet until I nodded and gave my best smile, then a wave of coos and applause overcame the room. Except, of course, from the broad-shouldered, dark-eyed stranger. He only sipped his drink.

"Thank you all for coming so far to see us on this day," I said. "I'm grateful that our family has so many good people to call friends. Please stay as long as you like. My handmaid will take your thoughtful and expensive birthday gifts on the way out."

The crowd chuckled, and Lina shot me a warning look. I shrugged with a bare shoulder and scrunched my nose at her in jest.

The only person who didn't crack a smile was my dark-eyed stranger. Was he made of stone?

I came down the stairs, greeted by men and women of the highest class. There were so many familiar faces: my father's coworkers, military comrades, and fellow community volunteers. My father was generous to the community, and his friends were generous to us, especially after my mother passed.

I was grateful to every one of them for it.

After a touch of small talk, I made it to the center of the room, where my father stood, proud as he always was. He wore his naval uniform - saved for only his best occa-sions - and his hair was pulled back as if he was still working for the king himself.

But my father was better than any king.

I flung my arms around him as soon as he stepped forward.

"You look absolutely dashing, Father!"

He chuckled, tapping my shoulders. "Always the flatterer! What's all this? This dress is most becoming, but I can't remember giving you my permission to grow up."

I leaned back and kissed his cheek. "I only grew because you gave me so much sun, Father."

He gave a hearty laugh at my teasing, and I took his arm and drank in the sound. There was nothing better than the sound of my father's happiness after so many years of heartache.

"Come let me introduce you to someone," he said, taking my arm.

We walked to the side of the room, and my heart pounded harder every time we took a step forward. I didn't want to jump ahead of myself, but we came dangerously close to the dark-eyed stranger I saw from the balcony, and everything in me wanted to know more about him.

Something was so inviting about him, even if there was something haunted behind his eyes... like the mist on the ocean.

My heart was frazzled with excitement as we stopped in front of the dark-eyed stranger, who was even more beautiful up close. His skin was delicate like silk, but his jaw and eyes were strong as iron. He was taller than I anticipated, with a firm posture that emitted great power.

Who was he...?

"I'd like you to meet my former naval captain, Theodore De Villiers, and his son, Jacques."

I had been so enthralled by the dark stranger that I didn't even see the older gentleman next to him. I sheepishly curtsied and held my hand out for them to kiss. The older man gave a polite peck. Jacques, however, only raised it next to his lips. He didn't kiss it.

"Your father has praised you a considerable amount, Miss Esmerelda," the older man said. "I was afraid he was exaggerating, but I'm pleased to find that he's quite accurate in his praises."

I smiled, tickled by the compliment. "My father should save some of those praises for himself. All of my accomplishments are from his spoils."

The men nodded in amusement, while Jacques only narrowed his eyes.

"Yes, your father was the best of us at sea," Theodore replied. "Saved quite a few of us—"

"—and was rescued plenty of times in return." my father finished. "We're even in terms of life-saving, I assure you."

"You're a hero among us, anyways."

"Stop your flattery, will you? You've already earned my respect and friendship, no need to keep earning it."

"Then I might earn your agitation just for sport."

The men laughed together, while I caught Jacques's eyes. He had his head cocked to the side, sipping his wine and watching me like an owl about to capture a mouse. His gaze was becoming less exciting, and more unnerving. There was something in his eyes... bitterness, perhaps? Anger? But whatever for? I had never met the man.

"Have you danced, my dear?" Father asked.

I turned back to him and shook my head with a smile. "Looking for a suitable partner, Father. All in good time."

"Perhaps someone nearby would be suitable?"

By the glimmer in his eye I knew he was teasing to something, but I decided to tease back.

"Are you volunteering, Father?"

"Me? Heavens no. You know I haven't the slightest ounce of rhythm."

Theodore cleared his throat. "As much as I would enjoy the honor of the first dance, I'm afraid I've forgotten all the steps after this blasted knee injury. Jacques, my boy, would you do the honor?"

Jacques - looking bored at the thought - nodded and left his drink on the table. He held out a hand, as if he was asking me to pay him instead of to dance. I took it with a smile, regardless.

"I warn you," Jacques said as he took me to the floor, out of the earshot of both our parents. "Once we dance, you'll lose interest in taking my hand again."

I giggled behind an open hand. "Is your dancing so bad?"

He turned to me slowly, his eyes changing from amused to something cold and foggy, like the winter sea.

"No," he whispered. "But once you find out who I am, you'll make your distance. Same as everyone else."

I swallowed, catching the seriousness in his tone. "Oh? And just who are you?"

He smirked. "You'll know soon enough… Whether you like it or not."

Turn the page for an excerpt from

THE FIVE PRINCES

A Choose the Ending Novel

A CHOOSE THE ENDING NOVEL

THE FIVE PRINCES

DEIDREA DEWITT

Available Now!

"And this is the ball gown of the late Queen Cerene of Aujina, who was said to be the most beautiful of all queens in our country's history."

I bet they said that to all the queens.

I wrinkled my nose at the puffy layers of red and gold lace on the ball gown locked away behind a massive glass case. The headless mannequin was constructed to be the same size and shape as the royal queen, and if I stood in front of the glass just right, it looked like I was wearing the dress instead of the mannequin. I shook my head at my reflection. Not my style.

I stood back as everyone in the tour group cooed, snapping pictures and taking selfies.

One of the other tourists leaned in towards me. "You know," he said, "I heard an interesting rumor about the late queen …"

"Marina!" the tour guide called over the crowd, walking towards me with her permanent smile. "What do you think of the dress? Wouldn't you like to wear a dress as lovely as this one?"

I cocked my head to the side, considering it.

That was a lot of lace.

"Nah," I replied. "I don't wear anything I can't roundhouse kick someone in."

The tour guide's smile widened, but it didn't go up to her eyes. "Well then!" she said, spinning around to the other tourists. "Let's continue!"

We continued to wander around the castle. It was stunning, to say the least. Twisted wood columns held up grand Greek arches reaching three or four stories high, while gold-and-diamond chandeliers hung from the ceiling. Each room was decorated with traditional gold and teal flower patterns, splashed with modern pieces of cherry furniture and white linens. My footsteps echoed against the marble floor as we walked deeper into the Grand Hall.

"If you look towards the ceiling, you'll see the great history of our dear country of Aujina," the tour guide said. "Starting with the first sunrise to the building of the Cyrus Tower, now the tallest building in the world. It brings in lovely tourists, such as yourselves."

"I came here for the food," another tourist said, squeezing the tips of her fingers together and raising them to her mouth. "This country is known for its famous fisheye soup. We're actually going to eat it tonight in this very castle with a special guest! I wonder who it is? Can you believe it?"

"Fisheye soup, huh?" I replied, trying not to outwardly cringe.

"Did you see the tower?" one of the other tourists asked us both.

I nodded. "My dad planned the entire trip. A train to the countryside, cultural museums, landmarks, the Cyrus Tower, and then the castle itself."

"Sounds wonderful!"

I rubbed the side of my face, nodding unenthusiastically. It was a wonderful trip, but it felt more like a field trip than a graduation present. My parents had arranged the entire thing, but Dad had business in Hong Kong and Mom had a fashion show in Milan, so neither of them had come with me. And God forbid I was left alone for more than twenty minutes. Dad hired tour guides, escorts, and even police officers to watch me for the entire two-week trip. How do you even hire a police officer?

I guess the CEO of a massive international trade company can do anything he wants.

As the tourists began to talk about fisheye soup again, I looked up at the intricate designs in the ceiling. There was a lot of history here, so different from the simple Californian mountains. Here there were turquoise temples, myths of ancient heroes and magical dragons, people who shape-shift from human beings to animals. The ceiling showed the battles of the past and the technology of the present. There was a long string of kings and queens painted around the border of the giant ceiling mural. One of the queens was painted holding a wine glass overflowing with deep crimson wine. The painter had done a shoddy job, though. It looked more like blood than wine.

My eyes fell from the giant painting to the mezzanine, meeting the gaze of a man with dark hair and a white suit.

He was looking straight at me.

He cocked his head to the side as he continued to look down at me from the indoor balcony. No one else seemed to notice him. By the clean cut of his suit and hair, I assumed he wasn't a worker. If he was, he was a well-paid one.

He kept staring at me and, not knowing what else to do, I waved. He gave a small nod and bow, then turned on his heel. After a few steps, he tripped, knocking into one of the statues by the entrance. The clattering got a few people's attention, but he didn't turn around. He grabbed the statue before it fell, set it upright, then walked briskly out of the room.

Did I know him?

"Next, let me show you to the gardens," the tour guide said.

We stepped out into Aujina's version of a June day, humid and sticky compared to the mountains back home. The air was thick here, but it wasn't unpleasant. The musk of the castle gardens hung in the air as we walked through them.

Finally. Nature.

There were fields and rows of roses, gardenias, lilies, and a hundred other flowers that I didn't know the names of but wanted to learn. The tour guide yammered on as we walked through the vineyards, looking at the thousands of grape clusters beginning to ripen.

I looked over my shoulder, back at the castle. How many years of history were wrapped up in this place? It wasn't the most popular country on the map, but it had its own charm. Dad talked about it often, as if it was the best place in the world. He often talked about his business trips here, showing me pictures of the great lakes, snow-covered mountains, and gentle countryside.

He always said we'd visit together. Instead, I got the hired help. It was always the hired help.

When we got to the gardens, the tour guide showed us around, pointing to various fruits and plants I had never seen before.

"And here we have the sweet and sour rambutan, King Cyrus's favorite fruit."

King Cyrus. He must have been hiding around here somewhere. It would have been interesting to meet the royal family. I didn't know a lot about them. My dad always went on about them, but I never paid any attention, to be honest. I knew the king and queen had died, and their oldest son, Cyrus, had taken the throne as king. He had a brother or two, I think, but I couldn't remember much else. Except that Cyrus was a twenty-five-year-old king, ruling alone. I was only a couple of years younger. I couldn't imagine not having either of my parents. How lonely must he have been?

I raised my hand to my neck, my fingers searching for the jade necklace my father had bought me.

It wasn't there.

Damn. The chain must have broken again.

I knew it was around here somewhere. I had been fiddling with it just before we reached the gardens. I wasn't about to interrupt the grand ramblings of Ms.

Plastic Smile, so I turned back to look for it without saying anything.

It wasn't expensive, but it was meaningful. Dad had bought it for me on my sixteenth birthday when we were together in a pop-up shop in Chicago. There were only a few times we took family vacations together. That was one of them.

Retracing my steps, I found it beside a bed of yellow roses. I inspected the broken chain and bent the clasp back into place.

That would have to do for now. Again.

Now to find the tour group. Not that I was interested in hanging out with Ms. Plastic Smile all day, but dinner was happening soon, and I had been starving for the last hour. If I lost the tour group, I lost dinner, and I wasn't willing to lose dinner.

I walked back through the gardens, following the path into the vineyards. There was a path that veered off to the side, leading to a maze of vineyards, vines stacking high above my head and creating an arched ceiling. There were pockets of sitting areas with benches. All of them were empty.

Except for one.

On one of the cherry-wood benches was a man in a navy-blue button-up shirt and white pants, reading a book. His black hair was pulled back in a man-bun, which made most men in California look like hipsters, but made this guy look like an ancient warrior.

He didn't notice me.

"Um, excuse me," I said, "have you seen the tour group?"

He raised an eyebrow before he raised his head to look at me. His eyes were deep set and a dark brown that brought a richness to his dark hair and wild eyebrows. He gave me a once-over, then looked back at his book. He turned the page.

"I have not," he said. "I told them specifically not to come this way."

"Ah, I see. Do you work here?"

"Does it look like I'm working?"

"You could be on your lunch break. I don't know."

He shut his eyes for a moment and sighed. "You keep talking. It bothers me."

"You don't answer my questions," I returned, annoyed at his attitude. "That bothers me."

He looked up from his page and opened his mouth to say something else. Instead, his eyebrows matted. Suddenly, he shut his book and leaned forward.

"You," he said, narrowing his eyes. "Have we met before?"

"No," I replied. I would've remembered that scowl if we had.

He tapped his fingers against his book in thought. His eyes widened for a moment, then he pulled out his cell phone. He swiped a few times and got up from his seat, shoving the phone in my face.

"This. Is this you?"

I looked at the picture. It was me with Mom and Dad on a trip to Italy last year.

"Yeah, that's me and my parents. But how did you …?"

He dropped his arm, frowning. "It's you, then?" He looked me up and down, pursing his thin lips.

419

"What are you talking about? How do you have that picture?"

He stepped in closer, leaning down to look me directly in the eyes.

"You …" he said. "You don't belong here."

He walked away, leaving his book on the bench. I leaned over and picked it up, running after him.

"Wait!" I called. "Who are you? Why don't I belong here?"

But he was already gone. The vineyard was too much of a maze to search for him forever, and after a few minutes I gave up. Dinner was more important. I could just hand the book off to someone else in the castle. It would have been easier to return the jerk's book to him if I had gotten his name, though.

I looked down at the book.

The Strange Case of Dr. Jekyll and Mr. Hyde

Huh. Maybe he was looking for the other half of his personality. The nice part that was destroyed by scowling and half-assed sentences.

I flipped open the book, hoping to see a name, but there wasn't one. Shrugging, I put it in my bag.

"Marina! We lost you for a moment!"

I jumped as the tour guide's smile came into view.

"Sorry about that," I said.

"Please, come with me," she said. "We're late."

The tour guide took me back through the castle and up the staircase.

"Is the dining room upstairs?" I asked. "Aren't we going to dinner?"

"Oh, dinner will be a bit later!" she said happily, as if it wasn't the most disappointing thing she'd said all day. "We have another stop before that. This way, please."

I kept following, down the wide hallways lined with crimson carpet and white tapestries with gold patterns. With how large this castle was, my feet were starting to hurt.

The tour guide stopped at the last door in the hall and knocked.

"Enter," a strong male voice said on the other side.

The tour guide turned to me. "Best smile, my dear."

She reached up and, taking me by surprise, pinched my face into a smile. Did she think I was six? I complied but dropped the fake smile as soon as she turned away.

The door opened to a grand parlor, with large leather couches and a bar at the back. I expected to see the rest of the tour group assembled, but there was just one person: a man in a white suit reorganizing the pieces on a chess board in the middle of the room.

The same man who had been watching me from the mezzanine.

He jumped up when he saw us, knocking over the chess board and pieces.

"How many times ..." he grumbled, looking at the mess he had caused.

He left the pieces where they were and stepped over to us, giving me a bright smile with his pale lips and dark eyes. He couldn't have been much older than I was, but the way he stood up straight, pulling his broad shoulders back, showed the maturity of someone twice my age. Clumsy perhaps, but mature.

He lifted his wrist, looking down at his watch. "You're seven minutes late, Catie."

She bowed deeply. "My apologies, Your—"

"You realize my schedule can't be rearranged," he said, tapping on his watch. "I have a meeting at 5:35. If that meeting is pushed back any further, it will cut into my video conference with New York. And if New York goes over its allotted time, that will push back my other tasks, and I'll lose possibly 30 minutes of sleep. That will disrupt my REM, and the entire balance of my sleep cycle for tomorrow's activities."

He kept tapping on his watch, frowning. Wow, this guy was worse than my dad. Why was I here to meet him?

He looked up from his watch, an eyebrow raised as if he'd heard what I was thinking. "You must be Marina?"

I raised an eyebrow back at him. "Yeah, that's me."

The tour guide nudged me. "Try to be a bit more formal, dear."

I frowned. "Uh … Yes … that is I?"

The tour guide grimaced. The man chuckled.

"Formalities are not your specialty," he said, tapping on his watch again. "I'll have to note that while scheduling."

"Scheduling what?"

"We'll talk about that in a moment. First, I must introduce myself."

He stepped forward, holding out a hand decorated in gold rings. I took it for a handshake, but he brought it up to his lips instead. He gently kissed the back of my hand, then put his other hand on top of mine. I'd never had a stranger kiss my hand before. Well, except for the guys I had punched in the mouth. That probably wasn't the same thing, though.

"Catie, please wait outside for a moment," he said.

The tour guide looked between us, then bowed and left.

"Allow me to officially welcome you to my home," the man said, still holding my hand. "I'm King Cyrus."

I drew my hand back. "King?"

He smiled ear to ear. "Yes. And it's an honor to finally meet you … Your Highness."

AUTHOR'S NOTE

Are you as ruined as I am?

I hope you enjoyed reading this book as much as I enjoyed writing it. I'm absolutely in love with these characters, to the point that I used to leave social events early just so I could spend more time with them! Beautifully dark and twisted inner conflicts are my favorite things to write about, as we all face our own personal battles of good and evil within ourselves on a daily basis. This is the absolute core of humanity: trying to win the battle of good versus evil within ourselves.

This story is meant to take place in an alternate Korean history, where the original three kingdoms never united and were instead ruled by an evil emperor. I kept the evil emperor distant for a reason. The real conflict of the story has nothing to do with authority, but instead, every individual's *response* to authority. This is why the story ends when Jaehwa resolves her inner conflicts, instead of having a final showdown with the emperor. The point of the story wasn't to overthrow wicked authority. The point of the story was for the characters to find strength and peace no matter the outside circumstances.

I tried to keep the setting as close to historical Korean culture as possible, however, there are a few inaccuracies that I'm aware of. One being the names. Historical Korean names were difficult for me to research, and even my students here in Korea struggled

424

with helping me choose names. So most of the names are more modern Korean names. It is true, however, that in historical Korea, family names were gifted to the best of the best. The poor did not have family names. Kim was one of the first family names created in Korea, and Sok was a popular family name in the time of the Baekje Kingdom.

I know that many of my readers will ask me which ending I choose for this book. The answer is… I don't know. I love all the characters so much! Saejun and Jaehwa were meant to represent a timeless, self-sacrificing love. Haneul and Jaehwa represent a relationship that endures brokenness, darkness, and uncertainty. And lastly, Kangdae and Jaehwa represent a relationship where it is safe to hurt and heal simultaneously. If there was a perfect relationship, I would say it combines all three; but since there is no such thing as a perfect relationship, I hesitate to choose which one is most important.

I would like to thank the people who supported me in making this book. To my beta readers, Becky and Ashleigh: you're amazing. Thank you for simultaneously being my biggest fans and my hardest critics. And special thanks to my readers - my lovely Tigers - who have supported me since the beginning. Your messages and comments have pushed me to create art I can be proud of, and I always look forward to sharing myself with you.

As you walk forward in troubled times and uncertain circumstances, I pray that you know yourself well. In the *Art of War*, Sun Tzu writes, "If you know the enemy and know yourself, you need not fear the result of a hundred battles. If you know yourself but not the enemy, for every victory gained you will also suffer defeat. If you know neither the enemy nor yourself, you will succumb in every battle." We cannot win the harsh battles of this life if we don't know our strengths and weaknesses. To understand our strengths and weaknesses and to accept them honestly and humbly is necessary to grow stronger, better, and wiser. And once we realize that we ourselves are our own worst enemies, we can start on the road to an inner peace that brings us victory no matter what our circumstances may be.

- Deidrea

ABOUT THE AUTHOR

Deidrea is a California native who currently works as an ESL teacher in South Korea. She has more than ten years of martial arts experience, resulting in her characters constantly getting punched in the face. When she's not fighting, writing, or traveling, you can find her reading philosophical literature or making pancakes.

For more information about her books and the CHOOSE THE ENDING series, please visit

www.deidreadewitt.com

CPSIA information can be obtained
at www.ICGtesting.com
Printed in the USA
BVHW081702220321
603177BV00005B/225